JOURNEY TO THE LAND OF
THE FOURTH DIMENSION

JOURNEY TO THE LAND OF THE FOURTH DIMENSION

by
Gaston de Pawlowski

Translated by
Brian Stableford

A Black Coat Press Book

ISBN 978-1-934543-37-5. First Printing. June 2009. Published by Black Coat Press, an imprint of Hollywood Comics.com, LLC, P.O. Box 17270, Encino, CA 91416. All rights reserved. Except for review purposes, no part of this book may be reproduced or transmitted in any form or by any means, electronic or mechanical, including photocopying, recording, or by any information storage and retrieval system, without permission in writing from the publisher. The stories and characters depicted in this novel are entirely fictional. Printed in the United States of America.

Introduction

Voyage au pays de la quatrième dimension by Gaston de Pawlowski was initially published in volume form by Fasquelle in 1912, in an edition of 2000 copies; a further 1000 were printed in 1913. The same publisher issued an expanded version of the work in 1923, augmented by striking illustrations by the Dutch Symbolist artist Léonard Sarluis, and prefaced by an elaborate "Examen Critique" [Critical Analysis], which proclaimed that version to be a definitive text. It is the expanded version that is here offered in translation as *Journey to the Land of the Fourth Dimension*.

The genesis of the work was a little more complicated than these dates imply, many of its chapters having previously appeared from 1908 onwards as short stories or brief exercises in speculative non-fiction—or hybrids of the two—in the periodical *Comoedia* [Comedy], of which Pawlowski was the founder and editor-in-chief. Some might be earlier in origin; in the "Examen Critique," Pawlowski states that he wrote his first futuristic short story in 1895 and was continually preoccupied with the book's subject-matter thereafter. Although he does not say whether any material from the 1890s is reproduced in the book, it is entirely possible that some individual items in the *Voyage* predated 1908. Although his earlier collection of fanciful vignettes, *Polochon: paysages animées, paysages chimériques* [Polochon, here used as the name of a person, is a slang term for a bolster; the rest of the title translates as "animated and chimerical landscapes"] (1909) contains some speculative material—including a story reproduced as Chapter XXI of the *Voyage*—it is highly unlikely to have used up the entire supply of such available material.

Whether or not any stories from the 1890s were recycled in *Voyage*, we can be certain that the 1912 text carries forward and elaborates a set of arguments first put forward in *La philo-*

sophie du travail [The Philosophy of Work], the thesis that Pawlowski wrote in order to obtain the degree of *docteur en droit* in 1901, which was published in the same year. (It is the only text by Pawlowski currently available for consultation of the Bibliothèque Nationale's *Gallica* website.) There is a sense in which *Voyage* is no more than a dramatic expansion and extrapolation of that thesis, lavishly decorated in parts with gaudy fictitious footnotes.

La philosophie du travail not only introduces the arguments about specialization, mechanization and the likely effects of the future advancement of science on human life that serve to generate the images of future history glimpsed in *Voyage*, but also the broader philosophical arguments regarding the limitations of materialism and the superiority of Platonic Idealism, the particular notions of the Atom and the Monad, and—most significantly of all—the fundamental thesis that the essential purpose of "forced labor" is to liberate time for freely-chosen activities, including physical cultivation though sport as well as mental cultivation by means of the arts.

Although *Voyage* is episodic and somewhat haphazard, it has a very definitive goal and destination, and that objective is to extrapolate to its logical conclusion the philosophy of human nature exemplified in *La philosophie du travail*. Given that Pawlowski was presumably working on the thesis during the late 1890s, in parallel with his early endeavors as a pioneering sports journalist, it is surely in that period that the text's origins are rooted, although numerous important modifications were introduced into the chapters penned between 1908 and 1912, and several others in those added in 1923.

The new material added to the body of the text in the 1923 edition consisted of additional pieces that had appeared in *Comoedia* between 1912 and 1914—Pawlowski was conscripted thereafter for the duration of the Great War to serve as an engineer in the "auto-service" and had to give up the editorship of the magazine—and between 1919 and 1923, following his release from military service. These new chapters were inserted at various points in the text, according to their approximate internal chronology—many of them, inevitably, in the relatively dour section dealing with the present day and the supposed development of the "Leviathan."

Pawlowski's wartime experiences inevitably affected his view of contemporary developments, and the chapters written between 1919 and 1923 are noticeably darker in tone than those written before 1914; this has the slightly unfortunate effect of making that early phase of the narrative more repetitive as well as more ill-tempered, but the resultant exaggeration of the patchwork is by no means inappropriate.

The 1923 edition employed the "Examen Critique" as a preface, as did a further edition published in Brussels by La Boétie in 1945, which was illustrated by Jean Tauriac. I have, however, placed it after the text of the novel in this translation, because that seems to me to be a far more appropriate location. It was certainly the last item actually to be written, and it reiterates a good deal of the homiletic material in the book, much of which had already been repeated more than once in the text—an inevitable side-effect of the "novel" being cobbled together from previously-published stories and essays. Reading the "Examen Critique" first, therefore, robs the text of some of its impact; although the future history mapped out in the book is not particularly suspenseful, it does have a developmental pattern that is better followed without too much forewarning. Furthermore, the heavy emphasis that the "Examen Critique" places on the role of the fourth dimension in Einsteinian relativity theory—an emphasis entirely absent from the text—would be bound to color the reader's perceptions if it were supplied in advance, in a manner that seems to me to be likely to distort the text's internal argument about the nature of the fourth dimension.

Pawlowski went on to write at least one more magazine piece referring to the future history sketched out in the book— Pierre Versins' *Encyclopédie de l'Utopie et de la Science Fiction* records an item entitled "Où allons-nous, ou le Savant Hydrogène du *Voyage*" [Where Are We Going; or, the Savant

Hydrogen of the *Voyage*], which appeared in *Les Annales* in 1925—but that was presumably a reflective commentary rather than an addition to its substance; he does seem to have regarded the 1923 edition as a definitive version. In consequence, no further text was added to the La Boétie edition, or to any subsequent reprints of the book, of which several more were issued after 1962.

Although Pawlowski was a very prolific writer—in an article in the February 1998 issue of *Le Visage Vert*, Eric Walbecq estimates his total production as the equivalent of 60 volumes—by far the greater part of his production consisted of unreprinted journalism. He published approximately a dozen actual books, of which *Voyage au pays de la quatrième dimension* is by far the best known. This reputation is partly due to its recognition as a highly significant example of early French science fiction; Versins reckons it a masterpiece of that genre. More significantly in the eyes of most literary historians, however, it was explicitly acknowledged—along with Pawlowski's many articles about imaginary inventions—as a significant inspiration of one of the masterpieces of Surrealist art, Marcel Duchamp's *Le Grand Verre* [The Big Glass] (also known as *La mariée mise à nu par ses célibataires, même* [usually translated, with deliberately excessive literalness, as "The Bride Stripped Bare by her Bachelors, Even"]).

The latter acknowledgement has given Pawlowski a considerable reputation as a precursor of Surrealism, and the credit is certainly well-deserved, but he certainly did not see himself as a Surrealist. Although the "Examen Critique" proudly proclaims that *Voyage au pays de la quatrième dimension* is "manifestly anti-Naturalist," the text itself declares that such anti-Naturalist movements as Impressionism and Symbolism—the evolutionary predecessors of Surrealism—were merely the other side of the same coin, and that the whole point of the author's imaginary journeys in the fourth dimension is to find a new stance outside the whole methodological complex. Although Léonard Sarluis' illustrations for the 1923 edition are certainly handsome, there is a sense that Sarluis' earlier association with the Decadent Movement put him somewhat at odds, philosophically speaking, with the author.

Pawlowski was proud to call himself a humorist, and justified the calculated *bizarrerie* of his work as a philosophical tactic—definitely a means, not an end in itself. He was as proud to be conservative in some respects as he was to be revolutionary in others, and his assault on Naturalism in the *Voyage*–which dismisses it as the literary arm of an excessive materialism—has the explicit purpose of restoring a much better sense of the *true* reality of things. Although, like the Surrealists, Pawlowski regarded our perceptions of "three-dimensional reality" as a kind of prison from which it is necessary to escape, his notions of both the means by which that escape might be made and the goal toward which the escapee ought to aim were much more distinct than those guiding the Surrealists.

What Duchamp found inspiring in *Voyage* was only a fragmentary aspect of the whole—essentially, the idea of the fourth dimension as an altered state of consciousness, a vital artistic resource and a stern mental challenge—and the use that he made of what he borrowed in *Le Grand Verre* is very different from the use to which Pawlowski put the notions in question. That is not to say that *Voyage* does not have other surreal touches; the laconic literary method of the early chapters has a deftly surreal quality about it, and the satirical vignettes describing the Second Scientific Era are also grotesquely inventive; its deliberate confusions of the organic and the inorganic were to be echoed in a good deal of surrealist art. Pawlowski recognized these elements of kinship himself, and his own art and literary criticism—some of which was contained in introductions to books and catalogues—is sometimes eager to acknowledge them, but when he commended Surrealist works it was because he thought they offered evidential support to his own thesis about the way the world was going, not because he thought his own work offered support to the Surrealist Manifesto.

The passage of time since the publication of *Voyage* has, however, emphasized its surreal features. Even a reader sympathetic to philosophical Idealism of the purist stripe that Pawlowski champions is unlikely to find the text's underlying argument convincing, and the feverish Platonism of the final chapters is likely to seem as bizarre, in its fashion, as the satirical vignettes parodying the potential excesses of science. The essential eccentricity of the whole exercise has, therefore, become further exaggerated in a seemingly-surreal manner. Pawlowski would probably have regretted this—because he was, in fact, only being wildly funny in support of deadly serious contentions—but it cannot be reckoned injurious to his work, and it has helped to maintain its modernity.

Much primitive futuristic fiction now seems so banal and unadventurous in its anticipations as to seem irredeemably quaint, but there is nothing banal about Pawlowski's future history. One advantage of attempting to extrapolate trends to surreal absurdity is that it encourages imaginative boldness, and the advancement of science and technology have been so much more rapid than early anticipators dared to imagine that only the boldest of imaginative leaps stood any chance, in 1895, 1912 or 1923, of accidentally discovering the big surprises that lay in store. The surreally hallucinatory quality of some of Pawlowski's futuristic vignettes—especially those dealing with "atomic dissociation" and future biotechnologies in the Scientific Era—has been given an extra edge by actual advances in 20th century science, which give the contemporary reader additional scope for appreciating their strangeness and wit.

Although it is more secure than its relevance to the history of surrealism, the importance of *Voyage au pays de la quatrième dimension* as a classic item of speculative fiction is also oddly problematic. As its title suggests, the book continues a chain of thought that first crossed over from speculative nonfiction to exemplary fiction in the work of the English schoolmaster and amateur mathematician Charles Howard

Hinton, whose essays on the fourth dimension and exemplary fables extrapolating the idea inspired his fellow schoolmaster Edwin Abbott to write *Flatland* (1884; initially issued with the by-line "A Square") and supplied H. G. Wells with the jargon supposedly underlying the theory of *The Time Machine* (1895). Pawlowski's notion of the fourth dimension is, however, not only markedly different from but significantly opposed to the notions developed by Hinton, Abbott and Wells.

The idea of the fourth dimension already had a complex history before it was introduced into speculative fiction. There is a sense in which the "dimensionality" of time was posited as soon as time began to be analyzed and measured by clocks and calendars, but clocks and calendars emphasized the cyclical repetitiveness of time and it was not until counting years began to map out history in a conspicuously linear fashion that duration became something that cried out for representation as a graphical axis. The development of co-ordinate geometry by René Descartes in the 17th century encouraged such mapping, although explicit description of time as a "fourth dimension" did not become commonplace until the 19th century, by which time the notion of further spatial dimensions had emerged from non-Euclidean geometry.

The prospectus for non-Euclidean geometry was first mapped out by Christian Gauss, but its actual development in the first half of the 19th century was undertaken by Nikolai Lobatchevsky and James Bolyai, whose work remained stubbornly obscure while they were still alive, as did the early work of Bernard Riemann in the same vein. The field became abruptly fashionable, however, in the late 1860s and 1870s, when it was taken up by Eugenio Beltrami, Félix Klein and Henri Poincaré and the physicist Hermann von Helmholtz began to apply the new mathematics to physical phenomena and the actual geometry of space.

The breezy popularization of the mathematical idea of a fourth dimension was then undertaken by Hinton in an article published in the *Dublin University Magazine* in 1880 entitled "What is the fourth dimension?" which was subsequently reprinted as a pamphlet, before being combined with other essays and stories in *Scientific Romances* (1886). Hinton had emigrated to the USA by 1886, and he continued his popularizing efforts there, with even greater success; he had also attempted a further dramatization of the idea of a fourth spatial dimension in the story "A Plane World," also reprinted in *Scientific Romances*, which describes a two-dimensional world and invites the reader to imagine the difficulty that a two-dimensional being might have in imagining our three-dimensional world. This notion was taken up by Abbott, who extrapolated it in his classic satirical account of *Flatland* before Hinton produced his own novel-length *An Episode of Flatland* (1906). In the interim, Wells' Time Traveler borrowed Hintonian jargon to explain the movement of his time machine as displacement in a fourth dimension.

To modern historians of science fiction, Pawlowski's *Voyage* seems, by virtue of its title alone, to be a continuation of this train of thought, but it actually had a different starting-point and constitutes a radically new departure. Hinton and Abbott both use fictional rhetorical devices to invite their readers to try to imagine that our three-dimensional world might only be an element of a larger four-dimensional one, but that is where they stop; they make no attempt to describe that four-dimensional hyper-world, which they regard—by definition—as essentially imperceptible, and thus imaginable only in abstract conceptual terms. Pawlowski, by contrast, only mentions hypothetical flatlands in a cursory fashion, because his primary purpose is actually to explore and attempt to come to terms, philosophically and psychologically, with a hypothetical four-dimensional reality.

Wells, having defined time as the fourth dimension, then sets out to explore future history by moving his time machine along its axis, constructing a sketchy but complete future history from a series of brief snapshots. Pawlowski—who is likely to have read *The Time Machine* (which was translated into French in 1899) but very unlikely to have read either Hinton or Abbott—does construct a complete future history of his own, but he does not do so by representing time as a fourth dimension; indeed, he regards time as an aspect of the deceptive mode of perception characterized by three-dimensional space. His fourth dimension is an extra spatial dimension, but it is also, and essentially, the dimension of the mind, of the imagination, of art and—fundamentally, in his definition—of *quality*.

By drawing a fundamental distinction—indeed, a crucial opposition—between the dimensions of quantity (time and space) and a hypothetical dimension of quality, Pawlowski is actually rejecting the essentially quantitative extra dimensions suggested by Hinton, Abbott and Wells. His extra dimension allows him imaginatively to move out of both time and space, so that he can look back on both from a new angle. This not only allows his narrative voice to compile a future history by looking at time from without, but—more significantly, in that voice's stridently-expressed opinion—to see what inert matter, living matter and human existence really amount to, and what potentials they contain. Nobody had attempted that before—and nobody has attempted it since. Whatever one thinks of the accuracy of Pawlowski's assessment, its originality and adventurousness are undeniable.

Even if the critical field of view is more narrowly focused on the phases of the future history developed in the course of the protagonist's fourth-dimensional excursions in *Voyage*, that too seems to be formed more in opposition than to than by continuation of previous examples. It does seem probable that some of the vignettes making up Pawlowski's future history owe some inspiration to the example of *The Time Machine*, although the only real clue in the text is the decision to name a future factory-worker—who serves no real purpose as a character—HG28, but the sum of that future history is very different from Wells' vision of the future in the pattern of its development.

Like *The Time Machine* and Olaf Stapledon's subsequent account of *Last and First Men* (1930), *Voyage au pays de la*

13

quatrième dimension attempts a comprehensive future history of the human species, extending to a climactic and conclusive fate, but that fate is so very different from the possibilities imagined by Wells, Stapledon and almost all other literary far-futuristic fantasies as to give Pawlowski's work a blatantly anomalous status. Like most of the kindred works cited, Pawlowski's straddles an awkward boundary between fictional and non-fictional formats, struggling to fuse them into a strong alloy, but its particular combination of formats is virtually unique. Its fictional elements are brief Swiftian satires, dressed in a scathing sarcasm that exceeds the ironic fervor of such august predecessors as Cyrano de Bergerac and Voltaire; its non-fictional embellishments range from delicate exercises in mock-autobiography to fervent sermons.

Although *Voyage au pays de la quatrième dimension* is not included in the definitive *Dictionary of Literary Utopias* compiled by Vita Fortunati and Raymond Trousson it is, in a sense, the ultimate Utopian satire in the 20th century "eupsychian" mode—which, according to Frank Manuel, largely displaced the earlier "eutopian" and "euchronian" modes, locating the ideal state of being in a hypothetical state of mind rather than a different place or a future time. In this respect, it is one of the most insistent works of Utopian fiction ever penned; it employs its flamboyant humor as a lure drawing the reader to an exceedingly earnest conclusion.

Although the "Examen Critique" casually drops the names of numerous scientists of which Pawlowski probably had scant knowledge until he set out conscientiously to research the essay, *Voyage* itself offers very little explicit acknowledgement of its sources of inspiration. Pawlowski must surely have been familiar, however, with Gabriel Tarde's "Fragment d'histoire future," first published in the *Revue Internationale de Sociologie* in 1896—when Pawlowski was still working on the doctoral thesis he was to submit to the Ecole des Sciences Politiques—and reprinted as a book (translated into English as *Underground Man*) in 1904. Pawlowski's future history has enough in common with Tarde's to be regarded as an extrapolation of its themes, but also sufficient difference from it to be regarded as a defiant ideological reply, calculatedly aimed towards the liberating light rather than the confining darkness in which Tarde regretfully leaves his philosophically-advanced descendants of modern humankind.

Despite its enthusiastic traffic in the absurd, *Voyage* clearly aspires to outstrip and overshadow such hypothetical progressive histories as Tarde's, Charles Renouvier's retrospective *Uchronie* (1857) and the Comte de Saint-Simon's account of the future of the human species in the posthumous *Oeuvres choisies* (1859). It sets out boldly to change minds, change lives and provide the final answer to all the problems of metaphysics. The fact that the book is rarely considered in this context, however, reflects the discomfort induced by its flagrantly bizarre comic elements, which must have seemed to contemporary readers—and still seems to many modern critics—to link it far more closely to two of its other likely influences: Alphonse Allais and Alfred Jarry.

Allais was a humorist whose contributions to periodicals in the 1890s were fairly prolific; they included numerous speculative vignettes based on contemporary developments in science and technology, which are very similar in content and style to Pawkowski's accounts of imaginary inventions and the vignettes detailing the Scientific Era that make up a substantial part of the *Voyage*. Had he not died in 1905, Allais would have been a perfect contributor to *Comoedia*. Jarry, who was considerably younger than Allais, but only a year older than Pawlowski, died in 1907, so Pawlowski never had the opportunity to publish his work in *Comoedia* either, but he too would have been very welcome in its pages; Jarry and Pawkowlski had more than literary interests in common, especially their powerful fascination with cycling.

Although Jarry discontinued his formal education at relatively early stage, he retained a fascination with science, having been briefly acquainted with Henri Bergson, the theorist of time and consciousness whose ideas form a key part of the philosophical underpinning of *Voyage au pays de la quatrième*

15

dimension. Jarry's swift Bergsonian response to the French translation of *The Time Machine*, "Commentaire pour servir à la contruction pratique de la machine à explorer le temps" (1899; tr. as "How to Construct a Time Machine") was a significant precursor, if not a key model, of the style and the content of Pawlowski's fictionalized essays.

Jarry became an important contributor to early French science fiction with *Le surmâle* (1902; tr. as *The Supermale*), but the posthumous *Gestes et opinions du Docteur Faustroll, Pataphysicien* (tr. as "The Life and Opinions of Dr. Faustroll, Pataphysician"), issued in 1911 by Fasquelle—who was to publish *Voyage* a year later—is even closer in spirit to certain aspects of Pawlowski's work by virtue of its bold celebration of contradiction, its hectic patchwork structure and its marked anticipations of surrealism. Contemporary readers could certainly be forgiven for considering Jarry and Pawlowski as two of a kind, although Pawlowski, unlike Jarry, was very tall—which presumably assisted his athletic endeavors—and enjoyed much better health, at least until he developed the middle-aged spread displayed in various surviving portraits and caricatures.

Pawlowski was undoubtedly familiar with at least some of the many other works of French scientific romance that appeared in the early 1900s, most of which took some inspiration from H. G. Wells. He was a friend of "Willy," for whom the science fiction writer Jean de La Hire had once worked as a secretary, and the short items incorporated into *Voyage* include probable derivations from science fiction novels by Gustave Le Rouge, Jean-Antoine Nau and André Couvreur (all of which are footnoted in the text).

In view of these complex and somewhat contrasted relationships with a remarkable variety of other proto-sciencefictional texts, it is no wonder that critics have never known exactly where to place *Voyage au pays de la quatrième dimension* in the generic spectrum, or exactly what to make of it. What is beyond question, though, is that there is no other Utopian, future-historical or dimensional fantasy novel like it—a fact that is surely sufficient to warrant its status as a classic of extraordinary fiction, and certainly makes it well worth reading.

Despite the thematic connections between *Voyage* and *The Time Machine*, it is almost certain that Pawlowski initially derived his notion of the fourth dimension from a very different source. The popularization of the idea as a mathematical conceit certainly owed much to Charles Hinton, but there were others avid to make use of the notion once the work of Lobatchevsky and Riemann had emerged from the shadows of obscurity. The book that did most to package the idea in a markedly different way was the third volume of Johann K. F. Zöllner's *Wissenschaftliche Abhandlungen*, known individually as *Transcendentale Physik* (1878; tr. as *Transcendental Physics*).

Dedicated to William Crookes, the English physicist who had become an important champion of Spritualism and its associated phenomena, Zöllner's book attempted to use the concept of a fourth spatial dimension to explain the various supernatural feats carried out by mediums; it is probably no coincidence that the two primary examples cited by Zöllner—tying knots in pieces of string whose ends are held tight or sealed, and importing objects into sealed boxes—are the two primary examples cited by Pawlowski. (Cynics like the American conjuror John Maskelyne pointed out that these were also two standard tricks of stage magic, and Zöllner's experimental subject, Henry Slade, had been caught cheating even before *Transcendentale Physik* went to press, but—like most scientists who took a stand on such matters—Zöllner refused to believe that he could have been duped.)

Further evidence that Pawlowski derived his notion of the fourth dimension from Zöllner is offered by his reference to its "German origins." Although any recent history of mathematics will inform the reader that the prospectus for non-Euclidean geometry was mapped out by Gauss, hardly anyone knew that until Zöllner advertised it prominently, quoting from the relevant unpublished manuscript in the first chapter of his book, which was given extra publicity when it was translated into English for Crookes' *Quarterly Journal of Science* in April 1878, entitled "On Space of Four Dimensions." It was that article rather than the whole text that first attracted attention in France, where Crookes' own experiments and popularizing endeavors were considered very newsworthy.

Zöllner's work pioneered the field of "psychic research" and its use of the fourth dimension to explain events that might otherwise be deemed supernatural was taken up enthusiastically by many ardent participants in the 19th century "occult revival." The fourth dimension and such notional offshoots as "the astral plane" became key explanatory resources of such movements as "Spiritism" (a French vogue invented by "Allan Kardec," which attempted to supply an underpinning science to Spiritualist religion) and Madame Blavtasky's Theosophy. It is significant that Marcel Duchamp was not alone in taking considerable inspiration from the *Voyage*; the novel was also responsible for the occult historian and novelist Jules Bois dedicating his study of *L'eternel retour* [The Eternal Return] (1914) to Pawlowski.

Pawlowski was personally acquainted with Bois— Walbecq quotes correspondence exchanged between the two—and also seems to have known Bois' immediate predecessor as the central figure in French occult scholarship, the would-be Rosicrucian magus and novelist "Sâr" Joséphin Péladan. Incongruous as it may seem, Pawlowski published at least one article by Péladan in *Comoedia*. How close this acquaintance was is difficult to determine, but the main text of *Voyage* does take the occult aspects of the fourth dimension more seriously than its author was prepared to acknowledge in the "Examen Critique," which is very careful to concentrate on more respectable affiliations. Although the various chapters dealing with the clichés of spiritism are written tongue-in-cheek, they fully accept the reality of the phenomena, and are perfectly serious in attempting a bold catch-all explanation of them.

It may well be significant that Jules Bois was a regular attendee at the weekly salon hosted by the famous popularizer of astronomy and champion of spiritualism Camille Flammarion, at which Flammarion's fellow astronomers and co-religionists rubbed shoulders with occult enthusiasts of more a colorful stripe and literary figures of various distinction; Victor Hugo had dropped in occasionally while he was still alive and Arthur Conan Doyle eventually became a regular English visitor. Scientists of many sorts, especially ones considered slightly unorthodox, found a warm welcome at Flammarion's soirées. Other regulars included Gustave Le Bon, a pioneering social psychologist who compiled a comprehensive history of civilization and produced a landmark work on the *Psychologie des foules* [Psychology of Crowds] (1905), who was also so struck by the near-simultaneous discoveries of X-rays and radioactivity that he undertook extensive laboratory experiments in physics in order to produce a definitive book on *L'évolution de la matière* (1905; tr. as *The Evolution of Matter*). It is from the latter volume that Pawlowski, who certainly knew Le Bon, borrowed his observations on "the dissociation of matter"—taking care to include a rare acknowledgement—and his related examples and statistics, while his depiction of the Leviathan draws heavily on the other thread of Le Bon's works.

Although Pawlowski does not appear to have been a regular visitor to Flammarion's salon, he might well have dropped in occasionally, perhaps in Le Bon's company, and it might have been there that he made Bois' acquaintance. At any rate, Pawlowski would certainly have been sympathetic to the polymathy of the salon's interests and the eclectic interplay of diverse ideas that its host encouraged. It was one of the last refuges of would-be Renaissance Men, of whom Pawlowski considered himself to be one of the last endangered specimens.

Although Pawlowski was a neo-Platonist in a much stricter and more orthodox sense than Péladan or Bois, and evidently considered occult phenomena as relatively trivial side-effects of a much more elevated and far-reaching Idealism, it is not entirely surprising that Bois found *Voyage* stimulating and inspiring, and the same must have been true of other occult theorists who read it. It is arguable that Pawlowski's work has closer affinities with such flagrantly mystical extrapolations of the notion of the fourth dimension as the works by P. D. Ouspensky translated into English as *Tertium Organum* (1920) and *A New Model of the Universe* (1931) and J. W. Dunne's highly successful accounts of *An Experiment with Time* (1927) and *The Serial Universe* (1934) than it does with any Surrealist fantasy or sciencefictional future history. Like Bois, both those writers were preoccupied with the notion of Eternal Return—a thesis that Pawlowski could not tolerate, let alone accommodate, but to which his version of the fourth dimension is more amenable and adaptable than he probably realized.

As well as these cultural contexts, of course, *Voyage au quatrième dimension* had a personal context, which was certainly highly relevant to its psychological genesis and contents. Gaston William Adam Pawlowski was born on June 14, 1974, in Joigny. His father, Albert de Pawlowski, was an engineer working in the research department of the Compagnie des Chemins de Fer de l'Ouest. He attended the Lycée Condorcet in Paris before going on to the Ecole des Sciences Politiques. Despite the fact that he took care to complete his doctorate, he does not seem to have had any intention of practicing law. Although he did publish one other work of social science before his thesis—the relatively brief pamphlet *Sociologie nationale: une définition de l'état* [National Sociology: A Definition of the State] (1897), which introduced the notion of the Animal-State redeployed in *Voyage* as the Leviathan—he was by then already working as a journalist.

Pawlowski first began writing articles for periodicals in 1894, before he graduated from the Ecole des Science Politiques, initially in connection with his chief hobby, cycling. He took a keen interest in the development of racing bicycles, and also in the parallel evolution of the automobile—an interest undoubtedly encouraged and assisted by his father's involvement in the development of railway locomotives. The first of the three periodicals that Pawlowski was to found, long before *Comoedia*, was *Le Vélo* [The Bicycle], the official organ of the Union Vélocipédique de France (the second was the short-lived *L'Opinion*, which played host to his political writings). By the time he graduated, however, Pawlowski had decided that his true vocation was humor, and the first professional magazine whose staff he joined was *Le Rire*, an established periodical that he was eventually to imitate when he founded *Comoedia* in 1907.

Pawlowski's first "novel" was a serial published in *Le Vélo* in 1894 while he was still a teenager, *Le record de Samuel Humbug* [Samuel Humbug's Record], but it was not reprinted in book form. He did, however, achieve book publication with *On se moque de nous* [They're Laughing at Us] (1898), issued under the by-line W. de Pawlowski rather than G. de Pawlowski, which he used on all his subsequent work. By that time, he had already begun writing brief accounts—usually only a few lines long—of imaginary inventions, which were to become a key element of his stock-in-trade. They were published in numerous different periodicals—Walbecq names six before adding "etc."—before Fasquelle eventually issued a collection in volume form as *Inventions nouvelles et dernières nouveautés* (1916). Although most are calculatedly silly—for example, a special kind of snail bred for use as a shaving device—some are ideas that have actually come to fruition, like a keyboard whose sounds are fed to a pair of headphones so that only the player can hear them.

In 1906, Pawlowski issued an unbound set of short texts as *Les billets de paysages animés* [Notes on, or Tickets to, Animated Lands], which were subsequently reprinted in the more substantial *Polochon: paysages animés, paysages chimériques*. Pierre Versins summarizes two other science fiction stories from that volume: "La faillite de la science" [The Bankruptcy of Science], in which Thomas Edison invents a translating machine; and the more ambitious "La véridique ascension dans l'Histoire de James Stout Brighton" [James Stout Brighton's Authentic Ascent Through History], whose protagonist journeys back in time by traveling at enormous speed from east to west, to the extent that he witnesses the disappearance of humankind. All of this work helped prepare the way for the pieces that formed the bulk of the first version of *Voyage*, in which their inventive spirit was carefully re-combined with and put at the service of the earnest concerns of *La philosophie du travail*. Pawlowski clearly intended *Voyage* to be his masterpiece, and presumably considered it as such throughout his life, just as other critics have done.

We can only speculate as to how Pawlowski's career might have developed had the Great War not broken out and required his conscription into military service, but that service did not slow him down. Although he was not directly em-ployed as a propagandist, he continued writing and publishing throughout the war, including many contributions to such mo-rale-building periodicals as *La Baïonnette*. Although he cer-tainly did not abandon comedy, he did set aside the phantas-magoric *bizarrerie* that had become his hallmark, concentrat-ing on humor of an earthier and more naturalistic kind. Many of his sketches and stories were collected in *Dans les rides du front* [a punning title, signifying, "In the Wrinkles of the Fore-head" but also readable as "In the Front-line Trenches"] (1917) and *Signaux à l'ennemi* [Warnings to the Enemy] (1918). The page in the latter volume that advertises the au-thor's other works refers to a collection called *Contes singuli-ers*, also dated 1918, but no copy appears to exist and it is probably a phantom title—*Signaux à l'ennemi* was issued in March (although dated April) and the advertisement is pre-sumably looking forward to a planned publication that could not actually be published due to wartime restrictions.

22

The extent of the personal disillusionment that Pawlowski suffered during the War, and the legacy of mournful bitterness that remained thereafter, is obvious in several of the passages added to the text of the revised edition of *Voyage au pays du quatrième dimension* issued in 1923, especially the diatribe featured in Chapter XI, which leaves the reader in little doubt as to the identity of the hypothetical writer whose fate the narrative voice bemoans. Gustave Le Bon expressed his own disillusionment very clearly in two books lamenting the break in the history of civilization that the war had caused, the second of which, a collection of aphorisms called *Hier et demain: Pensées Brèves* (1918), includes some futuristic items very much in tune with the text added to *Voyage*.

The effects of the Great War on Pawlowski's sense of humor probably never wore off entirely, but they were gradually ameliorated, and his spirits were doubtless raised considerably when he married Marguerite Mangin in 1921. He published few books thereafter, although his journalistic activities continued apace; his most prominent production in volume form, with the exception of the augmented *Voyage*, was *Ma voiture de course* [My Racing Car] (1923), which appeared in a pioneering series of "romans de sport" [sports novels].

Pawlowski suffered a fatal heart attack at his home in Paris on February 2, 1933, and was buried in the Père Lachaise cemetery. His vast and various book collection was sold off in 1938, along with much of his voluminous correspondence, which he had carefully hoarded; unfortunately, the items were sold piecemeal and the collection dispersed.

The La Boétie edition of *Voyage* added some confusion to Pawlowski's bibliography by rendering his by-line on the cover and spine as "G. de Pawlowsky," although the title-page has the correct spelling. That is the edition from which I have taken this translation, although it contains several other obvious typographical errors, and may well have others that are less easily detectable and corrigible.

The text inevitably presents certain awkward problems to a translator, many of which reflect Pawlowski's own difficulties in trying to broach and examine ideas to which "three-dimensional language" is unsuited. For instance, the translation of the word *pays* in the title as "land," although perfectly orthodox, is clearly misleading, "land" being an essentially three-dimensional as well as a sociologically-loaded concept. Had he so wished, however, Pawlowski could have used a vaguer or more refined term, and he presumably chose not to in order to illustrate the difficulty of adapting three-dimensional terms to his purpose; I have, therefore, done likewise, not only in that instance but others.

Brian Stableford

JOURNEY TO THE LAND OF
THE FOURTH DIMENSION

I. The Silent Soul

Having arrived in the land of the fourth dimension some time ago, I find it strangely awkward, as I begin to write my anticipated memoirs, to translate them into ordinary language—the vocabulary of which is, of course, conceived according to the givens of three-dimensional space.

No words exist capable of defining precisely the bizarre impressions that one senses when one elevates oneself permanently above the world of habitual sensations. The vision of the fourth dimension reveals entirely new horizons to us. It completes our comprehension of the world; it permits the realization of a definitive synthesis of our items of knowledge; it justifies all of them, even though they seem contradictory, and one understands that it confers a totality upon ideas which partial expressions cannot contain. The fact of enunciating an idea by means of words in common usage limits one to the preliminary assumption of three-dimensional space. Now, although we know that the three geometrical dimensions— length, breadth and height[1]—can always be contained in an idea, those three dimensions, by contrast, can never suffice wholly to construct a quality, be it a curve in space or a reasoning of the mind. Neither numbers nor words constructed in three dimensions can take account of that difference between the container and the contained, between idea and matter, be-

---

[1] Pawlowsky has "*largeur, hauteur et profondeur*" [breath, height and depth], using "profondeur" as a painter might, to refer to a horizontal rather than a vertical dimension; I have made the substitution in the interests of conserving clarity.

tween art and science, which is not measurable in quantities—
and which, for want of a better term, we call the *fourth dimension.*

It is not at all astonishing that, taking the part for the
whole, I should use the words *fourth dimension* in the course
of this story to describe the continuous ensemble of phenomena, incorporating into that ensemble what it is convenient to
call "the three dimensions of Euclidean geometry". In spite of
its imperfect name, one should not, in fact, consider the fourth
dimension as a fourth measurement added to three others, but
rather as a Platonic fashion of understanding the universe,[2]
without there being any need for him to dissent from Aristotle
on this point: as a means of escape, permitting the comprehension of things in their eternal and immutable aspect, and a liberation from modification of quantity in order to attain the
quality of facts.

I know that I could, in writing these notes, have recourse—as some philosophers do—to a conventional vocabulary, coining obscure words to mask the insufficiency of cur-

---

[2] Plato argued that the true objects of knowledge are not located in the world of sensory experience but in a world of
Ideas or Forms that must lie beyond it, of which sensory phenomena are only a sort of distillate or shadow. He suggested
that the disembodied soul might have direct knowledge of the
Ideas and that the process by which the incarnate soul increases its knowledge is one of *anamnesis* [recollection], in which
information is gradually and effortfully recovered from some
kind of subconscious reservoir. Pawlowski's narrator, in learning to perceive the fourth dimension, is, in effect, amplifying
the process of *anamnesis* in order to gain access to this subconscious reservoir, and hence the world of Ideas. This kind of
Idealism is contradicted by Materialism, which asserts that
nothing exists but matter in motion and that knowledge can
only consist of discovering associations between observed
phenomena—the fundamental assumption on which the scientific method is based.

rent language, but that would only serve to push the difficulty back without resolving it. I therefore prefer to recount these memories of my journeys in the land of the fourth dimension in the ways they presented themselves to my mind, without literary pretension, naively and in disorder, hoping for the reader's indulgence, and will be happy if I can merely evoke in his mind a few dormant ideas that no one, in our world, has yet bothered to awaken.

To begin with, despite the difficulties of vocabulary, and especially the impossibility of my classifying chronologically future memories that escape any notion of time, I shall attempt to retrace the mental path which, little by little and step by step, led me to the land of the fourth dimension.

Before anything else, it is necessary to establish that the process of being transposed—"transported" is the wrong word—to the land of the fourth dimension immediately over-turns the common notions we have of time and space. Natural-ly, therefore, it is by means of small observations contradict-ing these common notions that the attention is gradually at-tracted to the possibility of the great voyage that our mind may accomplish. These contradictions are frequent, in everyday life as well as in the opportunities of the loftiest scientific re-search.

Because presentiments make us afraid when they come true, we prefer to explain the leaps of our heart in terms of passionate causes rather than the obscure aspirations of the race, and, when we speak of the exact sciences, we avoid as subversive all indiscreet questions regarding the impossibility of explaining a curved line, parallelism, movement and, in general, everything that surrounds us.

Time, without the space that expresses it, is inaccessible to us, and space can only be explained to our senses in terms of the time we take to traverse it. By virtue of a sort of natural slothfulness, however, our mind avoids and dissimulates these contradictions, as if they constituted a veritable mortal danger.

27

In fact, it is necessary to recognize that, in the present state of our civilization, few minds can support without danger the abrupt destruction, or even the dissociation, of notions of time and space. These notions are so indispensable to us that we immediately feel terror and madness brushing our minds when we relieve ourselves momentarily of these two traditional crutches, which allow us to take our initial steps safely.

We feel, however, that we are perpetually surrounded by an immense unknown. We occupy a strange and ill-defined location *between* the sensible world and our consciousness; we remain timidly curled up in the depths of a ship that carries us wherever the waves of an unknown sea dictate, and we declare ourselves satisfied if our location remains subjectively much the same, between the four walls of our cabin. If, however, we were to take it into our heads to emerge briefly from our retreat and courageously direct our eyes outside, it would be easy to understand that nothing is less safe than our perilous situation in the ensemble of phenomena and ideas.

Could there be anything more uncertain, in fact, than the notion of time that appears to us to be fundamental? Certain undeniable facts of psychic notification, of future prediction, would be worthy of being courageously envisaged by science, if science were not terrified by the idea of emerging momentarily from its petty domain of known relationships, in which ideas are formulated like the steps of a minuet. We accept historical knowledge of the past as something perfectly natural, but is it not evident that the past, of which we are so sure, does not presently exist, and that nothing, in consequence, can permit us to prove its existence? We use, as a basis for that proof, objects that subsist and personal memories, although we know perfectly well that this material evidence and these intellectual memories are, in the final analysis, only present vibrations.

The future seems to us unknown, because we believe that we have no material vision of it. This is, however, a crude and superficial reasoning that is limited in its range once we understand that the world as it appears to us is only luminous because we have eyes, sonorous because we have ears, and solid because we can touch it—that it is only formed, in reality, of different, obscure and mute vibrations, immaterial in the absolute sense of the word. The past is made of nothing but present vibrations; why, I ask you, could the future, which is contained in those same vibrations, not be known in a fashion just as certain, if we had a true understanding of the totality of motion,[3] in accordance with which the entire universe would be seemingly modified for our sensibility?

When one has arrived in the land of the fourth dimension, when one is liberated forever from the notions of space and time, it is with this intelligence that one thinks and reflects. By virtue of that, one finds oneself confounded with the entire universe, with pretended past events. Everything, henceforth, is a world of forms and immobile and innumerable qualities, which are, in a way, merely the harmonious lines of the same masterpiece.

One can, of course, discern in this world, as in everyday life, different points of existence and link up events that connect them, but it is useless, for that purpose, to appeal to the habitual notion of time. Events are outlined in the manner of geometrical figures—or, better still, the contours of a marble statue. Nothing can have, properly speaking, a beginning or an end. Nothing subsists any longer but harmonious symbols. One understands then how poor and inexpressive words such as *Journey to the Land of the Fourth Dimension* are. In this intellectually superior state, *journey* signifies nothing, and the expression *fourth dimension* itself is nothing but the manifestation of a synthetic state rather than the analysis of a new quality.

---

[3] The mathematician and philosopher Pierre Laplace suggested that a "daemon" which had full cognizance of the present position and directional velocity of every particle in the universe would be able to extrapolate the entire past and future from those data.

As soon as one has arrived in this world of pure ideas, every expression of ordinary language becomes negative. The mind no longer operates with anything but the universality of things; its ideas are all possible, without any possible reaction. *The silent soul* is no longer disturbed by the noises of the world; they are no longer anything but conventional points, incapable of embracing the immortal unknown idea of the mundane, and confusing all eyes with that mysterious veil we call time.

These general notions of the relative existence of time were not, however, those which first appeared to me most clearly. I only understood the whole of their strange scope when, having already arrived in the land of the fourth dimension, I was able to know simultaneously what had happened in ages past and what would happen in centuries to come. The overturning of the habitual idea that one has of space, the abstraction of distances that I succeeded in realizing progressively, the discovery I made of the Flat House with two exits, and the fashion in which I traversed the Horizontal Staircase, permitted me for the first time conclusively to abandon our three-dimensional world and to travel in all tranquility into the unknown.

II. The Untied Ribbon

The first obstacle that one encounters, when one first ventures into the land of the fourth dimension, is the ancestral resistance of the body, conceived in three dimensions. The mind adapts itself quite naturally to the abstractions of space and time, but the body seems, at first, to be incapable of escaping apparent material necessity. Curiously, however, the first facts that pointed out the road to the fourth dimension for me were purely material. They demonstrated to me, with adequate evidence, how close we are, without being aware of it, to the conception of the fourth dimension—which, for a long time, has justly preoccupied all those who have devoted themselves to the study of transcendental geometry.

I knew that an attempt had already been made to take account of the curious abilities of a medium, explaining them by the existence of the fourth dimension. This medium tied genuine bow-knots in an extended cord whose extremities were held by trustworthy individuals. I knew, too, that it had been explained that the theorems of Lobatchevsky, Riemann, Helmholtz and Beltrami are the sole logical bases of any true theory of parallelism.[4] I did not, however, have the opportuni-

---

[4] The references here are to three of the mathematicians who made key contributions to the development of non-Euclidean geometry in the 19th century, Nikolai Lobatchevsky, Bernhard Riemann and Eugenio Beltrami, plus one of the first physicists to recruit their work to the explanation of actual phenomena, Hermann von Helmholtz. A fourth mathematician involved in that development, Félix Klein, is cited further down the page. Euclid had previously analyzed the foundations of geometry as a series of five postulates, the fifth of which was the "principle of parallelism," which states that a point displaced from a line can have only one line drawn through it parallel to the first; the first non-Euclidean geometries were derived by vary-

ty to establish for myself the possibility of similar experimental demonstrations until the day when, desirous of conserving a few letters that I had, I decided to tie a ribbon around a little box—which, I was told, had come from India. Once the knot was tied, I remembered that I had forgotten to place one letter in the box and, instinctively, while thinking about something else, I opened the box, put the letter in, and closed it again.

Only then did I notice that I had forgotten to untie the knot.

I reviewed the facts carefully, and was forced to admit, by virtue of the wax seal, that the knot I had made, and which absolutely prevented the opening of the box, had not been touched. The object undeniably avoided the ordinary rules of our three-dimensional space.

I remembered then that Félix Klein had demonstrated that knots cannot subsist in a four-dimensional space and I understood that the box I had before my eyes had been constructed outside any Euclidean law—that the curious object must have been conceived in India and materialized in France without the necessity to transport it materially.

Needless to say, after that extraordinary adventure I sought by every possible means to find a rational explanation for it. I had doubtless been the victim of a simple hallucination, and there was nothing to prove that the stray letter was actually inside. I opened the box again, this time untying the ligature. The letter was indeed there! Perhaps I had put it there before the first closure? But a little bit of wax had fallen on the forgotten envelope when I closed the box for the first time, providing indubitable confirmation of my memory. Materially, the fact was impossible to admit. Materially, however, I was obliged to concede its reality. I confess that the certainty was, at first, infinitely painful for me, for it overturned the funda-

---

ing this postulate so that there is (in Lobatchevsky's version) more than one possible parallel line or (in Riemann's version) none at all.

mental notions without which our mind goes astray and is set adrift.

Nothing is easier to accept, in fact, than the existence of unknown and invisible forces situated inside us, which can be externalized to provoke phenomena that are only surprising in appearance. Everything can thus be explained with the utmost simplicity. In haunted houses, for example, we always find some unbalanced young woman in the neighborhood, whose nervous force, unwittingly externalized, is sufficient to produce the strangest phenomena. From there to thinking that there are unutilized forces dormant within us, more powerful than all the machines in the world, is only a single step. A day will come when we shall understand that there exists within every human being a path of progress much surer and much easier than the external path that science is presently attempting to follow.

It is necessary to say, though, that all these phenomena, still mysterious because they are unknown, do not overturn anything in our habitual vision of the world. No one doubts that there are fluids other than electricity, but that never upsets the notion of cause-and-effect that forms the basis of our reasoning, and it is only when the relationship of succession seems to us to be inverted that our reason totters.

What mysterious intervention had been able to overturn the relationship of succession in the events of which I have conserved such a precise memory? I could not account for it in a plausible fashion at first, because it proved impossible to repeat the adventure as I wished. My traditional attention had been awakened; it was always necessary for me to untie the ligature to open the box.

I thought it, therefore, prudent not to advertise such an absurd incident—but I conserved the memory that had impressed me vividly. It was, for me, the first certain indication of the existence of a four-dimensional space in which *a ligature could not subsist, nor a locked room remain closed*, but I only understood much later how our traditional ideas of succession in time could be modified, and how that succession

33

might become void on the day when, thanks to the intervention of the fourth dimension, all facts become, in a sense, simultaneous: detached from any historical relationship of cause and effect, distinguished from one another only by their qualities.

III. The Innumerable Diligence

Some time after the adventure of the Hindu box, the existence of the fourth dimension was revealed to me in a more precise fashion by some observations that I made concerning the possible abstraction of distances.

I have always been somewhat distrustful of spiritual experiments, particularly reported legends of Asia. It is necessary to recognize, however, that Orientals often appear to have realized the suppression of space in a practical fashion and that evidence in this regard is abundant. Arabs, as everyone knows, can communicate over very long distances without recourse to the telegraph. De Lesseps witnessed it on the occasion of the concession of the Suez canal,[5] and it is equally well-known that Hindu ambassadors congratulated the Queen of England in London on a victory that her troops in the Orient were achieving at that moment. Have not trustworthy witnesses similarly reported, with telling details, how a Hindu can appear aboard a vessel that had quit the land several days before, deliver a message and disappear, his presence in India being established immediately afterwards? But these are simple materializations at a distance, which will doubtless obtain rational and scientific explanation one day.

More disturbing and bewildering is the observation that one can achieve a possible abstraction of space solely by an effort of will. Moreover, it must be said, all our contemporary effort has been tending for a long time towards a similar result, and we are already beginning to understand that progress can, in large measure, be realized by continually increasing the speed of our actions.

For a long time, economists have considered the sum total of the capital in circulation within a county as representa-

---

[5] Said Pasha signed the concession authorizing Ferdinand de Lesseps to build the Suez Canal on November 30, 1854.

tive of its wealth. That element is, however, insignificant by comparison with the *qualitative* element: the rapidity of labor and traffic. Indeed, whether it is a matter of capital or means of transportation, what it is necessary to obtain, before anything else, is a better return of labor, an increase in speed—and social life is increased 365 times over when one accomplishes in a single day what our ancestors, with the same amount of capital and the same individual energy, could only realize in a year. It is for that reason that, in certain countries that are highly advanced from an industrial viewpoint—America, for example—special engineers called *speed-merchants*[6] are only occupied with one thing: indefinitely increasing the speed of work, without any corresponding increase in general expenses (quite the contrary).

To take a commonplace example of this extraordinary transformation, it is sufficient to reflect momentarily on what simple day's journey once amounted to, in a humble diligence.[7]

To increase the services that could be rendered by a postal service thus conceived, it was necessary to multiply fantastically the number of vehicles. On the other hand, merely by perfecting the quality of the traffic, increasing the speed of the old diligence by replacing it with an automobile, it was possible for a single vehicle to cover 50 times the distance in the same day, and the service presumably works 50 times better without any need to increase the number of vehicles.

---

[6] Pawlowsky here invents the term *vitessiers*, whose translation I have likewise improvised. He is referring to the organizational principles pioneered by Frederick Winslow Taylor, converted into practice by "time-and-motion" studies. The publication of Taylor's *Principles of Scientific Management* (1911) caused a considerable stir the year before the *Voyage* appeared.

[7] A *diligence*, in this sense, is the type of coach that was employed in France as the principal form of public transportation of both people and mail before the advent of the railways.

Now, imagine that speed increased in an infinite fashion, and you will establish logically that, if such an increase in speed were possible, the same single vehicle would end up presenting itself at every stop along its route at every moment of the day. That seems unrealizable in practical terms because our material forces are insufficient and we can only conceive of movement in a three-dimensional space—which is to say, as a succession of situations. On the other hand, as soon as we have a total conception of the four-dimensional universe, that which was hitherto absurd becomes easily realizable, and we understand clearly that the same vehicle can find itself simultaneously in all the different situations at every moment of the day, since speed suppresses time on this occasion.

Our mind, which reasons in a four-dimensional space itself, is not astonished when it performs an analogous operation every day in making an abstraction from various situations and grasping at a single stroke the idea of the route as such, or of absolute speed. If we hesitate to apply these abstractions to the material world, it is because our natural weakness causes us to distinguish and categorize in time that which we call a memory and a present vision. A little reflection will suffice, however, to make us understand that, if our mind had the force necessary to evoke a memory as a whole, it would have as much effective reality as our present vision.

Every day, our four-dimensional mind incites us, in spite of ourselves, to disencumber ourselves of the material obligations of the three-dimensional world. Why do we not do, for our material actions, that which we do for intellectual reasoning? Why retake a road previously traveled? Why repeat an itinerary whose details we know in advance? It becomes an obsession when one runs the same familiar course every day. Why must we submit to the administrative formality that constrains us to retake the same steps we have already taken, to follow the same routes already traversed, to end up at a point at which we know in advance that we are bound to end up? Is there no new procedure that will permit us to escape this base and material obligation?

Already certain modern thinkers have done justice to the prejudice of the straight line. It has been demonstrated, for example, that in a world in which the size of its inhabitants increases and decreases the nearer they approach its center, the shortest route between two points on the spherical surface is a curved line passing via the equator, not the straight line that pierces a tunnel from one point on the spherical surface to another. Can one not conceive, equally, that in addition to these geometrical conditions of transport from one point to another, there exists a more direct process of abstraction, permitting the emancipation of the body and its abstraction from space, in the same fashion in which the mind acts, moving without physical displacement from one idea to another in four-dimensional space?

This idea was, for me, only a striking suggestion—until the day when, happening to be living in a village, I succeeded, solely by the desire of my mind, in catching the local diligence anywhere I happened to be, at any hour of the day, according to the caprice of my will acting in four-dimensional space. The phenomenon produced itself for me spontaneously, without rational explanation, and it was a long time afterwards that I realized that it was materially realized by what I call, for want of a better term, a transmutation of special atoms.

IV. The Horizontal Staircase

These initial steps in the discovery of the fourth dimension were particularly painful for me. They occurred, in fact, in direct contradiction to the geometrical notions, full of logic and common sense, which were familiar to me. After the first advertisement of the untied ribbon and the innumerable diligence, however, the notion of the fourth dimension had to materialize itself to me in an even more precise fashion, in a form that I had not foreseen, and which seemed at first to be nightmarish.

At very close intervals and in almost identical mental conditions, I found myself in the presence of staircases that were not constructed in a geometrical fashion—and, to begin with, nothing was more revolting to me than the negotiation of those sorts of staircases. Other people might, perhaps, not have been affected to the same degree. There are, in fact, people who—despite being well-educated or very intelligent—are insensitive to visual constructions and the equilibrium of things, and for whom every mechanical or architectural problem remains a closed book. They conceive the facts psychologically with their brains, but they do not seek to represent the events or ideas that they conceive materially to themselves. This is the case with writers who do not feel an imperious need, when they are analyzing a state of mind or a character, to do it in a graphical or musical fashion. It is evident, however, that this research is essential for the realization of a work of art. In our intelligence, properly speaking, there is no music, painting or literature; there are only obscure and silent impressions, and these impressions, all similar, are strictly self-contained. It seems difficult, in consequence, to have a complete artistic sensation if we neglect to examine the subject we are studying in all its aspects, according to all the information that our senses can give us. It is, however, a fragmentary fashion of envisaging things that is habitual to many people.

When, on the contrary, one experiences one of the greatest pleasures of the mind in discovering the universal harmony of entities in all these aspects, nothing is more painful, morally, than to see certain material constructions not realized in accordance with the eternal logic of things.

Now, among the architectural considerations that best symbolize our ideas, none is more seductive, albeit more complicated in its apparent simplicity, than the establishment of a staircase. The architects of yesteryear understood this very well and succeeded in working wonders in this respect. On the one hand, there are, as at Chambord, two intertwining staircases, which do not permit a person going up to encounter a person coming down; on the other hand, there are curious Gothic staircases whose savant helices seem to resolve all the problems of transcendental geometry. There are also, sometimes, and more simply, complicated staircases like those which still exist in certain old provincial houses; they intersect cleverly, each requiring several determinate landings. When one mistakenly takes the wrong staircase, one does not end up on the intended floor; one finds oneself above it or below it, and it is necessary to make a certain effort of the imagination to rediscover the general design of the labyrinth.

All this, however, is rapidly explicable, as soon as one gives it a little attention, and one soon realizes the reasons for the apparent illogic in the superposition of constructions of different eras, brought together over the centuries.

Much more disturbing is the problem of the staircase which, after an undeniable succession of steps, brings you to the floor from which you started. They are things at which one smiles the first time, believing it a temporary error, but they are problems which become frightening when one persists in seeking the problem according to the primitive principles of three-dimensional Euclidean geometry.[8]

And I admit, for my part, that I experienced a real relief on the day when I realized that if such staircases could exist, that their possibility could only be conceived in four-dimensional space, and only that this recourse sufficed to give a definitive explanation of the problem. Soon, I was even able to take a strange pleasure in passing through a few of these invisible residences, conceived by transcendental geometry, in which the floors are confused, where the first is not necessarily below the fourth, nor the third above the ground floor.

---

[8] Modern readers encountering this image will inevitably be reminded of the work of M. C. Escher (1898-1972), who depicted several "horizontal staircases," most famously in his *Relativity*, but Escher was still a teenager when this chapter was written, and *Relativity* dates from 1953.

IV. Spatial Abstractions

One generally forms a completely false idea of the fourth dimension, wishing to describe it in terms of the givens furnished by the vision of a three-dimensional world. One ends up, in consequence, with impossibilities—and, by definition, irreducible absurdities. One is often similarly mistaken, as I have said, in simply wishing to *add* the fourth dimension to the other three, as if it were only a matter of creating a supplementary dimension, rendering possible the extension, to infinity, of further "dimensions" completing length, breadth and height.

There again, without realizing it, one submits transcendental geometry to Euclidean definition; one renders all explanation impossible or absurd in advance. The fact is that Euclidean geometry, like all contemporary science, only operates in quantities, in *numbers* that divide our vision of the world into slices, cutting nature up into classes and categories. As soon as we want to begin on the most elevated research, we sense that this *quantitative* procedure is purely artificial, and that it cannot take account of the world entire. We know this because our consciousness, in contrast to our senses, is not constructed according to the vision of the three-dimensional world, but reveals to us, on the contrary, the fourth dimension—which is merely, in sum, the necessary complement of a total comprehension of the universe.

It is, therefore, above the *quantities* excised by science, that our mind perpetually reveals to us those *qualities* which know no scientific measurement, and which translate themselves materially to our eyes by virtue of the existence of *works of art*.

It is, therefore, grossly mistaken to think that the vision of a non-Euclidean world is opposed to our current vision of phenomena; in fact, it completes it.

42

The external world appears to us initially, according to our retinal sensations, in a visual plane of two dimensions; then the muscular sensations of convergence and accommodation permit us to distinguish the distance of objects and to conceive the third dimension. Only the mind, which possesses a divine spark superior to the senses, permits us to understand that, above the world of appearances and scientific constructions, a complete and continuous vision of the universe exists. Thus, we can, without any great effort, realize at every instant the abstraction of time, associating very different ideas with one another. We can avoid recommencing a reasoning already completed, and set forth on a new mental path already designed to return us to the same *mental location.*

Beneath the habitual three-dimensional vision, other, simpler ones can similarly be conceived. Yes, certainly, Euclidean geometry is for us presently the most comfortable means of grasping the universe, given the construction of our bodies and our centuries-old habits, but that does not make it a universal and indispensable form of sensation, Modern writers have tested this prejudice. Plane beings moving on a spherical surface would quite naturally conceive a geometry in which the sum of the angles of a triangle would always be greater than the sum of two right angles. Similarly, in a world derived of solids, our geometry might experience some difficulty in becoming manifest. Henri Poincaré has written some highly perceptively pages on this subject.

We can divide up volumes by means of surfaces; we can divide up surfaces by means of lines; we can divide up lines by means of points—but when it comes to defining the point, our Euclidean science fails and vanishes. When it is necessary for us to take account of the physical continuum, our powerlessness is extreme. We come to understand that science is nothing but a conventional language, which permits us to catalogue and classify certain fractions of phenomena that we detach from one another artificially, according to their qualities, but we begin to sense that science, like language, is incapable of translating the continuity that belongs to the world of qualities and cannot be defined by numbers.

The observations that we have just made immediately provoke an objection. If our *continuous consciousness* alone reveals to us the real existence of qualities—which is to say, the four dimensions united—how is it that our senses, developed according to the needs of the mind, do not perceive that fourth dimension with the same facility? Why must we have recourse to the numerical analyses of science and divide up the universe in three dimensions to render it intelligible?

The answer to this question is easy. Our world is, for us, in perpetual transformation—which is to say, in perpetual progress. Now, the vision of the continuous universe is opposed to any idea of motion or change. Our motionless consciousness participates in the universality of things; it has no need to resort to the fractionation of the universe, but it is not the same for the body. The mind, which only conceives absolute unity, employs an admirable artifice to create the world in its image, and multiplies it to infinity. It reflects itself in numbers; it parcels out its entire personality to fractions of the universe that it wishes to analyze and comprehend. Thus, for the mind, number, beyond the figure 1 is nothing but a mirage—but a useful mirage. It permits it to create artificial individualities, which it distinguishes purely as new qualities of the eternal unity.

It is impossible to understand space and the universe in an absolute fashion without being condemned, by the same token, to the divine immobility of consciousness. Just as the human mind creates gods in its own image, so it creates lines and numbers—but that is no more than a means of analysis, a scientific procedure of purely transitory demonstration.

Human activity is only possible with the vision of the three-dimensional world, which renders the world mobile for us; but that suffices to give us a better understanding of the necessary existence of a fourth dimension that completes its unity and renders it immobile in the vulgar sense of the word—because, when man attains unity, by virtue of that very fact, he kills the illusory contradictions of life.

As soon as one elevates oneself above the world of three dimensions—as soon as the mind, detached from the suggestions of sensation, recovers its integral power in the land of the fourth dimension—the activity of the three-dimensional world ceases, apparent mobility disappears and the abstractions of space and time become as natural in reality as they are in reasoning.

It was initially in automobiles, on very long journeys, that I succeeded in realizing my first abstractions of distance, of which I have long conserved the memory. The first time, coming back from Florence to Paris via Aoste, I completely forgot the fragment of the route between Ambérieu and Tournos. On another occasion, on the Route d'Espagne, it was the immediate surroundings of Tours that I omitted to traverse.

These material abstractions, on familiar journeys, were initially revealed to me by the veritable remorse that I felt, immediately afterwards, in observing my forgetfulness. It was as if all my atavistic senses were in revolt, as if in a protest of traditional logic, and I immediately tried to find the indispensable rational explanation that would have liberated my senses. Doubtless, being very familiar with the route, I must have confused an old memory with present reality. I thought I had forgotten a journey, when in reality I had accomplished it while thinking about something else. Certain items of irrefutable material evidence—the consumption of fuel, the indications of a kilometric counter and those of a watch—proved to me that it was not so.

Naturally, I still tried to think that there was nothing there but a collection of purely material coincidences and that I was the victim of an illusion. I experienced, moreover, a veritable cerebral fatigue in registering such facts and I tried not to think about them any longer, if only to escape those painful and material fits of remorse that I mentioned—fits of physical remorse much more discomfiting, when one is not accustomed

45

to the mysteries of the fourth dimension, than all the moral remorse that one can experience in the ordinary life of three dimensions.

VI. The Instantaneous Voyage

Interesting as they were, the first abstractions of distance that I succeeded in realizing in the course of automobile journeys were, for me, only elementary indications of the possibility of a journey to the land of the fourth dimension. Only the abstraction of time, however, could give me conclusive results.

It is curious to observe, in this respect, how many centuries-old prejudices are rooted in our minds when it comes to calculating the time necessary to accomplish an action or to conceive an idea. Fatally, we take for our base the average duration of human life. We estimate that this average time is necessary for the complete development of our personality. Furthermore, we cannot imagine that an important action or an idea of genius can become manifest without long preparation, without a historical series of successive actions—and we estimate the necessary time of gestation arbitrarily, according to the result obtained.

The idea of instantaneity is equivalent, for us, to that of nothing, and we cannot, for the most powerful reasons, support the idea that I have already mentioned, of a possible inversion of the order of succession in the development of a fact or an idea—and yet, many banal observations ought to demonstrate to us how puerile and inexact this way of envisaging things is.

In a dream, for example, when an external noise or an odd sensation disturbs our sleep, we immediately conjure up a long and complicated story that justifies and precedes the abrupt sensation. We dream that, after interminable preparations, we have set forth on a journey; that after a journey lasting hours, all of whose details are still in our memory, we arrive at its goal; that a catastrophe awaits us, and is taking us by surprise. It is evident, however, that the catastrophe has preceded our historical justification, even though we do not hesitate to consider it as the final moment of our dream. We suppose, in brief, a vain genesis of instantaneous four-dimensional ideas in imitation of the genesis of three-dimensional phenomena.

This need for preparation is found, to some extent, everywhere, even in very serious matters of scientific or artistic research that have nothing in common with dreams. Consider, in fact, what happens when a scientist makes a great discovery or a writer senses the emergence of an idea of genius. In such a case, the first concern of the inventor is not to recognize that the idea has come to him from an unknown source, that it has suggested itself to him involuntarily, but, on the contrary, to justify his discovery with reasoning invented after the fact.

With the best will in the world, the scientist will construct in all its elements, step by step, the pretended method that led him to make his discovery. Quite sincerely, he does not perceive that he is only justifying an involuntary intuition by means of the subsequent experiments, and that, in reality, he did not play any voluntary part in that instantaneous intuition.

The writer does the same when he tries to explain afterwards what his intentions were in conceiving a work of genius. In reality, the man, however knowledgeable he might be, does not know himself and is merely the humble servant of his immobile four-dimensional intelligence, beneath which he moves in an incomplete and transitory three-dimensional space.

Everything, in temporal terms, in subject to illusion. The duration of human life, sufficient from our point of view, is insignificant if one compares it to that of the stars, prodigious if one sets it beside that of inferior creatures, which are born, reproduce and die within a few seconds.

It is similarly worth pointing out that in the life of a man of genius, the truly creative act seems to occur within the short space of a few seconds. The rest is merely a matter of tuning, interminable variation and adaptation to vulgar prejudices constructed in three dimensions. In general, it is in the early years of their life that men of talent really conceive the ideas that will later make their intellectual fortune, and tomorrow's great man is only the fortunate inheritor of yesterday's wealthy child.

The duration of our actions, long and complicated as they may seem, is infinitely multiplied by the material difficulties of action or expression in a three-dimensional world. It often happens that a simple glance exchanged between two passers-by who do not know one another replaces years of communal life or complete intimacy, and the minds understand one another in an instant better than they would through the medium of their bodies in an interval of three long years.

We necessarily attribute a temporal duration to these intellectual flashes of total four-dimensional comprehension and, fugitive as they are, we suppose that they must last at least a few seconds. Even that duration is non-existent, however, for there is no possible duration in the world of four dimensions, and, in consequence, no necessary succession in actions that are, in sum, as simultaneous as all the distinct parts of a marble statue.

It was this apparently complex, but quite simple, notion that permitted me to explain, for the first time, the three little journeys that I had been able to make to the land of the fourth dimension.

These journeys were accomplished, if I might put it thus, on the spot, in depth and in an instantaneous fashion, in spite of all the difficulties—and I must observe once again that the words are unfortunately lacking for me to describe, in a language conceived in three dimensions, the admirable simplicity of these journeys without displacement: these extensive instantaneous excursions, which, however—to employ current language—comprised long and curious episodes. The first ones were devoid of much interest, but they surprised me by their strange novelty.

One day, therefore, without any apparent reason—I might almost say disinterestedly—I found myself in Paris, having gone past the Gare du Nord and the Gare de l'Est, in a little deserted square of provincial appearance where the Gare du Midi was. [9]

I cannot describe the strange impression made on me by that seemingly-abandoned building with the high roofs and walls of stone and brick, all of whose windows were closed and whose façade bore, in banal letters of gilded zinc, the simple words: *Gare du Midi*. Behind the building there was no railway, no movement.

By virtue of what materialization of ideas was this unnecessary and absurd station there, and why had the crossroads of memory erected it for me on this Parisian site? I did not even attempt to explain it to myself, and the more interesting journeys that I made thereafter soon erased this insignificant encounter from my mind.

---

[9] The actual Paris station from which most Midi-bound trains leave is the Gare de Lyon, which is located a long way south of the closely-associated Gare de Nord and Gare de l'Est; there are two other stations south of the Seine from which southbound long-distance trains depart, but neither of them is called the Gare du Midi (they are the Gare d'Austerlitz and the Gare Montparnasse).

VII. The Flat House

I have indicated in the preceding chapter how I was led to conceive that the development of the sciences is not effected, as is commonly believed, by deduction, but that, on the contrary, all the discoveries made by the human mind were due to the intuition of certain thinkers, whose conceptions often qualified as fantasies, although the recording savants subsequently appropriated them by verifying them.

It is to poets, to the imaginative, that the privilege has belonged since the origin of the world of discovering the secrets of nature, because that discovery is, in the final analysis, entirely internal, and its experimental verification nothing but a vain simulacrum. In failing to recognize the profound truth of certain poetic inventions, scientists have not neglected to reduce the domain of possible discovery, and one cannot stress too heavily the facility with which they set aside from their preoccupations certain problems whose existence is nevertheless undeniable. It hardly matters to Euclidean geometers that they give a ridiculous definition of parallelism: "two lines that only meet at infinity." They are content to smile when their approach to the squaring of the circle is criticized and they declare themselves satisfied when they have represented space and time as a succession of points occupied one after another by a moving object. Only definite quantities interest them, although such quantities are nothing but the reflection to infinity of the same unity; continuity escapes them and quality is, for them, a word devoid of meaning. Only quality and continuity, however, can permit us to rise above the commonplace world and glimpse, beyond pretended scientific certainties, the definitive certainty that never changes.

It is by this means, continually increasing our mental faculties, that infinity and eternity are eventually revealed within a moment, of which it is sufficient to increase the power,

51

whether in a past or in a future, in which eternity is nothing but a pure mirage.

It was doubtless under the influence of sharp memories encountered at certain moments in my thoughts that it was possible for me thus to accomplish my first instantaneous journeys to the land of the fourth dimension.

The discovery I made of the Gare du Midi situated in the heart of Paris beside the Gares du Nord and de l'Est was not, for me, the first revelation of the possible existence of "places in the world"—as we used to say—distinct from the ones that one normally sees, coexistent in the fourth dimension.

I remember, for example, a certain *green room* of which I established the undeniable existence during my childhood, which was situated exactly in between the final bedroom looking out from the façade of an old provincial château and the large room that came immediately afterwards and which occupied the entire wing of the château.

On reflection, adopting the ordinary three-dimensional point of view, that room had no door to the central corridor that served all the rooms, and its existence was geometrically impossible. It is no less true that no detail of the furniture of the green room, in the Empire style, was unknown to me, and I remember, even today, the periodic but entirely clear impressions I had of it. Moreover, that did not astonish me for many years, for it was customary to abandon certain rooms that were never used and to consecrate them permanently to memories of other times, In Paris, one cannot conceive of the existence of these forgotten rooms, but it seems perfectly natural in the provinces. It was that very fact that prevented me from taking a more particular interest in the green room during that period of my life. It is for that reason, too, that I only record the fact as a memory, without wishing to draw any other consequence from it.

Similarly, I only want to cite for form's sake the existence of an abandoned house that I discovered one day in the forest of Fougères, in which I went with some astonishment though rooms that were not constructed geometrically, whose vertically-arranged floors only comprised a single one internally. Since then, I have understood that these constructions are only explicable by the existence of four-dimensional space—but that did not become evident to me until the day when I discovered, in a quarter of Paris previously inaccessible to me and situated outside the habitual vision of three dimensions, an extraordinary flat house with two doors, one of which let out into the Place de la Concorde and the other on to the Terrasse de Saint-Germain. I have necessarily to employ the absurd expression *flat house* because I cannot find any words in our language capable of describing that house— which, in three-dimensional vision, would have been invisible in profile, whose facades could only be perceived at an angle, and whose entrance and exit were confused, distinguished only by the clearly-differentiated places in the world of three dimensions to which they led.

It is no less true that, after an initial atavistic revolt of my entire being, it was possible for me to pass through—in every sense of the phrase and quite naturally—the marvelous domain that was offered to me. Furthermore, it was not even a mater of personal displacement: the space seemed to come to me. This was not the "levitation" about which so much has been said, nor mental transport at a distance; it was something infinitely more simple than all that: a dissolution of the universe, unexpected and definitive. My immobility was analogous to that of the geometrical axis of a wheel rotating at top speed. I displaced myself while remaining still. My movements were only movements relative to myself. I benefited from them according to my desire, without contributing the least effort thereto.

According to every appearance, this reconstruction of the world was due to the power of my internal memories, which completed themselves and exteriorized themselves with a force that can only derive from the working of a highly-developed visual memory. The second door opened on to the

Terrase de Saint-Germain, but it was quite evident that, had my desire been modified, it might have opened somewhere else entirely.

Needless to say, the habitual preoccupations of modern life soon appeared to me to be infinitely paltry and pointless. The idea that thousands of men had been able to live in the world until then without benefiting from its complete vision seemed implausible to me. How long would that be the case? It did not take me long to understand that the question did not even make sense and that, from the viewpoint of the fourth dimension, the world cannot have a beginning or an end, properly speaking.

Nothing prevented me from achieving the same *displacement*—to employ the common expression—that I had succeeded in effectuating in space, by means of the fourth dimension, in time as well. I was thus permitted to enter into a relationship with that which had been and that which must be, all the while remaining motionless in the eyes of the vulgar, who have no understanding of the extreme mobility of the motionless philosopher and my power to explore, solely according to the caprices of my will, what are commonly known as future ages.

VIII. The Transmutation of Atoms of Time

It was, therefore, by displacements in space that the existence of the land of the fourth dimension was first revealed to me. Once again, I do not know how to explain these displacements by borrowing terms from a contemporary language constructed in three dimensions. I am forced, in spite of everything, to employ sketchy images, to have recourse to old expressions believed to be the preserve of alchemy, to describe an incident that is, however, quite simple and which should not be surprising, however unfamiliar one might be with the unity of viewpoint that characterizes the fourth dimension.

Just as one has recourse to the atomic theory to provide an adequate image of chemical combinations, I too am constrained to have recourse to an analogous hypothesis to explain in a rough fashion the displacements that one effects in the land of the fourth dimension; this imperfect explanation goes like this:

Whereas in displacement in three dimensions, the atoms forming a body are pushed back and replaced by other atoms composing another body, in the same way that a ship displaces the sea-water, displacement in the land of the fourth dimension is made by means of what was once called a *transmutation*.

The world of the fourth dimension being *continuous*, no movement, in the vulgar sense of the word can be produced there as in the mobile world of three dimensions. A displacement is therefore made by an exchange of qualities between neighboring atoms, and—to employ the same gross image as before—when a ship is displaced, it is the atoms of water in front of it that mutate into the atoms of the ship while, behind it, the atoms of the ship mutate into atoms of water.

This, if properly understood, is only an image of the most primitive sort, designed to explain, in the language of three dimensions, a procedure of displacement that has no

Euclidean character in the continuous world of four dimensions. It is, indeed, necessary to repeat that the atoms are only a convenient hypothesis. They do not exist in reality; there are only different qualities in a single physical continuum.

The atom is a conception of the mind, which isolates matter with all its attributes and all its qualities. The mind conceives the atom in its own image, thus extracting it from a complete and unique four-dimensional world, and it is an illusion of the senses that reflects the atom to infinity, as if by means of multiple mirrors, into the various appearances of an incomplete world of three dimensions. As soon as one is transposed into the land of the fourth dimension, movement, as we understand it, no longer exists; there are only changes in quality, and we remain motionless, in the vulgar sense of the word.

The same rough comparison permits a glimpse of the similar *displacement in time* that occurs when one is transposed into the land of the fourth dimension. In the same way that we suppose atoms in juxtaposition to explain space, we imagine, in order to justify time, a succession of moments that are, in a way, the *atoms of time*. Here, as with displacement in space, displacement in time is effectuated by means of a transmutation of the atoms of time—moments, that is—under the action of that philosopher's stone, the atom or, better still, the monad that is our mind. Again, it is quite evident that this is no more than a convenient hypothesis, and that, in reality, time is not composed of distinct moments but is a continuum whose quality alone can be modified.

When one has arrived in the land of the fourth dimension, these truths appear much simpler that all our scientific explanations of the three-dimensional world, and it is very difficult to envisage, without a certain amount of pity, the extreme ignorance of men of our time—by which I mean of our quality. It seems to me, however, that it should be easy for them to observe the strange opposition that there is between what everyday language calls *force* and *matter*, *mind* and *body*, *quality* and *quantity*—which is to say, between the world seen in four dimensions or only in three.

As they admire for the first time a new verity or an esthetic masterpiece that did not exist before, men often declare that the truth or the masterpiece is superior to everything that existed before, but do not ask themselves where that strange revelation can have come from. They freely repeat the assertion that observation and experience alone have formed their minds and bodies, but are not surprised abruptly to find themselves in the realm of knowledge when a new fact contradicts all that pretended acquired experience.

Art, in itself, is a perpetual contradiction of science. It proves to us that there is, over and above ourselves, a world of qualities on which we depend, that we know directly, and which permits us to judge in an instant the greater or lesser value of an artistic symbol conceived in three dimensions.

Without the existence of the veritable four-dimensional world known to our minds outside any idea of time and space, the evolution of species would be inexplicable, progress a nonsense, and art a folly. One cannot imitate a model that does not yet exist, and, without a model, the three-dimensional world would remain inert.

The men of today, bound by prejudice to three-dimensional space and, by the same token, to the division of a single movement into successive points in time, are in a situation not unlike that of an insect wandering indefinitely over a statue, which experiences its contours as a succession of events and never contemplates the whole. When one knows how to disengage oneself forever from that traditional inferiority, it seems, on the contrary, that one is abruptly established in the situation of an artist who admires the totality of the statue, sees it entire in a single moment and takes pity on the awkward insect which feverishly pursues its obscure route from one grain of marble to the next.

Personally, knowing now that there is neither time nor space, properly speaking, and that one can, when one knows how to liberate oneself from Euclidean prejudices, displace oneself at will within the present or the future, I have investigated with curiosity transformations of our world over the course of centuries: transformations that are, in the final analysis, merely the same motion designed in its entirety outside time.

Thus, I was enabled to make strange discoveries in the course of these journeys in the land of the fourth dimension, and clearly to understand certain problems that still confound our contemporaries.

Hopefully, the reader will excuse me the slightly unaccustomed fashion in which I shall proceed, not needing to pass from one period of history to another. The evolution of humanity being only a single motion—a single statue, to resume the comparison I made above—it is entirely natural that I mention successively, without any necessary order, the head, an arm or a leg—by which I mean the year 200, 1912 or the time of the Golden Eagle. All these eras, like the parts of a single body, form a simultaneous whole for me, the numbers of the years being analogues of the classification numbers that a sculptor might employ for the display of different parts of the same work.

IX. The Leviathan

It is, therefore, somewhat at hazard and in no particular order that I shall recount in the chapters to follow the strange philosophical journeys I made in the land of the fourth dimension, leaving it to the reader to derive the intellectual scenario of these romantic adventures. These journeys were always accomplished on the spot, at the moment when I least expected them. I often found myself mentally transposed, without transition, to the land of the fourth dimension, without having made any effort to go there, the crossroads of multiple memories having gradually replaced the banal three-dimensional world by reflection.

The conception of these journeys was, I repeat, instantaneous. Time does not exist, in fact, in the land of the fourth dimension; whatever the multiplicity of observed details might be, it is impossible to conceive them in any but a simultaneous fashion. Later, wishing to transcribe these memories in the three-dimensional world, I was naturally led to remake them in the form of a story, and I projected in time impressions or events that could not be revealed to me in space and time. For greater convenience, I thought I ought to classify successively, following their aesthetic line, events that only form, in sum, a motionless curve.

To employ the language of the third dimension, I shall therefore say that in my memories of future ages, I had first to combine all the events that passed in our own century, the singular era of the *Leviathan*. There is no more curious study than the period, contemporary with this book, when there reigns without division a colossal microcephalus, superior to men and enveloping them like the cells of a gigantic body. Personally, I admit that these surprising revelations of a present period that I believed I knew astonished me even more than my visions of future ages, and I have hastened to impart them to my contemporaries.

After the disappearance of the Leviathan, it was granted to me to know strange events that unfolded in the *Scientific Era*. These events were perhaps sketchier, less subtle than those which characterized the transitional era of the Leviathan, but they are no less curious to describe.

Thirdly, I shall preferentially group the journeys that I made to the era of the *Golden Eagle*—unfortunately, it will be very difficult for me to transcribe my memories that strange period, the most curious of all. In the era of the Golden Eagle, in fact, the fourth dimension becomes familiar to all men and it is impossible to translate what will happen then into three-dimensional language.

I should add, finally, that I have always experienced a certain timidity in exploring that philosophical age, very distant from ours, because, although it is relatively easy to describe future three-dimensional centuries without danger, it becomes very difficult to *come back* from the age of the fourth dimension when one has committed the imprudence of venturing into it.

Now, my primary intention is to report these curious notes on the age in which we live, and I am proud of the moral hesitation that has permitted me to remain bound to the modern world, to return to it *and not to remain forever in the future*. When the mind rises up into the fourth dimension in a work of art, it finds itself entirely prepared for eternal and conscious immobility, and death is no longer anything but a mere escape. When that escape occurs in advance of any creation, however, the infinitely painful impression of nothingness subsists in isolation; that is the great weakness of Oriental philosophies.

As for journeys into the past, no one will be astonished not to find any of them in the course of this story, for these sorts of journeys are impossible. Only the future exists at this moment in the land of the fourth dimension. The past no longer exists, since it is entirely contained within the present, and it is sufficient to evoke ones memories internally with sufficient will-power to know everything that has happened in the past until now.

In the course of this story, I shall relieve myself of the responsibility of explaining every time the exact conditions in which some event or other was revealed to me. That is not, in fact, of any importance. Whether they occur in the course of a stroll in Paris or the countryside, or during my sojourns in the Flat House with two doors, my journeys, I repeat, are always instantaneous. They do not, therefore, occupy any tangible place in the events of my quotidian life; they never modify it and are not confused with it.

The most important and disconcerting event of the time of this book—whose consequences, for that reason, I hasten to advertise—was, beyond any doubt, the unexpected, gigantic and, quite incredibly, *unnoticed* emergence of a new being, superior to man, tightly enslaving him, which robbed him of the sovereignty of the world without his even suspecting it, and which assumed his succession in the scale of living beings. This colossal animal was afterwards called the Leviathan.

It is truly curious to observe that all the veritable thinkers, all the philosophers, had foreseen its appearance, and that they had even given it a name, as Hobbes had done, but without, it seems, having taken their own predictions seriously.

Yes, certainly, there was no lack of abundant previous talk about certain social transformations; mention had been made of judicial links between men; the birth of civil societies and the social contract had been exposed; numerous volumes had been published on the subjects of the social organism and contemporary mechanization; some had even gone so far as to draw close analogies between that organism and the human body—but no one had taken it to the level of literalizing an analogy that was more real than anyone thought.

At the beginning of the 20th century there were even some very curious newspaper articles that touched, without suspecting it, on this important question. When, for instance, it became practicable to film microbes, people marveled to see on the screen the swarming and hyperactive life of innumerable tiny creatures that live within our own bodies. They even went so far as to formulate the idea that the worlds we know might perhaps be little corpuscles forming parts of a gigantic and unknown body—but such analogies remained purely literary.

In fact, during the centuries that man has considered himself the uncontested king of the world, he has not been able seriously to admit for a single instant, in the depths of his being, that this sovereignty might be endangered by superior organisms that he considered to be entirely his creations and entirely subject to his whims.

Certain symptoms, however, might have disturbed him at the present moment. With a little more perspicacity, and less self-confidence, it would have been easy for him to discern the definitive constitution of the superior and veritable being: the colossal Leviathan that would subjugate and crush him.

Firstly, there were strange social maladies, which demonstrated, beyond the shadow of a doubt, that the individual life of social cells was not as complete as people believed. People witnessed, in art, literature and music, the birth of works which lost more of their individual character with every passing day. Here, there was a judiciary affair that transformed itself into a social malady; elsewhere, some musical or literary school that made it understood, without any doubt, that an author was now no longer master of his work, and was reproducing overly general ideas that he did not understand very well himself. Finally, and most importantly, it was in the moral domain that strange indications were given. Some individual crimes and indelicacies involving only isolated individuals were considered as negligible; certain acts insignificant in themselves, but having a social bearing, certain material assaults against the mechanization of the State, took, by contrast, first place.

No one, however, appeared to glimpse the formidable revolution that was taking place in the world, the very curious consequences of which I should like to outline.

X. The Voluntary Slaves

People who had not lived in the century of the Leviathan could not, I am convinced, form an exact idea of what that monstrous animal really was. Some considered that there was nothing at stake but a symbol, that by Leviathan it was necessary to mean a moral collective, a community of ideas, scientific methods and actions that crystallized out at the same time quite naturally. That is a conception that it is important to destroy in the interests of truth.

The Leviathan was a very real animal, which dominated man without being placed above him in the scale of living beings, contrary to the opinion of zoologists of the era, who allotted that place to the Superman.[10]

Yes, certainly, the Leviathan was reminiscent of the human organism in many respects. It was formed materially of living cells, but grouped in the manner of a colony of protozoans deprived of synergy and incapable of conscious centralization.

The Leviathan was reminiscent of those marine hydroids forming a colony of polymorphous individuals which specialize in five different functions. Some are the individual consumers that, by means of a network of common canals, take responsibility for the nourishment of the whole. Others, in the form of elongated and sensible fingers, observe the colony's surroundings. Others, covered with stinging hairs, serve as the fortifications protecting the retreat. Others, finally, are the reproductive individuals, sometimes faithful to the colony but sometimes of vagabond inclination, drawing away to live their own life.

---

[10] It is arguable that *surhomme*, the equivalent of the German *übermensch*, is better translated as "overman," but I have employed the English usage that became most common.

In these primitive colonial animals, as in free colonies of ants or bees, the consciousness of a general end to be attained—the plan of action—does not exist in certain individual directors of the colony, as it does, for example, in the brain of a superior animal. The communal idea remains in the Universal Consciousness, and the individuals of the colony, guided by simple material needs, instinctively divide up the necessary roles and increasingly specialize, by virtue of the law of minimum effort, in an identical function, to the extent permitted by the present administrative intelligence of protozoans.

The Leviathan owed its success to this inclination to minimal effort, as represented by the horror of general responsibility and ideas that encourages men to specialize in anonymous, unvarying tasks and to serve.

It is therefore necessary to reject all the legends that tend to represent the Leviathan as a fabulous being, endowed with intelligence, passions and vices: as a vicious animal, deliberately crushing human beings and incorporating them purely for its own pleasure. Undoubtedly, within its gigantic body, men became no more than simple cells, but they gladly accepted that diminution of their own individuality. We shall see why.

At the beginning of the modern world, Estienne de La Boétie, in his admirable *Discours de la servitude volontaire* or *Contr'un*, noted the tendency that all men have to serve, for the simple reason, as Plutarch put it, that they do not know how to pronounce the syllable *no*.[11] It is not weapons that pro-

---

[11] Estienne de La Boétie (1530-1563) was a close friend of the skeptical essayist Michel de Montaigne, who wrote a poignant memoir idealizing their relationship and published much of his friend's work posthumously, in 1571—but not the *Discourse on Voluntary Servitude* cited here, which he considered too controversial; it was eventually published in 1576. It is a passionate diatribe against tyranny, asserting the sovereignty of the people and denying the divine right of kings—hence the

tect a tyrant but five or six people that surround him "to be the accomplices of his cruelties, companions in his pleasures, procurers of his sensual indulgences and sharers in his plunder.... These six have 600 who profit under them, and these 600 hold 6000 in their grip... and whoever would amuse himself by unraveling that network will see, not 6000, but 100,000, millions, which the tyrant sustains by that thread, whose end he holds..."

Consider from the height of a mountain the valleys that extended beneath your feet, with their towns and villages, where 1000 individual interests coexist and rub elbows with one another, with their patchwork of innumerable differently-colored fields testifying to opposed desires and appetites; how marvelous to think, then, that millions of wills and conflicting ambitions are maintained in order and equilibrium solely by the prestige of a central power personified by a single man who does not know them. It is not, therefore, from on high that power comes, as one imagines impatiently when one is young in experience, but from below—by voluntary servitude, as La Boétie puts it—and the history of peoples is nothing, in the final analysis, but a continuation of natural history.

In a State composed of individuals, as in a body composed of cells, progress is a function of the enslavement of the mass. From that general progress, the elite profits in intellectual activity and the mass in intellectual inaction; the two things are equally good, depending on the ambition one has.

What Estienne de La Boétie could not, however, foresee in the monarchical times in which he lived, was that voluntary Servitude would be even more absolute under a scientific republic than under a tyrant.

---

alternative title *Contr'un* [Against One], signifying opposition to dictatorship. The Belgian press that published the third edition of *Voyage au pays de la quatrième dimension* was named after La Boétie as a statement of its political ideals, in an era when tyrannical fascism was considered a more dangerous avatar of the Corporate State than communism.

To the extent that the State takes an anthropomorphic form in assuming a resemblance to the human body, the brain—which is to say, the tyrant—is rendered responsible for communal actions, and is credited with intellectual reasons that can be debated, admired or blamed. Let us also add that, its desires being human, they might chance to be *good* if the tyrant conserves his common sense and his intellectual free will.

The Leviathan is entirely dissimilar. Here the brain no longer exists as in the arbitrary tyrannies of kings or in the benevolent tyrannies of ancient republics directed by their elites towards intellectual goals. The Leviathan, following the model of the marine Hydra, repudiates as illusory any idea of central consciousness and considers the human body and the social entity alike as simple colonies of polymorphous individuals, specialized according to material needs whose mere juxtaposition forms the entirety of the community.

This might well be taken as a triumph of the three-dimensional conception of the world, only accepting as real the transitory relativities of material groupings. The Leviathan, although superior to man in quantitative terms, by virtue of its colossal mass, was an extremely primitive animal in qualitative terms. Only bringing men together in terms of their material functions and not their minds, it was, in the final analysis, no more than a materialistic caricature of the *Golden Eagle* that was to be born several millennia later, in the time of the Great Idealist Renaissance—when it was understood, thanks to the fourth dimension, that three-dimensional material groupings were no more than provisional hypotheses and that union could only be achieved by minds in the continuum of a communal consciousness.

Without the total intelligence of the fourth dimension, however, the only possible communism, that of minds, is unrealizable, and the vision of the three-dimensional world engenders the primitive and wretched communism of a Leviathan, as low in the scale of living beings as the most primitive of animal colonies, but with the new peculiarity that the most advanced creatures—by which I mean humans—play the role of protozoa within the colossal grouping.

This abasement of human being was not at all surprising where the masses were concerned. Long stripped of ideals, and no longer believing in anything but material appearances, they had only too great a penchant for a voluntary servitude that represented, to them, blissful and irresponsible specialization—which is to say, minimum intellectual effort. When it came to the elite, however, this same voluntary servitude was liable to astonish a superficial observer. Nothing was more natural, though, if one will deign to recall that, in the time of the Leviathan, the elite too had progressively lost all the beliefs that had once constituted its strength, and no longer thought of any but immediate needs.

Since Estienne de La Boétie rightly wrote his *Discourse on Voluntary Servitude* for the masses—fortunately, some centuries before the republican law that punished the vindication of actions considered criminal—it is regrettable that no other pamphleteer has since thought of publishing for the powers-that-be a *Discourse on Voluntary Abdication*—a *For All* instead of an *Against One*.

If all evidence suggests that political power really does arise from a voluntary renunciation by the masses, all evidence similarly suggests that revolutions arise from a voluntary renunciation of power. The masses experience a slothful joy in feeling dominated and led. They very often suffer miserably, but they await the God or Prince Charming who will take responsibility for saving them by magical means; they never imagine that their release might depend on an effort that comes from within themselves, towards greater dignity, professional capability or nobility of mind. They wait, fetishistically, for a miracle, complacent in their mechanical and specialized irresponsibility.

The revolutions that have actually been accomplished in the history of the world do not give the lie to these absolute principles. One might believe, to begin with, that it is enslaved elements within a country who are rebelling against their rulers, but if one examines things a little more closely, one is not long delayed in realizing that revolutionary movements always spring from a source within the ruling class, and that it is from there that the order comes which pushes the masses forward.

For a superficial observer, this order—a veritably suicidal decision—might appear to emanate from dishonest agitators seeking to swim in or fly above troubled waters, while mystic apostles, for the profit of their dreams, naively clamor for the masses to embrace the voluntary servitude that they are pretending to fight; in reality it is the ruling classes from with the order is emitted, consciously or not, and the order to revolt cannot be followed unless the ruling class has already confirmed its abdication some time before, by voluntarily renouncing moral and material privileges in which it no longer believes or of which it is weary.

It is, in fact, sufficient to enjoy something no longer to have the desire for it, whether it is a matter of fortune or life. A certain degree of health is therefore necessary to kill oneself, and people who kill themselves do not wish to do themselves harm; people drown themselves in summer, but hardly ever in winter. In politics, it is the same; a relative social well-being is indispensable to the organization of reforms and revolutions, summer suits them better than winter, and it is generally the rulers who clamor for the abolition of privileges of which the abuses that they wish to alleviate attract them all.

When the Leviathan began to grow, it therefore found immediate and unexpected support among thinkers and artists, among those who had previously pretended to represent individualist ideals. Specialization increased every day and voluntary servitude to social functions received joyous consent.

One may talk about neurasthenia and collective maladies of the will, but that had nothing to do with it. It was with the fullest consciousness in the world that the elite was the first to become disinterested in general ideas and the direction of affairs. Five hundred years after the proclamation of the rights of man came the *proclamation of duties*, which enslaved everyone's individual authority to the conditions of the collective and which recognized the indisputable superiority of the scientific organism that governed the world.

Although they were self-conscious mortals only benefiting from a short life span, men no longer thought, as they once had, of pursuing the universality of human knowledge, of seeking individually to know everything about the world. Each individual remained, immutable, where hazard placed him, accomplishing his social function without protest, suffering or dying at his post, as soldiers had done in times past. Moreover, with the ever-increasing demands of specialization, it was very difficult, after a passage of several years, to change position. Differentiated from infancy by scientific education, ignorant of everything that did not concern his own employment, a man would have been nothing but a useless wreck if his situation had been altered.

Only the formidable Leviathan benefited from these specialized activities. A monstrous and unconscious Hydroid, it replaced with its material universality the intellectual universality that had once been the prerogative of the human being.

It was by muted movements and inexplicable communal ideas that the existence of the new being was initially revealed. When, little by little, all men came to understand that it was not for themselves and for their own wellbeing that they were working, but for some dark and mysterious Unknown, and when the distinction became ever-more-obvious between their own wellbeing and the social wellbeing in which they were collaborating, there were a few muffled individual rebellions, as a frightful despair took possession of humankind entire—but by that time, the scientific organism and specialization had already done their work.

Outside social functions and economic organization, life no longer seemed possible to these specialized men—and slowly, without any possible goal, they desperately pursued their obscure tasks, like miners in the depths of a pit, or like globules circulating automatically, nourishing themselves, defending themselves or succumbing inside the bloodstream. They were working for a being that they did not know at all, which they had never understood and which did not know them, just as a man is ignorant of the work of the flesh in which he lives.

XI. The Morality of the Leviathan

It was at the beginning of the 20th century that one might, if one had been paying sufficient attention, have been able to discern the first infantile wails of the Leviathan.

Unfortunately, in 1900 and the years that followed, people did not have a very clear vision of the era in which they lived and blithely persuaded themselves that they had reached the final phase of civilization.

When one considers the entire history of our planet at a single glance, one can hardly help smiling at such a pretension. All things considered, man was not much different in 1912, for example, than he had been at the origins of humankind; he would only have had to be abandoned by himself in a forest for a few weeks for him to recover, without great difficulty, the habits and manners of his ancestors; the war subsequently demonstrated this. He knew nothing of his destiny, he was absolutely incapable of exerting any authority over his life; he did not even know what that life might be; with regard to the soul, God and death he was still as grossly superstitious as primitive tribesmen. It must not be forgotten, of course, that he had nothing at his disposal then, by way of a body, but the habitual organism common to all animals; he allowed himself to be mysteriously led through life by his animal instinct, and his true nature immediately got the upper hand when he was exposed to any sort of physical danger.

Whatever the clothes, laws, titles or honors were in which they dressed themselves up, all men found themselves equal in confrontation with danger, before danger—and in such circumstances, these so-called civilized beings often showed themselves inferior to their own domestic animals. That did not prevent the men of the 20th century from considering with pride the distance they had traveled and gladly imagining that the evolution of living beings had terminated with man.

If people had been able, in that era, to detach themselves temporarily from that absurd human prejudice, they would not have been long delayed in discerning the imminent domination of Earth by the Leviathan. Evidently, at the beginning of the 20th century, people felt that something in the world was undergoing a transformation; they spoke freely of an *era of transition*. Some affirmed that ancient traditions were in complete decadence, which was true, others that the scientific world had modified ideas in many respects, which was also true; but they attributed to these changes a purely temporary significance, due to habitual variations in fashion.

With regard to the specific concerns of morality, however, it would have been easy to understand that this transformation went far beyond the simple ethical discussions of previous eras. It was easily observable that individual Christian morality had been abolished, that the violent attempt to rescue the moral individual attempted by Kant had undermined itself; but people were content to say that the era was immoral—or rather amoral—and no one troubled to enquire where that indispensable morality, which had guided the world since its origins, had gone. A few minutes of attention would, however, have sufficed to reveal to the men of the time that the morality in question had, if I might put it thus, been unceremoniously devoured by the new Being, the Leviathan.

No one bothers to inquire what the antecedents were of the cells that compose the human body. Whether they have appropriated their water, their phosphorus or their nitrogen from the right or the left, whether they have been taken ready-formed, in the aftermath of a catastrophe, from another organism, as if by an animal's claws, is of no importance if, at the present moment, they are rendering the services expected of them. The same was true for the *cellular humans* composing the Leviathan. It was of scant importance, in the 20th century, to be acquainted with a man's antecedents, to know whether his anterior life had been free of any suspicion. It was of even less importance to be acquainted with his family, since one only had to deal with him, and every individual, at the present

73

moment, had equal value in terms of the services that he could render to the social body.

This point of view even extended to the most illicit cases. The summary execution of a man who had compromised the safety of the social body was easily comprehensible; but the old judiciary theories by which a man was still punished, five, ten or 20 years afterwards for a crime that no longer interested anyone were no longer explicable. All the old theories of expiation, heredity, traditionalism or family were on the point of disappearing; one thing alone was relevant: success at the particular moment, effort judiciously accomplished in the *social moment* in which it was fitting to attempt to succeed. That alone was important to the Leviathan, and its consent was necessary for individual effort to be attempted with success.

By contrast, all the isolated individuals, all the thinkers, all those who wanted to act outside social opportunities, were looked upon with very jaundiced eyes, and it was felt that they were intervening inappropriately and in a dangerous fashion in a time that was not made for them.

Alongside an indulgence, which profoundly disturbed traditional humanists, for immoral actions that only stained the conscience, that era also demonstrated, on the other hand, a veritably excessive rigor in treating immoral actions affecting the collectivity—and this seeming illogicality misled the researches of all the psychologists.

If a man had committed all the indelicacies in his private life, if he were defective in a thousand ways, if he were morally rotten in the most odious fashion, that could not hinder his success on the day that he intervened opportunely in some communal action. If, on the other hand, a man had lived the irreproachable life of a thinker, with austere and pure morals, he found himself discredited forever, crushed within a few minutes in the formidable organism of the Leviathan, if he intervened at the wrong moment in a social action. This was, in fact, the way that it had always been in the human body when it was a matter of cells. It is, I repeat, curious to observe that no moralist of the 20th century was able to explain, by

74

analogy, the strange disturbances that were then occurring in public morality. The enterprise, however, would not have been without its dangers.

About 1923, for example, a writer who took it into his head to denounce the stupidity, ignorance and incapacity of the masses was excluded from all the newspapers, whatever their opinion might be. Indignation would have been general if that same writer had affirmed that evolutions and wars, those apparent rehabilitations of popular initiative, were always decided outside the masses, to whom it was sufficient to throw, as the price of their services, the brief animal joys of a tragic mid-Lent or a few bloody scraps of offal.[12] Let us finally add that he would not even have been understood if he had demonstrated that, under the sovereignty of the Leviathan, the role of the masses had become even more amorphous. In industry, as in war, the human being was no longer anything but the obscure servant of machines and materiality, but—even more incredibly—a formidable egalitarian Revolution had been able to turn the world upside down after the War, sweeping away the old capital and replacing intelligence with manual labor, not only without the collaboration of any popular movement but without the masses even being aware of it. This is true to the extent that when this Revolution, the greatest of any century, was accomplished, there were still people awaiting it, dreading it or wishing for it. It was still not understood, in fact, that the reign of man was over and that nothing would any longer be known than the anonymous mass composing the Leviathan.

For that mass all the basest demagogical flatteries were brought to bear, for to denounce the mass would have been, by the same token, to unveil the imbecility of the Leviathan.

---

[12] The festival of mid-Lent had perforce to be celebrated frugally; the second reference to "*une curée sanglante*" refers to the practice by which hunters throw a few scraps of their quarry to the hounds that have actually brought it down, while retaining the good meat for themselves.

It was forbidden, on the other hand, to be interested in personalities, to claim that, among the people like everywhere else, there were prodigious differences of intelligence and aptitude between individuals. Any impulse of charity, pity or fraternity for an isolated individual was severely reprimanded as subversive. One had to admire the totality of mass composed of homogeneous individuals—which is to say, the Leviathan, formed of identical cells differentiated not be nature but by social destination, like the "civilians" who are taught to march when they arrive in a regiment.

XII. The Murder of Style

At the beginning of the 20th century, the Leviathan, still young and not yet fully formed, had powerful moral enemies to vanquish, of which the greatest, without any doubt, was style.

Style is as old as humankind. It was to style that the development of the human mind was owed, on that alone that the individualism was still based that permitted heterogeneous individuals to escape social unification within the unique body of the Leviathan. In order to combat it, a muted campaign of denigration was launched. There was an attempt to persuade all literate people that style, properly understood, was nothing but a brilliant assembly of words, a game of showmanship without veritable reality, which was ill-accommodated to the documentary precision of triumphant science.

No thought was given to the contradictory fact that it was by the constant practice of the natural sciences that the Comte du Buffon had once been led—and quite naturally—to offer a eulogy to style when he was welcomed into the Académie. It was forgotten that its style, far from being an external manifestation, constituted, on the contrary, the very essence of a human mind, and that it represented, properly understood, the sole continuous principle created by man in contradiction to fragmentary natural law. Style was, in sum, the permanent opposed to the relativity of life, the only method that man had invented of triumphing over death and oblivion.

Style, in past centuries, had manifested itself in a hundred different ways. In the State, it was represented by constitutions and laws; in the family, by hereditary principles; in private life by morality; in public life by the voluntary contribution of each citizen to the State's intellectual needs. In the fine arts, style was manifest in an even more precise fashion. By releasing immortal forms, tracing the definitive rules of architecture, synthesizing the traditions of mastery, style had permitted man to create, above and beyond natural contingencies, an imaginary world formed by all his works, immortal and solely capable of resisting, in the course of centuries, the slow modifications of evolution.

Little by little, in all social sectors and the most various actions of everyday life, superior men had acquired the habit of submitting their passions or momentary needs to the inflexible control of immutable rules; often—in the matter of honor, for example—they had preferred to die rather than debase or transgress them.

It was doubtless easy to object that these rules, always arbitrary and artificial, might turn out to be bad, but the objection cannot stand up to serious examination. If a rule of style, in morality as in architecture, happened to be erroneous, it was thus condemned in advance and was not viable. On the contrary, when it resisted collision with facts, maintaining itself over the centuries, one could be assured of its necessity, of its reason for existence in a superior world of ideas, even if that necessity did not appear evident on first inspection—which is why it is often said that an endeavor, even an infamous one, can have a certain beauty when it is pursued persistently, because its beauty proves, by its permanence, that it is not infamous above and beyond the prejudices of the moment.

The first endeavor of the Leviathan was, as can be imagined, to destroy at any price the style that was irredeemably opposed to its development—and the spirit of scientific analysis, born a long time previously, supported its efforts marvelously.

Already, since the French Revolution, social style had been extensively compromised, and the Empire had provided a sufficient indication of the marked tendency of social cells to group themselves into a homogeneous body. At the end of the 19th century, style in ideas was aggressively attacked by certain analysts who, following the example of Renan,[13] at-

---

[13] Ernest Renan (1823-1892) was a controversial skeptical historian, widely reproached for his representation of Chris-

tempted to break the straight line of our intellectual life, to separate it into many critical fragments, applied successively to the meager events of everyday thought. German influence, delivering muted combat to our Mediterranean creative enthusiasm in the 19th and 20th centuries, had not left our thinkers untroubled; experimental methods did the rest. Henceforth, in fact, there were immutable principles directing each individual; the synthesis of ideas was replaced by an everyday analysis, but an opportunist criticism; the *tabula rasa* of our convictions was transformed into a dissection-table on which the cadavers of ideas appeared in rapid succession, all equally subject to analysis.

In politics and diplomacy, these new procedures were likewise welcomed without difficulty, and it was not understood that this fashion of extracting all permanence from general external relationships, by submitting them to the critiques of the moment, destroyed all public security, and consigned individuals to fatalism, neurasthenia and disgust for any fecund and consequential effort.

A curious and final indication of protest was what was called in that era "anti-Semitism." For centuries as is well-known, the Jews had lived in a state of perpetual expectation; they had remained, from the material as well as from the moral point of view, simple nomads. For them, no definitive certainty, no future promise of the divinity, no permanent monument, no immortality on Earth or in Heaven, but the daily relativity of a wandering people. Quite naturally, when style was very nearly dead, the Jews did not fail to take the first place in all things, for their remarkable critical procedures happened to correspond exactly with the analytical procedures required by the Leviathan. They were accused, quite unjustly, of intrigue, for it was our world that had converted itself, in different ways, to their ideas, while they had only conserved their own.

---

tianity as a mere mythology; the reference here is to his methodological approach, eventually summarized in such works as *L'avenir de la science* (1890).

Unconscious of all interior regulation, deprived of all style in their artistic productions as in their daily lives, the men of the 20th century no longer formed anything but an immense mass of differentiated cells, deprived of moral direction, which, quite naturally, agglomerated themselves gladly into the material body of the Leviathan. External social form replaced from then on the internal style of which it was nothing but a gross caricature. It was imagined that this gave them complete independence by delivering them from all ideals, but it only succeeded in serving the basest needs of material life.

This decline was particularly rapid for anything connected with Letters and the Fine Arts. For example, a scholar writing a history of religion undertook to describe the ceremonies of all the cults and the powers imagined by the priests, but the idea never occurred to him to investigate, outside material appearances, the possible interior needs of human thought, the creators of the various great currents of which individual cults were only gross materializations.

A literary man, in the time of the Leviathan, was similarly ignorant of the fact that the subject is unimportant and that the interior rhythm alone marks the vale of a writer, whether of verse or prose. Versification was mistaken for poetry and anecdote for prose; the interior music of style had been killed.

Painters and sculptors, wishing to be free of a traditional craftsmanship that had once permitted 15-year-old pupils to collaborate in the works of their masters, became bogged down in lamentable material difficulties and labored in matter, under the thumb of nature, without ever attaining the secondary, superior nature that is art. The portrait stylizing a human being was forbidden to them; their lesser decorative art treated gods, tables and basins identically. There were no longer anything but journeymen molders copying material contours. The interior music of lines and harmony of style had been killed there too.

Accidents of happenstance were grasped, fugitive impressions; gross caricatures, inspired by the sensations of the moment, replaced the eternal types dreamed by the artists of antiquity. The Leviathan knew only accidental juxtapositions of matter, it did not know the formidable universal consciousness that unites all the arts in the same style, which permits a Beethoven to awaken philosophical ideas and a Gluck architectural splendors.

XIII. The Theater of the Leviathan

At the beginning of the 20th century, it was in the theater, above all, that it would have been easy to observe the progress realized by the Leviathan. Indeed, the theater, better than any other mode of expression, permitted the formation of a clear idea of communal aspirations and the liberation of average morality. Like the orator, it did not address itself to an individual, but to a crowd. Furthermore, the theater was never more honored than during this period of transition. It seemed that men were now incapable of feeling an individual artistic pleasure and that art was no longer anything to them but a collective hallucination.

I have already observed how profoundly the new social morality of that era differed from the old individual morality. It was no longer inside himself, in the depths of his conscience, that a man now sought reasons for action, but outside, in social necessity. There gradually resulted, in consequence, a sort of fatalism, of submission, which bent the masses to the omnipotent will of the Leviathan.

The theater offered an exact expression of this transformation. When an author undertook, in his play, to develop characters, he did not interest the audience at all; he even made them indignant when his internal ideas seemed dangerous and hazardous to the coherency of the social body. A deceived husband killing his wife became inadmissible; a playwright, criticizing the morals of his time, was seen as an insupportable misanthrope whose divagations could scarcely be tolerated. Even the classical glorification of physical individuality was inadmissible; any manifestation of esthetic beauty, any exhibition of nudity in the theater, seemed unfitting or out of place. It was not that personal morals were more corrupt in that era than in any other, but that did not interest the Leviathan, and it was solely in the name of the social body that people protested against the public honoring of the human body.

With the progress of science and the leveling of ideas, all discussion now seemed futile; conversations in salons no longer existed, private correspondence did not interest anyone, and the editorial content of the great newspapers, instead of revealing personal opinions, was nothing but base demagogic flattery, further debasing the most abject and most ridiculous instincts of the masses.

In the theater, the dialogue that would once have painted the internal evolution of a thought was soon replaced by material representation determining situations by external social signs: by means of furniture, décor, the wealth or otherwise of the characters. This is what explains the incredible success, in that era, of mute cinematography, which sufficiently satisfied the majority of the public by means of its material indications. The determinist theater was pushed, in that era, to its extreme limits; it was considered adequate, in some plays, to indicate the characters' states of minds by movements in a crowd, external noises, the distant whistle of a railway train or the color of the scene's lighting. Modern décor indicating milieu replaced antique masks indicating character. Given the equality of all human cells before the omnipotence of the Leviathan, it was understood, in fact, that the same external causes would determine the same sentiments in all the characters and symbolize them.

This forced equality was, moreover, found in the same era in all the social institutions that had prepared the way for the advent of the Leviathan and had permitted that monstrous being to develop in all liberty. Universal suffrage in political matters, equality of birth—which was to realize, a few years later, the suppression of inheritance—and many other things concurred in giving the Leviathan the equal and homogenous elements that it needed for its formation.

It was for that same reason that it was not always understood, in that era, what the deeper significance was of the so-called workers' movements that were developing irresistibly.

Many artists and thinkers were offended, in their most intimate convictions, as they observed that people did not hesitate to sacrifice themselves, on every occasion, to the most vulgar personalities. More than that, excellent workmen no longer understood the orders they received from their syndicates, enjoining them to lower the standard of their work to that of their least capable companions. Neither party, adopting the old individualist point of view, could understand that this homogenous equality was indispensable to the cellular formation of the Leviathan.

Assured in the present, that equality had also to extend into the future; the uncertainty as to what the next day would bring that reigned after the War only served to prepare the state of mind that had to be engendered. People soon adopted the habit of living from day to day, without worrying about the future; thrift was no longer anything but a memory, money was spent as it came in; knowing that its value was subject to variation, no one any longer built with future centuries in mind, but according to the needs of the moment.

In politics, the situation was graver still. A Republican of 1789 worked for all of humankind; a Republican of 1923 did not any longer work for his country, for his party, or even for his electoral interests, but for himself, furtively and day by day. Laws, all the beauty of which had formerly been in their generality and their permanence, were no longer voted for any but particular cases, according to the needs or the appetites of the few, and no one was liable, on that basis, to embark upon any long-term commerce or industry. Only courtiers and intermediaries were able to bring off coups, making rapid fortunes, living as parasites on the labor of others, without creating anything but ruins. In that era, it was not immediately understood why the prestige of statesmen and governments was diminishing every day; it was because in reality, they too were no longer leaders but simple cells functionally differentiated within a single homogeneous organism.

Dramatic production, which always reflects the mores of a time exactly, followed this general movement. Care was not longer taken, as before, to construct a play exposing a general idea or describing an eternal human character; successions of amusing little scenes were written, each one in the moment when it was played but without any necessary connection, without any notion of wholeness. They were written for a particular theater, a particular public, a particular interpretation, a particular season, for the fashionably nuances of the day. Success was desired at a determined moment and no one, in that time of relativity, any longer thought of immortality, as had once been the case.

Alongside the theater proper, a no less valuable indication was offered, in that epoch, by the characteristic evolution of music. Instead of an individual piece of music or the personal artistry of a singer alone on stage, praise was initially lavished on a symphony orchestra or a voice that only played the role of a secondary instrument. Then the sung theme, the last vestige of humanity, progressively disappeared. In the same way that, in the solar spectrum, beyond the colored rays visible to the eyes, there are ultra-violet rays whose presence can be indirectly observed, there was in music, as in dramatic composition, a sort of symphony superior to human expression, inaccessible directly, whose existence was well established scientifically, but which could not be defined in direct, exact and purely sensual terms. There was a sort of social harmony no longer corresponding to individual rhythm, dominating and enveloping man, a new scientific "Marseillaise" devoid of charm, inspiration and harmony but harmonically precise according to the laws of acoustics, which properly belonged—as was only understood much later—to the colossal Leviathan, which was gradually developing its formidable and complex framework.

XIV. The Rejuvenation of Cells

I have tried to explain in the preceding chapters how the development of scientific ideas had progressively prepared the way for the Earthly manifestation of the Leviathan.

Deprived of all internal principles, having rejected all belief in an eternal and immutable substance, men no longer admitted anything but the most absolute determinism by way of moral regulation. If human ideas really only depended on external combinations, if thought really were no more than the result of purely material encounters, it was ridiculous any longer to admit free will and individual responsibility. Every action accomplished by a man being determined by innumerable causes over which he had no control, it became just as absurd to accuse him as to consider that he knew his own mind. Good and evil actions were no longer distinguishable; they were no more than simple phenomena, essentially similar: facts that the scientists ought to observe and record with neither affection nor anger.

It became evident, on the other hand, that the only true *value* on Earth could only be a material value—which is to say, a *force*. The stronger a man was, the more violently he acted, as a living cell, according to his instincts or desires, the more he would pass for a perfect man. That was, in sum, the justification of all actions previously considered immoral, the facile excuse for all laxity, and the certain discredit of any bravery or virtuous action. The best-equipped man was nothing, properly understood, but the plaything of his destiny; one should certainly not admire him for his powerful actions, since he was not their true author, but one ought to fear, respect and obey him, as one obeys, without any possible discussion, an irresistible natural force.

It was understood that a focal point was necessary in such conditions, and the idea was joyfully welcomed of a material grouping capable of codifying nascent anarchy and replacing the vanished principles with a scientific organism modeled on the natural organism of the marine hydra. With the Leviathan, the metaphysical principles of old, conclusively rejected by science, were still driven out, but an organism was nevertheless obtained that was seemingly capable of taking their place.

Perhaps, however, the Leviathan would never have developed completely if a new scientific discovery—that of perpetual rejuvenation—had not provided definitive permission. Without being aware of it, and even though they had rejected forever the moral principles of times past, men instinctively followed the same customs as before, quite simply because they lived, in the final analysis, in the same fashion as their ancestors.

Whatever progress science had made in the rapidity of instruction and the more perfect organization of life, it remained no less true that men were born as they always had been, passed through a naïve and enthusiastic period of infancy, and then the reflections of maturity, to finish up in the authoritarianism of old age. And inevitably, as in the good old days, they observed that their ideas were modified by experience, and that high positions and authority came with age. As before, it was in the hands of the oldest that cunning—which is to say, power—lay, and, quite naturally, still as before, social ideas were instinctively inspired by the development of human life. Old men, with the best will in the world, continued discrediting the ideas of youth and praising those that were compatible with the decline of life, classifying passions and ideas in accordance with the age in which they are experienced rather than according to their intrinsic value. It was for this reason that love had been rapidly discredited by Government legislators, as it had been disdained by the sages of old. Only artificial procedures of reproduction were honored; the disabused studies and sad, inconsequential researches of maturity were reputed, as in the time of the ancient philosophers, the most elevated achievement of humanity entire.

All desire for immortality had been suppressed, all future constructions for the family or the race; humankind had been robbed of all belief in tomorrow, but it had not been possible to prevent human life from reproducing in miniature, by the stages of its evolution, the life of a nation, thus ensuring that human cells would remain identical in time, as in space, for the sake of the Leviathan's good health.

Suddenly, the sensational discovery of the rejuvenation of cells arrived to modify the ancient morality even more profoundly than years of materialist philosophy and science had been able to do.

To begin with, the Government legislators affected to treat this discovery as a simple laboratory game. Obviously, it pleased them to think that their old age or their maturity might henceforth be prolonged indefinitely at their discretion, and that they would thus almost certainly escape dreaded death. They therefore limited themselves, at first, to taking advantage of the new discovery by maintaining themselves as they were. Then, little by little, sure signs of rejuvenation were observed in the faces of each and every one of them.

An old man, who had still been wrinkled beneath his white hair a few months earlier, returned after a short absence with graying hair and a young face. He excused himself with a smile, saying that he had perhaps overdone the treatment without being aware of it, and stoutly renounced all juvenile ambition. Nothing, in fact, was worth more than maturity, each one of them declared—and, as rejuvenation exercised its influence on their character, it was understood that no one, among the government personnel, was prepared to exchange his morose gravity for the infantile joys of youth.

In spite of all these declarations, one could not fail to observe, after a few years, that the oldest legislators in the Council of Ministers, as a result of their successive transformations, no longer looked any older than 18 or 20. It was not long before the effects of this transformation were felt in the deliberations of the Government.

Needless to say, this transformation, so rapid among the greatest legislators, was even more prompt among the public. In a few months, the entire population had become definitively young, enthusiastic and joyful again—and you can hardly imagine, even approximately, the profound change that was then produced in mores.

The determinist theories being indisputable, people continued, as before, to take them for their guide—but the veritable danger that might be presented by theories of violence, youth and strength was perceived for the first time when they were applied by young men who were veritably young and strong. So long as they had only been professed by morose philosophers, they had not had any real influence on mores; they were bitter fancies of old men and their effects remained purely theoretical, since those same old men simultaneously extolled the authority of the most aged and the irreducible supremacy of experience.

It was only in the presence of that childish populace, that the terrible practical consequences these ideas might have were understood. Thanks to the facile excuse of determinism, all acts of violence, all infamies and all crimes came to be not merely acceptable but—which was far more important—materially perpetrated. For the first time in the history of the world, the ancient morality slumbering in the depths of men was definitively attained and the gravest disturbances would have been threatened if that childish populace had not, in its insouciance, fortunately set aside the methods of rejuvenation and welcomed, as a deliverance, the nascent empire of the Leviathan, which brought a measure of order into the chaos.

It was admitted then that it was absurd to want to mobilize the human cells at the same invariable age, and that a certain evolution was necessary between birth and death. To halt the course of life, not to grow old, was, according to all evidence, not to augment human activity but, quite to the contrary, to rob man of all motive for action and to plunge him into despair by forbidding him the essential characteristic of life that is change. Change is nothing, in fact, but the endless course of desire. Desire disappears when it is realized and eternal youth was only, in sum, a total realization, just like death: a conclusive arrest of material life.

Perpetual youth was henceforth the sole prerogative of the Leviathan whose cells were indefinitely renewed—and that was the beginning of its ruin, for it became, at that point, a material three-dimensional being avoiding evolution, which is to say, life.

Without the sense of the fourth dimension which prolongs him in the past and the future—to employ the language of three dimensions—*man would be, in fact, nothing but a material three-dimensional being, without arbitrary freedom, without will, without the power of decision, always submissive, in the present moment, to the same actions in the same circumstances, like a falling stone or a reflected ray of light.*

Without the awareness of the *future* and the *past*—which is to say, of *progress* and *tradition*—completing the present sensation of three dimensions, in a word, without the awareness of the fourth dimension, placing the mind outside time and space, man would not be superior to a pebble. He would be no more than a soulless body—and that soulless body was that of the Leviathan.

XV. The Century of the Soulless Body

The most curious aspect of the extraordinary development of the Leviathan at the beginning of the 20th century
was, as I have said, the universal and unconscious consent of
the human cells that served the monstrous animal as fodder.

Already, for a long time, science had affirmed the theory
of materialism sufficiently for no one in the world to be able
to believe in the necessity of a soul directing the human body,
or a king directing the social body. It was thought that the life
of the whole did not consist of anything but the life of cells,
and that no central immaterial point could really exist within
that whole. The ancient idea of a mechanical construction
grouped around a spiritual core had been abandoned, although
that theory had been strongly favored by all primitive civilizations.

It had been decided that the whole was no more than a
composite of parts, and all those who thought that that the
superior being only existed as a function of its constructive
cells—which is to say, human beings—were reassured as to
the intentions of the Leviathan.

Furthermore, the notion of that collective being was by
no means new. Thomas Hobbes was an admirable man in the
sense that he, first of all, dared to write in 1651, at the head of
his introduction to the *Leviathan*, that if nature is the world
that God constructed and governs by His divine artistry, then
man, for his part, by means of his industry, produces in imitation an artificial animal—and that formidable animal, that
Leviathan, is Society, the State.

Hobbes extrapolated this analogy quite extensively. All
the habitual maladies of man are found again in the State: for
instance, a man who has read libertarian tracts in favor of tyrannicide has contracted hydrophobia; he perpetually desires
to drink pure water, but it fills him with horror. Athens and
Carthage died of bulimia. The agitation of humble folk is ana-

logous to that of ascarid worms. Leisure and luxury engender lethargy...

This is certainly what was most powerfully and precisely conceived in establishing the materialist theory of the State. For Hobbes, there is nothing in intelligence that does not originate in sensation. Our general ideas are nothing but an addition or a subtraction of bodily images that exist independently, and knowledge cannot be incorporeal. The State, similarly, is nothing but a collection of individuals, but grouped by the social sensations that are egoism and fear. In a state of nature, man is a wolf to man, as Plautus put it,[14] for, men being equal, war and anarchy are their normal condition, since nothing limits their appetites and their desires. It is the need for security that makes men renounce their individual strengths to the profit of a unique strength, and that social contract creates absolute sovereignty.

As for religion, it is the daughter of imagination and fear. It is nothing but base superstition when the fearful imagination is individual; it is a useful means of government when that imagination and that fear are collective.

At the time in which Hobbes lived, this materialist analogy between the social body and the human body was little more than a literary image designed to be mentally striking; in the 19th and 20th centuries, with the scientific development of evolutionist theories, it took on a singular importance. It is by its own initiative, it was thought, and by a more complete adaptation to its environment, that matter becomes organized, groups itself into cells, into organisms, and into living beings of ever-increasing complexity and originality. The idea of a creator, as well as that of the old dualism between the soul and the body, no longer made sense. Only the old social contract

---

[14] *Homo homini lupus*, quoted from Plautus' *Asinaria*, was cited by Hobbes in *Leviathan* as a truism, although less cynical translators prefer to capture the intended rather than the literal meaning by rendering it as "to a stranger, man is a wolf."

dreamed up by Hobbes, inspired by dread or the quest for the least effort, sufficed to explain the formation of collectives of living beings, and the most recent arrival among them: the State, the Leviathan.

Far from being reduced to slavery by a superior authority, organic cells, like social cells, group themselves quite willingly and for their greater good. Voluntary servitude is not granted to the advantage of an elite but to that of the sovereign mass, and nothing exists outside the materials which, in combination, compose the edifice.

Furthermore, philosophers themselves had taken care to reassure humankind as to the consequences of the development of the social organism. Spencer had made it understood that within such an organism, the whole lived for the parts and not, as in the human body, the parts for the whole.[15] Claude Bernard had brought a reassuring scientific precision to this point; "Vital properties," he said, "are, in reality, in the living cells; everything else is arrangement and mechanics."[16]

What was forgotten only in the 20th century was the question of who had conceived the plan of the edifice or ordained the preliminary harmony of mechanical movements— for, in the end, although adaptation to the environment can explain the simple practical modifications of existing organs, its obscure present instinct seems insufficient to foresee future constructions or combinations of an order so superior that they seem pre-established and arrive at the ultimate terminus of its evolution: that very intelligence that material evolution is claimed to prepare.

---

[15] Herbert Spencer gave a name to the science of sociology, and lent such considerable support to selected aspects of Charles Darwin's theory of evolution by natural selection that many of the assertions nowadays grouped under the heading of "Darwinism" really ought to be called "Spencerism."

[16] Claude Bernard was a pioneering physiologist whose *Introduction à l'étude de la médecine expérimentale* is considered a masterful definition of scientific method.

How have certain plants demanded that butterflies and the wind ensure their reproduction? What superior council of wild bees has conceived the hive? What were the organs that decided to establish three canals in the ear giving the awareness of three dimensions? And, even supposing that the entire future is potentially contained in matter, how can we explain the maintenance of a unique plan of assembly between the local, often antagonistic, patterns of local progress realized by divided matter?

It is, in truth, a great error that the 20th century made in mistaking the shadow for the prey and limiting its knowledge to relative and fragmentary three-dimensional hypotheses, ignoring the unique and continuous universal soul, released from any prejudice of time and space, which the mind alone can attain in the fourth dimension, and whose thoughts and actions are translated into material appearances, fugitive and unreal because they are three-dimensional.

XVI. The Marquis' Heirs

Still ignorant of the fourth dimension—which, outside prejudices of time and space, permits us to conceive the universal Idea particularized in every one of us—and entirely resistant to *unity*, the 20th century was not mistaken when it only saw in the Leviathan the sum of an addition of three-dimensional bodies, a colony of material ideas comprising no central heterogenous element: a body living normally without a soul, in sum.

Where the error became gross, however, was when the 20th century became persuaded, by analogy, that the same theory must apply to man and that thought, properly understood, was merely a phenomenon emanating from organs, having no other origin than the matter composing the aggregate of the human body. What seemed to encourage this error was the observation that thought came into being and disappeared with this aggregate, that its vigor dependent on it, and that no one had ever been able to conceive scientifically of a soul without a body.

When one has raised oneself up to the fourth dimension, this way of thinking seems as puerile as a man would who, looking through a window and seeing thousands of mirrors placed on a plain, reflecting the rays of an invisible Sun towards him, decided that each beam of light was produced by a mirror, and that breaking the mirror would obliterate the radiance. Yes, undoubtedly, every human body is a mirror necessary to the universal consciousness, but one does not put out the Sun—the unique source of all light—by breaking a mirror; nor does the immortal Idea disappear along with a body that has reflected it momentarily.

More than that: the reflection, once emitted, does not die with the mirror and, in the same way that luminous rays once launched into the relative three-dimensional world are brought back to their point of departure by gravity, having followed millennia-long elliptical courses, creating a pure sunlight to replace a vanished Sun, thought too does not die; the purified idea shines eternally when the fugitive body that reflected it in a flash of genius is no longer but a distant memory. Thus, the action of the dead is greater than that of the living, because it is redeemed from matter.

Unfortunately, the considerable progress of science since the end of the 18th century had impassioned minds to the point of forgetting this in the 20th century, and of misunderstanding these fundamental ideas—which, suggested by the fourth dimension of the mind and completing the givens of the three-dimensional senses, had until then been the only thing allowing human intelligence to brave, by a thousand means, the odious simulacra of death.

Since the beginnings of civilization, in fact, man had been able to create a spiritual life, of which he remained the absolute master, and which set him far above other animals. Thanks to the laws, mores, social constitutions and principles of every sort that he gave himself, his mentality elevated itself further every day, and his immortal ideal seemed bound to escape natural laws forever.

It was, therefore, as we have said, these permanent and continuous moral rules that had to be destroyed at any price to create the Leviathan, and it was science that was charged with that heavy task.

In developing the study of natural phenomena, the philosophers of the 18th century gradually accustomed the human mind only to hold as true the immediate testimony of the senses and, as a consequence of examining matter, it was believed that it was three-dimensional. Nothing was any longer admitted but laws of nature, and every social edifice seemed to be a vain scaffolding, hypocritical and outdated.

There was one man of that time who dared to push the new theories to their ultimate consequences: the Marquis de Sade. With implacable logic, and in a form sometimes worthy of the Encyclopedists, without omitting a single detail, he developed the new program that the thinkers of the following century would adopt: more falsehood and more hypocrisy; the torch of philosophy—which is to say, of science—having dissipated all the ancient impostures, it would be appropriate to hold to the role dictated by nature and no longer listen to anything but our instincts; man would seek to develop his emotions as much as possible in the direction indicated by nature, and, pain being greater than pleasure, pain would be the principal agent of success.

It is by wounding the trees that one obtains the finest fruit; cruelty is the essential order of nature. This, in contrast to false Christian ideas, orders us to do to others what we would not want them to do to us. The strongest reason is always the best; Bismarck, Nietzsche and the most celebrated novelists of the 19th century have not said anything better. It is regrettable that Sade compromised the reputation of his works by absurd erotic bluster, which permitted his immediate heirs to erase his name from literary history; if he had only held to the philosophical ideas that he expressed on the eve of the French Revolution, his place in the history of ideas would be that of a venerated ancestor. It is sufficient to reread the principal works of the writers of the 19th century to be convinced of that.

In his *Origin of Species* and his *Descent of Man*, Charles Darwin only confirmed, point by point, all the Marquis' assertions, restoring the natural instinct of selection to primacy. The economists, from T. R. Malthus to John Stuart Mill, similarly ratified the brutality of such assertions. The writers and artists hesitated for a part of the 19th century, but they too were soon converted, in the presence of the incessant progress of science, to conclusions imposed by natural laws. Romanticism enslaved artists definitively with scientific doctrines. It was for this reason that literature, at the beginning of the 20th century, was nothing, in sum, but the rigid application of rules imposed by the French Revolution and then applied by the Empire, and that the supremacy of instinct brought man—who had thought momentarily that he might become God—to the simple rank of the animals that had preceded him.

This moral decay would have been insufficient to permit the realization of the Leviathan if the scientific organization of the entire world had not also offered the universal matter necessary to the creation of the new being. Man, reduced to the state of a social cell, having no other law than natural instinct, was no more than the plastic matter of the new being; the general bond charged with uniting these various elements was furnished by the scientific exigencies of the new organization. The world was no more than a colossal being, all of whose parts remained interdependent, and none of which could live separately from the whole. A malady felt at any point on the globe immediately echoed throughout the universe; an arrest of function in the nutrition or the nervous system of the Leviathan immediately compromised the life of the entire being.

The cells, incapable henceforth of independent life, no longer knew anything but their natural instincts. Deprived of any general idea, they could no longer aspire to the superb isolation of the individuals of old; mental life no longer appeared to be their own; that formidable hydra the Leviathan represented the external form of a purely mechanical three-dimensional economic State, in which carefully equilibrated needs and material appetites took the place of morality and the social contract.

Only the Leviathan could have a material scientific tradition exceeding the duration of human life. Every link with the past was, by contrast, forbidden to the human cells who, living under the dominion of natural law, could only be aware of the sensations and appetites of the moment. The divine Marquis de Sade was the veritable father of the precept "Live life," which the best dramaturges of the 20th century illustrated. Since the 18th century, moreover, favor was transferred, in novels, to domestics drawn from the common people, who tortured the hearts of marquises and gave great social lessons while expressing themselves, doubtless by force of habit, in the third person in order to make their claims.

Almost everywhere, in the most various manifestations of human activity, attempts were made to cut traditional roots, and that unremitting war was manifest in the smallest details of everyday life. In painting, in sculpture, in music, everyone wanted to innovate loudly, no longer taking account of the centuries of research and experience that had gone before; painters no longer had any craftsmanship or technique; sculptors retained no memory of it except by the intermediary of their assistants. As for musicians, they deliberately rejected 20 centuries of natural grace and harmony maintained by generations of thinkers and poets.

This pursuit was even more marked in the establishment of educational programs, in the suppression of classical studies; an artificial wall was elevated in front of every child, between the present establishment of incomprehensible results and the study of causes and logical rationality of actual facts. One felt henceforth that one was still living on the legacy of the dead, but the cemetery gate was firmly closed and no one any longer learned about the sufferings and joys, ambitions and efforts of intellectual ancestors that had gone forever.

Without being aware of it, humankind had only killed the true artists and savants by accusing them of reaction. Honoring, by contrast, sorcerers and tricksters, it had no alternative but to fall back inevitably into the grossest fetishism. By the same stroke, it rid itself of the Idea that it wanted to combat and the Science that it wanted to maintain, and that deplorable decadence delivered it, defenseless, to the inconsequential artificial grouping of the Leviathan: that monstrous and brainless creature from which all direction was expected.

XVII. The Birth of Humor

It was not until a long time after the death of the Levia-than that a clear understanding began to emerge of the moral complicity that had allowed that colossal being to develop, and the laborious and obscure labor of its adversaries that had succeeded in breaking it up. That muted and profound conflict had begun towards the end of the 19th century, between natu-ralists and humorists, and even though the adversaries had changed their names along the way, they had never ceased to represent the two contending parties until the end of the strug-gle.

Since that hypothetical first day when the first man opened his eyes to nature, and then reflected on what he had just seen, nothing had, in fact, been modified in the history of human thought. There was still the double movement of flux and reflux, aspiration and respiration, that perpetual oscillation between the immediate givens of consciousness and the in-formation regarding external phenomena furnished by the senses. Where, in that perpetual process of coming and going, was human personality really situated? No one could say, ex-actly. Mid-way between the relative and the absolute, judging moving events according to an internal and immutable yardstick, man sometimes looked outwards at the changing phenomena, sometimes inwards at the immutable notions to which he compared them.

Almost always however, by an instinctive need for spe-cialization, man settled on one or other of these attitudes. When he affected only to consider external phenomena, to analyze them scrupulously and to attribute a character of truth to them alone, he posed as a scientist and a naturalist, he be-came a disciple of Aristotle. When he affected, on the con-trary, only to interest himself in internal notions, only to attribute reality to the mystical life, he became a Platonist and only found truth in the world of ideas. It might seem astonishing that an exclusivity that was as intransigent in one direction as in the other did not always seem ridiculous. It is not very difficult to understand, in fact, that a scientific analysis is non-existent without an immutable and unchanging principle that permits the observation of *relative* movements, and that, on the other hand, an artistic or moral synthesis is only possible on the basis of analysis. One cannot analyze without an analyst; one cannot synthesize in the absence of elements.

As things were, this infantile verity did not appear at all clear to the scientists and literary men of the 19th century, who, enthused by the ever-increasing discoveries of science, abandoned all synthesis and decided no longer to accept, in human research, anything but analysis. Naturalism invaded everything; it soon passed from the natural sciences into literature and art, by way of psychology. Nothing was any longer produced but exact descriptions, scrupulous analyses, monographs on the family, anthropometric lists, and realistic photographs that were called "slices of life;" painters applied themselves to becoming scrupulous color photographers or passive interpreters of instantaneous impressions. And as, quite naturally, synthesis still remained the unconscious and unacknowledged basis of these works, it seen became instinctive, devoid of choice—and, in consequence, lamentable.

Something more serious happened that had hastened the birth of the Leviathan. By virtue of repudiating the existence of an internal consciousness, men—who could not, of course, do without it—took it into their heads to project it externally, to fabricate a fetishistic and social conscience. In the same way that, in the natural life of the body, certain reflex, habitual and commonplace actions no longer require the intervention of the brain, in the new social body of the Leviathan, a series of commonplaces, customary necessities and arbitrary principles formed something like a vast exterior consciousness: a monstrous bulb that was the caricatural consciousness of the Leviathan.

As in the times of primitive religions, men surrendered a part of their responsibility in favor of supernatural rules, social superstitions and reputed inevitable necessities: pretended fatalities of the race, which they decorated pompously with the name of natural laws. Logically, *instinct* resumed its primacy. Instead of governing themselves, men imagined that they were governed by external laws, and with the progress of naturalism they unknowingly favored the monstrous and abnormal development of the State, then of the Leviathan.

It was then that the inevitable movement of Platonic reaction came to light.

So perilous did the enterprise seem that it was in a conciliatory and ironic form that it first presented itself, and those were the beginnings of humor, unknown until then in the world, born of the abnormal development of 19th century Science. Humorists, irreducible individualists, pretended at first to be prodigiously interested in the conquests of science—and, in fact, set about studying them carefully, impeccable analysis being the preliminary condition of any good synthesis. Their rigorousness in the application of rules was that of jurists and sportsmen.

Humorists, therefore, studied nature; they pretended to be more naturalistic than the naturalists, more enamored of discoveries than the scientists themselves; in a few steps, they attained the extreme limits of scientific reasoning and then they pretended not to perceive that it had limits; they continued their analyses and deductions in the void, thus demonstrating, by means of absurdity, what the limits of science were. Up to that point, they had only employed the Socratic method; they had been content to treat injury with injury, in the manner of homeopaths. Soon, when they felt stronger, they resolutely resumed the path of synthesis and, empowered by their acquired science, were now able to produce the art-work of which they dreamed. Only then was the total seriousness of their campaign understood, and the full scope of their pretended buffoonery.

XVIII. The Revolt of the Apes

Had the humorists been content to demonstrate by means of absurdity the limits of three-dimensional pseudocertainties, their seemingly negative work would have been inconsequential.

When, on the other hand, they set out to demonstrate that, beyond these limits, *something else* must exist, and that doubt and negation represented, in the final analysis, positive realities completing the notion of the universe, certain minds began to understand the profound meaning of the fourth dimension.

At that moment, a few individual revolts became observable which, in the name of symbolism, broke away brutally from external naturalism and tried to adopt a purely subjective vision of the universe.

To tell the truth, the symbolists were only unconsciously copying in the subjective what the naturalists had done in the objective. Imposing the form of their mind on the World as the materialists were imposing the form of the World on their minds, they were likewise men of the moment, repudiating all tradition, similarly ignorant of that humanism that unites all minds, outside time and space, in the superior world of a universal consciousness—but while the materialist, photographing the external three-dimensional world, had some chance of moving other men by presenting them with familiar objects, the symbolist, by contrast, photographing his fugitive constructions of the three-dimensional world, presented images that were not merely incomprehensible to other men but very often incomprehensible to the new person that he became himself a moment later. It was because idealist, as well as materialist, endeavors were always conceived in three dimensions in the time of the Leviathan, that they were sterile, and powerless to reveal the great mysteries of the human soul.

Humor alone, by contrast, was to open the great highway that was to lead a few millennia later to the Great Idealist Renaissance, in the Age of the Golden Eagle, when, the fourth dimension being familiar to all men, love replaced the lie that could not admit a communal consciousness.

Humor in its conscious form, was born, as we have said, as a reaction against the absurd vanity of three-dimensional scientific "certainties." It was not sufficient, in fact, to have decreed the suppression of the soul for it to cease to exist, to think and—as always—to submit the relativity of three-dimensional phenomena to the perpetual control and contradictory criticism of the immobile, eternal and continuous four-dimensional consciousness. Humor was, in this sense, a sort of intellectual safety-valve, and the materialists of that era, who pursued their sarcasms and their anti-clerical hatred of obsolete and outdated religions, proscribing mystics, ideologues and poets, did not understand for a moment that humor was their sole adversary, reborn in a new form—but prudently masked with buffoonery, in order to be able to say anything without hazard, like the fools of old. Certain more subtle minds successfully divined that humor hid something, but thought that it was a timidity of the heart; they saw nothing in it but a psychological accident and did not glimpse the reality of a new world in the sallies it made, in the manner of an adolescent Christopher Columbus.

And yet that humor, which—this time with a conscious rigor—set out to attack the highest philosophical speculations, dated in its unconscious form from the earliest eras of the world. At the same time that he invented God, man created the Devil, for one without the other would be impossible and inexplicable; good only acquires its significance in the presence of evil, and nothing can exist without its *contrary*. Humor, in this sense, does not only contradict, it completes. The known loses all its savor without mystery. The relative discontinuity of three dimensions can only subsist as a function of four-dimensional continuity—and without immobile eternity, temporal movement would be meaningless. Humor, as a principle

104

of limitation, gives life to the world; as a principle of contradiction, it permits us to understand it—and that is why it sometimes qualifies as divine. Humor, at its birth, was the intimation—which finally became conscious—of the fourth dimension.

This fourth dimension, in the earliest eras of the world, could only be glimpsed by the mind. It was what was called, for want of a better word, consciousness. Thanks to that entirely internal notion, man could construct an integral idea of nature, complete the sensorial notions of three-dimensional space with the fourth dimension, internally perceived, and thus judge the universe entire.

It required many centuries of research for that notion, simple as it was, to be clarified in the human mind. It was understood that all the homogeneous information furnished by the senses had no intellectual value if it were not completed by the judgment of the mind; people sensed, even though that heterogeneous internal notion had no particular location in the mind, that it had total dominion. It was similarly understood that it alone could furnish the necessary bond between the past and the present, suggest notions of permanence, eternity and art—but no philosopher had succeeded in establishing the exact nature of that intimate sense and, for want of anything better, the fourth dimension met the expenses of all religions. The good news that it gave to human intelligence was projected externally; external objects were invented that were called the absolute, eternity, god or the infinite, and it was not understood that human intelligence was the centre of the world, that it alone united, in a complete fashion, all possible knowledge capable of revealing nature to us in its wholeness.

The Leviathan itself was always ignorant of that intimate science of the fourth dimension and the principle of contradiction on which the life of the mind is built. It knew neither hatred nor sacrifice; devotion was meaningless to it and love unknown. Excluded from evolution since the affair of the rejuvenation of cells, deprived of all intellectual life—since its social regulation, based on science, did not admit contradiction—the Leviathan suppressed all individual initiative, and even the functions of the reproduction of the race were confided to laboratories. The law-courts were suppressed, individual revolt no longer being recognized outside the medical domain. Everyone knew that the Leviathan, based on scientific "certainties," could not be mistaken, and a tide of *ennui* soon descended upon the entire human race.

It must be admitted, however, that it was not the work of humorists that reawakened the human cells from their dangerous lethargy; the extraordinary adventure of the apes struck a more resounding chord, and had an even more powerful impact on the masses.

People immediately began talking, with astonishment, about a gorilla couple locked in one of the cages at the Museum that had been able, by virtue of patient labor, to slide back two bolts, open the door and hide by night in one of the vivisection laboratories--where their keepers were planned to commence long and interesting experiments on their two offspring, which had been removed from their loving company the previous day.

There were excited comments regarding the frightful audacity of the mother, who, taking possession of various surgical instruments, had not hesitated to murder two of the Museum scientists and then flee to the roof, carrying her children.

This individual revolt, coming from a mere animal, had a considerable impact on the human cells of the time, whose children were sacrificed every day to the needs of science without provoking any protest on their part.

Certain examples of sensibility and devotion given by animals were recalled: timid hens protecting the nests of their chicks in the face of danger; seagulls that risked their lives to help a wounded companion; respect for ancestors among bears; wild beasts that only killed when driven by hunger; nostalgic monkeys which grieved bitterly over a flower from their homeland.

A revolutionary party soon formed, composed of a few thinkers who did not hesitate to denounce the Leviathan as nothing but a monstrous, unconscious fetish constructed in three dimensions, and incapable, by virtue of that very fact, of usefully ruling the world.

Thousands of people who had abdicated their personalities to the advantage of the social colossus understood how chimerical their hopes had been, and that there was no other truth or moral life than in the individual.

That was the commencement of the slow disintegration of the Leviathan.

A curious thing: the monster, to which contradiction was unknown, remained passive throughout the time that its trial was conducted before the tribunal of public opinion. Little by little, the reawakening of consciousness became complete, and it was understood, on the day when people wanted to be done with its omnipotence, that the omnipotence in question had been dead for a long time.

One might think that, after the death of the Leviathan, there would have been an idealist renaissance. One was certainly advertised, in order to calm minds, but the material scientific organization of the world was so complex that it was science yet again that monopolized the renaissance to its own profit. A communism without authority was replaced by the pitiless dictatorship of an elite that was the reign of the Absolute Savants.

In the chapters that follow, I shall relate certain curious and strange events that were revealed to me in the course of my journeys, which sufficiently characterize that brutal and authoritarian period in the great history of the world.

XIX. The Dissociated Dog

Among the monstrous adventures that marked the beginning of the Scientific Tyranny, it is necessary to pay particular attention to the extraordinary history of the Society for the Commercial Exploitation of the Planet Mars. Earth was, at that time, on the brink of disaster; a tiny incident might have resulted in its complete disintegration, save for an implausible combination of circumstances.

It is well-known that scientists have been preoccupied for some time with the possibility of communication with the planet Mars. The most favorable place for attempts at interplanetary communication had finally been determined, and an immense experimental field had been set up there.

The results obtained were kept strictly secret. It was, in fact, a financial organization with a capital of several millions that had resolved to establish the necessary communication, and it was understood that the organization in question was entitled to the exclusive benefit of any secrets that might by discovered by this means.

For a long time, the results were negative. Immense luminous triangles or circles were described on the ground, and it was even decided one day to go to enormous expense to reconstitute luminously, on a base of 400 kilometers, the construction of the square of the hypotenuse. No conclusive response came from Mars. [17]

---

[17] This method of attempted communication had been employed by the hero of Gustave Le Rouge's *Le prisonnier de la planète Mars* (1908; available in a Black Coat Press edition, with its sequel, as *The Vampires of Mars*); it had earlier been suggested by the American astronomer W. H. Pickering, but Pawlowski is far more likely to have run across it in Le Rouge's novel

The attempt was then made to reproduce on the ground, but in black light,[18] the diagram of a phonographic impression. This time the result was immediate, and the company's telegrapher, trembling with emotion and amazement, recorded a radio telegram that undoubtedly originated from the planet Mars, and was written in French.

"Yes," it said, "that's very intelligent."

It was thought at first to be a joke played by the enemies of the Society; soon, though, it was necessary to yield to the evidence. The communications became more active and precise instructions were given by the Martians regarding the means by which communication might be facilitated by means of fluids capable of traversing space.

It then became clear, amazingly, that ever since the invention of wireless telegraphy, the Martians had kept track of everything that happened on our planet, and that they were acquainted with the smallest details of our life. Needless to say, these communications remained secret, the Society jealousy conserving the information it was able to obtain from the Martians.

Relations developed further every day. Important questions were asked of our neighbors about the way in which one could obtain energy cheaply by the dissociation of matter.

For a long time, in fact, since the prophetic work of Dr. Gustave Le Bon, the discovery of radium and the researches of Sir Ernest Rutherford on the means of breaking the atomic bond, the question had urgently preoccupied all the scientists on Earth, It was well-understood, in fact, that matter, hitherto considered as inert and only able to return energy that one had

---

[18] "Lumière noise" [black light] was a term used by Gustave Le Bon in *L'évolution de la matière*—on which much of the substance of this chapter is based—to indicate electromagnetic radiations outside the visual spectrum. Le Bon construed such radiations, or "effluvia" [fluids], as phases in the fatal return of matter towards the condition of ether—i.e., the gradual and inevitable decay of matter into energy.

first imparted to it, was, on the contrary, a colossal reservoir of energy. Thus, according to Dr. Le Bon, if one were able to dissociate, for instance, a one centime copper coin weighing a gram, one would obtain 510 billion kilogram-meters, which is about six billion 800 million horse-power if the gram of matter were dissociated in a second.

That quantity of energy, appropriately redistributed, would be capable of driving, at 36 kilometers an hour, a 500-metric-ton goods train a little more than four and a quarter times around the circumference on the Earth. To effectuate the journey with the same train, powered by coal, it would be necessary to dispense 2,830,000 kilograms of coal—which is nearly 200,000 francs instead of a centime.[19]

Alas, though, in order to transmute a gram of matter it was necessary to expend the greater energy of ten billion kilograms—and that transmutation, by ordinary means, would not have been economic but ruinous. It had, therefore, to be admitted that the question of the practical dissociation of matter, in addition to its scientific interest, was of serious economic interest to the financiers.

The Martians' response was satisfying, but incomplete:

"No time to give you explanations; are immediately sending effluvium to dissociate whatever object is beside your apparatus."

The object in question happened to be a simple lamb cutlet on a plate, representing the telegrapher's lunch; she had absent-mindedly let it go cold beside her. A few seconds later, it became evident from the scorch-marks and little fires produced all around it that the cutlet was slowly dissociating, and the Board of Directors, immediately alerted, came running.

---

[19] In the La Boétie text the figure 2,830,000 kilograms is misrendered as 2,380,000; although the mistake might have been Pawlowski's. I have corrected it to the figure given in Le Bon's text. Le Bon gives the necessary expenditure as 68,000 francs, but Pawlowski's figure is presumably corrected for inflation (which was of course, steep during the Great War).

For long hours, the scientists studied the phenomena that were unfolding with veritable terror.

At first, the symptoms of dissociation seemed to be localized at the extremity of the cutlet's bone, but it was soon observed that the disintegration was gradually spreading to the entire cutlet, and then to the walnut that was beside it. There was no doubt that the phenomenon of dissociation was not localized, as in the observations previously made with radium; it was, on the contrary, like a faculty of disintegration that transmitted itself rapidly—which would soon reach the surrounding objects, the house, the country and perhaps the entire Earth.

How could such phenomena be contained? How could their development be arrested? The interplanetary telegraph apparatus, destroyed at the start by the fire, did not permit any request for urgent instructions on this subject. Furthermore, the phenomena were beginning to take on a truly frightening intensity. The dissociation was visibly proceeding in fits and starts; now it was a matter of simple burning, then violent detonations shook the walls, knocking over the onlookers. In a few minutes, perhaps in a few seconds, they would doubtless witness a total destruction, a veritable explosion of the entire universe.

It was then that something happened that was very simple, but which nevertheless sufficed to modify the history of the world.

Suddenly, while the consternated scientists stood dumbstruck around the mysterious table, a dog belonging to the workshop janitor—who happened to be passing by—bounded into the room, grabbed the cutlet and ran off with it into the fields. Immediately, everyone else launched themselves in pursuit.

The animal seemed to have gone mad; it was leaping about randomly, the hundredfold multiplication of its strength permitting it to outpace the most skilful aviators sent in search of it. At last, run to earth from all directions, mad with pain,

111

burned by the infernal cutlet that it had swallowed, it hurled itself into the river.

For the next two months, there was a succession of terrifying phenomena to beggar all human imagination. The river was transformed into a veritable volcano, spewing out boiling water, overflowing in a single surge, and then disappearing into the Earth, only to reappear abruptly, a few hours later, to resume its normal course. Mad things occurred in that interval, whose story one hardly dares to record. It seemed that the dog's spirit, similarly dissociated, influenced the frightful phenomena that were produced. The waters of the river were covered at one time by a thick fleece of hair, at another by inchoate embryos.

One day, when the dog's master, along with other curiosity-seekers, had gone down to the river, they saw that an enormous hairy tail projecting vertically from the waves and waving, while an immense tongue of water swept the banks and died out at the very feet of the fearful master. Evidently, the dog's instinct had dissociated in its turn, and an inexpressible terror had been conceived.

Then, all the phenomena calmed down; the dissociation stopped—no one knows exactly why—and the scientific world recovered, if only for a few months, the calm of times past.

XX. A Visionary

It was in the 33rd year of the Absolute Savants' reign, at the very moment when human science seemed to have reached its apogee, when a visionary, by means of criminal outrages contrary to all scientific wisdom, turned the world upside down at 48 degrees, 50 minutes and 30 seconds of north latitude and zero degrees, one minute and eight seconds of east longitude on the collective terrain A-327, at ground level.[20] (It had been impossible for some time to designate localities in any other way, all the towns being confused and superimposed 11 deep on the surface of our marvelous planet.)

Science now reigned alone as absolute mistress and everyone was divinely happy to live in a world organized by her. A machine had been invented, in fact, to create that belief. The horror of the first outrages was only too palpable and there was temporary anxiety about the insufficiency of the projections of iodoform designed to calm minds.[21] It was a matter of criminal acts perpetrated on three exhibits in the Great Central Museum, and the monstrosity of those acts denoted such an aberration of mind that everyone was confounded.

For a long time, in fact, these exhibits had been the last in the world still comprised of *living animals*, the sole survivors of terrestrial fauna, which recalled those distant eras when man still shared his home with the thousands of animals from which he had descended. These curious specimens, occupying three special palaces, were three in number: a dog, a

---

[20] On a modern map this map reference leads to a point somewhere north of Alençon, but Pawlowski is, of course, using the Paris meridian rather than the Greenwich one; the relevant location is in the south-east suburbs of Paris, probably the spot on which the author was writing.

[21] Although chemically related to chloroform, iodoform is not normally used as an anesthetic but as a dressing for wounds.

flea and a horse—but no one knew those ancient names any longer.

The first was, it was said, a bizarre creature, always on all fours, with a depressed skull, pointed ears, often pronouncing the same words—*yap! yap! yap!*—and devoid of all mathematical knowledge. It had been classified among the ferocious prescientific animals of the *anti-elephant* genre because of its hairy trunk—set behind rather than in front, as in the elephants, and designed, it was believed, to withdraw nutriments from the body.

The second animal, lodged in a grandiose palace, was scarcely larger than a grain of tobacco, but it made prodigious leaps. It was thought to date from the chaotic period during which the Earth had been encumbered with blocks of stone, which rendering walking more difficult. It was mute, as ignorant as the other, but livelier.

The third animal, finally, was of considerable size. Walking on all fours, like the first, it made a sort of whinnying sound without any practical implication, sniffed the air and struck the ground with its foot. This fashion of self-expression, analyzed by calculation, had furnished nothing intelligible. According to vague items of information surviving the second deluge, it was thought possible to baptize it with its old name, inasmuch as it could be reconstituted—the *Soliped*—even though it had four feet rather than one, as the name appeared to indicate; it was assumed, in consequence, to be a degenerate specimen: a monster.[22]

These three animals were nourished, with great difficulty, with a synthetic artificial grass costing 2000 Europeans a roll, since all vegetation had had been suppressed on Earth by order of the Great Central Laboratory, the pernicious example of the loves of plants being disastrous to social order. By virtue of a laudable sentiment of scientific probity, people had

---

[22] Soliped actually means "whole foot" rather than "single foot," being used to contrast animals like the horse with those with "cloven feet," such as goats.

abstained from teaching them to read, to calculate or to study the workings of interplanetary trains, in order to conserve them as they had once been—and also for fear the admirable electric engraver employed for the instantaneous education of all young citizens as soon as they emerged from the *birth machine* might be subject to a fatal return of ignorance by induction.

For a long time, in fact, the reproduction of the human species had been entrusted to special biological laboratories, and sexual love, the joy of the ancient world, was unknown to the mechanically-minded citizens of the new scientific State.

The assault upon the collections of the Great Central Museum was actually committed by the son of a high functionary of that establishment: young Antimony, a descendant of the noble Stibine family.[23]

From an early age, Antimony had given evidence a strange character, rebellious against all scientific information; it had been necessary to send him back four times to the engraver, whose fuses he continually blew by virtue of his obstinacy. When he came of age at 14 and a half he was refused the social joys of artificial marriage in the special State workshops responsible for the necessary sample-collection. His father died of shame and his uncle Kermes fell gravely ill.[24]

Antimony passed entire minutes dreaming instead of calculating. Sometimes, he spent a long time looking at his work-companion Benzamide, and asked her what reason there could be for the differentiation of the sexes. Benzamide, intrigued and quite disturbed, searched the logarithm tables for the answer, but could not find it.

---

[23] "Stibine" derives from the Latin term for antimony, Stibium, which gives the element its chemical symbol, Sb.

[24] Kermes is the common name of an insect related to the cochineal beetle, which was once similarly used to produce a red dye. Antimony sulphide, commonly known as antimony red, was also used as a pigment.

A year later, contrary to all custom, Antimony had not wanted to have his brain taken out in order to have it replaced, as everyone else did, by a 12-tier electric filing-system, and that evidence of thoughtlessness had conclusively plunged the families Sb_1O_2 and Sb_3O_4, the young man's closest relatives, into desolation.

Such antecedents foreshadowed tragic adventures.

For an entire year, Antimony became increasingly depressed; he no longer listened to the quotidian phonographs, was disinterested in the course of vibrations, and spent long hours in contemplation in front of the three living animals. Then he went out, arms dangling by his sides, to watch the chemical clouds drift across the sky between the artificial trees, spending days in the sunlight and going to bed when everyone got up at the electric dawn.

Sometimes, he wandered the streets like someone suffering from hallucinations, murmuring: "I love... I love..."—but he did not know what.

Mysteriously, in order to escape from his ennui, he then set about constructing a strange harness composed of interlaced cords and asbestos straps. Sometimes, he slipped into the deserted walkways of the Museum, went as far as the Soliped's cage, took new measurements and returned home to work in secret.

When everything was ready, he waited patiently for the great festival of Benzilic Aldehyde and, taking advantage of the general inattention, took possessions of the three living animals. With frightful courage, he imprisoned the living flesh of the Soliped in a network of straps, leapt on the monster's back, succeeded in taming its wild resistance, and set about exciting it by voice and gesture. The Soliped soon bounded forwards, carrying the visionary with it on its mad course.

The anti-elephant followed, gamboling and releasing its strange and terrible cry: "Yap! yap! yap!"

As for the jumping animal, it had immediately lodged itself in the anti-elephant's fur, and let itself be carried off without resistance or fright.

The abomination of desolation then spread throughout the entire world, and a long S.O.S. of terror maddened the 11 tiers of science.

Like a whirlwind, the frightful cavalcade ran along entire autotracks, was engulfed in tunnels, launched itself over balloon-bridges, precipitated itself down parachute stairways and miraculously evaded the thousands of items of security apparatus spread by science over the entire world.

Magnetic roads were short-circuited, rivers resumed their courses, and a veritable blade of grass grew in a laboratory; thus science knew every shame.

The scientific world was then so thoroughly mechanized, in fact, that it was defenseless against an individual initiative that it had not foreseen, and the slightest dust of intelligence, lifted by the wind, was able to throw that gigantic clock out of order.

Innumerable films, taken in flight, showed Antimony smiling in his crazy course, quite transfigured, sitting up on the Soliped—which he regarded avidly—shivering and gripping its living flesh. He was seen to bound forward, then stop abruptly on the summit of some mountain, while at his feet, stretching up towards him, the anti-elephant, indubitably tame, gently licked his hands.

It was not until the following evening that they were able to regain control of the disaster. It was observed with amazement that the animals had come to no harm, and they were returned without difficulty to their palaces.

As for young Antimony, even though he too had suffered no injury, it was decided his action could have had no other provenance than a sadistic counter-scientific madness of the third degree. He tried to explain, vaguely, that he had obeyed an irresistible inner desire, akin to a mysterious atavistic instinct, but he could give no reasonable explanation of his outrage and convinced himself that his criminal action had not satisfied the irrational aspirations that were devouring him.

It was decided to intern him in the laboratory where he worked and to monitor him closely for a year. Given the marvelous progress accomplished by science, the prisons and dungeons of old were long gone, and it is understandable that the new world took great pride in that reform, which placed men on a par with gods. To tell the truth, there was no difference between the condition of citizens submissive to the superhuman State and that of ancient convicts, except that the convicts of old enjoyed freedom of thought and the spectacle of nature. Prisons no longer had any utility in such circumstances.

The strict surveillance to which Antimony was subject was scarcely favorable to him. It revealed new scandals much more dangerous to public order than his assault on the Museum collections. It was thus that the terrified Absolute Savant learned what strange questions Antimony asked Benzamide regarding the utility of the sexes. His outrage reached its maximum when it was reported to him that Antimony and Benzamide were having frequent quarrels. In the new scientific world, all discussion was, in fact, unknown, since all discord could be immediately regulated by calculation.

The danger to the State became immense, but it was necessary, in order to bring a formal accusation against Antimony, to find a pretext that would not awaken any suspicion. He soon furnished one himself by writing, contrary to all the laws, an implausible manifesto from which all equations were excluded and which rested on nothing but ideas! For a citizen of the Superhuman State, that was a work of folly.

Antimony was arrested that same evening, and the Absolute Savant breathed more easily.

XXI. Dead Love

It was on the happy occasion of the great worldwide feast of the Acceleration that Antimony was brought to trial.

Since the already-distant hour when Kilowatt, the man with the rubber fingers, had opened the doors of the Workshop and released the radiant effluvia of the artificial Sun upon the world, hundreds of citizens with phosphor-bronze brains had been hurrying madly through the arterial highways and winding venous streets crying: "Ninety-three! Ninety-three! Ninety-three!" What this signified was that the net output of the new State dynamos had attained 93 per cent.

The scientific satisfaction was general, for everyone believed that the progress of the Superhuman State was now solely dependent on the increase of social speed. Human cells had been preoccupied with nothing else for a long time. Abundantly nourished with arsenophenol, provided with arms of bismuth, electrified brains and bacterial dust-covers, all they had to do was perform their functions in narrowly delimited conditions and their happiness, in accordance with the exact givens of science, could only increase.

The Superhuman State, by complete contrast, remained perfectible. It had been taken in the earliest days of humankind for a simple juridical fiction, but with the unbounded progress of science, its living reality soon became undeniable. The replacement of a human cell was, therefore, an insignificant natural occurrence; the death of the Superhuman State, by contrast, would entail that of all the people who could not live artificially without it.

One after another, surrounded by universal respect the members of the Central Brain arrived on the roof of the State Palace and descended by the electric elevator to the Hall of Science, where the annual ceremony of the Acceleration was held.

119

The 118 State Scientists were there, sitting at their keyboards, impassive and mute. Above them, majestically enthroned, under the direction of the Absolute Savant, were the 20 Old Men of Yesteryear, the ancestors known to humanity by means of books now destroyed in the interests of the safety of the Superhuman State.

Everyone knew that judgment would be passed on the visionary Antimony in the first ten minutes of the session. To tell the truth, the madman's idea hardly seemed worth such an expenditure of time, and the citizens with brains of bronze were trying in vain to figure out the true motive that might have led the 20 Old Men of Yesteryear to interrogate the lunatic in such solemn circumstances.

It was rumored in the crowd that Antimony had been diverted from the straight path by a sojourn of three months in the disaffected deserts of ancient Europe, and his assault on the collections in the Great Museum was recalled. All that the people and the 118 State Scientists could determine was that a capital accusation of scientific imprecision hung over him. Only the Absolute Savant and the 20 Old Men of Yesteryear understood the disturbing gravity of the debate, for they alone knew that, thanks to them, Love was extinct in the world and that its resurrection might bring down the Superhuman State.

A few seconds passed and the session was opened. Blue rays succeeded the red rays and Antimony appeared, introduced by an automaton and powerfully shackled by hypnoses of both feet. Briefly, his frank, clear and luminous gaze wandered indifferently to the dome, criss-crossed by the instantaneograms of the provincial journals, then settled, abruptly and ardently, on Benzamide, who was sitting on the witnesses' bench, waiting anxiously.

Suddenly, the keyboards were activated and the Absolute Savant got up to summarize the ideograph of accusation.

Antimony claimed in his manifesto:

Firstly, that a *qualitative* reasoning ought to replace the scientific methods of the State, based on the illusions of time and space, in directing human cells.

Secondly, that man, without recourse to the Superhuman State, by the cultivation of *his own will*, would be able to tame the elements, fly in the skies, float without material support, and even escape death.

Thirdly, that with the increase of that same *individual will*, man would be able to displace himself instantaneously from one place to another, no longer subject to the infantile rules of space.

Fourthly, that this formidable augmentation of individual power could, undoubtedly, *only be produced as a function of other passions, unknown today, but whose nature it was urgently necessary to research in the history of past centuries.*

As this last paragraph was read, the 20 Old Men of Yesteryear felt themselves going fearfully pale. What, then, was this terrible force of Love that had contrived to come back to life in the cinders of an abolished world to challenge their omnipotence? Was science not the most powerful thing of all, then? It was necessary to settle the matter.

When the reading of the ideograph had finished, violent emanations of protest traversed the hall, and the Absolute Savant, addressing himself to Antimony, went on, sternly: "I cannot understand why, when you were under observation, you asked that your ideas be submitted to laboratory assistant Benzamide, the daughter of the illustrious Anthracite, with whom you conducted your studies. You have affirmed that, without her approval and presence, you cannot do anything. She is here today, in front of us, and I must warn you that this opportunity to explain yourself is the last that you will be given."

A long silence descended.

Haggard, with eyes aflame, Antimony looked at Benzamide; his effort of comprehension seemed frightful. The 20 Old Men of Yesteryear followed the scene with anguish, ready to intervene; the 118 scientists, completely uncomprehending, stared at the accused impatiently. Benzamide, in her turn, studied Antimony with a lively curiosity, as if she were seeing him that day for the first time. The experiment was infinitely perilous; it was necessary that it cease immediately, and the Absolute Savant got up nervously.

"In the absence of any explanation on the part of the accused," he said, dryly, "We shall suspend the session for three minutes, in order to permit Benzamide to draw conclusions. She alone knows the accused's ostensible works well enough to be able to testify in his favor."

Without knowing exactly what she was doing, Benzamide shut herself up alone in the laboratory adjoining the session hall. Her ideas were in turmoil, theories and methods dancing before her eyes as if seized by madness.

Violently, she tried to bring order to her thoughts, to look into herself. Fortunately, she was not in any doubt. Was not her father the glorious inventor of the system of repopulation of the artificial State that had replaced whatever primitive and outdated method had previously been in use? Nevertheless, she was not like other daughters, and strange ideas sometimes got into her head. Often, when she worked with Antimony, she had abrupt fits of annoyance when the young man employed methods that were not hers. Alone among all her companions, however, she did not like her name; she would rather have been called Narcotine or Codeine.

Two minutes went by; then, suddenly, without knowing why, Benzamide felt hot tears running down her cheeks.

Instinctively, the young woman got up, took up a test-tube and conducted a rapid analysis in the Atomometer: water, 983.0; sodium chloride 13.0; mineral salts, 0.2; albuminous matter, 5.0.

I'm going mad, she thought. *There's nothing outside science; this madman is dishonoring the State.*

The third minute having elapsed, Benzamide went back into the session hall, resumed her place, and, with a movement of the head, signified that she had nothing to say; then she looked away.

There was a click, and a see-saw motion; Antimony slid on to the iodoformed table, inert.

No objection having been raised by anyone—even Benzamide—and Antimony posing a danger to the State by reason of his madness, the judges, exercising their discretionary power, proceeded by themselves, promptly and without further ado, to replace his brain with a logarithmic machine in arsenic bronze, of the regulation model furnished by the State

Thus, the spectators of that tragic scene soon saw Antimony leave, a docile automaton devoid of personality or thought, to mingle with the crowd of slaves of the State outside, awaiting the scrupulously regulated mechanical impulses of the Master of the Workshop.

And while Benzamide, her head bowed and her thoughts in disarray, went back to her social father's laboratory, the 20 Old Men got up and went into the Privy Council Chamber. There, still trembling at the dangerous experiment they had just attempted, they looked at one another slowly, without saying anything. They alone, in all the world, knew that something immense had just been destroyed forever: something fabulous, with which ancient humanity had lived for centuries; something that might have put the state in peril simply by virtue of the pronunciation of its name.

And over Love, definitively dead, over the ashes of the Divine Sufferance of yesteryear, assured henceforth of the passivity of citizens of bronze with automatic hearts, they were finally able to glimpse the colossal triumph on the artificial world, forever submissive to the claws of the Superhuman State.

In the street, the docile crowd cried again: "Ninety-three! Ninety-three!"—which signified that the net output of the new central dynamos had reached 93 per cent.

XXII. The Fear of the Thing Unknown

"Materializations developing from the eye! Materializations developing from the eye!"

This statement, repeated 100 times over, drove Paris mad at the end of the 20th century.

For a long time, war had been non-existent, its very name forgotten, and the nations of the Earth enjoyed extremely polite diplomatic relations. No one will be astonished by that when they learn that armaments had developed to unprecedented proportions, and that the admirable progress of science did not permit them to be distinguished from other industrial productions.

Peace was universal. There were no more armies, no more soldiers. When a nation had a grievance against another nation, it contented itself with killing 300,000 or 400,000 people by means known to itself alone; the heads of State exchanged hypocritically affectionate radio messages of condolence, accepting the lesson or trying to take their revenge, according to their strength, but nothing, externally, seemed to trouble the cordiality of their accord.

In every country, war had become endemic; it was no longer anything more than a feature of science and of the general peace. Civilization thus appeared to have reached its apogee.

Grieving minds sometimes regretted the barbarous era of brief, declared wars in which only military personnel were exposed, and which subsequently engendered veritable periods of peace, but they dared not say so, and scarcely to think so, so despotic were the police of the Absolute Savants who governed the world.

It was, specifically, in the last year of the polar oscillation of the 20th century that a sequence of pacifist reprisals desolated humankind.

The Northern Gauls having abruptly raised their customs duty on alimentary peat-mud,[25] the Petty Prussians, vegetarians all, threatened by famine, sent 6000 aerial tourist helmets to Paris by devious routes, which they sold at a knockdown price to the central hatters in the *arrondissements* of Argenteuil and Saint-Germain.

A few clients having lost their sight on trying on these helmets, it was established—fortunately in good time—that each item of headgear contained two particles of radiumite, which turned out the optic nerve within minutes without leaving a trace.

The affair having been hushed up, as usual, by the Savant's censors, it was announced in all the art magazines a few weeks later that, out of deference to Germanic high culture, the Parisian Academy of Music would put on a grand French season in Berlin, designed to make the masterpieces of modern vibratory orchestration better known.

This announcement caused a sensation in Berlin society, where everyone had a passion for the new music—which, inspired by the old impressionism in the medium of painting, left each instrumentalist in the orchestra to play in an independent fashion according to his own inclination. The synthetic whole recomposed itself in the mind of the listener, who had only to plug his ears slightly to obtain a better sense of the general harmony, just as the connoisseurs of old had squinted

---

[25] The word "tourbe", here literally translated as "peat," is also used metaphorically to mean "mob" or "rabble," thus setting up a play on words with the other item employed in this paragraph, where "casques de tourisme aérien" (literally suggestive of some kind of special headgear worn by tourists traveling by air) might also signify "6000 head of airborne tourists." Pawlowski's prophetic gift had evidently allowed him to glimpse the future of cheap air travel that is now our present, as well as the routine exposure or civilians to acts of war, although he was wrong about the omnipotence of the Absolute Savant.

in order to appreciate the luminosity of an impressionist canvas.

The French concerts in Berlin were extended over several weeks. Every day the musicians caused the most curious and discordant notes to be heard, and their inharmonic folly reached such a point that it was necessary to cover all the theater windows to avoid the deadly effects of the vibrations shattering the panes. The French musicians seemed evidently expectant.

On the last day, having called upon the collaboration of an eccentric American orchestra and a few Italian violinists, the strange and profound musical vibrations were abruptly interrupted by a powerful explosion in the suburbs of the capital, which cost the lives of 63,000 people: the colossal nitrogen fertilizer factory in Schweidenburg had just blown up.

Everything worked out as well as it possibly could; the French musicians interrupted their concert as a sign of respect for the dead, the Margrave of Brandenburg himself distributed splendid baskets of bulbous begonias to the artists to thank them for their assistance, and a collection for the victims was organized in Paris…

A terrible anguish subsequently gripped the capital of Northern Gaul. All enlightened minds understood, in fact, that the Schweidenburg catastrophe, caused by the French orchestra's expert musical vibrations, would bring terrible reprisals.

They dreaded the return of the pink poison clouds or the explosive migratory birds that had done so much damage, and the Absolute Savants themselves were afraid of discovering themselves disarmed against the ever-possible treasons of their *subconscious*: a direly ill-protected mental domain on which the enemy had already made several disturbing hypnotic espionage raids.

It was, in consequence, a sort of relief for them when inspectors came to tell them that a poor workman in the Home Theater distribution factory had been strangled that same night by a phantom that had materialized progressively in the darkness of his bedroom. First, a luminous eye the color of emerald had opened about two meters above the ground, then a blurred head had manifested itself, from which filaments of matter soon extended in the form of muscles, arms and hands. These filaments, like the tentacles of an octopus, had rapidly ramified around the neck of the terrified unfortunate, and had provoked death by suffocation. A dozen identical cases were identified the following day in the suburbs of Mantes and Château-Thierry—which is to say, at the very extremities of the Parisian agglomeration.[26]

These materializations at a distance were not entirely new and, despite all the danger they posed, the means of combating them was known. Had not 3000 analogous phantoms, captured ten years before and subdued by hypnotism, been employed for some time in draining marshes and the more repugnant sorts of refuse-disposal? This time, however, what troubled feeble minds was that each materialization started with an eye. Not, we hasten to say, that in that scientific era the appearance of an eye in the darkness was capable of frightening even the most timorous of people—but everyone knew that Petty Prussian phantoms materialized feet first, and the primary appearance of the eye disconcerted the observers.

The Colonial Academy, meeting the next day, awoke greater anxiety in Paris by proving definitely that this was a matter of *Oriental* reprisals, doubtless due to the prohibition of exports of white worms, and that the Petty Prussians had nothing to do with it. Indeed, it is well-known that the Far Eastern mentality is, in every respect, the inverse of ours. Orientals fear the rod and scorn death; their cooks peel their vegetables outwards, instead of bringing the blade towards them as ours do; they write from right to left; and their painters, when they

---

[26] Mantes is about 35 kilometres west of central Paris, Château-Thierry about twice as far away to the east, so the capital has not yet extended nearly as far as Pawlowski here estimates in jest, although it is considerably bigger than it was in his day.

have to paint a large mural, first draw the eyes of birds, then the beaks, the feathers, and finally the surrounding country-side. The fact that these phantom materializations began with the eye was an indisputable indication of oriental action.

Paris was therefore plunged once again into the fear of the unknown. Imaginative people, precisely describing all possible catastrophes to themselves, were dying suddenly of heart attacks on perceiving the slightest unexpected noise; others no longer dared venture into the streets; almost every-one experienced an unhealthy terror when they abandoned themselves to sleep. The more the waiting was prolonged the more extreme this nervousness became. People got to the stage of hoping for the worst catastrophes in order to be libe-rated, at whatever price, from an unbearable nightmare.

It was, therefore, a veritable explosion of joy in Paris that greeted the arrival of the first *male shells*, engendered in their course by female shells of a very old type—which, incontesta-bly, came from the Petty Prussians although they bore ostensi-ble American trademarks.

No one wanted to believe, at first, in reprisals so gross and infantile. Everyone ran to the impact-points to see these familiar—exceedingly familiar—shells, of which no one any longer had any atavistic fear. They laughed and sang in the streets; open-air balls were organized, as of old; a great dis-tributor of electric nutriments was even seen to set up chairs and tables on the pavement of the boulevard, in the ancient manner.

The joy was so great and popular gaiety so extravagant that the Absolute Savants themselves forgot for 45 minutes to operate the simple lever controlling the old magnetic appara-tus they had designed long ago to deflect shells in case of an attack, and dispatch them with precision to the scrap-metal yard established for that purpose on waste ground near the Creusot foundries.

Everyone believed that the good old days of puerile bombardments with shells had returned; no one yet suspected the inconceivable horrors that impending scientific progress had reserved for humankind.

XXIII. Universal Levitation

It was not long after the 20th century that man began to dominate nature and really to command the movement of the Universe. Until then, he had scarcely made progress, and it was only with difficulty that one could distinguish differences between a caveman and a man that lived at the beginning of the 20th century, utterly ignorant of himself and the Leviathan that surrounded him.

It is sufficient to recall, for example, the stupidity and general incomprehension that greeted the periodic return of Halley's comet in 1910. The men of that time probably attached less importance to that astronomical event than Chaldean herdsmen living 7000 years before them had. No scientific conclusion was drawn from that important encounter; no one, however intelligent, thought of making practical use of the providential passage of the wandering star for any industrial or scientific end. And yet, the men of that time did not have the excuse of not knowing about radioactivity, and that alone should have put them on the road to the marvelous discoveries that were to follow a few years later.

When one compares that extraordinary indifference to the frenetic activity that reigned on Earth when it was decided to capture a comet, one remains veritably astounded by the thought of the gigantic strides made by humankind in that short space of time. That formidable step, it must be admitted, was entirely due to the sensational discovery of the general law of *universal levitation*—which, completing that of *gravitation*, previously known in isolation, explained the general movement of the universe. It was, in sum, the definitive revelation of two antagonistic forces of attraction and repulsion, association and dissociation, two contrary energies on which depended the appearance and disappearance of worlds—in a word, of matter.

How had people not realized sooner the necessity of that contrary factor? They asked themselves that in astonishment. Kepler alone seemed to have been preoccupied with laws of energy but it was with a truly surprising indifference that Laplace had hastened to set the question aside. Newton's law was sufficient to explain everything. In the same way that ancient religions supposed a *deus ex machina* at the origin of the world responsible for giving the primal impulsion to creation, the physicists were enthusiastic to accept the energy of matter—the primitive and rectilinear movement of nebulae—as an undemonstrable axiom.

Once this point of departure was accepted without discussion, *universal gravitation* sufficed to account for everything else regarding the formation of worlds. The primitive nebula, agitated by a rotational movement, successively emitted rings under the influence of centrifugal force; these rings broke up like smoke-rings and, under the influence of attraction, condensed into spheres, forming planets. When the central nucleus was of sufficiently restricted dimensions for no further rings to be detached, it condensed in its turn into a central Sun. All that was quite exact, but no one dreamed for a moment of seeking the origin of centrifugal force that formed each solar system, and which, combining thereafter with attraction, permitted each planet to describe its regular ellipse around the central Sun.

When the structure and laws of the tiny solar system that is the atom were definitively discovered, it was easy to resolve this problem and to explain the gigantic universe clearly by means of the microscopic one. The comets themselves, of a matter often less dense than the relative vacuum of a pneumatic machine, were no more than alpha particle equivalents traversing the immense interplanetary voids of the atom-universe between the solar nucleus from which hydrogen is dissociated and the planetary electrons in fixed orbits that gravitate around it.

After that, people no longer thought about anything but utilizing the formidable rectilinear force that the comets possessed, in imitation of primitive nebulae.

Indeed, on the day when the dissociation of terrestrial matter in considerable proportions began, in order to extract useful energy therefrom, people observed, with amazement, a slight augmentation of the day, and then the year—which is to say, a slight slowing of the Earth's movement around the Sun. Insufficient notice was taken, at first, of this deceleration, due to the dissipation of a part of our centrifugal force. By compensation, in fact, attraction had made itself felt and had drawn the Earth proportionately closer to the Sun, thus re-establishing, almost exactly, the length of the year.

It was no less urgent to repair these losses of centrifugal energy as quickly as possible, and people immediately began to think of capturing the radiant force of comets. It was a triumph of the new science that soon diverted a part of the energy of Halley's comet; that was, properly speaking—I repeat—the first act of veritable royalty that man exercised upon the universe.

There was then, as usual, a quickly-restrained period of excess. In the joy of triumph, people went so far as to utilize all that newly-amassed centrifugal force and amused themselves, purely out of pride, by considerably augmenting the speed of the Earth's rotation. The days were no longer more than a few hours long—until the day when, the speed of rotation having reached exactly 17 times the initial speed, alarmed telegraph messages were received from the Equator, saying that men and objects were no longer adhering to the surface of the Earth. The planet's rotation was then returned, progressively, to its former speed, and people contented themselves with storing the new forces, as before, solely for the needs of industry, without thinking any longer of the momentarily-glimpsed *direction of the Earth*.

XXIV. The Enlargement of Memory

In the year of Transmutation, when the Social Surgeon performed the first successful cephalotomy, substituting a calculating sponge for the left hemisphere of the brain, he had scarcely any inkling of the formidable consequences that his audacious intervention would have. He proposed, in fact, quite simply, to operate on another young man who had initially emerged from the Workmen's Teacher Training College, and to transform him into an elite subject capable of calculating in a few minutes all the new income-tax bills. He scarcely imagined that this operation would soon permit all the curiosity-seekers in the world to journey into past history and to observe for themselves, in the minutest detail, events that had taken place several centuries before.

It had already been observed, however, in the course of surgical operations, that new methods of anesthesia did not, strictly speaking, suppress sensation, but amplified it in the manner of a microscope. In the course of a minor surgical operation, the patient, locally anesthetized by cocaine or ether, perceived the work accomplished by the surgeon magnified a thousand times, like an image of a cinema screen—and it is conceivable that it was this magnification that relieved the pain of all its acuity. Without suffering, the patient became a mere spectator of an immense operation, soft and muffled, accomplished by cotton-wool giants.

When it first became feasible to anesthetize the brain, these phenomena suddenly took on an unexpected character. It was no longer the dimensions of the world or the surgeon's instruments that appeared to be formidably enlarged in the patient's mind; it was old facts stored by the memory in the deep layers of the brain, which were abruptly brought back to the plane of immediate consciousness, in the broad light of day.

To the great astonishment of all the observers, the trainee teacher, while subject to the operation, became delirious, swore that he would let two three-*sou* items go for a franc and that he would make nothing on the camembert. At the same time he gave such precise information regarding life behind the lines during the Petty War of 1914 that the bemused scientists embarked upon a rapid enquiry. It revealed that an ancestor of the trainee teacher had been a profiteer in 1918 and that it was undoubtedly his ancient impressions that his descendant had perceived directly during the operation.

It is evident, in fact, that innumerable memories slumber in the deep layers of the brain, not merely of a particular individual but of his ascendants. Many an infant folds a newspaper instinctively or scratches his ear in the same manner as a grandfather he never knew. Certain reflexes and certain instinctive repugnances come to us from an unknown ancestor. But there is much more; one often *recognizes* towns or landscapes that one sees for the first time; one experiences seemingly-ancient admirations or sympathies for art-works or people one recognizes without ever having seen them before. This is because we live superficially, with the sensations of the moment and memories of the day before; we are ignorant of the immensity of an unexplored subconscious in which billions of sensations and ideas of people who have preceded us are often enclosed.

Thanks to the skillfully-localized anesthesia of present layers of memory and the hyperesthesia of the subconscious, the scientists of that era were soon able to organize veritable voyages into history. They all volunteered to effectuate soundings of the past—and just as aviators had once competed to break altitude records, *voyagers in the subconscious* became keen rivals to travel the furthest possible distances into History.

That was a strange time, when people absented themselves from the present for months to live exclusively in memories unexpectedly brought back to the surface by the anesthesia of contemporary memories. Unsuspected details

134

were thus obtained of life in past centuries—and as the present era, uniquely devoted to Science, was no longer very entertaining, the explorers of history became more numerous every day.

This fashion was brought to an end by legislation when the scandal of the celebrated scientist Sodium broke. By virtue of a line of descent of which history had not conserved any trace, Sodium, retracing his memories by elimination, ended up by incarnating one of his ancestors in his own person: King Caribert, who, even though married to Queen Ingoberge,[27] had been seized by an irresistible passion for his two chambermaids, one of whom was named Marcovèphe and the other Meroflède. The fact was not unknown, being recorded in the Chronicles of Saint-Denis, but no one had realized the force of the passion in question. When the scientist Sodium arrived at that era of his ancestral memories, he found himself so content with his two chambermaids that he deliberately refused to redescend through history to return to the marvelous century of Science.

This example might have been pernicious and upset the perfect social equilibrium in which the citizens of that era lived. It was therefore decided, by means of the successive hyperesthesia of recent layers of memory, to bring Sodium back to his own time—but Sodium, who was familiar with all the methods that might be employed to force him to leave his two chambermaids, suffered such a fit of despair that he committed suicide in History. In that same year, the Scientific State banned voyages in the subconscious, on pain of death, and the mathematical and fastidious life resumed its normal course, as before.

---

[27] Caribert (521-567) was a Merovingian king of the Franks, who married Ingoberge (519-589) in 540.

XXV. Man Cut In Two

In year 23 of the New Era, dating from the Mastery of the Atom, the obstinacy of scientists almost led humankind to ruin for a second time.

After the death of the Leviathan, it was understood that thoroughgoing materialism possessed no serious basis, and that it ought to be definitively abandoned. If the Leviathan was dead, it was assumed, it was doubtless because its gigantic body had been constructed in three dimensions, neglectful of the necessary support of the fourth internal dimension to which human existence was owed.

Since the most remote times, in fact, it had been known that life was nothing but a perpetual sequence of actions and reactions between the external and internal worlds, and that this double movement, this *contradiction*, was frequently represented in ancient religions by the symbol of respiration. As soon as the Leviathan disappeared, the opposition of the human personality to the external world was better and more distinctly understood, and it was affirmed that consciousness, properly understood, was nothing but an internal and innate sense of the fourth dimension. This internal sense was found at the same time to furnish the key to the great problems of space and time; it permitted the integration of all human notions, the reconstitution of the entire world outside any idea of space and time, forming a unique whole, without beginning or end, describing in a single line what had been taken until then for the successive actions of centuries.

Immediately, as science was unable to stop at simple philosophical intuitions, and had to have immediate recourse to the enlightenment of analysis, the most extravagant experiments were carried out on the human body. The ancient assertion of the mages of old concerning the necessary intervention of an even number in all human constructions was taken up again, on a new basis. The considerable mistake was, however, made of neglecting, for the moment, the odd number that was found in all ancient myths and which completed—whether it was the number 12 by the number 13, or the number six by the number seven—the calculation of divine unity. They simple stated the fundamental duality of all superior beings, and undertook, in the laboratories, to cut men in two, in the vertical sense, in order to facilitate a complete analysis.

Needless to say, no sooner had the operative technique been developed to a high degree of perfection than such operations came to seem quite natural.

Those first experiments were not crowned with any success. It seemed, however, logical, by working along a vertical plane passing through the bridge of the nose, to separate a man composed of two similar halves, and who, properly speaking, was nothing but a duplicate being. Unfortunately, I repeat, this analysis did not yield any satisfactory result. Although it had been possible for several centuries to section a human being horizontally, conclusively depriving him of the double usage of certain limbs, the vertical operation remained impossible.

In transverse section, veritably marvelous operations had been realized. After accomplishing the banal ablation of two arms and two legs, that of the trunk was similarly successful. By means of simply-excavated channels, the head was enabled to live in isolation without any difficulty. They even succeeded in isolating the brain by horizontal section, then a layer of the cerebral substance. Although the body, thus reduced, presented two opposed and symmetrical parts, it undoubtedly continued to manifest all the characteristics of life.

On the contrary, the vertical section—seemingly much more logical and much simpler to achieve, since it resulted in the subsistence of two complete halves, each having one eye, one ear, one lung, one auricle, one ventricle, one cerebral hemisphere and so on—always had the effect of instantaneously extinguishing the very sources of life, as if life were, in reality, only due to an antagonism, a *contradiction*, between similar organs, one positive and one negative.

137

The scientists of that time, in their obstinacy, were not at all discouraged; the division of man that they could not obtain anatomically they attempted from a purely psychic point of view. Little by little, they succeeded in training the human race, then much diminished by science, and dividing it into two clearly-opposed classes.

On the one hand, there was what came to be called *neo-materialists*, constructed in the image of the Leviathan, among whom all consciousness was abolished, and who only conserved a three-dimensional vision of the world. Their purely reflexive movements were sustained by the everyday needs of social life; they knew no other orders than the scientific regulations of the external world; their discipline was absolute, their science very complete, their intelligence totally extinct.

On the other hand, there was what came to be called *idealists*, who were deprived of any means of relating to the external world of three dimensions. Their lot was, in reality, that of ancient Hindu fakirs and their internal life developed in strange proportions. Provided solely with the sense of the fourth dimension, they were entirely ignorant of time and space. For them, phenomena did not succeed one another; for them, there were soon no longer any phenomena at all.

The scientists of the Great Central Laboratory were at first intoxicated by the results they had obtained; they had finally, after their fashion, completed the analysis of man; they had decomposed and had power over the separate elements making up his life. Their enthusiasm diminished when they came to understand that these elements, thus separated, were incapable, either on one side or the other, of reproduction, and that humankind would soon be extinct forever. They had successfully isolated what had previously constituted, for them, the idealist element, but it proved that the element in question could only react in contradiction with the material element. Only by the reunion of the two elements could the eternal flame of intelligence—the immortal life that, until then, had guided humankind to its highest destiny—be reignited.

The scientists imagined that they possessed all the elements of the problem, having analyzed human intelligence to its extreme limits, but it proved that human intelligence could only manifest itself in its three-dimensional symbols. They had acted in the fashion of chemists who had isolated all the simple bodies composing a crystal, but who could not find in that analysis the geometric form of the crystal, which had entirely disappeared.

Thus, after centuries of research, progress and analyses, the scientists found themselves brutally returned to their point of departure: the profound ignorance that everyone had had, in the earliest ages of the world, of the origins of life, of the undeniable but always ungraspable reality of ideas. It soon became necessary to make use of the coarsest procedures, utterly unworthy of science; it was necessary, at all costs, to reawaken passions that had supposedly been abolished forever, to revert to the ridiculous exploit that the men of old had called *love*.

Humankind, differentiated into passionless materialists and idealists detached from any phenomenal preoccupation, now seemed incapable of feeling the erotic passions of old. It was necessary to appeal to two despised beings that had been conserved in the Museum as mere ethnographic specimens, and who lived in the most absolute scientific ignorance. They had to excite the most vulgar passions in this primitive couple: jealousy, cruelty, envy. They had to dress the man in sumptuous ornaments, in the manner of prehistoric males, to provoke in his companion the outrage of being abandoned or badly dressed. When she finally complained to the chief warder that she did not have a stitch to wear, they began to understand that humanity would soon be saved. The rest was a matter of time, and ancient creatures conformed with the complexity of primal ages eventually began to emerge from the State incubators, whose intelligence came to life once again.

It was, as if by a miracle, the rebirth of man: the lamp of Psyche lit up again for centuries on end, still mysterious, still incomprehensible but, as ever, saving humankind continually from the successive failures of science.

XXVI. The Photophonium Catastrophe

It was some time after the death of the Leviathan that the terrible Photophonium catastrophe occurred, which turned the scientific world upside down.

The tyranny of the Leviathan, which had weighed upon man for a long time, had taught the majority of scientists a lesson. It was finally understood that if a colossal personality, superior to man, had been able to form in the world, incorporating human beings as simple cells, the fault lay entirely with the absurd and prideful certainty of materialists who, admitting nothing but positive discoveries and rejecting any idealist theory, had thrown themselves into the monster's mouth, in accordance with naïve and ancient predictions.

This vanity of wanting to know everything by the sole means of the testimony of the senses was, however—it had to be admitted—quite puerile. The senses, as they existed in the men of old, were nothing but five little windows opening upon nature in different places. Outside the senses, the world was nothing but a collection of obscure and silent vibrations and, according to whether these vibrations were more or less frequent in each second, they were perceived by one or other of the senses. Thus, from 32 vibrations per second to 3600, it was the ear that perceived them in the form of sound. Beyond that, the vibrations were unknown. Further on, the eye began to perceive vibrations at 40 trillion a second (red light) and lost sight of them at 756 trillions (violet light).

In addition to the vibrations perceived by the ear or the eye, others exist in nature, some of which are perceived by the nose, the tongue or the skin, others by the thermometer, photographic plates or registered by electrical apparatus. Theoretically, therefore, nothing prevented man from having other senses analogous to the eye or the ear, permitting him to perceive countless beauties that were unknown to him, and it was known that certain animals, since the origins of the world, had been able to perceive phenomena to which man was blind: the pigeon's instinct of orientation and the dog's sense of smell provided that more than adequately.

During the period of the Leviathan's tyranny, it was supposed that that superior animal, a newcomer in the scale of beings, must have retained innumerable unknown sensations to its own advantage, but it was also thought that it had not perceived things in the same fashion. How had it translated the sensations of light or sound? Had there been a transposition or a synthesis of all those vibrations? Had it surrendered itself to unknown orgies of vibrations inaccessible to man? No one ever found out—but once it was dead, for fear that a similar tyranny might reappear on Earth, nothing seemed more pressing than to renounce the positive doctrines of old in order to launch resolutely into the research of the unknown.

Before anything else, there was a matter of transforming human sensations, of augmenting their intensity, developing senses beyond known limits and gradually creating, as required, new senses that would permit people to have a more extensive understanding of nature. A special institute was immediately founded: the *Photophonium*, dedicated to the upbringing of human beings endowed with a superior sensibility. It was proposed to enhance each sense somewhat in every subject, causing him to perceive vibrations hitherto reserved to senses superior to his, and eventually liberating the sense of sight, whose former functions would be replaced by an inferior sense, in order to render it disposable for the possible vision of the invisible.

The results were not immediate, but after three successive generations they exceeded all hopes. Soon, the old sensations were improving every day; it was no more than a game for the pupils of the Photophonium to experience the sensations of odor and taste via the intermediary of touch. In their laboratory experiments, it was no longer necessary for them to put chemical products into their mouths or smell them in order to recognize them; it was sufficient to touch them. Progress proceeding in parallel for the entire body, the most distinguished among them clearly perceived luminous sensations by means of the ears. It was, at first, only a vague, opaque light, like the sensations experienced by a myopic individual considering a distant landscape; then, new nervous receptors having been placed behind the tympanum by the Laboratory's scientists, the sensations became clearer; an arrangement of optical mirrors easily rectified the divergent views obtained by the ears, and the former vision of the eyes, realized henceforth by the former auditory sense, was perfect.

To tell the truth, this did not constitute a goal even while it was being pursued, but merely a preliminary step. What was necessary, in fact, before anything else, was to liberate the superior sense of sight from its former functions and to educate the eye in such a fashion that it was able to perceive new, superior vibrations hitherto inaccessible to man. For that, a special optical apparatus had been invented: the *Aphanoscope*—which, it was thought, would permit the invisible to be seen.

Snobs—for they are found in every epoch—naturally took pleasure in these novelties, in order to appear not to sense things in the same way as everyone else. Numerous concerts were thus arranged in which the sounds were perceived by smell and by taste, in which good music was sampled after the fashion of a wine-tasting. There were also fine spectacles put on, which the aesthetes of the moment took pleasure in seeing through their ears.

During this time, serious research continued at the Photophonium; people waited anxiously to know what the first sensations perceived by the disaffected eyes might be, and the ocular apparatus of the pupils was progressively improved to this end. Electric stimulators were placed in direct communication with the eyes, which could already perceive X-rays through opaque bodies and discern hitherto unknown influences and vibrations in the atmosphere.

It was at this moment that the frightful Photophonium catastrophe occurred, in the course of a final session that took place in the great amphitheater, in which the attempt was made to obtain a clearer and more distinct vision of invisible things on the part of the pupils.

First, there was one loud scream in the hall, then others; the pupils could *see*, and as they saw more, their agitation became extreme. Habituated as they were to calm scientific methods and to logical and well-balanced deductions, they saw all the sensations of the past abruptly surge forth before their eyes: all the vibrations accumulated in the air over centuries, all the wasted words; all the evil influences, desires or hatreds; the phantasmal apparitions of the ideas of old; *and their terrible future consequences*.

They saw everything that nature, in its wisdom, had hidden until then from the infancy of human beings, by offering them the art-work of selective sensation. For them, it was as if a frightful storm had suddenly broken out in the hall. Perceived in the form of luminous impressions, that disconcerting chaos deranged their minds and broke the aphanoscopes with which they were surrounded, unleashing a tempest in their crazed brains.

In disarray, they tried to flee, but their cleverly-trained hands no longer encountered anything along the walls but unfamiliar taste sensations; the howls of the spectators could only arrive in their brains in the form of violent odors, and the lights in the hall made a frightful buzzing din in their ears.

Almost all of them, broken down and demolished, piece by piece, like overcomplicated machines, succumbed to that terrible trial. When the hall was finally evacuated, nothing was found there on the following day but the janitor's little cat licking itself, calmly looking around from time to time—with eyes adapted by the habit of centuries—at those phantom ideas which, as everyone knows, are always drifting slowly through the atmosphere.

XXVII. The Ferropucerons

I have had the great pleasure of spending a short time with Hydrogen, one of the 12 Immortal Old Men who preceded the formation of the Cellular State and who were the only ones to conserve the memory of time past.

The manner in which I introduced myself to him in the new world, across a distance of centuries, by means of the fourth dimension, was infinitely intriguing to Hydrogen—who, knowing that I could not communicate in any way with the citizens of the Cellular State, willingly allowed me to circulate freely, equipped with an identification number, and took some pleasure in telling my tales of olden times.

Between the primitive era of humankind, which came to an end around the year 2000, and the definitive reign of Absolute Science, many years of an infinitely curious intermediate era elapsed. Indeed, man was already in possession of all the mechanical discoveries that were the glory of the scientific world, but he was still submissive to all the traditions of prehistoric thought, and that formed a strange mélange of new and old ideas that often gave rise to the craziest conceptions.

All the renewed joys of Byzantine decadence were rampant then, formidably increased by the colossal support given to them by new scientific discoveries—and one can certainly imagine that humankind might have rolled into the abyss of madness if the prodigious interventions of the 12 Old Men had not put an end to those excesses, regulating and disciplining the new bronze-brained citizens of the Cellular State by means of the Magnetic Tempest.

Among the mad adventures that marked the decadence of the ancient scientific world, Hydrogen told me about one that troubled many a brain at the time.

It was on the occasion of one of the great airborne hunts that were held in the forests of the East by the mayor of

Suippes; the latter, then 212 years old, had organized an aerial hunt conceived in imitation of the falcon-hunts that had been held in prehistory. Little unmanned monoplanes, shaped like birds, were released into the air, and racing airplanes had to seize that prey at an altitude of 1500 or 2000 meters, in the manner of falcons.

The hunt was saddened by the unfortunate fall of aviator 671-98, who, having fallen from a height of 3000 meters, spent at least 37 hours in hospital and came out of it quite disfigured and unrecognizable, the majority of his principal organs having been replaced by grafted organs taken from calves, dogs or monkeys.

Needless to say, there was much anxious discussion the following day of the unknown causes of such a fall. Unfortunately, the aviator could only give vague indications regarding the matter; he did not understand what had happened to him at all. His artificial bird was certainly the most prodigious that had been constructed to date; it bore no resemblance to the gross frameworks of canvas and wood that had been employed, a few hundred years before, in the early days of aviation. It was a veritable bird, faithfully reconstituted down to the slightest detail, which had been ingeniously endowed with sensibility.

Little mirrors, specially designed for hunts of the falconry genre, reflected the prey to be seized, affected the magnetic current and modified its direction without the aviator even having to preoccupy himself with it. Gusts of wind and the turbulence that one sometimes encounters in the atmosphere provoked the required reflex movements in the least of the creature's organs in good time. It was a completely articulated artificial bird, anticipating all outside influences: an infinitely docile creature, in which any accident was rigorously impossible.

And yet, the facts spoke for themselves!

671-98 had only noticed one thing: that at the moment when he had lost equilibrium, one of the wheels mounted on the fork that served as the bird's feet had appeared to be displaced in a lateral direction—and that slight imbalance had doubtless been followed by the machine's fall.

That provided no precise indication, and it was decided to examine the machine more closely.

The artificial bird had remained very nearly intact; a few repairs sufficed to put it back in order and technician 15-20 wanted to try it out straight away. He took it up to 50 meters—then, suddenly, one of the wheels was clearly seen to rise up to the height of the right wing. The apparatus lost its position of equilibrium and fell heavily to the ground.

The same thing happened a dozen times over in different situations, and the bird had to be taken into a hangar, where experts examined it piece by piece.

The motor was started up again with the machine stationary. Suddenly, at the moment when it was least expected, the right foot elevated itself once again to the height of the right wing, brushed it slightly, moving slightly to the left, then fell back to the ground. There was no doubt; it was necessary to yield to the evidence: the artificial bird, endowed by its maker with reflex movements, *appeared to be scratching itself.*

The wings of the bird were rapidly examined with a microscope, and the amazement of the experts could not have been greater on discovering little iron lice within the weave of the silk, of a species absolutely unknown until then, which seemed to have been born on the aircraft and to be unable to live anywhere else.[28]

It was these imperceptible little parasites that provoked the corresponding reflexes on the part of the artificial bird. No doubt remained on this point: the mechanical bird was scratching itself.

---

[28] Strictly speaking *pucerons*—the adaptation from the Latin exists in English as well as French—are aphids, or a "plant-lice," but as the artificial bird is a synthetic animal, it seems preferable to use the term "lice."

Needless to say, the scientists lost themselves in conjectures on the nature of these lice. In that era, people were still entirely imbued with absurd evolutionist doctrines and spontaneous generation seemed simply nonsensical. They devoted their ingenuity, therefore, as best they could, to explaining how ancient lice, feeding on iron filings and living on the wings of airplanes, had been able to transform themselves by adapting to a new environment. It was even suggested, by virtue of their color being identical to that of the wings of the artificial bird, that they represented a curious case of mimicry.

They had not the slightest suspicion of the disconcerting prodigies that were to turn that transitional humankind upside down a few years later, with the appearance and the decadence of living machines.

XXVIII. Industrial Love

It was only in the mid-20th century that an inkling was finally obtained of what Love might be. Since the origin of the world, that question had legitimately preoccupied all thinkers and all psychologists, but no one had so far been able to come up with a satisfactory answer.

People sensed, deep down, all the absurdity and all the pettiness of the sexual passions between men and women, but the force of those passions could not be denied. In response to the slightest inclination, the greatest men did not hesitate to throw away their entire lives, renouncing the noblest ambitions, and one thus caught a glimpse of a colossal underutilized or ill-directed energy. It was a relief when it was understood, with the progress of civilization, that all this was merely a matter of an obscure primitive instinct that had awaited, in order to develop normally, the appearance of the scientific world, colossal factories and gigantic business affairs.

The love of women, which was merely a base physical penchant, was bound to be succeeded by the love of civilized man for his industrial creations: for the work that he had conceived and to which he devoted all his life. Certain follies of the past immediately became clearer. What did the absurd age-old jealousy, the immoderate love of sacrifice and the inadmissible personal pride of men with regard to women signify, without that industrial explanation? How, similarly, could the seduction be explained that the complications, cunning and trickery currently employed by women were able to exercise on well-organized masculine brains?

Everything in primitive love was veritably absurd and disproportionate. It could often happen, for instance, that a man loved two women, sincerely and profoundly, at the same time and, when that was discovered, showed a distinctly ill grace about it. Why, equally, did a man, when he was a lover,

149

accept the existence of a husband, when a husband did not accept that of a lover?

Great military feats had, it must be admitted, furnished a useful nourishment to these unused forces of the human mind. Generals had been known who loved glory more than anything else, devoting all their efforts to bringing off a victory, gladly resorting to any subterfuge to succeed and not hesitating to sacrifice their own lives if required—but it has to be recognized that these were barbaric games, unworthy of a more advanced civilization, which involved the needless sacrifice of a large number of human lives. Industrial love, it is true, sometimes also involved many human sacrifices, but the results that it pursued were much more worthy of tempting a civilized man.

Progressively, towards the middle of the 20th century, the old love disappeared almost entirely from the upper classes of the nation; it was now only found among the lowest class, where it replaced—quite advantageously—the sad alcoholism and stupefying agents of old.

The great industrial magnates devoted themselves entirely to their works, and were not long delayed in recovering, massively magnified, all the despairs, all the amorous joys, all the triumphs and all the deceptions of primitive love. It was no longer a matter, in the ferocious struggles of industries, of making money, if one could not render a factory more beautiful and more prosperous, and amorous passion soon far surpassed the simple love of money.

The most celebrated adversaries of that era bore the two greatest names in France: they were the Chevalier Bloch de Lille and Prince Weill de Jeanne d'Arc. The former had been for many years the director of the colossal factory making Greasy Filaments, a new product which, by reason of recent discoveries, was used more than any other in the land. The latter was the skillful proprietor of the English Filament Company, whose concurrence was a serious threat to Greasy Filaments.

The story of these two great industrialists dominated the news for a long time.

Chavalier Bloch had a great affection for his factory. He had known it when it was very small, had dedicated himself to its development, and had formed it piece by piece—but it was beginning to show its age a little when the Fatty Filament arrived on the scene.

Prince Weill, for his part, had got involved with the Fatty Filament when it was in full bloom. He had acquired it from an Englishman who had gone to Japan with a young newly-formed overseas company. Prince Weill scarcely saw anything in his enterprise but the façade. It flattered him to have in his possession the Fatty, which was as famous and as universally admired—justly—as a beautiful racehorse, but he did not have the kind of affection for it that leads to a long communal life and the memory of difficult years spent together.

It was then that Chevalier Bloch, seduced by the new production-methods and the young and vibrant appearance of the Fatty Filament, began to commit inexplicable sins. Furtively, he favored the concurrent factory, secretly becoming one of its principal clients, and committed the worst follies on its behalf. Is it necessary to relate that the Fatty, in spite of all his advances, never belonged to him, and that Chevalier Bloch, humiliated and ruined, was content to rediscover his old Greasy Filaments, damaged and impoverished by his error, but still capable of devotedly assuring his upkeep again? Is it necessary to evoke the tragic drama that put a final end to the affair: the moral suicide of Chevalier Bloch, who mechanically destroyed the old factory that he did not love and whose benefits were sold in order that he might become a simple workman in the Fatty that he loved; and finally, the industrial murder of Prince Weill, whose entire factory was destroyed one day by an unspeakable sabotage due to jealousy?

These were events whose multiple amorous contradictions tempted the feuilletonist novelists of the era, but which I shall limit myself to recording.

151

XXIX. A Machine Revolt

On the third intercalary of the first scientific period, overseer HG28 flew into his factory manager's office like a gust of wind, crying: "Boss! Boss! Come quick! The electricity's fizzling out!"

Given the mores of the time, this obsequious mode of addressing the factory manager is sufficient demonstration of HG28's state of agitation. The factory manager followed him immediately to the workshops and there, in the automatic lathe section, he saw that strange things were indeed happening.

Undoubtedly, the reality was not at all in accordance with HG28's affirmations, and the electricity was not *fizzling out*; there were, however, inexplicable losses in the transmission of power and a sort of oily sweat was escaping from the arrested dynamos, which streamed away without it being possible to determine its precise origin.

Salts had escaped, climbing up the walls of their vats, and were now heaped up against the factory's main door. Some automatic lathes had stopped abruptly while working at top speed, their principal mechanical parts breaking clean off and their controls twisted in every direction, without the intervention of any external force that might explain such deformations of the metal.

The engineers were contemplating these strange phenomena in silence. They had already known for some years, in fact, that a strange and unknown life had animated the metal; how it might be poisoned, subject to overwhelming fatigue, stimulated—like tin or platinum, for example—with sodium carbonate or calmed with bromide or chloroform. They were no longer unfamiliar with the way that an iron bar, after receiving a shock or being subjected to a rapid expansion at a particular place, repaired its substance and became much stronger at exactly that place, just as a broken bone in the human body becomes more resistant at the point where it has knitted.

Nevertheless, they had not thus far attributed to matter a veritable life analogous to the life of plants and animals, and they asked one another anxiously whether new and disturbing discoveries were not being made on this subject.

It was necessary, in fact, to recognize that, since the formation of the globe, nothing of that which constituted life could have come to us from the sky. In the beginning, the Earth was nothing but a gaseous mass, then matter in fusion; it was from that primitive matter that plants and animals had later emerged, by cooling, and that is sufficient reason to think that life as we know it was pre-existent in minerals.

The most primitive cell is already a complex edifice. Below that, it is thought that bacteriophages[29] exist: veritable parasites of microbes, entities more primitive still, but living, since their influence suffices to modify the hereditary characteristics of microbes. But if one considers life as emanating uniquely from the physico-chemical properties of certain bodies: carbon, oxygen, hydrogen, sulfur, phosphorus and metallic catalysts, ought one not to seek even more distant origins within the very constitution of the elementary atom, that veritable but infinitesimally small universe whose modifications and planetary movements suffice to create or absorb energy, and which, by a marvelous alchemy, know no other differences between bodies than those of the number of electrons gravitating around a central nucleus?

Is not life already in play in the movements—the actions, one might say—of inert matter drawn into eddies in water or the wind? And when one considers that the entire solar system is nothing but a grandiose imitation of the atomic world, is it not evident that what creates, for our minds, the penetrating

---

[29] Although the entities subsequently called bacteriophages had first been detected in 1896 by Ernest Hankin, the term was not coined until 1917 by the French-Canadian biologist Félix d'Hérelle.

charm of descriptions that poets have given us of nature is the obscure kinship that unites, over centuries, the movements of clouds, seas and forests with those of our various and ever-changing thought?

These facile observations had been reinforced, in recent times, by curious observations made of advanced machines. The metals, intensively worked that had been employed in their construction, reinforced and coated in numerous chemical materials, had become organisms of a sort, of a genuinely new kind, capable of engendering unprecedented phenomena. The perpetual transmission of electric currents and the impact of Hertzian waves had provided these ultra-modern metals with properties more curious still. In certain cases, veritable recurrent maladies had been observed to occur in machines, rather like vices, identical to those that had once decimated the working class. Obviously there was no question, strictly speaking, of alcoholism or tuberculosis, but the defects were analogous.

By virtue of curious affinities, it had been noticed that certain steels, when they were in the presence of certain chemical compounds that pleased them, appropriated particles of them over time, forming a shell that soon influenced their own organism. It was by this means that certain machines had their health entirely ruined by the abuse of the soap-suds used to reduce friction during their operation. Other machines seemed to be endowed with mobility; disturbing displacements of matter were observed: bosses produced at certain points on the surface, grooves in others. Undeniably, molecular labor was tending in a particular direction, and it was observed that this direction was no longer that of the canteen, but always that of reservoirs containing chemical products. These displacements were evidently due to an internal effort of the metal, progressing like molten metal but without losing its qualities of resistance.

Finally, as in cases of cancer or fibroma, there were molecular transformations of matter, transmutations of metal that would have enchanted the alchemists of old. Certain items of steel transformed themselves gradually into bronze, pieces of tin germinated into iron and patches of gold were observed in the lids of sardine-tins.

There was soon a veritable agitation in the factory, a precursor of definitive revolt. Certain machines became ataxic, others were afflicted with Pott's disease.[30] For long weeks it was necessary to drown the workshop in iodoform vapor and surround the principal items of automatic machinery with tampons imbibed with chloroform. One sensed, however, that some muted and distressing project was in preparation throughout the factory, like a general strike or a revolt of finally-liberated matter.

On the fourth intercalary, the pressure of the current having been inadvertently increased, all the machines abruptly flew into pieces like shattering glass, twisting their arms, and collapsed. Throughout the day, the terrified engineers again bore witness to a dangerous displacement of matter, which formed into balls and rolled slowly but smoothly towards the doors. For a while, they thought that the Human Limb Depot next to the factory was going be destroyed by the moving blocks of matter. This depot contained incalculable riches: heads, arms, intestines and human hearts held in store following operations, which were used on a daily basis for grafting, in cases where damaged organs needed replacement.

On penetrating into the guard-room, the blocks of matter, charged with electricity, did indeed galvanize all these stored body-parts—which began to speak, walk and escape in every direction. It took two or three days to regain control of them and bring all the scattered organs back to the depot. In the meantime, their crazy and whimsical excursions sowed terror in the town, particular among the women. As for the matter, it

---

[30] Percival Pott was an English doctor who have his name to a quasi-arthritic affliction of the lumbar vertebrae; its citation here continues the running analogy between the typical afflictions of the automatic machines and those of their human predecessors.

was necessary to tame it by means of artificial gel and afterwards to dispatch it in barges, with infinite precautions, to the Arctic Ocean.

This was one of the most troubling incidents of that agitated era, for it was dreaded every day that this bad example might be followed by the machine-tools of other factories. Radical measures were taken in this respect: obscurantism was built into mechanical matter and machines were surrounded by a network of wires designed to intercept and channel all outside influences—and for some years thereafter, calm was restored.

XXX. The Industrial Plants

It was after the machine revolt that people gradually began to comprehend that man was not the unique master of creation, but that animals, plants and things must play a large part in the general life of the universe. Already, on thinking about it more attentively, they had taken account of the immense industrial superiority of vegetables—which, without colossal factories or ingenious and complicated mechanisms, succeeded with all the simplicity in the world in producing the most complicated materials in the universe.

A simple seed, germinating in the ground and then extending a few roots, a stem and leaves, was enough, according to the particular nature of the plant, to produce the most unexpected effects. From the same ground, one such grain, as it developed, could draw the richest coloring materials, another subtle perfumes, and yet another fruits capable of nourishing human beings in a substantial or delicious manner. What savant, what magician, calling to his aid all the resources of science, could have accomplished such prodigies with such simplicity?

From the chemical point of view, plants similarly outstripped the best-equipped scientific laboratories. Without recourse to complicated apparatus, they fixed carbon, where the soil had only given them carbonic acid; they created living matter, where it had furnished them nothing but inert substances. By themselves, in a word, by means of invisible processes that were doubtless bafflingly simple, plants realized the improbable transmutations of one simple substance into another of which the philosophers, alchemists and scientists of times past were only able to dream.

A violent reaction against traditional industrial chemistry was rapidly produced in the scientific world, and the fervent study began of the extremely ingenious mechanism of vegetable life. Was it not infinitely more skillful to capture that life—since it could not be reproduced—than to try in vain to counterfeit its effects?

Soon, with the aid of progress, there was a veritable hatching of industrial plants, cleverly adapted, profoundly modified and capable of reproducing on a large scale the phenomena of which nature had thus far produced, so to speak, only sample specimens. Undoubtedly, these new plants, thus adapted to new functions, were very different from the plants of old; they resembled those animals whose breeders had formerly developed some part useful for nutrition, which soon assumed monstrous aspects. Agricultural factories were, therefore, installed on considerable tracts of land. Forests composed of adapted trunks, fields of vegetation whose stems alone were conserved, took on the appearance of immense workshops entirely subservient to the needs of production.

Roots and stems alone subsisted between the ground and the machines. The soil, profoundly modified by chemical products and thermal or magnetic currents, guaranteed an exceptional fecundity to the vegetal stems, whose other extremities terminated in vendors' show-rooms. Veritable marvels were immediately realized in this fashion. A few hours sufficed for transmutable matter to be incorporated into the soil, aspired by the stems, transformed, poured out on to display-tables, packaged and dispatched to the four corners of the universe. Mass-production was carried out by this means of perfumes, dyes, nutritional pastes and chemical products of every sort. It was an era of intense overproduction.

During the early days of this industrial adaptation of fields and forests, certain old men of previous eras complained about the transformation of nature, which definitively suppressed everything on the Earth's surface that had formerly constituted its grace and beauty, but their esthetic opinion had no value in that industrial epoch and people only laughed at their complaints. It was only a few years later, when the adapted plants had gradually lost the memory of their primitive state, that people began to understand the profound implications that such regrets might have.

The industrial plants, deprived of the joys of reproduction, maintained in a state of excitation, became bad-tempered, underhanded and cruel. Little by little, chemical products no longer being enough for them, they developed tentacles on the surfaces of their leaves analogous to those of the *Drosera rotundifolia* once described by Darwin, which nourishes itself on insects that it seizes in order to absorb their substance.[31] Sometimes these tentacles were enormous, and the demands of the plants became limitlessly voracious. It was necessary to feed them on dogs, cats and rabbits.

The spectacle of plants that had become carnivorous, disdaining the old and gentle nourishment of the soil, was infinitely repugnant. Their roots gradually lost their alimentary functions, but they developed the former sensibility of their tips in an extraordinary fashion. They soon became veritable organs, analogous in many ways to the brain, which formed underground. As before, sensations were transmitted by the roots, and movements effectuated, without it being possible to discover animal nerves and muscles in the plant.

This primitive sensibility, as it developed, gradually led to the disintegration of the ill-centralized plants and the radicular extremities were soon transformed into little sensitive mushrooms, isolated and useless, stupidly bumping into stones in the ground, fleeing or seeking the light, often traveling long distances through the soil.

The industrial plants were soon no longer producing anything but noxious substances, dangerous toxins or fragments of ill-digested animals, and the true cause of this degeneracy, which the obstinate old men had prophesied, was realized.

The plants were dying of ugliness.

Deprived of those ornaments that nature, in spite of its frugality, had judged indispensable, they were dying, no long-

---

[31] *Drosera rotundifolia* is the insectivorous plant commonly known as sundew; it does not, if fact, have "tentacles." Pawlowski might have confused it with the more spectacular Venus fly-trap.

er having the beauty that had once been their whole strength to excite their activity.

Attempts were then made to console them by painting brilliant flowers on the factory walls, and decorating the machines that imprisoned them with barbaric medleys of color, but it was a futile effort; soon, all the industrial plants died, one by one, of having been deprived of their flowers.

XXXI. The Phantom Hunt

The failure of the industrial plants did not discourage the scientists of the Great Central Laboratory, whose ambition was insatiable. They merely attempted to direct their researches in a more skillful fashion, no longer addressing them to inferior beings but to superior animals, in order to realize their fervent desire to capture inimitable Life.

Already, researches concerning the fourth dimension seemed to prove that the various bodies of living beings were composed of three external dimensions and a sort of fourth dimension completing their intimate structure. That was, in sum, the only possible justification that could be given for the irreducible difference that had been observed since time immemorial between inanimate objects and living beings.

This fourth dimension had been revealed to humankind, since humans uttered their first stuttering grunts, by the functioning of intelligence. It had also been revealed by the first hypnotic researches effectuated in barbarian times. In that distant epoch, the duality of the personality had already been established; curious phenomena had been recorded due to the creation of the phantasmal double that emanated from the hypnotized subject, remaining by his side, linked to him by a simple thread of imponderable matter.

It had even been observed, from the outset, that the hypnotized subject, no longer reasoning in three dimensions, became absolutely unintelligent during these doublings, while all the phenomena of consciousness were localized in the double, representing the fourth dimension.

With the progress of science, these phantoms had undoubtedly been restored to their true status. They were no longer, as had once been believed, evil beings, mysterious and extraterrestrial, but simple emanations of living individuals, forming part of their personality—and, in consequence, submissive to their initiative or to their subconscious.

161

A few skillfully-made observations had proved, from the start, that animals, primarily endowed with instinct, were more clairvoyant in these matters than intelligent men and that these very simple manifestations of duality were more easily sensible to them than to their masters.

The scientists even cited the story of the clairvoyant lady who, while walking in the countryside with a friend who was not endowed with second sight, had declared that she could see the phantom of a dog walking in front of them. Her word was doubted until the moment when, as they went past a farm, a cat was seen to come out of the farmhouse, make as if to cross the empty path and stop abruptly at the moment when it encountered the phantom of the dog, which had just crossed its path. Suddenly, its fur bristled and it extended its claws, breathed noisily and, panicking, returned at top speed into the house from which it had emerged.

Animals, therefore, better than humans, clearly discern the phantasmal emanations scattered throughout the universe.

When the day came when people understood how useful it would be for the new factories to appropriate the vital fluid lost here and there in the form of useless phantoms, they directed their attention to animals with a view to tracing down and capturing these errant forces. Instead of letting phantoms frighten timorous spirits needlessly, permitting them to upset items of furniture, haunt houses or abandoned châteaux, devoting themselves to all sorts of absurd endeavors, they tried to capture them in order to put their vital forces at the disposal of science. Special three-dimensional traps were set up nearly everywhere, each containing a four-dimensional living seed as bait, and use was made of numerous clairvoyant dogs, analogous to the hounds of old, to drive the phantoms towards the traps. There was then an energetic—sometimes terrifying—beating, which lasted several months.

Gradually, all the howling, desperate phantoms were made captive in public workshops, enclosed in machines that imitated—roughly, but adequately—the different organs of the human body.

To begin with, it was imagined that life was definitively subject to the orders of science and that the imprisoned phantoms would be constrained to animate the three-dimensional machines in which they were imprisoned as in cages of flesh. Gradually, though, it was necessary to admit the comprehensive failure of this new attempt. The imprisoned phantoms no longer stirred themselves; they did not produce any useful work; they could only live in total independence. In order to act, they needed the fantasy and the liberty of vanished eras. Emanating from exceptional individuals they could not submit to a social discipline. Sons of imagination and not of science, they were beyond the reach of orders and reasoning; dream-artists for centuries, indicating possibilities outside time and space to human beings, the phantoms were incapable of being artisans of the real.

People therefore limited themselves to imprisoning the phantoms forever in simple bodies—and industrial life, disembarrassed of these troublesome elements, calmly pursued new researches towards the rational unknown.

XXXII. The Supermen

It was entirely natural that the industrial research carried out to capture life prepared the way for the appearance of the first supermen, a more rational creation that provoked a lively and legitimate curiosity in the scientific world.

Furthermore, certain philosophers, for several centuries, had delighted in the anticipation of the arrival on Earth of these marvelous beings, and their poetic renown had preceded the noise that the scientists of the Great Central Laboratory made about their new superhuman products. There was, however, nothing particularly strange in the fabrication and education of supermen in a century in which surgical techniques had obtained extreme limits of perfection.

By pursuing the attentive study of the human body, it had been determined that it was, in fact, composed of two very different sorts of cells, some immortal, devoted to the reproduction of the species, others mortal and perishable, giving the body its terrestrial appearance and equipping it, for some years, for the functions it had to fulfill.

Properly understood, the life of immortal cells was no different from that of amoebas, which reproduced themselves perpetually by duplication. In the same way that, in primitive animals, there is neither mother nor child, properly speaking, but a simple duplication, the reproductive cells constituting the ovules never die, save by accident; they duplicate themselves indefinitely, living as long as the race that they perpetuate. When it comes to forming a new individual, they are content to sacrifice some among themselves for the transitory and plastic formation of the mortal body of a new individual.

The body of a human being, therefore, is of no definitive importance; it is merely a simple temporary ornament. By contrast, the reproductive cells interest us because they are immortal, because they *conserve* and collect within themselves, without necessarily having to *transmit* then, the characteristics and improvements of the race.

It is on this very simple principle that the construction of supermen was established.

After isolating the reproductive cells of a few handsome specimens of the race, it was enough to educate them, over many years, by grafting them successively on to individuals of every species, human beings or animals. This method was similar to that employed on the schoolchildren of old, who were placed successively in a series of preparatory schools. Instead of bothering with the whole body of the schoolchild, the operation was limited to placing the productive cells of the future supermen in different bodies, in which they could complete their instruction, acquiring good breeding and experience.

Carefully-labeled cells destined to engender the bodies of supermen at a later date were, therefore, grafted, for observational purposes, on to lions, birds, whales, dogs, poets or scientists. As for the body itself, it was ingeniously prepared in the most marvelous fashion. The body of the future superman was, in effect, only a simple tool, an indispensable but subordinate plastic form whose value depended entirely on the value of the central reproductive cell that was incorporated into it.

Furthermore, for a long time, savant humankind had been able to establish a fundamental difference between the general direction of the body and the body itself. Since the most distant eras, all the way back to the creation of those primitive instruments called the bicycle, the automobile and the airplane, men had understood how easy it might be to complete their body by adjoining new mechanical limbs to it, augmenting its power without violating natural laws in any way.

A cyclist, after traveling a few kilometers, felt awkward when it was necessary for him to return to walking; he had lost the habit, stumbling and feeling disorientated without the instrument of transport that had become indispensable to him. It had similarly been observed that an automobilist or aviator, in case of danger, instead of letting go of the steering-wheel or the joystick, clung to it forcefully. He sensed, in fact, that, far from being an instrument independent of his body, the automobile or airplane was no longer anything but an extension of it, and the instinct of conservation drove him to keep that augmentation of his strength and increase in his being in his possession for as long as possible in the presence of danger. Like a telegraph-operator clinging with all his strength to his apparatus in the case of a shipwreck, calling for help, the collective instinct of social conservation had replaced the old instincts of a man who had nothing but his own natural resources to call upon in the world mechanized by science.

With animal grafts, whose techniques advanced so rapidly during the scientific era, this artificial growth of the body was no longer anything but a game; assisted by snobbery, the game soon resulted in a few exaggerations. Just as automobilists had earlier been seen successively to adopt 6, 8, 12 and 24 cylinders, certain people thought it interesting to augment their vital forces indefinitely. Men with four lungs, three hearts or double nervous ignition acquired by grafts, eventually became a common sight, along with supplementary spare limbs for normal walking or mountaineering.

Needless to say, from the moment of their creation, haste was made to give the benefits of all these advantages to the supermen, and animal grafts were complicated by even more cumbersome mechanical grafts.

When, after years of education, the productive cells of the supermen were finally grafted into fully-developed bodies, the unfortunates were supercharged with all the latest scientific developments. Soon they were no more than deformed, monstrous creatures, equipped with telepathic telegraphy and calculating machines, walking encyclopedias uniting all human knowledge within themselves, subject to a central distribution console. To support this formidable mechanical assemblage, they had recourse to multiple grafts and adjunctions of innumerable limbs; the supermen were somewhat reminiscent of many-legged human elephants, deprived of all plastic beauty, which had to be immobilized, for the sake of public safety, in the halls of the Central Museum.

The scientists dared not admit their disappointment; they hid these monstrous beings invented by their pride—which were ignorant of beauty, common sense and generosity—from all eyes.

All this would have remained an event of no great importance in the history of the world if that same year had not seen, in the vicinity of the Great Central Laboratory, the disappearance of a young woman of great beauty who, for a long time, had not concealed her scorn for the scientists of that Laboratory and who lived resolutely, in opposition to the preoccupations of the era, a life entirely devoted to grace and elegance. This disappearance remained most mysterious; there was talk of vengeance, vile vivisection, irreducible hatred of beauty engendered by science, but the power of the scientists of the Great Central Laboratory was so great, at that time, that the affair was classified as a legend and never had any consequences.

XXXII. The Conjuration of Larvae [32]

When the wall of the Great Central Laboratory began to displace itself slowly and smoothly to be swallowed up in the door that gave access to the Institute's great library, it was understood that something abnormal had just happened in the scientific world, and that the causes of the curious phenomena must be investigated immediately.

Many years before, the ideas of matter and evolution had been profoundly modified; it was admitted that the old prejudice which made evolution into an inimitable model had evidently been stripped of all foundation, and it was in another direction that man must seek the natural course of progress. It was not without a smile that people recalled the distant era of the glorification of the beauty of labor, the benefits of association and the marvelous ascension achieved by nature since the world's beginning in creating ever-more-complex creatures.

It was, curiously enough, sociology that had first indicated to scientists the age-old error that they had got into their heads in such an absurd fashion. In fact, the history of societies proves to us that, in every era, men have striven, not to work, but, on the contrary, to deliver themselves from all material cares by making other men or machines work in their stead. In the same way, when a man accepts the social contract that binds him to all others, he only yields to a simple kind of sloth, seeking to specialize himself and only to accomplish one part of the general effort, only repeating the same action

---

[32] The French word *larve* carries a double meaning that is not readily translated into English, the latter language having only retained one of the Latin root-term's original meanings in common parlance. As well as referring to the larva of an insect it refers to a kind of ghost or specter, often of a malevolent character. The new meaning imposed on the tern in this chapter echoes and transforms both originals.

endlessly, thus following the law of least effort. This is why exceedingly unhappy individuals, in a socially inferior condition, have often preferred to remain in that state than to attempt an effort that might have raised them up, and it is similarly for that reason that great conquerors and the masters of the world have always found plenty of docile subjects preferring to obey their orders or those of another rather than make the necessary effort themselves. In every case, whether it is a matter of masters or slaves, it is always *the least effort and the least danger* that everyone seeks to achieve, some from on high and others from below.

Nature, in its successive creations, has done nothing but indicate in advance the pretended forward march of civilizations. It is by the law of least effort that work and matter have always been directed; it is by virtue of that same law that increasingly complex associations are created in elementary atoms, always better satisfying *the desire for sloth* that rules the world.

Contrary to what was believed in the early eras of science, *the dissociation of matter* is not, therefore, a diminution, a return to nothingness, but rather an effort that matter makes towards idea, in order to return to a superior individualism after being enriched by the multiple experiences of association. Association in an organized body is, on the contrary, nothing but a pause, a specialization diminishing the primal universal activity, a moment of sloth to which a rapid dissociation will eventually do justice. The Hindu philosophy—which preached a return, not to nothingness, but to nirvana—was the only one in ancient times to glimpse that true march of the world towards individual perfection.

When the researchers of the scientific era had finally understood that fundamental verity, they gradually ceased to interest themselves in complex organization and they attempted, on the contrary, to return to basics and to release, so far as they could, the *elementary atom* containing in embryo all known forces and all imaginable possibilities.

This elementary atom, ancestor of all simple bodies and all known energies—this *larva*, as it was eventually to be dubbed—was finally released, reconstituted by synthesis in its primal state, as it exists at the beginning of worlds when it is no more than a simple particle of a nebula.

Unfortunately, it has to be admitted, these larvae, cultivated in great quantity in the Great Central Laboratory, were not adequately monitored. There were some, naturally enough, that escaped through the walls, and others that lodged themselves in material objects situated in the environs of the Laboratory. A strange series of phenomena, calculated to distress the scientists of the day, was immediately produced.

As in the most terrifying ancient times, the Earth was seen to open up, fabulous creatures spontaneously generating and dying of some fault of construction, in the fashion of prehistoric monsters. There were public monuments that began to move, to groan like veritable living beings, and others that set off across country in formless masses, like block of matter melted by consequence of some incomprehensible molecular labor.

Visibly, these artificial larvae, too rapidly germinated, incapable of remaining isolated, full of modern ideas and disorganized by centuries of organization, were attempting to escape their formidable individuality by associating themselves randomly with matter, improvising around themselves hastily-constructed and ill-conceived entities.

It was briefly feared that this movement of organization might overtake all matter and turn the world upside down. Luckily, the phenomena gradually diminished by dispersion. From time to time, there were occasional disconcerting apparitions of unnamable phantoms and bizarre movements of material objects that could not be explained, but the association of matter did not go any further, and the monstrous products of these larvae, unaccustomed to the environment, did not take long to perish.

The experiment, as may be guessed, was not renewed; it was, however, from that moment on that people began to understand more fully what *the life of matter* was, and no longer to consider material objects as simple inferior creations unworthy of human consideration. Everyone feared to trouble anew the formidable reservoirs of unknown forces and energies that nature hid, and men prudently continued to live their lives in the immense cemetery of the world, which they now knew to be populated by the living dead.

XXXIV. Body-Letting

I understood very early on, perhaps in my dreams of infancy, that there had to be a means of sustaining man in the air much safer and much simpler than mechanical aviation. Aviation is, in fact, a rough scientific solution, an entirely external transitional method, which can only interest barbarians. Gravitation is a force that must be vanquished and neutralized by developing forces innate within us. Furthermore, we know that these forces are real because we can, in certain pathological cases, observe their effects outside a human body from which they have escaped.

Clinical observation has been made of a young hysteric who felt impressions of burning or freezing directly when the water in which she had washed her hands was thrown, while she was not present, into fire or on to ice. Similarly, the displacements of furniture and the materializations that exteriorization of force can produce are well-known. In all times, man has understood instinctively that he can, by cultivating his will-power, combat external influences and counterbalance the natural forces surrounding him solely by his own personal forces. At all times he has sensed that he can shield himself from attraction, rise up into the air and hover above the ground, without requiring recourse to any mechanical stratagem.

This preoccupation is found in all religions; it forms the basis of all moral beliefs, all artistic symbols.

It is in dreams, especially, that these indications become more precise. With a great contention of will and a continued effort of mind, it does not take long to feel that one is losing contact with the ground and that, without making any movement, one has set oneself a little way above it. Unfortunately, it always takes a painful effort that requires sustained attention, and the equilibrium obtained is never very satisfactory; one awkward shift, one ill-timed movement, and the threat of falling is immediately urgent—without, however, being realized.

When I arrived in the land of the fourth dimension, I learned without astonishment that during the Scientific Era this mode of locomotion was much in favor—but people had been gradually obliged to abandon it by reason of the cerebral fatigue that it provoked in all its adepts, and especially the extraordinarily grave social disorder that had resulted from it.

Levitation applied to material bodies, in fact, demands considerable nervous effort. The mediums who, while sitting on a chair, have succeeded in leaving the ground and going to set themselves, along with their chair, on a table, always experience extreme fatigue following that excessive effort. When the subject is well-balanced, that poses no other inconvenience but to himself, but when there are losses of nervous force, or when that force is misdirected beyond the single task that one is trying to accomplish, it expands in all directions, drifting aimlessly, and results in very curious phenomena. These are generally objects that form in mid-air, unknown to the person, or displacements of existing objects without any possible control.

At the time when levitation became a fashionable mode of transport, there was a considerable quantity of lost force which extended thus, at hazard, through the towns and the country, only awaiting an opportunity to manifest itself and provoke the most distressing phenomena.

While it was only a question of insignificant manifestations, it was not very serious. From time to time, one observed that telegraph poles were growing beards; mechanical objects or items of furniture sometimes acquired the faculty of sight, hearing or smell. Such events were as surprising as they were distressing, but people soon grew used to them.

Unfortunately, when the vagabond forces began to attack factories and socially useful machines, the danger of tolerating such abuses was recognized. Soon, light-distributors began to talk or sing; thick clouds, suddenly solidified, formed dangerous reefs into which aviators crashed; ships and trains were transformed into bouquets of roses or bottles of eau de cologne—and worse catastrophes threatened at every moment.

The scientific government had therefore formally to prohibit all transport by levitation, and any other cerebral effort designed to utilize the human will outside the prescriptions laid down by the regulations of general policing.

It was then that, to get around the difficulty, people took advantage the method of exteriorization formerly indicated by spirits, which consisted of abandoning one's material body by a simple effort of will in order to displace what had formerly been called one's "astral body."

The inconvenience of such a method was to remove, by the same token, any material possibility of action from the traveler. By means of astral bodies we can, indeed, move from one place to another with the greatest ease in the world and sense what is happening there, but we can only communicate with persons using their material bodies if they put another material body at our disposal, abandoned by its own astral body and consequentially empty.

Needless to say, the Economical Travel Companies immediately got a grip on the problem, and organized special hotels almost everywhere, in which one could find everything one needed to be able to act on arrival. A man could, for example, leave his material body empty in Paris, transport himself by thought to Marseilles and there find, in the special hotel, an empty "spokesman" body that was put at his disposal, permitting him to take care of all his business in the city, communicating with his clients. During the period of the lease, the astral body of the newfangled spokesman would take a stroll in the country, without any worries.

Unfortunately, this method, simple as it was, was also not long delayed in causing grave inconveniences. Skillful crooks exploited the situation by obtaining information. When they were sure that the material body of a known individual was empty in Paris, during his mind's absence, they made haste to abandon their own bodies—as one does an old suit of clothes—and to take up lodgings in the body of the known individual, which they then refused to quit. Use was widely made of a system of psychic anthropometry permitting the identification of people by their external appearances rather than their mental imprints, but deplorable confusions resulted nevertheless, particularly in conjugal relationships. These abuses were such that new measures, even more rigorous, had soon to be taken.

Furthermore, persons possessed of socially interesting situations hesitated to leave their material bodies and travel any distance. Fear of a theft, a substitution of their identity, almost always restrained them. Who knew whether, during their absence, the astral body of some miserable street-urchin might not animate their material body and make it commit misdeeds of the worst sort?

This was, as one might imagine, a period of surprising adventures, and one can only laugh at it when one thinks of the extreme simplicity of the fourth-dimensional procedures that were later to sweep aside all these barbarous methods.

XXXV. The Garden of Planets [33]

In the days when the Great Central Laboratory was beginning to achieve omnipotence, a feeling of hatred for what
had formerly been called, in barbarous times, Beauty gradually developed in everyone's mind. Already, in the most ancient
eras, thinkers who lived for pure ideas had excluded poets
from their republic. [34] Much later, at the same time as the first
mutterings of the new science, the total practical uselessness
was proclaimed of the ancient magical, religious and literary
formulas that had cradled the infancy of humankind.

To begin with, all religions, whose symbolism appeared
excessively naïve, were suppressed. Then, little by little, literature and the fine arts—religions no less powerful, but just as
naïve—had been attacked. Why invent false histories, why
fabricate entirely imaginary heroes? The men of the scientific
age had less and less understanding of the necessity of these
puerile fables that did not correspond at all to the practical

---

[33] The French title of this chapter, *Le jardin des planètes*,
echoes the name of *Le Jardin des Plantes*, the principal botan-
ical and zoological gardens in Paris.

[34] This reference is to a famous passage in Plato's *Republic*, in
which the philosopher suggests, perhaps somewhat tongue-in-
cheek, that artists might have to be banished from an ideal
state whose citizens aspire to a precious calm of mind, because
they devote themselves to nourishing the well of the emotions
instead of furthering the empire of reason. Aristotle famously
disagreed, although Plato was more of a poet than Aristotle
ever was. The problem was, however, restated in Félix Bodin's study of *Le roman de l'avenir* (1834; available in a
Black Coat Press edition as *The Novel of the Future*), whose
author was driven to wonder whether the ideal of social per-
fectibility was compatible with the ideals of Romance—and to
conclude, a trifle reluctantly, that it was not.

176

realities of the moment and caused everyone to waste precious time. In the beginning, the writers and artists tried of their own accord to accommodate their productions to the taste of the day, by offering the public rigorously exact analyses of reality, scientific reports minutely established according to nature, or works of decorative art narrowly applied to the immediate needs of life, but it did not take long to decide that all these were merely useless illusions and a gulf was hollowed out, definitive and profound, between the fine arts of yesteryear and the scientific dreams of the new world.

Soon, the ideal being entirely displaced, one could not consider without suffering ancient monuments surcharged with fetishistic figures designed, no doubt, to avert bad luck; one could not read without disgust the literary lies of the great poets of old who tried to hide their own sensations and personal adventures behind the inexact faces of imaginary heroes. Elegance was henceforth entirely within the usefulness of lines or the indication of movement; beauty was to be found in force, charm in speed.

Nevertheless, during that transitional era, all not all the experiments that were made were exclusively scientific or ungraceful. There were very pretty ones among them that would have seduced the poets of times past.

Undoubtedly, when the first exteriorizations of nervous force were provoked by levitation, there were—as we have just seen—certain phenomena well fitted to alarm sensitive souls in the scientific world. Under the influence of the imagination of the individuals present, the nervous force dispersed in the air materialized in the most various forms. Here they were enormous larvae, terrifying animals, there immense viscous protozoans, which sometimes borrowed the forms of inanimate objects or scientific instruments in order to manifest themselves.

The confusions that were created between material objects and living beings did not take long, however, to furnish precious indications regarding the nature of things. It was rapidly understood that, if the human personality could duplicate

177

itself, that of animals, plants and even material objects could equally well support the same duplication.

We have seen how, during that period, certain people acquired the habit of only displacing their immaterial body when they traveled, forsaking incarnation for a few hours, lodging in a material body vacated for the occasion hired to them by a hotelier. These journeys, soon forbidden by the Great Central Laboratory because of the disorder they provoked within the State, were still tolerated in certain limited conditions in the era of holiday resorts and in a place specially designed by the Absolute Savants, which was named the Garden of Planets.

In this era there was a very curious fashion, followed by certain sensitive individuals—writers and poets—who still conserved the cult of emotions of times past. Every year they gladly adopted the habit of incarnating themselves for a few days, or during the entire holiday season, in the material bodies of animals or flowers. This delicate and charming custom necessitated infinite precautions and an entire special organization. The bodies of flowers or animals had to be prepared for this purpose by expelling the immaterial personalities, in order to permit people desirous of rest or reverie temporarily to occupy these fragile shelters. The Garden was monitored in a very particular fashion to ensure that no accident would trouble these peaceful retreats.

Some people spent exquisite weeks in this way in the same greenhouse or field, enjoying all the advantages of animal or vegetable life to the full—much better than the ladies of old had who played at being shepherdesses—sometimes even abusing, without modesty or restraint, borrowed bodies that were not their own.

This delicate fashion ameliorated to some degree the rigors of the Scientific Era, which was still in its early stages, and one could not help observing, in this regard, how all these scientific possibilities had been anticipated, in an obscure fashion, by antique religions and the naïve minds of the 19th and 20th centuries. When the Egyptians placed useful objects and weapons in tombs, respectful of a dead person's mortal remains, it was with the intimate conviction that the material doubles of all the funereal objects would be used by the defunct individual in the afterlife. As for the spiritualists who believed in the evocation of the dead, they also liked to imagine that the soul of a dead young woman might gather the souls of dead flowers placed on her tomb in one of their naïve cemeteries.

I, having arrived in the land of the fourth dimension, have no need to say how primitive all these old beliefs in survival appear when one knows that death does not exist and that life, short as it may appear, has no value in duration but only in quality, outside of infantile notions of time and space.

These notions of the doubling of the body and the mind contained in ancient beliefs were, therefore, directly realized on Earth, during life. They were no more than a means of taking a holiday, available to everyone—infinitely banal, in sum, and placed under the surveillance of a scientific laboratory.

This charming custom too came to an end in a rather abrupt fashion, however, in the wake of painful incidents that desolated the Garden of Planets. That nickname was given to the large walled garden because it contained large fragments of extraterrestrial matter—bolides, as they were once called—perhaps detached from unknown other worlds, which had descended upon our Earth one night at that spot. Soon, they had been surrounded by strange vegetation, completely unknown to our naturalists until then, which was one of the principal curiosities of the Great Museum.

It was imagined that these strange and marvelous plants were vegetables analogous to ours, and no one hesitated, by virtue of the attractions of mystery and novelty, preferentially to choose these plants in order to place the doubles of vacationing poets therein. At first, things went very smoothly, but then a number of intellectual deaths were recorded, fearfully. Some minds on holiday in the planetary plants did not come back to their normal bodies.

179

Others, which did come back, explained the frightful and savage battles they had been forced to wage against the spirits of these unknown planets, which represented, in other worlds, the veritable inhabitants of foreign lands. Curious information was thus obtained about the universe, but it was necessary to put a hasty end to those murderous holidays, which cost the lives of the last poets of times past.[35]

There was even some suspicion, at the time, that the Absolute Savants of the Great Central Laboratory had premeditated these bizarre deaths, exciting the curiosity of the poets, their age-old enemies, and deliberately sending them forth on a calamitous adventure from which they would never return.

---

[35] This image recalls the plot of the first winner of the Prix Goncourt, *Force ennemie* [Hostile Force] (1903) by John-Antoine Nau (Eugène Torquet), in which an inmate of a lunatic asylum is plagued by the disincarnate soul of an extraterrestrial, obtaining a graphic account of the invader's nightmarish native world.

XXXVI. The Materialization of Three-Dimensional Nightmares

Many people do not know of the existence of certain Japanese mice that are deprived of the sensibility of the third dimension. They can move easily on a lacquer tray but they never succeed in escaping it when it comes to getting over its edge. They completely lack the awareness of vertical displacement; they only comprehend two dimensions, and only ever go back and forth or left and right on the same plane, somewhat reminiscent of those chickens that are hypnotized by a unidimensional straight line traced on the ground in chalk.

One might think, at first, that this is simply a matter of an atrophy or a lesion in some nerve-center; it is known, in fact, that certain animals, after an accident or a bite, can become completely disoriented or turn in circles until they are exhausted, without recovering consciousness of the equilibrium of things. This is not the same thing; the little Japanese mouse, in a normal and healthy state, can only conceive two dimensions. It is quite capable, organically, of climbing, of displacing itself vertically, but that is a concept it lacks, and the idea never occurs to it.

In the same way, creatures that only know three external dimensions, like human beings, cannot conceive that it is as easy to exit from a locked room via the fourth dimension as it would be for the Japanese mice to get down from the rim of a tray—as easy as it would be in time, when one is old, to look down upon oneself as a sick child from the bedside, or in space, to hear the doorbell ring and to see oneself enter the room where one is sitting.

Nevertheless, when the useful idea of the fourth dimension was adopted by human beings at the end of the Second Scientific Era, it did not take long to comprehend that the

181

problem did not end there, and that new ideas about space would inevitably modify other phenomena. The world of dreams immediately attracted the attention of researchers and savants, and it was quickly realized that this ungraspable but real world, in which human beings had for centuries taken refuge for a good third of their lives, was nothing more, in sum, than *a two-dimensional world*—and that it was solely for that reason that the events unfolding there had no direct effect on the human body.

People had automatically adopted the habit, in dreams, of fleeing from imaginary dangers, escaping catastrophes, of desperately thwarting the enterprises of terrible assassins—but that, properly understood, was nothing but a game. After a few seconds of terror, it was sufficient for a person to wake up, thus recovering his three-dimensional senses, to understand they were nothing but chimeras of no importance.

When human beings became gradually accustomed to the idea of the fourth dimension, however, their faculties became extraordinarily overexcited and singular accidents were soon produced in dreams.

There were people who were found in the morning cut in two in their beds by the wheels of a locomotive. Others found themselves, after a night of nightmares, feverishly walking on the ceiling, their heads down and feet up. One fat man was discovered crushed in his bed, flattened as if by an incredible steamroller—and it was known that the man had long had a recurrent dream of an immense stairway slowly invaded by an inundation of molten lead, which ended in a rock-face from which the only means of exit was a minuscule mouse-hole.

These various events attracted the attention of the scientific world by virtue of their extreme gravity. A few subjects were chosen from among those familiar with the fourth dimension to undertake a minute examination of the world of dreams and to make personal observations of the disturbing events that were happening there.

After a few nights of observation, they came back in a state of terror. One of them, despite very energetic self-defense, had had his right arm devoured by a steam-crocodile with the body of a cow. Another, having spent all night running back and forth from one airplane to another with incredibly heavy little bags, had eventually been deprived of his last items of clothing and the bones of his skeleton, in open country, by a flock of white clouds that had shown themselves to be pitiless.

These new phenomena left no more room for doubt: the dreams that had, until now, added charm to life—the dreams that had been the sole replacements, during the tedious Scientific Era, for the fairy tales of old, which children awaited with joy as they went to bed in the evening—were becoming real, and presenting the most formidable danger that humankind had ever faced.

By dint of externalizing his imagination, of researching all the joys that the use of the fourth dimension might give him, man had not taken precautions against the third dimension that he was instinctively introducing, little by little, into his dreams, thus giving them all the dangerous reality of quotidian reality.

Certain braggarts—poets, of a sort that is found everywhere—declared themselves enchanted by the adventure, and undertook fabulous hunts worthy of mythology. They realized in dreams all the heroic exploits that the ancients, by some strange presentiment, had only imagined. Strengthened by the impunity that their entire possession of the fourth dimension assured them, they delivered themselves to all excesses in their new three-dimensional dreams. They amused themselves by jumping in front of express trains traveling at top speed; they threw themselves from the tops of high monuments, hurled themselves upon swords, had themselves attached to the muzzles of loaded cannon. Sometimes they amused themselves by carving entire armies into pieces, remaining intact under intense fire. Sometimes, they gave themselves the exquisite sensation of going alone and unarmed into the dark underground passages of châteaux, populated by phantoms, or reconstituting solely for their own pleasure the most famous orgies or massacres of antiquity.

Unfortunately, such fantasies were not without danger. These materializations of objects entirely formed by the will of sleepers and constituted in a tangible three-dimensional fashion soon became cumbersome. In the morning, the houses of the seers would be found heaped with broken wagons and bloody chairs, and fusillades or cannonballs, materialized in three dimensions, sometimes reached inoffensive passers-by and set fire to entire towns.

Severe regulations therefore had to be enacted in that era, against sleepers capable of maintaining themselves in four-dimensional dreams, constraining them to take a special potion every night that prevented all dreams. Four-dimensional imaginations were restricted, no longer permitting any excursions but those in time—which, at least, passed unperceived, remaining invisible. They only inconvenienced the people of previous eras, who, confronted with these interventions—incomprehensible to them—attributed them to hazard and fatality.

Finally, three-dimensional dreams were forbidden, on pain of death, to persons incapable of taking refuge in the fourth dimension, experience having sufficiently demonstrated that all dreams were not subject to the human will, but that they were engendered, on the contrary, by a subconscious common to all beings, whose true nature would not be revealed until much later, in the Age of the Golden Bird.

XXXVII. The Giant Bacteria

The beginning of the second scientific era was marked by the establishment of the definitive tyranny of the 12 Absolute Savants and by an inconceivable offense against humankind committed by the Great Central Laboratory.

For a long time it had been understood, in the regions of African Europe and Atlantis, that something extraordinary was in preparation in the Great Central Laboratory, but precise information was lacking.

From its frequent instructions and the measures that it ordained in the industrial world, it was imagined that the Great Central Laboratory was concerned with the general wellbeing of humankind. People were, therefore, surprised to see communications with the external world becoming rarer and rarer, and to observe that the vast palace was gradually being transformed into a sort of inaccessible fortress. It was forbidden to come within two degrees of its borders; no one, in any case, dared venture into that dangerous zone.

Nothing in that vast plain, to tell the truth, betrayed the presence of any fortifications, but it was known that asphyxiating barriers and radiant cordons capable of reducing the hardest steel to dust gave adequate protection to the borders of the Laboratory on the ground and in the air. It was understood that this retreat and magnificent isolation were indispensable to the efficient conduct of scientific research and no one was unduly astonished, at first, by these formidable defensive precautions. Anxiety increased, however, on the day when the rumor spread at the speed of light that tons of culture medium had just been poured into the conduits of drinking water and the equatorial rivers, undoubtedly originating from the Great Central Laboratory.

Everyone was familiar with various means of destroying dangerous microbes and protecting themselves therefrom, but they did not have the necessary serums in great enough quanti-

185

ty to defend themselves against the mounting flood of invisible enemies. Amazement, consternation and, finally, terror, took hold of all minds when it was learned that the Great Central Laboratory was refusing to reply to all radiograms, and that it would not consent, under any pretext, to concern itself with the frightful epidemics that seemed imminent.

There was no doubt about it; the Great Central Laboratory was carrying out an unknown and terrifying plan, and people could no longer count on its assistance. Rapid analyses however, established the fact that the most frightful diseases—syphilis, yellow fever, encephalic herpes, rabies, tetanus and many diseases long-forgotten by virtue of energetic measures taken against them—were present in all the conduits and were accumulating there, ready to introduce themselves directly into the human organism with a virulence that defied all commonly-employed methods of defense.

The bacteria from the Great Central Laboratory were not, in fact, microbes like any other; they had been specially bred in particularly favorable conditions. They could not be compared to humble bacilli growing in the body, combated on a daily basis by the organism, overwhelmed by the number of their enemies, weakened and then eliminated.

The general panic would have had grave consequences if the fortunate intervention of a Japanese scientist who happened to be there had not abruptly averted the danger in the most elegant fashion.

Far from trying to destroy microbes, this physician had had the excellent idea of conducting research into the origins and causes of gigantism among them. Thanks to his discoveries, the means of increasing the size of these primitive organisms, which had formerly been called microbes, and allowing them to grow to dimensions perceptible to the naked eye, had already been known for some time. Originally, his discovery had had no object save facilitating medical studies, but at that particular moment it saved a substantial fraction of the human race.[36]

Thanks to tons of a special nutriment that was manufactured in a matter of days, the dangerous bacilli in circulation slowly grew in size, becoming visible to the naked eye—and, by the same token, henceforth incapable of introducing themselves into the human organism.

The only amusing aspect of this adventure was the excessive extent to which the manufacture of his precious product was taken. People were soon fearful of the invisible enemy, and had such faith in the salvation that the new nutriment offered them that they made it in vast quantities; as a result of flooding all the channels, they soon found themselves in the presence of microbes as large as small domestic animals.

It was an infinitely repugnant spectacle to see thousands of long silvery serpents, enormous crabs, viscous sponges and gelatinous hedgehogs—representing the terrible bacilli of the day before, and secreting hideous poisons—first heaping up in the streets, then being swept into the rivers. A few were kept for the sake of curiosity; others were stuffed, in memory of the terrible danger that everyone had been in—but these momentary distractions soon gave way to new anxieties.

---

[36] This idea, too, echoes a recently-published scientific romance: André Couvreur's *Une invasion de macrobes* [A Macrobe Invasion] (1909).

XXXVIII. The Disgust for Immortality

When the terrible danger of microbial cultures was averted, after an initial reaction of joy, there was a pause for reflection and people wondered what the reason might be for the sudden hostility of the Great Central Laboratory. To what new dangers were they exposed? They had every right to fear anything. Then, by means of words and surprised gestures communicated by wireless photophone, they eventually understood the unexpected reasons for that abrupt rupture between the Absolute Savants and the human cells. A great revolution had turned the great Central Laboratory upside down; six months before, the Absolute Savants had finally found the source of life itself and the formidable secret of immortality.

The secret was undoubtedly not unique. It apparently involved hundreds of methods, ancient procedures designed automatically to renew the cells of the human body and to render men practically immortal by prolonging life indefinitely. It was remembered then that no death had occurred in the Great Central Laboratory for a very long time. Did its occupants intend to maintain a monopoly on immortality, to make a selection of human beings, annihilating the weakest from now on? All sort of conjectures were made on this subject. At first, fear held them back; then, as the news of the discovery of immortality spread throughout the entire world, there was a vast irresistible rush towards the Great Central Laboratory, a spontaneous gathering of crowds such as had not been seen since the prehistoric era of Medieval mysticism.

People dragged themselves along on their knees, skinning them on the stones in the road; others threw down any precious objects they might have in front of them, offering their entire fortunes, without thinking of the absurdity of such offers made to scientists who possessed the empire of nature. There were ardent supplications and touching pleas made on behalf of beloved wives or children. Finally, when it was understood that all the supplications were in vain, there was a brutal, torrential surge, an unleashing of all the animal forces of humankind denied the secret of immortality, determined to take possession of the Great Central Laboratory at any cost, in order to extract its formidable secret—by force, if necessary.

Armies were organized, in a puerile fashion, as far away as the lands of the Far North. It was like a general awakening of the survival instinct, a last desperate spasm of the civilizations of old towards immortality, the hope of an inaccessible tomorrow. Cadavers piled up around the Great Central Laboratory, pulverized or liquefied by projections that volatilized them, single rays scything down entire armies.

Then, little by little, discouragement set in and a strange sort of madness took hold of all the combatants. In every city there were cases of collective delirium: mystical conversions wrought *en masse*; a sort of domestication of the will; a general enslavement meekly accepted, as if with pleasure; a respectful and almost joyful submission to the unknown and mysterious desires of the Great Central Laboratory.

Evidently, the Absolute Savants had acted directly upon their minds by some occult means. Perhaps they had discovered the ancient secrets of the mastery of the will and suggestion at a distance. It was understood that an absolute empire of immortal savants had now been established, crushingly and irredeemably, upon the entire, brutally tamed Earth.

It was a period of boundless triumph for the Great Central Laboratory. The Absolute Savants no longer died. They lived on, always the same, and 1000 years went by in this fashion without any apparent modification. Then, one day, the first death in the Great Central Laboratory was announced— and then another. They were initially thought to be accidents, but it was soon necessary to yield to the evidence. The oldest Savants were allowing themselves to die without appearing to take any precaution against it. It was understood, given their incomparable science, that such acts could not be involuntary.

189

What strange weariness of life had contrived taken possession of these men, who had seen everything, known everything, explored everything and for whom life was no more than a perpetual recommencement devoid of interest and the unexpected?

It was learned, with even more astonishment, that births were taking place in the Great Central Laboratory.

Attempts were made to justify these events in the eyes of the crowd; it was claimed that certain savants had judged it preferable, for the future of humanity, to renew their being entirely, assuring a line of descent that was merely, in sum, a simple prolongation of their personality.

Was it a protest of nature, an irresistible return to the normal course of things? Did scientific immortality not bring with it an unnatural fatigue and an infinite lassitude? It is permissible to think so, but the Great Central Laboratory never admitted it. It was only much later that the total absurdity of that *quantitative* immortality was perceived, when people understood that true immortality only exists *qualitatively*—by means, so to speak, of the creation of immortal masterpieces of beauty or bounty, the only things that can attain infinity.

XXXIX. The Rat

The satisfaction that the scientists of the Great Central Laboratory felt when they were sure they had discovered the secrets of life—and, in consequence, of immortality—was nevertheless legitimate, but for other reasons.

Since the remotest eras of the world, humankind had vaguely sensed the utter ridiculousness of death, the total absurdity of that annihilation of the body at the very moment when human beings were able to gather the fruits of their experience and labor. For a long time, people had consoled themselves for that absurd lapse by inventing poetic fictions about a future life. Then, these primitive fables having been smashed and obliterated by the positive discoveries of science, the entire world had been abandoned for centuries to the darkest neurasthenia. Why make any effort? What was the point of having admirably reshaped life and transported paradise to Earth if one could not profit from it—if, after a few years, one was bound to disappear like the most primitive and most abject of animals? Mechanisms were reparable; their life could be prolonged indefinitely, but no one was capable of doing as much for the human body, even though it was composed of simple elements and only required to be quite naturally renewed in perpetuity! After a period of about seven years, all the parts of the body were naturally renewed; why, then, could that renewal not be ensured indefinitely?

Proud of their discovery, the Savants of the Great Central Laboratory initially had only one thing in mind: to subject the world to their domination, to become masters of the life of the entire Earth. I have explained how they succeeded, by simple magnetic methods, in calming the exasperation of the crowds that rushed the Great Central Laboratory after the conquest of immortality—how, by suggestion, they subjected to their will, joyfully and without restriction, a multitude whose rage had taken it, the day before, to the limits of madness.

In the years that followed, this domestication of the masses became even more complete. The whole world was already nothing but an immense, infinitely delicate mechanism composed of an inextricable network of wires, controls, conduits and radiant effluvia, and there was an evident necessity for an absolute order, an exceedingly powerful authority to maintain equilibrium in that vast overcomplicated social machine.

This complexity increased further when the crowd was domesticated, classified into different specialisms by the Savants of the Great Central Laboratory. Masters of the sources of life, the scientists at the Laboratory gradually modified the traditional forms of the human body. The slaves employed in forced labor had their muscles specially developed, while their brains, reduced to an indispensable minimum, were complemented by helmet-meters obedient to the slightest directions issued by the Laboratory. Other individuals, charged with intellectual labor, were, so to speak, *disarmed* entirely, from the physical point of view, and reduced in advance to powerlessness should they ever attempt—however improbable it might be—to rebel.

These specializations, multiplied to infinity, were, moreover, welcomed joyfully by the people, who felt completely reassured by this state of dependence. They understood that they were part of a social whole; they found themselves less isolated and better maintained—and, in their new functions, they exaggerated the joys of specialization to the point of folly.

Unfortunately, this formidable organization supposed the Great Central Laboratory's total dominion over the entire Earth, for the smallest unexpected speck of dust might be sufficient to block the movement of that colossal clockwork. In the beginning, this autocratic organization of the world did not proceed without a few catastrophes. First of all, as you might remember, there was the frightful vegetable conspiracy that put science in peril. As a result of playing with the sources of life, transmitting the essential fluid, by way of experiment, into inanimate objects, then into plants, there were certain losses that escaped the strict attention of the Great Central Laboratory. Nothing was more frightful than the abrupt increase of newly-conscious plants, invading the cities and the countryside, getting hold of the transmission wires and diverting the electric current—a crisis that could only be brought to an end by propagating a microbial disease in the nascent forest.

Distress, at that moment, reached its maximum. The historic dangers once presented by wild beasts or earthquakes were still remembered, but the profound mystery of the antediluvian forests that liberated the oxygen on which we live, the invasive madness of fevers, and the troubling enigma of animate plants was unknown. There were also, in that era, a few resurrections in the ancient cemeteries, which made a considerable impact on opinion.

Those were, however, merely beginners' mistakes. Much more perilous, a few decades later, when the scientific world seemed conclusively organized, was the appearance of a simple rat, forgotten in the general destruction, which emerged from some unknown hiding place and which roamed the conduits tranquilly for six months, causing unexpected short-circuits, the destruction of mobile machines and interminable interruptions to transport, postal and supply services.

Once, in the times when the world was not yet civilized, the destruction of the rat would have been quite simple. It would have been sufficient to take up a gun, bait a trap with a little lard, or hunt it down with a ratting dog. In the admirable world of science, such procedures had become completely impracticable. The brains, deprived of bodies, could not be risked in such an adventure because of their physical inferiority. The colossi with aluminum brains were equally incapable of carrying out a so complicated a hunt. All their movements were regulated in advance, all their actions determined electrically; their personal initiative would have been insufficient in confrontation with the thousand whims, the unforeseen leaps, disappearances and unexpected movements of one conscious and independent rat.

It required 18 months of continual work in the Great Central Laboratory to put an end to that formidable enemy, which put the order of the entire world in peril and which thwarted, by means of its natural instinct, the cleverest schemes of the scientists. The security of the Great Central Laboratory itself was at stake, had certain communications been interrupted, certain wires cut.

It was necessary, little by little, by means of unprecedented prodigies of science and skill, to tame the rat, to suggest human ideas to it, to commence its education, to make it understand the rudiments of science—and that was certainly the most admirable project that the Great Central Laboratory ever attempted.

When that was done, when the mentality of the rat had been elevated to the complexity of a scientific brain, its capture was child's play and its annihilation saved the mechanical world from the greatest peril it had ever run.

XL. The Woman-Specimen

With the autocratic development of Absolute Science, the feminist question was no longer even posed. Life was prolonged indefinitely by the progressive replacement of different parts of the body. Human beings no longer died, as they once had, unless they wanted to, and diseases were henceforth unknown.

The very ancient sense that had once been called *instinct* in animals and *the survival instinct* in humans—which is nothing more than an interior awareness we have of different phenomena occurring in our bodies, a certain prescience of dangers that might be posed by various foreign germs—had, in fact, been developed in a particular fashion. While that internal awareness was developed to the highest possible degree, the deadliest diseases were nipped in the bud. For the first time, when there were no more physicians, medicine became something other than charlatanism and there was no longer any recourse to the vague indications of unconscious empiricism, as in olden times.

Quite naturally, the question of the reproduction of the species became equally uninteresting. Women were no longer distinguished from men by their work and their occupations, or even by costume. Human beings resembled the primitive androgynes described by antique religions. Suffice it to say that the mere idea of maternity no longer crossed anyone's mind.

Furthermore, thanks to energetic measures take in that respect by the Great Central Laboratory, all of what had once been the principal preoccupation and joy of humankind became something definitively unknown and profoundly scorned by scientific beings who had no personal understanding of what the word meant and considered love as an historic memory, an animal lapse, interesting only in the contexts of natural history and simple anatomical investigations.

What the scientists of the Great Central Laboratory did not say at that time, in order not to attract unnecessary attention, was that they had thought it a good idea to conserve, in a laboratory annex prohibited to the public, a curious couple representing a man and a woman as they had once existed on Earth.

This special laboratory had been furnished in a very particular fashion with fetishistic objects in an obsolete style. The chairs there, instead of being made of articulated iron to support the arms while reading or carrying out laboratory research, were formed out of curious multicolored cushions representing flowers or birds, supported by fragments of natural wood similarly cut in the form or flowers or arabesques. There was no scientific apparatus in the entire house; instead of a physical recreation laboratory, there was a large room in which the couple ate as people had in the past, without discernment, toxic pieces of dead animals cooked over a fire, or vegetables not yet decomposed. On the walls, instead of diagrams of energy-distribution, there were more flowers and imitation animals, cast in bronze or painted, which attempted to reproduce, as in the time of human naivety, natural scenes.

Only one invention appeared genuinely new and practical: that of simple cotton wicks steeped in mineral oil, which, ignited at the end, procured light without wires or generating-stations—in a word, without any social disposition. That was a veritable masterpiece of invention by the scientists of the Great Central Laboratory.

The couple who lived there comprised two handsome specimens of the human race. The Absolute Savants had named the woman-specimen the *Queen*, to serve as a reminder, by analogy with bee-hives, of the reproductive role that she was intended to play. As for the man, by reason of his favorite occupation, he had been given a quaint and ancient name; he was called the *Poet*.

These two beings had a strange life, completely isolated from the new scientific paradise, having no relationships with anyone but the Great Absolute Savant who directed the Central Laboratory.

To maintain the woman-specimen in her primitive state, the attempt had been made, by laborious research, to reconstitute her environment exactly and to put at her disposal everything that might delight her age-old tastes and irresistible penchants.

Firstly, around the palace in which she lived, beyond the ditches, an admirable complex of mirrors had been established, which reproduced exactly everything that took place within the palace and the images of the people therein. The woman-specimen was thus able to spend long hours on the terrace, contemplating her own image within the image of her own palace from a distance—and she went back in every evening sadly, to recount all the beauties that she had seen, passionately jealous of the happy woman who lived in the magnificent palace across the way, and who, in spite of her frightful ugliness, had someone with her, who remained kneeling before her all day long, who loved her, was preoccupied with her and thought of nothing but saving her from the slightest fatigue and the most minor annoyances. The poet, who had spent entire days at the woman's feet without being able to attract her attention and without daring to interrupt her reverie, protested a little, for form's sake, when the question of the ugliness of the neighboring princess was raised. That was a continually-renewed source of quarrels between the poor man-specimen and his tyrannical companion.

The scientists of the Great Central Laboratory, through the intermediary of homunculi—which is to say, insignificant and automatic little beings created by science—sent the woman new presents every day, designed to satisfy her most secret passions. They offered the woman-specimen ankle-boots in which it was impossible to walk, hats in which one was unable to see one's surroundings, clothes too small for the body they were supposed to contain, or books of ancient philosophy that

197

were impossible to understand, but whose presence on the surrounding tables flattered her ignorance.

Similarly, to promote her role as a queen bee, they had taken the trouble to create in the palace, outside the bedroom designed according to an ancient model, dangerous and unexpected places where she might meet the poet: cluttered lofts sown with traps, romantic caves furnished with oubliettes garnished with scythes an swords, and a place that no one could exactly locate in the darkness.

There was also, for the purposes of reproduction, a bush in which everyone knew, from a reliable source, that several venomous serpents were always coiled up, and a very tell greasy pole terminating in a carefully-balanced little nest. By this perpetual variety, the scientists of the Great Central Laboratory had gone to great lengths to satisfy the young woman's taste for adventure.

In spite of all these kindnesses, however, the Queen remained sad and melancholy; she often summoned old Hydrogen, the doyen of the Absolute Savants, and chattered to him for a long time. She explained that the Poet did not understand her, that she was made for life with a man of action. Hydrogen's visits multiplied, and that was the commencement of an unprecedented scientific scandal, which spoiled the beginning of the Second Scientific Era.

XLI. The Poet-Type

It was in the third year of the Second Era (old style) that the scandal burst which nearly brought down the 12 stages of science in a definitive fashion.

A restaurateur who happened to need to put in an important order for formic acid, addressed himself to his supplier by radiophotogram, in order to interrogate his correspondent's face directly as to what his commercial intentions might be. The radiophotogram having, by virtue of an unfortunate glitch, traversed the walls of the secret Palace where the woman-specimen was kept in company with the poet-type, the astonished restaurateur saw a scene on the screen of his apparatus that he had scarcely expected. In company with the woman-specimen, Hydrogen, the Absolute Savant of the Great Central Laboratory, was reconstituting ancient actions of animality, of a sort that history textbooks depicted in times past, without a thought for the frightful prohibitions and rigorous laws that he himself had enacted on that subject.

As might be imagined, a few of the restaurateur's clients happened to be there, curiously surrounding the screen; then a crowd of homunculi interrupted their slave labor so that they too might study the strange spectacle. An entire disorganization of minutely-regulated work throughout the entire city soon ensued; this interruption had repercussions in distant cities, and frightful complications were momentarily feared.

When the Great Central Laboratory was hastily alerted, there was an unprecedented scandal, and all the doors were immediately closed, with an absolute prohibition against anyone coming near it.

Meanwhile, in the palace reserved for her, the woman-specimen was greatly amused by the idea of the terrible scandal that would break when her husband, the poet-type, was surprised by it.

199

She had, in fact, undertaken to horrify that insatiable dreamer, with whom she was imprisoned for the purpose of perpetuating the race and who persisted in dreaming about the stars all day long, and celebrating his companion's beauty in every fashion, in verse and even in prose—for he was a true poet.

Often, in the secret hope of provoking an unwonted fit of anger, the woman-specimen had told the poet-type that she was deceiving him with Hydrogen, but the poet-type had not believed her, because she was beautiful and old Hydrogen was fearfully ugly. The woman-specimen had then attempted to explain the moral reasons that drove her to deceive her poetic companion: quite genuinely, she did not understand poetry at all; she found that perpetual quest for the unreal utterly ridiculous; she could not imagine that anyone could see the appeal of tall stories and fairy tales. By contrast, Hydrogen's scientific certainty, his effective and material power, was infinitely seductive to her; she hoped that her companion the poet might kill Hydrogen and take possession of his scientific power.

She had tried a little harder every day to excite his jealousy of his rival, but had never succeeded. The poet did not believe her, in fact; for him, the woman was a divine being, all sensibility, intelligence and beauty, which nature had created to be understood. Her changing character, her abrupt mood-shifts, made a new woman every day, and the poet delightedly studied his own reflection every day in that ocean of passions, ever-changing and yet always the same, as if in the mirror of his own mind.

The poet had no desire to kill Hydrogen, firstly because he was not at all jealous, unable to suppose for a single instant that the other's gross materiality could have any attraction for the woman, and also because he was blissfully happy. Sometimes, for pleasure, he had tried to show jealousy; he had even killed a homunculus that, out of sympathy, had told him the truth, but in the most powerful of his fits of anger he instinctively employed the most subtle and surest means of not learning anything compromising.

Furthermore, violent and brutal acts were not the sort of thing he did; the practice of poetry had elevated him to higher summits; he addressed the stars intimately, upset the universe, struck down the gods; he wanted the objects of which he had made use, even for an instant, to be broken after he passed by; he would have fought an army of giants on his own. He was, in a word, a proud poet—which is to say, an infinitely timid creature, for whom the slightest reality was sufficient to throw him into confusion. The mere idea of learning something untoward terrified him; he was afraid of everything, even clouds, because every object, even the most futile, was for him filled with inextricable problems, imprecise threats and disturbing phantoms; like a child, he was only happy when he could amuse himself with picture-books or believe that the Moon only existed as a function of his desires.

When the woman-specimen incited him, directly or indirectly, to kill the Absolute Savant she described a brilliant future for him in which they would be masters of the Central Laboratory; she told him that, as possessors of the universal science, they would then be like gods. He did not believe it; he replied that there was something else beyond what she saw, that ideas alone were certain, that divinity was within us. Then his eyes lost themselves in the sky, attentively following the ideas that floated slowly by—as certain animals sometimes do when watching unknown things pass through the air.

When the Laboratory scandal broke, undeniable and inevitable, the poet did not give way to the fit of violence that the woman-specimen expected of him. There was no movement of revolt, nor even of surprise. To him, a material novelty counted for nothing; only the moral fall of his ideal appeared to affect him. For several days, he did not reappear; he was only seen in the ethnographic collections of the Laboratory, actively seeking a nail from past ages and a rope of the ancient sort, which had not been woven by the scientific world. It was even rumored that, above the nail that he hammered into his bedroom wall, he drew a naïve image of the

Earth's satellite. No one knew why. It was simply observed, some time afterwards, that he had died of asphyxia, and the loss was regretfully recorded by the Curator of the Great Museum's collections.

Hydrogen resumed his place in the Council of Absolute Savants, and good explanations were given to the people and homunculi of the extreme devotion that the great scientist invested in his studies of ancient questions, perilous and devoid of contemporary interest.

As for the woman-specimen, there was great anxiety on her behalf. An incomprehensible thing: when she learned of the disappearance of her companion, she exhibited an immense despair. Henceforth, having no one on Earth to torment, her life was pointless. To avoid any complication, the wise decision was taken to declassify her; she was retired from the collections, in spite of the historical interest she presented.

Her ancient brain was replaced by a model 327 phosphor-aluminum box and she was lost, unconscious and docile, in the servile crowd of homunculi.

XLII. The Massacre of the Homunculi

A scientist who considers the nature of things in his laboratory will always remain ignorant of the possibility of repugnance or disgust. However noxious the compound he is examining might be, he will taste it, if necessary, with all the tranquility in the world. Compounds are nothing to him but unknown chemical composites, always the same.

In the wake of considerable progress of science, men ended up examining everything from that special scientific angle; for them, all the phenomena of nature became equally interesting, without it being possible to establish any meaningful distinction between a chemical reaction, for example, and a violent passion experienced for good or evil. Above human beings, moreover, were placed the machines that ensured the existence of the entire world, and the materializations of collective intelligence that took the form of great factories were put well ahead of simple individual manifestations of thought. By virtue of an entirely natural tendency, the artificial animals created by man to serve his daily needs were also objects of much sympathy in that era.

People had already noticed, in the earliest days of civilization, that the new kinds of machines were breaking violently with the artistic traditions of the past and were, by contrast, reminiscent of the creations of nature.

The automobile had been the first instrument of current usage to give some indication of this direction. In barbaric times, the automobile had been imagined somewhat in the manner of a Greek temple or an item of Louis XV furniture; its mechanical parts had been willingly concealed beneath a stylish body-work modeled on a Roman ship or a Sedan chair, and the most fantastic projects were then proposed. It required the intervention of *necessity* in order for it to be understood how old-fashioned that way of thinking was, and how ill-fitted to the new ideology.

Racing cars, designed according to the immediate exigencies of speed, were the first to indicate the path that would have to be followed. At first, artists qualified them as monsters; then, gradually shedding ancient prejudices, they celebrated their new harmony and imperious beauty. Soon, when the automobile had conquered its new form, solely thanks to the indications of empiricism, it was finally understood that it simply realized, without anyone having been aware of it, the complete and logical structure of a new animal.

From the head, with its eyes and voice, to the black evacuation-mechanism of the exhaust-pipe, the automobile behaved like a simple animal, with the same weaknesses, the same fainting fits, the same fever at certain hours of the day, tempered by the sudation of the radiator, the same recovery of strength at nightfall, the beating heart of its valves, the vertebral column of its transmission, sending movement to the motive hind-limbs via the intermediary of a differential in the form of a pelvis, while the front wheels felt their way along the road. The circulation of water, the circulation of oil and the electrical nervous system were as many distinct networks dictated by imperious logic—as if, in all construction, certain natural laws demanded the same forms, the same processes. The new creature was distinguished from natural creatures by the idea of the wheel and gears, but that was all that distinguished it from them.

No one saw anything in this but an amusing resemblance, as long as man was credited with a divine intelligence superior to matter—but when materialism had made further progress, when people began to see all phenomena, material or moral, as nothing but a simple juxtaposition of molecular forces, they asked themselves whether the artificial animals could be logically distinguished from natural animals by anything other than their imperfections.

The question became even more vexing as the artificial animals were further improved. Almost everywhere, at the beginning of the scientific era, homunculi designed to play the roles of the slaves of old were beginning to be constructed for industrial and domestic use.

These homunculi varied in form according to the functions for which they were designed. A homunculus responsible for supervising the work of automatic lathes in a factory was obviously not the same as a homunculus in charge of a telegraphic station or the preparation of toxic products in a laboratory. All of them, however, were constructed in approximate imitation of the human body; all of them were endowed with adequately-regulated reflexes, and the perfection of their mechanism was such that people often had trouble distinguishing a homunculus, in the course of his work, from an ordinary man.

It is necessary to add, moreover, that the scientists of the Great Central Laboratory had imparted a certain elegance to the perfect realization of the dream of seekers of old. They had doubtless had recourse to the famous recipes of Paracelsus in constructing their homunculi. The latter were not, as they ancient alchemists had imagined, little creatures devoid of gravity, sexless and equipped with supernatural powers. On the contrary, the scientists amused themselves by making them as similar to humans as possible, with the secret hope that, by faithfully reproducing the forms of nature, their creations would become ever-closer to nature.

There were even, at that time, strange laboratory homunculi into which nervous fluid appropriated from certain animals was transmitted, and which, little by little appeared to be giving evident signs of independence and initiative.

Almost everywhere, with too much haste, the instinctive development of homunculi was encouraged. Their makers watched avidly for the birth of human vices within them; their caprices were complacently encouraged; their desires were developed.

All of this was merely a distraction of superior scientists, until the day when it was perceived, with terror, that the individual initiatives and secret vices of homunculi were definitely not those that had been expected.

Constructed solely in accordance with scientific logic, the homunculi adapted themselves narrowly to the new world; they appeared to be better equipped for the direction of the new civilization than old-fashioned human beings.

When their projects were revealed, there was a long period of struggle, debate, and then anguish. Some people argued that a homunculus was only a machine, at the end of the day, posing no real danger; others explained that, according to the materialist theory, there was nothing absurd in thinking that these new creatures might have the same authority and the same initiatives as a man.

Certain suspicious occurrences, certain inexplicable assassinations, unleashed general panic; people were afraid, and no longer wasted time in debate. The homunculi were destroyed *en masse*. Doubts caused the scientific challenge issued by natural forces to be renounced. For weeks on end, these mysterious beings fully armed by human industry were executed.

Some time afterwards, but too late, people asked themselves whether they might not have yielded to an impulse of unthinking fear—but no one had any regrets when, according to certain reports, they learned that several homunculi, as they died, had wept in pain and fear.

XLIII. The Two Savages

When one has surveyed in detail, as I have, all the centuries that follow the one that produced this book, one is literally stupefied by the extraordinary pride that the men of the 20th century took in the extremely petty progress of their nascent civilization.

Yes, undoubtedly, at that moment, man could still have avoided great disasters and resumed, without futile detours, the idealist path that anterior civilizations had traced. He preferred, on the contrary, to deliver himself unreservedly to science, expecting everything from mechanization—and it was that insane error that led humankind to the brink of oblivion.

If, however, one examines the situation of the human beings of the 20th century, one can easily see that their situation very closely resembled that of prehistoric humans: the same absolute ignorance of the causes of everything, the same gross fetishism, content with vain appearances, empty words and hollow definitions. Humans inhabited their bodies as *foreigners*, living, in the final analysis, like sheep or oxen, automatically accomplishing organic functions, submissive to their instincts, obedient to natural necessity, without any true control, without any useful influence on their destiny.

Towards the end of the Second Scientific Era, all of that had been completely changed, I freely admit, by the veritable progress accomplished by science; a man of 1912 abruptly transported into that strange, entirely mechanized, world would have been very surprised. No more diseases, or deaths, strictly speaking, but bodies entirely reconstructed, sometimes spending long months in repair-shops; cemeteries replaced by temporary storehouses, resurrections effected routinely, according to the disposable credit of the social budget; the heavy burdens of maternity replaced by embryonic grafts carried out on animal nurses; the different utilization of the senses, their amplification, new vibrations perceived by new senses; the suppression of language, its replacement by algebraic transmission—so many things that profoundly disrupted the traditional habits of old.

The simplification of useful movements had, moreover, brought much calm and order to the scientific world: no external noise; silent cities with very rare passers-by and without apparent conduits; everything being done by remote control, without any difficulty at all.

It was not just the ancient pleasures of the theater that were obtainable at home, without putting oneself out, by means of simple collective suggestion. Even performances had been replaced, in the majority of cases, by simple impressions of performance giving the illusion of pleasure and success. Information, news, the announcement of important discoveries and collective recommendations were all similarly done by suggestion, without any loss of time or needless displacement.

The sole defect of this excessive social aggregation was the gradual destruction of all individual initiative, all ambition, all independent activity—and, by virtue of the suppression of individuality, the progressive development, without anyone being aware of it, of the absolute omnipotence of the Great Central Laboratory.

At first, this exaggerated centralization had given welcome results by constraining people conclusively to resolve social problems that had previously seemed insoluble. Thus, with ever-increasing concentration of the means of production, when there was no longer more than one factory in every region of the world, functioning automatically under the direction of a single manager, everyone had to agree that the factory could not belong solely to the heirs of the formidable trust that had constructed it. On one side, in fact, one found oneself in the presence of a sole proprietor, and, on the other, of all the consumers who, producing nothing, had no means of purchase at their disposal. From that very exaggeration of the problem, an organization almost immediately emerged for the distribution of products necessary to life.

Unfortunately, if that admirable organization produced fortunate results for the collective satisfaction of material needs, it progressively reduced individual initiative and, by virtue of wanting to subjugate matter to their needs by means of machines, men made themselves into nothing more than simple cogs in a social machine.

This was exaggerated to such a point that, a few years later, two savage aesthetes from God only knows where, who had avoided the progress of science, being physically constituted as people had been at the beginning of the 20th century—and, it was thought, of different sexes—appeared in African Europe and, without the slightest effort, imposed their tyrannical will upon the scientific world for several months, without anyone being able to discover a practical means of reducing them to powerlessness.

No mechanism had, in fact, been anticipated by the Great Central Laboratory for that sort of combat, and no individual then had a sufficiently general and flexible intelligence or a body sufficiently complete to oppose by himself the crazy enterprises of the two savages.

The scientists of the Central Laboratory could not leave their posts without precipitating the immediate ruination of the entire world; the specialists among the common people could not seriously oppose these complete human beings. Fortunately, the two savages vanished of their own accord one day; one of them was simply heard to say to the other, employing the spoken language of old: "We've seen enough of them!" Then they left, without anyone being able to find out, afterwards, to which part of the world they had retired.

It was at that moment that all the dangers of specialization began to be appreciated, and the full value of developing a complete little world within each individual. It was the dawn of a new era, in which the cultivation of the will and the exploitation of the internal forces of human being began to assume top priority. The scientists knew that that cultivation would inevitably produce unexpected and surprising results,

but no one then suspected the formidable reservoir of unknown energies that the human body represented.

XLIV. Beyond Natural Forms

It is genuinely very difficult, in borrowing the primitive language of the 20th century, to explain in a satisfactory fashion the confusing phenomena that afflicted the final years of the Second Scientific Era and, at the same time, anticipated the Great Idealist Renaissance.

It was, very specifically, the introduction of the fourth dimension into the constitution of the human body that provoked the gravest disorder in the natural order of things. While that concept had been nothing but a simple philosophical discovery, a theory—interesting, to be sure, but solely limited to the domain of ideas—one had only to laud the enlargement that it brought to human thought. On the day when the fourth dimension entered the physical domain of quotidian life, however, unprecedented turmoil resulted on the surface of the globe.

To begin with, the advanced thinkers who had the idea were content, in their voyages of exploration, to make use of specters and phantoms, which temporarily furnished them with the supernatural bodies that they needs in order to incarnate their thought. They were thus able, without any risk, to abandon their human bodies for several days. Leaving them to tick over, and borrow spectral forms that sufficed for displacement in the fourth dimension.

Gradually, however, with the continual practice of this new sport, people began to try to adapt their own bodies to the greater demands of their thought. Why not try to bend their material envelopes to the new ideas?

Improbably, they succeeded, and irreparable disasters soon ensued.

It is, in fact, understood that the human body is constructed according to the givens of three-dimensional space. The bony frame is established according to that provisional vision of the universe; the organs are contained by the muscles

211

and the skin in a three-dimensional space. When people tried to contort the human body to the demands of the fourth dimension, it was exposed to the most serious disorders. Without any apparent wound or visible opening, certain organs were transported outside the body and, under the natural pressure of the muscles, grouped into indescribable masses, escaping any familiar regulation and any precise anatomy.

One could not say, admittedly, that the body, thus modified, was crushed, broken or disintegrated; it continued to live, but without presenting the habitual appearance of the human body in three-dimensional space.

This terrible lesson had made a deep impression on certain scientists, who resolved no longer to expose their bodies to similar accidents and quite naturally, took advantage of domestic animals to incarnate their four-dimensional minds temporarily. Their human bodies were deposited in the Great Central Laboratory, where they were maintained in readiness, and in the meantime, our explorers took great pleasure in utilizing the bodies of unlucky animals.

In this manner, certain scientists, like the generals of old, had innumerable mounts die under them—or, at least, reduced them to the state of misshapen organisms previously unknown in three-dimensional space.

There were also people who never came back to reclaim their human bodies, and of whom nothing more was ever heard. Signs of intelligence were simultaneously observed in certain animals, and people became anxious in consequence. Might not some dog or horse wandering in the street be one of the most notorious scientists of the Great Central Laboratory?[37] People in doubt had to take infinite precautions not to

---

[37] The citation of these particular examples is likely to remind the reader that the persistence of familiar animals is one of the most evident inconsistencies in the narrator's reconstituted future history; the horse and the dog had once been so completely forgotten that the last surviving specimens were known as the Soliped and the anti-elephant.

mistreat donkeys or geese that might be incarnating the minds of the noblest representatives of the human species.

Numerous cases of animal madness became manifest in subsequent years, and it was necessary to create a special insane asylum. No one dared try to kill these bizarre animals in fact, and people came to have the same respect for them that Oriental peoples had once had for sacred animals. Animal madness assumed the most human forms. Giraffes were observed which refused all nourishment and imagined, by night, that they were grazing the stars. Horses attained the prideful folly of spending their days moving through the fields in military formation and whinnying in a warlike manner. Dogs, eternally faithful to all the people they encountered, perished of grief in thinking of the thousands of masters they would never see again. There was much talk about an ostrich which believed that it had swallowed a celebrated scientific textbook and which dragged itself along the ground, crushed by its supposed weight. A calf, crowned with flowers, drowned itself in a pool with two springs of parsley in its nostrils.

These various divagations of scientists in animal bodies gave rise to a thousand puerile or grotesque incidents, but the Great Laboratory remained unconcerned until they began to take on an erotic character. Under the hypocritical pretext of supernatural experimentation, most people were, in fact, only borrowing these animal bodies to re-enact in an uncontrolled manner ancient procedures that were strictly forbidden, and which were only too natural.

Preparations were therefore being made to prohibit incarnations, on account of their bestial aspects, when it was realized that the greatest danger resulting from the introduction of the fourth dimension into the physical domain was, on the contrary, its excessive spirituality. As soon as the physical body, under the influence of the fourth dimension, lost its natural three-dimensional form, as soon as it became capable of spiritualizing itself in order to pass through walls or displace itself in time, it was gradually reabsorbed into the continuum, dissociating instead of disintegrating, as before—and in that new death, it was the soul that devoured the body.

The prohibition of suicide by the mind was thus announced, but it was no less obvious that, in future, the greater reality must be sought beyond natural forms, not in transitory three-dimensional appearances.

XLV. Immortality in Ideas

The Idealist Renaissance that was gradually substituted for the Second Scientific Era permitted, for the first time, clear reasoning and a glimpse of the real future of humankind.

It was astonishing, now that all ideas seemed quite simple, that they had not occurred to the human imagination sooner, and that it had required the costly and dismal experience of the Leviathan and then the long and depressing scientific domination of the Great Central Laboratory to demonstrate the insufficiency of materialistic concepts. That was doubtless because the assumptions made by science had been insufficiently clarified and their ultimate consequences had not been extrapolated.

Only one man, in the ancient era of materialism, had had the courage of his convictions and pursued it to its extreme limits, and that man was Blanqui.[38] Meditating in the solitude of his cell, while he was imprisoned by governmental justice in the Fort du Taureau, he wrote a curious pamphlet entitled *Éternité par les Astres*, whose rigorous logic ought to have had an impact all his contemporaries.

---

[38] Louis-Auguste Blanqui (1805-1881) was France's most notorious revolutionary socialist. Imprisoned under Louis-Philippe, he was released during the 1848 revolution, but was so troublesome thereafter that he was imprisoned again even before Louis-Napoléon's *coup d'état*. When the Second Empire collapsed he was briefly released but was imprisoned again as swiftly as before, this time in the Fort du Taureau in Brittany; he was elected president of the Paris Commune but his jailers would not release him to take up the appointment. It was after that, in 1872, that he wrote the pamphlet cited by Pawlowski, whose title is deliberately echoed and transfigured in the title of this chapter, "L'immortalité par les idées."

Here, in summary, are some of the conclusions to which Blanqui's thesis led:

The universe is infinite, but we cannot understand what such a representation means, because the notion of infinity is scarcely accessible to the human imagination. At 40 kilometers an hour, it would require 250 million years to reach the nearest stars, and the Earth, with its prodigious speed, would require 100,000 years to reach the star 61-Cygni.

Now, all that is accessible to us is the nearest part of the universe, that which is effectively part of our daily life. The immensity composed to innumerable worlds only begins, so to speak, beyond that. However, all that these worlds reveal chemically is the presence of scarcely 100 simple entities, always the same. It is with these meager 100 elements that nature must forge all the material combinations in the universe, and these combinations, although innumerable, are, by definition, mathematically limited. Inevitably, therefore, there will be solar systems analogous to ours; equally inevitably, in extrapolating this research to infinity, there will be solar systems rigorously similar to ours in the slightest detail, including Earths whose history is exactly similar to that of our Earth. [39]

If one does not lose sight of what the word *infinity* signifies and if one keeps in mind, on the other hand, that material combinations are limited by the number of simple bodies, it is impossible not to admit that, at the moment when we are writing these lines, other identical persons—counterparts or doubles—are writing the same words in other identical worlds. This is a game of mirrors that it is necessary to pursue logically to its most extreme consequences: the action that we would

---

[39] This argument was reproduced, without acknowledgement, in an essay by the English Marxist scientist J. B. S. Haldane entitled "Some Consequences of Materialism," collected in *The Inequality of Man and Other Essays* (1932). Another of Haldane's essays, "The Last Judgment," provided the blueprint for Olaf Stapledon's future history *Last and First Men* (1930).

have performed yesterday, *our other selves* have performed or will perform; every possibility of our life must have been realized, or will be realized, in another world.

Let us finally add that the identity of action is not merely simultaneous; it also exists in time, in the past and in the future; it exists in *every second*, for it is necessary to limit ourselves, and Blanqui to the most rigorous conclusions, and to keep them to a minimum—and that is, in fact, the serious insufficiency of this theory, for, here again, it is necessary to continue to infinity the infinite fragmentation of time. In a word, we bump into infinity at the very moment when we were on the point of escaping it, and thus fall back into the eternal critique of discontinuous science formulated long ago by Zeno of Elea.[40]

From this *scientifically* exact theory, Blanqui draws rather melancholy philosophical conclusions: everything that we have personally done and everything that we will do in future, a double has already done or will do; it is the definitive negation of all ambition and all progress—but it is also the sincere conclusion at which one must arrive by *pushing materialist theories to their conclusion*: a sincere conclusion that would have been sufficient to demonstrate, even before the birth of the Leviathan, the radical impuissance of three-dimensional science in the presence of problems of continuous four-dimensional quality.

In that primitive era though, pushing conclusions to the extreme was reckoned to be a utopian's game or a humorist's joke, and no one hesitated to affirm unsmilingly that the only certainty must be sought in relativity!

---

[40] Zeno of Elea formulated the famous paradox of Achilles and the Tortoise, which Pawlowski takes as proof that time and space are not infinitely divisible; he was acquainted with it via Plato's *Parmenides*, named for the leader of the pre-Socratic Eleatic school of philosophy. It is not, however, obvious that the objection is sufficient to demolish Blanqui's thesis, or is even relevant to it.

217

A very different procedure was followed in the Great Idealist Renaissance. People attempted to research, ahead of anything else, aesthetic unity, moral originality and the absolute heterogeneity of all material support, and to get closer to the immortal and continuous type uniquely furnished by the four-dimensional mind.

It was considered that the world must be conceived, not by three-dimensional analysis, but by four-dimensional synthesis and that increasing generalization only corresponded to the legitimate aspirations of humankind.

It is, in fact, by an ever-greater centralization that ontological progress is manifest; it is by the association of ideas, by ever-more-powerful syntheses, that the human mind makes progress. That is what religions and ancient philosophies symbolized very aptly by the progressive purification of the soul passing through ever-more-elevated spheres.

The study of man from this viewpoint produces precious information. While the body, only disposed in three-dimensional space, is fatally devoted to disintegration—which is to say, to a sequence of partial or total reconfigurations—during its life and at the point of death, the human mind attains the fourth dimension and, by virtue of so doing, possesses immortality; it can envisage, in the same instant, past or future phenomena; it can elevate itself, by abstraction, above material contingencies and participate, in reality, in the universal and immutable substance of things. On the one hand, material senses furnish it with the provisional elements of an analysis of the three-dimensional world; on the other, the intimate sense, consciousness, gives it the notion of the fourth dimension—which is to say that it completes the continuous representation of the universe outside what is conventionally called space and time, vain props from which the Idea releases itself, like a completed cathedral denuded of its fragile scaffolding.

Everyone knows that in a true work of art the subject or the scenario is only a provisional sacrifice made to materiality, and that the esthetic quality of a line or an idea is entirely independent of the subject chosen. A masterpiece reveals itself to us spontaneously outside any material explanation, and all critical analysis is merely coarse afterthought. The absolute and the infinite are not materially definable, they are *a priori* joys that artists alone can attain.

One sees, now, how pitiful and sterile it was for the first men to pursue infinity or immortality in space or in time—which is to say, in the illusory domain of the senses. When people understood, by contrast, that infinity only existed in *quality*, that immortality was to be found, so to speak, on the spot, immutable and graspable by the mind in the domain of pure ideas, humankind resumed its forward march with confidence, assured of the usefulness of its task, knowing henceforth that a new idea was a creation worthy of that name, and that no double, as Blanqui thought, could rob the man-God of the idea of immortality, which had sprung fully-armed from his brain.

Death for the body is nothing but the end of a physical oscillation that is called life; for the mind, it is nothing but the end of a mental hesitation that is called thought. Death is, in a word, nothing but the end of a *contradiction*, provisionally useful for the search for the truth, but which becomes pointless when that verity is attained.

Only in the Age of the Golden Eagle was it understood that, outside of any idea of progress in time, this total verity could be attained by an act of faith, intelligence or love, and that such an act, instead of having a relative value—a social value as in the three-dimensional world—always acquires an absolute value in the world of ideas. In the physical domain, in fact, the murder of a man is, for instance, more serious than that of an insect; in the moral domain, on the contrary, only the desire to commit murder is important, and its gravity remains immutable in relation to the mind that conceives it.

Similarly, in the three-dimensional world, a new contradiction, an idea of genius, dazzles humankind by the incalculable social consequences that it might have; in the purely intellectual domain, on the contrary, the most timid movement

219

of a solitary and sincere heart towards infinity is often worth more than a flash of intelligence; the value is measured by its innate quality and not by its quantity, and it is for that reason that the humblest are sometimes closer to immortality than the greatest.

Immortality, it was understood in the Age of the Golden Eagle, is potentially attainable at any moment by a thought released from the three-dimensional world, escaping thereby from the illusions of time and space. One divines, without it being necessary to insist, that it was rarely attained during the long period of scientific tyranny that preceded the Great Idealist Renaissance.

XLVI. The Stations of Infinity

As might be imagined, the Great Idealist Renaissance did not come about instantaneously following the long scientific era that had succeeded the 20th century.

For years, men had got into the habit of obeying the orders of the Great Central Laboratory; social life had been entirely mechanized, down to the last detail, and the new idealist tendencies, understandably, could not reform such deeply-rooted mores in a matter of hours.

The various checks suffered by the Absolute Savants of the Great Central Laboratory had proved, beyond a shadow of a doubt, that there were others things in the world than numbers and quantities, and that science was quite insufficient to satisfy all human aspirations. It had proved possible, without much effort, to prolong life, to grow and nourish fractions of the human body separately, to attach them to other living beings; it had even proved possible to communicate animal life to plants and vice versa—but it had never been possible to *create* life.

Several times, undoubtedly, someone had imagined that the creation in question had finally been obtained, but they had always discovered, eventually, that the life was pre-existent, even in simple bodies. As for materialist theories, their insufficiency had been demonstrated on the day when someone had had the courage to push them to their final consequences and their impuissance was particularly marked when the attempt had been made by their means, to touch upon the great questions of immortality and infinity.

To limit nature to a certain *number* of simple bodies, always the same, combining them in various fashions, *to infinity*, was to recognize fatally, developing the ideas of Blanqui, the inevitable existence of identical combinations distributed throughout the universe. From that, as we have said, combinations being limited in number, it is necessary to admit that by

221

continually searching, one must find an Earth identical to ours, other Earths where individuals identical to us will do what we have done, or what we might have wanted to do—and not only once, but an infinite number of times. And that, better than any other demonstration, suffices to prove that materialist combinations are incapable of taking account of the very nature of things.[41]

One understands very quickly, therefore, that it is not in material combinations that it is necessary to pursue the quest for the infinite but, quite to the contrary, on the spot, within ourselves, by an ever-greater increase in our intellectual faculties and an ever-more active research of pure ideas.

Time and movement are, in fact, only purely relative expressions, and the quality of life is quite independent of its duration. A nebula takes millions of years to coalesce; a scientist can imagine that agglomeration in a moment of reflection so brief that no human instrument can measure it.

Furthermore, in the life of a man of genius, truly useful, generative ideas only take a moment of reflection so brief that it escapes all measurement, and the rest of such a life is merely devoted to the popularization of that idea of genius. Similarly, a violent shock, a threat of danger, and imminent death, can endow the brain with more activity and more memory in a few

---

[41] It is, in fact, not obvious that the mere possibility of infinite duplication is sufficient to prove anything of the sort—although, of course, the whole argument breaks down as soon as it is admitted that the universe is finite (as Gustave Le Bon had alleged as a corollary of the proposition that matter is in a state of permanent decay). Even in 1923, Pawlowski was writing before the discovery that the universe is expanding had been fully formulated or popularized, so he had no inkling of what would ultimately come to be called "Big Bang theory." The Blanqui thesis has, however, since been transferred in its application to a hypothetically infinite multiverse of parallel alternative universes—in which context its falseness, if it is false, still remains somewhat less than obvious.

seconds than interminable years of banal life could contrive. Given this, the duration of a life hardly matters, so long as one succeeds in prodigiously increasing the faculty of thought. Patient researches were undertaken in this direction, but they were, unfortunately, quickly compromised by scientific methods of which it was very difficult to get rid at the beginning of the Great Idealist Renaissance.

Laboratories of an entirely new kind were, therefore, soon created, in which willing volunteers attempted to *depart for infinity* as people had once departed on long voyages. They were, properly speaking, new stations that the civilizations of old had never anticipated, from which people departed on a daily basis on journeys inside themselves. Innumerable precautions were taken to ensure the safety of these strange voyages made on the spot, whose goal was to escape, to the greatest possible extent, the ancestral exigencies of time and space.

It was from the body, a burdensome accessory, that all the ancient ideas of relativity came; it was from that mass of sleeping cells that it was necessary to be released as quickly as possible, and the first step that was taken was to isolate, without any danger to life, not only the central cells that represented the personality of each voyager, but also the very essence of those cells.

The voyager was prepared, for a month, for that *instantaneous voyage* by means of philosophical readings and artistic visions of increasing purity. The education of the will commenced with an analysis of Plato's *Parmenides*, and terminated in purely musical sensations, mathematical music permitting more complete syntheses than the other arts and evoking the maximum of possible memories. In that sense, the new *stations of infinity* were slightly reminiscent of the theaters of barbaric times.

The first results thus obtained were fairly satisfactory. In a few seconds, the voyagers could often access, not only almost all the present ideas, but also, in the same instant, the past ideas accumulated in the living cell since the origin of the world—but that was all. Their rapidity of thought had increased in incalculable proportions, but they were not united, as had initially been hoped, with the infinite—which is to say, with the universality of things.

Between the three dimensions of phenomena registered by the senses and the fourth dimension, suggested by consciousness, man remained suspended mid-way, enclosed in a personality conclusively abstracted from any idea of time and space. The voyager no longer situated infinity, as before, outside himself, no longer exteriorizing it in a gross fashion in the form of some sort of divinity; infinity was located within him, where his consciousness had formerly been situated.

It was understood then that the stations that had been constructed for departure on the quest for infinity were, at the end of the day, only coarse scientific establishments analogous to those that might have been conceived a few years earlier by the Absolute Savants of the Great Central Laboratory.

Fortunately, after this deceptive hitch, another way, clearer and more luminous, opened up for the Great Idealist Renaissance—and that way was prepared in an unexpected fashion by the discovery that was made, at the same time, of *resurrection*. Men who had been dead a few days before, had been successfully resuscitated, returning for the fist time to tell the frightful story of the moral tortures they had endured during the time when their spirits had found themselves permanently separated from their bodies.

Conscious, exactly as they had been before their deaths, they had experienced the frightful regret of wandering amid the people who had been dear to them, witnessing their grief without being able to console them, without being able to let them know that they were beside them. These men had understood that only one truly superior idea existed in the world, capable of clarifying all others, and that this pure idea was love.

This was not a matter, of course, of love such as it was understood in the barbaric centuries, but of that universal sympathy capable of uniting all living beings in a narrow sense, which would develop in incalculable proportions if the living were able to comprehend the frightful isolation of death and which would permit the accomplishment, in a single moment of common enthusiasm, of progress that centuries of timid and suspicious civilization had not been able to effect.[42]

For the first time, thanks to these new notions, the Great Idealist Renaissance began to understand that infinity could not be discovered by the mind, but by the heart. The attempt successively to attain all the ideas in the universe could only fail miserable. On the contrary, in mingling all beings in the same common love, infinity would come to us. It was no more than a unique and individual creative act, uniting in an instant what all the reasoning in the world had been unable to summarize. Universal love was hope perennially renewed, the communal forward march of all beings, the supreme and definitive synthesis forever opposed to the hostile and solvent analysis of science.

These were, at first, only vague and imprecise ideas, but they soon developed to find their full justification in the Age of the Golden Eagle.

---

[42] Although Pawlowski is an atheist, considering God to be merely a fictitious invention made in man's own image, he is a conspicuously Christian atheist; his philosophical God-substitute is universal Love, and—as we shall shortly see—even incorporates a crucial Last Judgment.

XLVII. The House of Bodies

Although it has always been very difficult for me to estimate years with precision in the course of my journeys to the land of the fourth dimension, I think I can affirm that it was exactly 2000 years after the Declaration of the Rights of Man and the Citizen that the Great Idealist Renaissance abolished mechanical slavery and proclaimed the Rights of Matter and Nature. It had required centuries of civilization and crude scientific labor for that idea, simple as it was, to succeed in making itself manifest.

When one has traversed the centuries to arrive in the Age of the Golden Eagle, one cannot comprehend that humans had needed to subjugate matter for so many years and to surround themselves with mechanical slaves, just as people in the 20th century could not accept the human slavery of times past—and yet, it has to be said, that liberation could only be achieved after centuries of preparation and progress.

In abolishing slavery, moreover, the Great Idealist Renaissance was only following and completing the same movement towards liberty that had been in development since the origins of the world, but which the sociologists had been unable to recognize or appreciate in full. Particularly in the 20th century, at the beginning of the Scientific Era, work had been blithely glorified in a ridiculous fashion. Without realizing it, people had confused the *free activity* of the human mind, from which all its glory stems, and *forced labor* rudely imposed by the necessities of the material body—and, by extension, the social body. And yet, it had already been evident for a long time that that frenetic and unhealthy glorification of social work was in contradiction with the most legitimate aspirations of humankind—that it conflicted brutally with the highest ideals of thinkers of genius as well as the basest desires of the crowd.

An attentive examination of past civilizations had sufficed, however, to reveal that humans, since the remotest times, had done all they could to obtain, not the right to work, but the right to leisure; that they had tried, in every fashion imaginable—by means of force, toil or dreams—to escape, as much as possible, from the material exigencies of life.

Asiatic potentates, conquerors and lords of every species had constructed society in the unique hope of obtaining for themselves the necessary tranquility to develop their minds, and when the great ancient republics were founded, their first concern had been to ensure the leisure of the all-powerful kings who were their citizens. Thus, in Athens, the enviable rank of citizen was limited in its numbers, each place corresponding to an assured source of State revenue. Three slaves worked in the mines for every citizen, and Xenophon proposed the creation at Piraeus of a hostelry for foreigners whose revenues would augment those of Athenian citizens. Rome similarly levied tributes from the entire world. After the fall of the Gracchi, the Roman Senate had undertaken, as Pericles had before, to protect the life of citizens. The colossal exploitation of the world served to liberate the citizen-kings from all material preoccupation.

In all times, this formidable example was followed. By means of slavery, by the abuse of force or moral authority, the best endowed men always attempted to free themselves from the material labor necessary to life in order to devote themselves entirely, according to their aptitudes, either to sloth, to crude bodily toil accomplished in play or to intellectual research—the only sources of pleasure. The weakest took refuge in superstition, sleep or alcohol.

With the progress of science, people naturally thought it appropriate to substitute mechanical slavery for human slavery, and to transfer the forced labor previously imposed on men to inert matter. That transformation, already foreseen in antiquity by Aristotle, was only a displacement of the same principle: people still living at the expense of the environment,

227

subjugating the natural forces the surrounded them, destroying in order to live.

During the Scientific Era, people blithely imagined that the world had changed, but they were only imitating ancient methods; at the very most, an authentic progress in ideas had made it clearly understood that material work ought not to take first place in the preoccupations of humankind, that it was nothing but the ransom of inferior obligations, and that its sole utility was to procure the leisure necessary to the development of human thought. They were so enraptured by the new machines, though, and by the discoveries of the Great Central Laboratory that they often forgot that the mechanical slaves were, for humankind, a means of liberation and not an end.

When the Great Idealist Renaissance arrived, it was finally understood, on the contrary, that excessive mechanization was a heavy intellectual burden and that human progress would consist of a gradual reduction of this over-cumbersome mechanical personnel. As the notion of the fourth dimension became common to all men, as the mind became gradually accustomed to liberating itself from the body and traveling freely at whim, the utility of machines conceived solely for the needs of the material body diminished in astonishing proportions.

Already, thanks to progress, the old processes of alimentation no longer existed and the nutrition of cells was effected electrically by simple diathermic currents. Thanks to the displacement of the immaterial four-dimensional mind, means of transport were unnecessary. As defenses against bad weather and hiding-places the habitations of old were similarly unnecessary. It was sufficient to shelter the material body, and for that purpose an immense city was constructed, called the *House of Bodies*. As for the ancient symbolism of spoken language, books and works of art, that too became unnecessary with the transmission of thought, much more rapid and complete than the crude hieroglyphic languages of past centuries, which used words to imitate ideas.

Except for the House of Bodies, therefore—the last vestige of the material necessities of old—our world, in the time of the Great Idealist Renaissance, gradually resumed the appearance that it must have had in prehistoric times—and I admit that, during my first journeys to that very remote future era, I naively imagined that I had returned, without realizing it, to the primitive ages of the Earth when humankind did not yet exist.

It was only then that people understood the extent to which the obscure impressions of the naïve poets of old who called themselves lovers of nature—who found as much joy and emotion in inanimate objects as in the characters of novels and who discovered more sincere and true humanity in landscapes than the hypocritical lies of human language—had been justified, in spite of their imprecision.

Nature and matter, definitively freed from their slavery, resumed all their glorious expansion in the time of the Great Idealist Renaissance—and if, for the civilizations of old—the human race might have seemed to have died forever in the great House of Bodies, for those who knew and understood, it was only then that it established its definitive reign and blended itself forever in the universal soul of things.[43]

Let here be no mistake about it, though: this new state of nature had no relationship, however distant, to the infantile return to primitive mores prescribed by the tender utopians or anarchistic ascetics of old; it represented, on the contrary, the ultimate progress of a transcendental science, the coronation

---

[43] The narrative becomes a trifle anthropocentric at this point, after which it seems that the human race constitutes the intelligence of the universal consciousness, as it were, single-mindedly. What has become of the Martians who so blithely dissociated the lamb cutlet, and the inhabitants of other worlds like the one glimpsed in the Garden of the Planets? If they are included in the orgy of universal love and limitless telepathic communication, the narrator surely ought to have some interesting things to tell us about them.

229

of the patient and laborious effort that the genius of man had pursued obscurely for thousands of years.

After the false departure of the Leviathan, a premature materialist caricature of a spiritual union that only the Golden Eagle could realize in the fourth dimension, the First Scientific Era had, it will be remembered, exalted and developed mechanization to the point of subjugating the individual to his own slaves. In the Second Scientific Era, progress having been of a much higher order, all that obsessive mechanism tended towards simplification, then disappeared. Minuscule items of apparatus, utilizing formidable natural forces, sufficed to supply the needs of millions of people. Everything was accomplished in silence, in an invisible manner, at the behest of human will-power, by means of influences and radiations—and, in that universe mechanized to an extreme at which one no longer saw the machines, thanks were rendered to the men of old who, for centuries, had lived in a mechanical inferno to prepare a future that they could not even discern: no more transmissions, no more wires, no more rails, no more ships or aircraft, no more apparent monuments raised by human hands, but the immense forests of old, the terrestrial paradise of legend, haunted invisibly by millions of men communicating with one another mentally, consumed by a spiritual activity inaccessible to our understanding and comprised, for each one, by the thought of all.

At the most, in the era of the Great Idealist Renaissance, men resumed their corporeal bodies for a few hours every year, as if putting on their working clothes, in order to fulfill a social obligation. The human race, thanks to the patient scientific labor of past centuries, had tamed nature and abandoned itself to the active mental leisure glimpsed by antique civilizations.

XLVIII. The Golden Eagle

As I have already explained, the Great Idealist Renaissance overturned all the old ideas about death, infinity and immortality. It was understood that, far from being a quest for the absolute, human intelligence was, in sum, only a simple reflection of that absolute, seeking itself, as in a mirror, in the fragmentary and provisional contradictions of time and space.

It was understood that the entire history of progress, since the origins of the world, was there, and that the Spirit, the sole creator, had projected, wholly within itself, the world as we knew it. That Spirit, quite naturally, had not revealed itself at first in the image of human intelligence, but it was always the same thing that presided over chemical differentiations and then the biological development of the natural forms of every creature.

That was an idea so very different from ancient ideas, a conception that so profoundly overturned human existence, that the men of that time were the only ones able to grasp it— and one can only smile, it must be said, in thinking about the preoccupation with survival, the folly of corporeal immortality, that possessed the men of the early ages of the Earth.

That first phase of the Idealist Renaissance was designated in a rather curious fashion, which demands a few words of explanation: it was called the *Age of the Golden Eagle*, or sometimes, more familiarly, that of the *Golden Bird*. This was intended to recall the instinctive and rather naïve belief of the metaphysicians of old who imagined that every human action had a corresponding intellectual double and that every grouping of ideas must be represented somewhere by a real being, which they called the Golden Eagle. It was moreover, of that supernatural creature that the ancient alchemists made use when they wanted to exercise some action at a particular point on the globe. Instead, for example, of converting all the inhabitants of a town by preaching, it was sufficient to act upon the

231

Golden Eagle that represented the town for that action to be felt by all the individuals that epitomized the single personality of the supernatural being.

The Golden Eagle of the Great Idealist Renaissance, properly understood, was that which had been called Love in many centuries of primitive civilization: not material love in its generic sense but the expansive and profound sentiment, the desire for submission of the individual to universal beauty, that gives love all its grandeur.

When one looks back over the naïve beliefs of past eras regarding love, and when one thinks of the observations that psychologists were able to make on a daily basis, one cannot help experiencing some astonishment in thinking that its divine mystery was so long hidden from human beings. It was easy for them, however, to observe how weak and contradictory the link was that united a petty physiological function with the formidable idea that was conceived of it. For want of the ability to apply the violent instinct that he had within him to objects other than animal passions, man had accustomed himself to find all the nonsense and absurdities that such a contradictory problem could present quite plausible.

It would have been possible to observe 100 times a day, though, that the intellectual passion had no relationship with the physiological function; poets and thinkers had certainly sensed, obscurely, that the greater an amorous passion became the more distanced it became from its material realization. They were even able to affirm that the most sublime terrestrial amours were often those that remained free of materiality, whether they were made in reality, like that of Dante and Beatrice, in a poetic dream, like that of Tristan and Iseult, or in the mystical passion of believers. It was equally possible to observe, since the time of Ovid, and even before him, the aberration of a madly amorous mind and the manner in which it was capable of mistaking the real merits of the person beloved, imagining virtues in accordance with physical charms.

Evidently, human beings, since the beginning of the world, were in pursuit of a dazzling ideal that they themselves had created, often in fragmentary form, and which they felt the need to materialize in the only way they knew, whatever frightful disillusionments that realization had in store for them.

Some poets and novelists had certainly dreamed of transposing the love of women into that of humanity entire, preaching universal fraternity and love of one's neighbor, but they were the vague formulas of thinkers, which could not correspond to any reality in a three-dimensional world, and it had proved more convenient to affirm that all great artistic or humanitarian passions were nothing, in the final analysis, but sexual perversions.

It was the clear and profound revelation of the fourth dimension that finally permitted humankind to find the way for which it had been obscurely searching for centuries, and definitively to resolve the most irreducible antinomies. Until that day, in fact, certain notions had appeared to be utterly irreconcilable. If ideas were real, if matter was nothing but pure phantasmagoria, if unity, by definition, escaped all modality, what, after all, was matter? What was the phenomenal world that opposed itself to the absolute like the Evil Genius of legend locked in combat with God?

If the human soul had an existence of its own, and it hardly mattered whether or not it was attached to a material body, then what use was the material body? How could that unacceptable duality be reconciled? How could that Idea, sufficient in itself, representing the universe entire but nevertheless opposed to the natural phenomena observed by science, be explained?

When people had examined the essential nature of the fourth dimension in depth, all these questions seemed infinitely clear and easy to resolve; all objections crumbled of their own accord. Consciousness, whose screen once seemed to be opposed to three-dimensional sensations, was no more than the fourth dimension bringing about the definitive synthesis of

233

the world, permitting the mind to seize the very substance of phenomena at a stroke, without the intermediary of any notion of space or time.

The absolute and unity, expressions previously devoid of sense, obtained their exact signification when it was understood that they could be clarified by the necessary notion of the fourth dimension.

Love followed the same evolution in this new vision of the universe; it was understood that it was no more, in sum, than the obscure pantheistic instinct that had been encouraging humankind for centuries to pursue intellectual unity in communal thought, in an irresistible sympathy of homogeneous elements.

All the ancient dissimilarities, conflicts and antagonisms were solely due to the fragmentary fashion in which people had been content, until then, to study the universe. When all these divergent rays of thought had found their common focal point in the four-dimensional synthesis, natural variations were no longer anything but harmonic manifestations of a single common thought. And from matter, formerly judged inert, to the noblest speculations of the human mind, the world was now no more than a single soul, living the same life, an emanation of a single diverse thought that was named, in memory of the naïve beliefs of old, the Golden Eagle.

This union of minds, of the same time and all times, by the direct path of the fourth dimension—by the subconscious, as one would once have put it—had nothing blissful or passive about it, though, although no one had believed otherwise in the times when humankind still dreamed of naïve celestial sentimentality and eternal paradisal adoration. More than ever, contradiction engendered an intense intellectual life in which opposition alone, as in all the mind's operations, was able to motivate thought.

What ensured that all effort became useful and positive, however, was that each individual action of intelligence concurred with the same continuous whole—just as, in a statue, all the lines, because they are opposed, unite to perfect a single masterpiece—and that love had replaced hatred since the language of the four-dimensional soul had been substituted for the fragmentary hypocrisies of three-dimensional modes of expression: hypocrisies contained in the concrete words of language as in the relative formulas of science.

After overturning all human traditions and mores, sincerity, imposed by the direct reading of thoughts, had engendered love and created, in the spiritual domain, a sort of state of nature, this time transcendental, that marked the definitive liberation of the human mind.

Every man understood, in the Age of the Golden Eagle, that he was but one fragment of a single statue—whether an eye, nose or finger did not matter—that he was only one act of the same intelligence, and that he desired the beauty of the whole with all his heart, his duty was to devote all his strength to make the part that was confided to him as beautiful as possible. That detail of the whole, his personality, immortal as the whole outside time, was the art-work signed with his name for all eternity within the universal art-work; it was the "I" marking his place in the universal continuum. It was not important whether the act was one of intelligence, faith, revolt or kindness, provided it was worthy of the whole; on the contrary, woe betide the man if his "I" was nothing but a defect, a lack or a fault, forever.

XLIX. Resurrection

I admit, sadly, that, since the day when it was given to me to reach the era of the Golden Eagle, I have been confronted with a dearth of expressions to translate in an appropriate manner the strange revelations that overwhelmed me there.

At the outset of my motionless displacements in the fourth dimension, observation was easier for me. I undoubtedly experienced, at first, a sort of anguish, a perfectly comprehensible hesitation. The men of the 20th century are so habituated to moving in three-dimensional space that they recoil, as if before death, when it suddenly becomes necessary for them to envisage the possibility of moving in four-dimensional space, and it seems to them that something in their brain might break if they make the effort necessary to pass from the world of phenomena to the continuum.

The first time that they try, for example, to escape from a sealed room and move outside it, they are afraid and they hesitate, as they hesitate again when the possibility is demonstrated to them of making a voluminous object—their body, if necessary—pass through a keyhole or form a bow-knot in a taut cord. Their physical nature rebels, as it has already rebelled against the idea of a vision passing through opaque bodies or a human voice making itself heard all over the world—but these are only the hesitations of a debutante, which dissipate when mental life gets the upper hand over physical life.

The fourth dimension, in fact, is nothing but a fashion of expressing the qualitative reality of the universe, which does not correspond in any respect to apparent mathematical realities. To assimilate space to algebraic representations, to see in the grandeur of space the idea of multiplicity, is a naïve error into which the first German researchers fell who took the trouble to research non-Euclidean geometry.

When, with further practice, the true nature of the fourth dimension is glimpsed by the mind, one understands immediately that the fourth dimension has been in current usage for centuries, under the names of consciousness and the subconscious, and that, properly understood, it is only the passage of that substance without which the three-dimensional universe cannot have any real explanation.

At the beginning of the reign of the Golden Eagle, which succeeded the Scientific Era, ideas were rapidly modified and the universe evolved in a new way, no longer in quantity in time, but in quality in all times.

As I have already said, it began to be understood that Love had a significance infinitely greater than had previously been thought, and that the obscure instinct that had led a passionate lover to desire all women or a philosopher to love all humankind, and even nature entire, was nothing, in sum, but a naïve expression of the *communal consciousness* that unites all beings.

The great pantheistic aspirations of past centuries soon found their definitive justification in the realization of that *great work* which the alchemists of old had glimpsed. It was no longer simply metal that could be transmuted at will by the medium of a common agent, it was all the manifestations of nature—the most dissimilar beings and things—that could be transmuted in what were previously called space and time, thanks to the complete intelligence that was then obtained of the fourth dimension.

It is there, unfortunately that the modes of expression at our disposal all come to a stop, utterly impotent to describe such events.

Imponderable, without measure, without space, the intellectual universe as it was then offers nothing comparable to the phenomenal idea that we are able to have of it. And, to speak the incoherent language of today, we could not claim that it was definitively dead then, if we did not know that, delivered forever from dependence on time, no longer having, properly speaking, a beginning or an end, its empire extended to the very eras in which we think we live, as to eras presently elapsed.

While humankind limited its vision to three-dimensional possibilities, its obscure aspirations to immortality remained inexplicable and absurd. How, in fact, could one conceive an infinity succeeding the end of life, a superior state of the soul engendered by the decrepitude of the mind that precedes physical death, a resurrection after decease that could, in itself, justify the miracle of a providential complicity?

When the fourth dimension had released humankind from the prejudice of succession in time, the union of the souls of all times in the same time—excuse the expression—explains, as well as the predictions and visions of the future of past eras, the natural resurrection of the souls of the past that were elevated to the superior plane of the mystic life by an act of intelligence or faith. For, just as a superior mind retains an indelible memory of the beauty and forgets the ugliness of life, so the Universal Consciousness only retains the thoughts that serve it, and that is the whole mystery of the Last Judgment advertised and foreseen since the origins of the world.

By the same token, one understands the cowardice of the men of old who postponed the superior life until after their death, instead of understanding that they could only attain it in the most intense moments of life, by will and not by miracle, solely by means of quality and not by advancement in time.

Few people of the 20th century, alas, saw those of future ages who extended a hand to them and lived alongside them; few lived again, during life, outside time. There is nothing astonishing in that, since we ourselves, who have glimpsed future ages as well as pasts and presents, are incapable of talking about it without employing the absurd expressions of "past" and "future" imposed by three-dimensional language, which signify nothing when one know that reality and personality can only exist in terms of quality. The word "resurrection" itself implies a false notion of succession in time although the true resurrection can occur at any moment in life, for a mind that realizes, at the humble or sublime combat-

station at which it is placed, a desire for the unique Consciousness.

L. The Invention of the World

The Idea invents the world, which develops like the hero of a novel. It is not indistinguishable from it, any more that the geometric form of a crystal is indistinguishable from the matter of the crystal, but it is what suggests the characteristics of the innumerable aggregations of forces, those associations of ideas that we call matter. The four-dimensional Idea is eternal and immutable, without measure and without age. It manifests itself in the symbols of three-dimensional matter that now appear to us in motion, and in a state of perpetual becoming.[44]

Consider a work of art attentively. You will not have any trouble distinguishing the material, three-dimensional part of it, submissive to time and space—which is to say, that which reveals an epoch or a substance—and, on the other hand, an idea, often a simple line, that reveals the fourth dimension, which is that of all times, which does not depend on evolution or civilizations: an immortal idea that escapes space and time. Matter, here as elsewhere, is nothing but an assembly of provisional hypotheses. Pure Art has no history; it cannot evolve.

Does that mean that the vision of the three-dimensional world is useless? Far from it; it is, for the eternal Idea, a method of abstraction, a possibility of motionless movement, of improvement in quality—in a word, of intellectual life. Without that partial vision, we would be unable to generate within our minds the procession of hypotheses that are facts, until we recognize in our place of exile the image that leads to our birthplace. The vision of the three-dimensional world permits us to evoke the possibilities of the Idea type, but it is, we re-

---

[44] This state of "perpetual becoming" is, according to Henri Bergson, the essence of our actual experience of time, as opposed to our measurement of its apparent dimensionality by means of clocks, calendars and historical and geological calculation.

peat, only a method of abstraction, and the fourth dimension alone, furnished by our consciousness, allows us to attain Reality.

As I have already said, these principal notions, and others, more clearly evident at the time of the Great Idealist Renaissance, overturned all the ancient prejudices concerning death, infinity and immortality. The entire history of evolution appeared clearly as a continuous creation of the mind *inventing the world*, in accordance with a Desire that imperfect three-dimensional language would have judged pre-existent, but which it would be more correct to call *co-existent*, formal appearance being nothing but the qualitative reasoning of the universal consciousness engendering time and space, a *thought* resulting, in a word, in a *character* once posited.

In any case, the laws of natural selection and evolution have long seemed insufficient to explain the prodigies of mimicry, the plan of the nervous system or a beehive, or the involvement of insects in the fecundity of certain plants. How, for example, can one explain the rational construction of the mechanism of the eye or the ear, without intelligent premeditation?

When one has traveled the ages that will follow the 20th century, one knows how man, still under the influence of more elevated desires suggested by his consciousness, will be able to increase the power of his vision by developing in the retinal layer, as well as rods and cones, new nerve-endings sensitive to ultra-violet rays. Is it also necessary to mention, at the beginning of the Great Idealist Evolution, the appearance in the inner ear of a new canal, circular in this instance, giving man an indispensable sense of balance in four-dimensional displacements of the body?

In auditory sensibility, in fact, it is to the three semi-circular canals that man that man owes the notion of space and a sense of balance in the relative positions of three-dimensional bodies. It is true that one can subject an animal to irregular movements of rotation, rolling or turning somersaults following experimental action upon the horizontal canal, the anterior vertical canal or the posterior vertical canal, each canal corresponding to a distinct spatial dimension. When the first attempts were made employing the fourth dimension for bodily displacements, a fourth canal developed *in a circle*, surrounding the three others, to combat the painful sensation of instability with which all those who practice levitation are familiar. Unfortunately, as I related in a preceding chapter, the old body could not accommodate itself to the fourth dimension, the organs no longer having a fixed relationship to a particular axis, and the new circular canal was no more resistant to disintegration. The adventure nevertheless demonstrated, yet again, that matter is modified according to the indications of the Idea, that the Idea alone created the desired function and the organ itself.

Matter, in fact, has no independent existence; it is only a hypothesis of inventive intelligence, and, in the relationships of its new position, reveals new values around it, ever-richer and more numerous vibrations.

The history of civilizations is similar. When one studies attentively the role of writers, poets and artists, one easily understands that their effect on mores involves similar procedures. In accordance with their eternal internal desires, they propose new situations and ever-more-elevated thoughts; the offer exemplary superior heroes to humankind, and their creations, by virtue of a natural illusion, and subsequently projected into the past, serving generations to come as real models.

History itself does not escape this idealist transformation; the most ordinary events of life, the passions that are, in reality, the basest and the most instinctive actions are generalized four-dimensionally by historians as by poets, recast in a legendary form and represented not as they were, but as it would have been desirable for them to be. One cannot reasonably pretend that all these legends correspond to reality or that they are automatic creations of matter; they are imaginations proposed by the Idea, anticipations inspired by the eternal desires that are inside us and whose development we foster, a little more each day.

By virtue of that perpetual creation, what was merely a simple fiction eventually becomes a reality. As a result of hearing tales of legendary prowess or the virtuous actions of imaginary beings, human beings become accustomed to the possibility of these exemplary lives, gradually incorporating these supernatural events to quotidian life, and the man of today is always, in a way, the son of the fictitious heroes of old. When the gods materialize, when heroic legendary deeds become true, the poets are there to offer new, even more elevated, models to humankind; it is by this means, taking examples from an imaginary past, that man draws closer—without a shadow of a doubt—to the absolute type desired by the Idea.

Immortality, eternity, infinity, the absolute and progress: such ideas are not located, in the final analysis, either forwards or backwards in time, nor are they subject to any necessity of space; they are always present, always accessible and cannot be subject to any quantitative evolution. When one understands these notions better, simple as they are, one ends up attaching less importance to physical life and the phenomena of birth and death than was previously attributed to them; one understands that they are only, quite simply, experimental modalities of the Idea.

Undoubtedly, to facilitate the task they had undertaken, people strove to prolong the period of three-dimensional aggregation that was once called human life; they succeeded without difficulty, to an extraordinary extent.

Nevertheless, it has to be said, the question lost much of its former interest in the new era; it was realized that, in the final analysis, the average man had lived as long as he needed, that the length of his life, that his life itself, depended solely on his own will—life being, after all, merely a useful but provisional hypothesis of the Idea. It was, at the end of the day, with their own consent—by virtue of discouragement or the inability to realize a personal creation—that the men of old slowly allowed themselves to die; it was consciously that the

243

men of the Great Idealist Renaissance allowed the material instrument of their body to disintegrate, every time they understood that they could no longer expect anything.

Living for a slightly longer or shorter period is of no importance in the history of the world as soon as one has attained the Idea that can create life and invent ever-new appearances, since it imagines the world. One then understands the relativity of the three-dimensional world, which, created in a determinate form by the Idea, was incapable of making a proper decision and had to repeat the same actions in every case, eternally.

The fourth dimension, on the contrary, permitted man to anticipate events outside time and, in preparing the causes, to exercise choice, varying the actions in every case according to his whim. For the sense of the fourth dimension advances ahead of man; it is what is called *the sense of the future* in a world of three dimensions; it is the creative Idea existing qualitatively outside Time and permitting the human mind to explore all the epochs of the world in the present.

If the subconscious appears to us unfathomable and immense, it is because it is nothing but the Unique Universal Consciousness and because, by its means, we can reunite all the ages and all the consciousnesses of the world—those that we call yesterday, today and tomorrow—immobile and immutable, behind the moving mirage of the phenomenal world.

LI. The Secret of the Atom

In concluding the transcription of these notes taken in the course of my journeys to the land of the fourth dimension, I want to try, for the benefit of the men of the 20th century, briefly to unveil the mystery that still separates them from future times—or, to put it better, superior ages.

I know that, instead of writing this novel of ideas, I could have contented myself with a brief philosophical summary that would have had more prestige among the specialists of a scientific era. Unfortunately, as we shall see further on, if the great philosophers of times past had only ever ended up with decidedly relative conclusions, their thought would have remained permanently imprisoned in three-dimensional mathematical hypotheses. I have therefore thought it preferable to follow the literary path, which permits, by means of its images and symbols, an approximation of *continuous reality* instead of a collision with the algebraic division of words, and to attempt a synthesis of all the ways of knowing, from which no mental initiative would be excluded—especially the most extravagant. I should add, finally, that a preliminary enlargement of the mind appears to me to be indispensable before touching fruitfully on fundamental realities that remain inaccessible if one does not liberate oneself progressively from the prejudices of space and time.

When we examine our "established certainties" we observe that they only exist in relation to a *contrary* whose measure is unknown.

In the mental domain, humor, which is the internal sense of a necessary contrary, reveals to us *the relativity of our certainties* with respect to the absolute.

In the mathematical domain, the flexible theories of relativity only extend between two infinities, and it is never possible to pass, according to Zeno of Elea, from *extreme divisibility* to the *indivisible continuum*. Matter, life, thought, movement, space and time can never be conceived in finite *unities* without being functions of an *infinity*.

Now, in order to avoid mistakes: that infinity is not a purely theoretical external hypothesis, as people affect to believe; it is an inherent condition of the finite, to the point that one can say without absurdity, in the language of three-dimensional space, that *infinity* is always necessarily contained in the *finite*.

It is, therefore, *as if* a supplementary dimension must be added in every circumstance to our relative three-dimensional concepts in order to integrate them into the real Unity, and it is that supplementary value, representing the *contrary* or the *infinite*, that we have called *the fourth dimension*, for want of a possible expression in three-dimensional language.

In reality, this fourth qualitative dimension, escaping all prejudices of space and time, absorbs rather than completing the quantitative dimensions; it is merely a passage from divisible matter to indivisible Unity. It is not a dimension, properly speaking, but the provisional idea that we form of *that which our world lacks* in order to reintegrate its Unity. This is so true that it "adds itself" as easily to the unique dimension of a curve as to the two dimensions of a circle, curve and circle being the pure esthetic qualities inaccessible to geometrical divisibility. From that, moreover, arises the absurdity of the would-be squarers of the circle who, like seekers of perpetual movement, attempt to reduce the indivisible continuum to finite quantities.

The fourth dimension being merely a necessary passage from the fragmentary to the continuous, a mental voyage from the relative to the absolute, from the divisible to the indivisible—in a word, from the multiple to the unique—one definitive question arises: *What is Unity?*

One can conceive of it *a priori* in terms of the divine, but that is merely to beg the question, a further acknowledgement of the eternal dualism, irreducible in its various aspects, between God and the world, soul and body, spirit and matter. For

246

if we agree with Pythagoras and Heraclitus that all truth is in the Unique—of which other entities are only formal appearances—it is impossible for us, without the aid of the fourth dimension and the principles of relativity revealed in the 20th century, not to oppose the phenomenal world of three dimensions to the Unity, or, if we want to fuse them, not to suppress the phenomenal world in the process as something inconceivable, deprived of all utility, since everything exists in a complete and perfect fashion in the divine unity. It was for this reason that, in ancient philosophy, absolute materialism led to the denial of the Idea and logical idealism to depriving living beings and things of all personality—an antagonism inevitable while the scientific prejudice of space and time persisted.

Deprived of the ability to redescend from Heaven to Earth, it thus appeared more logical, in the earliest phases of human thought, to start from where we are and go back from the complex to the simple to discover the primitive element of whose innumerable forms, it was thought, the world was *composed*. By progressively dividing matter up, it seemed, we ought to discover the indivisible primitive element; the *Atom*—a magnificent but redoubtable name. For the atom, having become, from the moment of its birth, the property of theorists of divisibility—which is to say, scientists—found itself materially *divisible* after Democritus, since it possessed extent, remaining no less *measurable* for the theorists of the 20th century. The latter, no longer seeing anything in the atom but a mass dependant on speed, undoubtedly idealized matter but—by the same token, and with reason—removed all substantial reality from it, leaving it solely accessible to quantitative calculations bounded by infinity. We are, remember, now only talking about the atom of the chemists and physicists: a complex composite; a veritable miniature solar system, no longer having any relationship with either the name or the idea of the atom.

Among the philosophers the conception of the primitive element was immediately elevated, thanks to Pythagoras, to the supreme unity, the only unity: the *Monad*—also a magnificent name, but even more redoubtable to bear than that of the atom. For, while it was necessary, according to the honest and luminous genius of Leibnitz, that the monad alone took account of the whole universe, we had the truly hallucinatory surprise of seeing that monad, that *unique* "which contains the entire world in its coils," multiplied in infinite number to follow the infinite division of matter. Although the monad had the singular advantage over the atom of being an unextended formal atom, it did not escape the scientific mirage of the three-dimensional world, which leads us to see at the bottom over every phenomenon, not *a unity always the same*—which is the truth—but as many total unities as there are phenomena, which is to say, an infinity, which is absurd. Provided with all the qualities of the unique, containing within it the entire history of the universe, prototype of composites, moving without doors or windows solely in quality, engendering those moments of the mind that are bodies, reducing even time and space to the logical order of reasoning, the monad of Leibnitz ran aground in *the multiplicity of the unique* and in the miracle of pre-established harmony, which made, for instance, words and thought coincide.

When one has traveled the great circular road of the Fourth Dimension to attain a clear vision of the unique Unity, all these genius steps of human thought, moving as they are by virtue of the fashion in which they often disturb the veil of mystery, appear rather disconcerting in sum. When, in fact, in the three-dimensional world, we consider the same statue from 100 different angles, the idea never occurs to us to believe in the existence of 100 actual statues. In the same way, in the four-dimensional world, the idea never occurs to us to attribute a distinct substantial reality to each of the three aspects of the unique substance.

THE ATOM IS UNIQUE. There is, in the universe as we know it, *but one single atom*; or, if one prefers—the two words being equivalent in their absolute sense—*but one single monad.* The great secret of the UNICITY OF THE ATOM,[45] unintelligible without the aid of the fourth dimension, summarizes within itself all the enigmas of the world, posed 100 times over in the course of the centuries, never resolved and always more impenetrable, by the very reason of the progress of Science. Its revelation in the Age of the Golden Eagle was, for the human mind, like a flash of enlightenment, but it is more difficult of access for men of the 20th century, blinded as they are by the quantitative prejudice of the infinitely *small*—although no real grandeur exists but in quality—and by the puerile mathematical artifice of the unique unity being infinitely divisible into as many unique unities as there are phenomena.

For want of expressions in three-dimensional language, let us simply say that it is *as if* the unique Monad, unextended, without doors or windows, were sufficiently great to *contain within itself* all the phenomena of the Universe, which are only thoughts and associations of ideas imagined in a logical order of reasoning that we call time and space. It is because they have become accustomed, over centuries, to the convenient scientific hypothesis of *divisibility*—compensated by that of *infinity*—that men have believed for so long in a substantial reality appropriate to each phenomenon, although each phenomenon is nothing but a distinct idea of the same unique Consciousness. And one remains confused in observing that the greatest of metaphysicians, Leibnitz, after having given his Monad all the inevitable and evident characteristics of universality and unicity in pure quality, outside time and space, lost himself lamentably in the naturally infinite multiplicity of the unique atom, to remain, in spite of everything, imprisoned in

---

[45] Although the word unicity (*unicité* in French) has been dropped from many modern dictionaries it was once in common usage among philosophers who wanted, as Pawlowski does, to add a further emphasis to the notion of unity, simultaneously embracing the notion of uniqueness.

the scientific prejudices of the relative world of three dimensions.

Subjectively, the unique atom is known as our *consciousness* with respect to all our immediate perceptions and *the subconscious* with respect to the values escaping our field of distinct perception. In reality, THERE IS BUT ONE CONSCIOUSNESS or unique atom, comprising in quality the whole universe. *Our pretended individual consciousnesses are, like living beings and things, only momentary ideas and associations of ideas of the unique Consciousness.* Because our relative consciousness symbolizes in accordance with the absolute consciousness, we may say that everything happens in the universal consciousness as it does in our own minds and that, in short, metaphysics ought to be fused with psychology.

There is, therefore, nothing external, superior or miraculous outside of us, for our intellectual life is the very life of the universe, and its expression the very highest.

If our thoughts, thanks to their contradictions, are the most fecund and the most elevated of the Universal Consciousness, it does not follow that they are the only ones. The principles, the fixed ideas—the reflexes, one might rather say—of the Universal Consciousness are personified by matter; from that comes the permanence of physical laws, a permanence entirely apparent and relative, since time and space are only modes of expression of thought, incapable of distinct substantial reality. Everything is contained within the unique Consciousness, everything moves relatively to the same rhythm, without any necessity for pre-established harmony; a second may be longer than 1000 years if it is greater in quality, without anything indicating that it is, and without it even being so, since quality alone is real.

Certain thoughts engendered by an encounter of ideas in the Universal Consciousness, outside time and space, can similarly appear fortuitously in minds that perceive them passively, from which come premonitions of the future and visions at a distance. Equally passive are the materializations of ideas that are called monsters and the actions of nightmare figures developing their character independently of our will and in contradiction to it. We do not always do exactly what we intend and our ideas are linked to innumerable other ideas of the unique Consciousness; make no mistake, though: the unicity of the Universal Consciousness suppresses neither our personality nor our free will—entirely to the contrary, as we shall see.

The unicity of the ATOM, CONSCIOUSNESS or LIFE are so many different ways of envisaging the same unique substantial reality. The human personality germinates in the Universal Consciousness in exactly the same way that an idea develops in the human mind or a seed in the soil. Life—which is to say, character—once given, development belongs to the new "relationship of ideas" that is the created being. It is not by gathering a bouquet that one creates a living being, but by planting a seed.

The human personality is the free development of an initially-determined character in contact with neighboring personalities. Its field is love—which is to say, the union of all personalities in the communal consciousness. Its mission is the contradiction that accentuates characters—which is to say, the differences in which the unique Thought lives. To borrow the ancient symbolic language: man is freer than God; he is His superior, as the work of art is to the author, since it is more complete than he is in the relevant particular. For God is not All, since He seeks to realize himself and, without the creations that are His thoughts, he would remain as non-existent as the human mind would be without thought. The world, in the Universal Consciousness, is, in this sense, here a relative certainty (physical laws), there a contradiction (human works), and one might say that the human personality is God's sense of humor.

Perfect and homogeneous agreement would be a moment of death for the Universal Consciousness whose life is composed of thoughts—which is to say, of contradictions—for, if contradiction ceased within itself, the contrary would have to

251

be outside. By the same token, the Universal Consciousness would cease to be the Unique Being, it would no longer be anything but one of the ideas of a higher Unique, completely inaccessible to our understanding...and so on, to infinity: a simple game of mathematical mirrors that we cannot admit into the real domain of pure quality.

How can we know what is happening in the unique Consciousness of which our personalities are only thoughts, freely blooming in contact with other thoughts, like a plant in its environment? Quite simply by examining what is happening in our own minds. In the same way that there are good and evil thoughts within our minds, miserable thoughts that eliminate themselves in a final judgment and sublime thoughts that will overshadow the others forever, so our personalities are distinct in quality and in vigor within the Communal Consciousness, but all are equally free to persevere in their being, until they attain their ultimate consequences. Just as, in literary composition, an author is no longer able to bend the actions of a character whose nature he has determined to his whim without depriving him of life, so the Universal Consciousness can no longer bend to its whim the thinking being that it has created and which henceforth acts within it and for it, for better or worse.

We are, therefore, in reality, characters in a novel invented by the unique Artist, but the organic growth of his work depends on our character, our style and our interaction with the rest of the World. In that capacity alone can we become aspects of the Universal Consciousness, immutable components of its Work of Art.

From that, undoubtedly, stems the eternal success of literary fictions, which symbolize, without being aware of it, the Life of the universe. From that stems the sense more profound than we think, of that great imagined comedy that we call the Comedy of Life.

As Psychology contains the knowledge of the Unique— and is superior to it, as the knowledge of the Work is of a more elevated order than the knowledge of the author—it is now appropriate to ask ourselves what Science is.

When we set out for the land of the fourth dimension, Science appeared to us, justly, to be open to criticism, for it aspired to impose itself on the only real and complete certainty, superior to man and subjugating him. But since we have attained the sole Unique and Continuous Reality and, beginning from that reality, have followed the development of thought as it invents the world and, more particularly, each character from which human Personality emerges, our point of view has been inverted. The *individual*, seen as superior to the Unity, has regained control and Science appears to us as his most subtle servant, as a purely speculative method of analytical abstraction, permitting *understanding* but not *creating*, which remains the most personal and the most original hypothesis of the human personality. And three-dimensional vision, so puerile when one imagines that it attains continuous reality, becomes an analytical method of genius, which, by hypothetically removing one pawn from the crowded chessboard that is the Unique Consciousness, permits all the others to move.

Mathematical divisibility is, therefore, a metaphysical hypothesis indispensable to analytical reasoning, but psychology alone permits us to attain the physical reality of the world: creation and life.

Epilogue

Why have I returned from that dazzling land of the fourth dimension, from those distant and yet present eras in which the intelligence of things is complete? To begin with, I admit, sadly, it was a base sensation of material anxiety that advised me to abandon these journeys; after that, there was a more noble and more precise sentiment of a moral duty that enjoined me to resume a projected work of art: a personal creation uniquely capable of permanently capturing the fugitive grace of a movement, the spark of a thought—which is to say, a new aspect of the Unique Idea, revealed to the world for the first time.

It is, therefore, to this book that I have returned instinctively, and that alone has always indicated to me, in an irrefutable fashion, the location at which I ought to act within the universal order of things. I have returned to my work because I felt the imperious need to remind men that the false certainty of science is deceptive, and that the immense mystery they imagine around them is created every day, uniquely within them and by them.

One always returns to one's faith or one's work, and the fervent artist is very similar to the humble believer. There is but One Reality and if death can dispel the vain illusion of the three-dimensional body, it can no longer reach those who have glimpsed, if only for an instant, the immortal four-dimensional Idea and the creation of pure Forms beyond space of time.

I have returned irresistibly to this book, because, although the hypothesis of three dimensions leads only to the mundane world, the complete four-dimensional intelligence becomes death-like if it does not if it does not do battle in contradiction, and if love does not develop in the struggle. I have returned, because Prometheus' chains are always a finer burden than triumphant fire. "When you were born," the great

254

poet Saadi[46] wrote, "you wept and everyone around you was laughing; make sure when you die that you are laughing and everyone else is weeping." Our double duty is contained in these words.

We must act with discretion and generosity, for we know now that everything that surrounds us is really part of us, and that in hurting others it is ourselves that we hurt. But if love is, in consequence, the most sublime form of egoism, egoism is, by the same token, the most elevated form of love, for it is in demanding everything of ourselves that we best serve others. Above all else, therefore, wherever chance has placed us, we must elevate our personality to superhumanity with honor and courage, and release it from three-dimensional prejudices. We know that we have nothing more to expect from the *Author* that creates individuals, while the Author expects everything of us, who are creating the *Work of Art* by living it.

All mystery is henceforth in us, all imagination superior to the universal consciousness, good or evil, solely dependent on our will. Sole inventors of the world, we live in a magnificent fairyland in which the humblest objects are thoughts and the greatest individuals are souls.

Since the consciousness of the world is within us, let us learn how to laugh at appearances; let us learn, above all else, how to conduct ourselves internally like immortal heroes, and no longer as men.

---

[46] The famous 12th century Persian poet Sheikh Muslih-ud-Din Mushrif ibn Abdullah, who used the pseudonym Saadi, or Sadi, was the author of the *Bustan* [The Orchard] and the *Gulistan* [The Rose-Garden]; the proffered quotation is derived from the latter volume, first introduced to the West in the 17th century.

CRITICAL ANALYSIS
(Used as a Preface to the 1923 Edition)

The need to prepare a definitive edition.

From the beginning of 1895, when I wrote my first story about the exploration of time, until 1912, when the first edition of this volume appeared, the *Journey to the Land of the Fourth Dimension* remained, for me, in perpetual development: published in fragments according to the intuitions of the moment, taken up again, revised and then completed, its publication as a whole did not put an end to the work that my mind devoted to it, to the extent that it seemed difficult, in certain respects, not to talk about it exclusively at every opportunity.

The majority of books, once published, detach themselves from the author in a process of birth and become stranger to him than they are to the eventual reader. This book, by contrast, remained present in my everyday life, a passionate but ever-fleeting reflection of those marvels with which enlightenment dazzles us if we have the courage to leap forward instead of remaining crouched tremulously on the edge of that abyss which seems, as on ancient maps, forever to limit the known world of our ancestors.

I had eventually to decide, though, to release a definitive edition of *Journey to the Fourth Dimension*, present fashions no longer permitting one to spend nearly 30 years thinking about what one might write. I did not wish to do so, however, without adding a preliminary critical analysis of the book, which will, I believe—by explaining its inclinations and revealing the genesis of its ideas—allow it to be read with greater pleasure and fruitfulness.

Manifestly Anti-Naturalist, this book is a Novel of Ideas.

Manifestly anti-naturalist—for nothing human exists outside the realm of artifice, a product of passionate Belief in the unique and total creative power of the Idea—this book was, in its origin, an attempted escape from bourgeois certainty, a revolutionary protest against the scientific tyranny of the moment. It was, above all, an attempt to write a novel in which the principal character would no longer be a human being but an Idea, a novel whose plot would unfold in the realm of Thought and whose adventures would consist of the modifications of its character.

These modifications of character are forms of style, passing reflections in the same mirror, fugitive impressions from various angles. If, in fact, style—which is to say, the character, the intrinsic movement and the life of a mind—is necessarily *one* and indivisible, all the possible forms of human thought, serious or frivolous, instinctive or experimental, must be permitted to it, however contradictory they may be and by the very reason of their fecund contradictions; for, as all creators know, only the coupling of male and female ideas can engender life.

The first chapters imagine a new aspect of the World.

The first chapters of *Journey to the Land of the Fourth Dimension* are specifically designed to subvert the received order of our reasoning, to open up the possibilities of a new way of thinking by modifying the situation of the observer relative to that which he observes. Now, in the domain of the Idea, whoever says "possibility" also says "realization."

Everything imaginable exists.
Affirmation cannot be conceived without Negation.

It seems evident to me, contrary to current opinion, that everything imagined exists, purely by virtue of being imagined, and that this existence has a reality other than that of so-called realities. A material realization is nothing but a partial death, a caricatural crystallization of an Idea. The Idea, on the other hand, is replete with infinite possibilities and its certainty derives precisely from the fact that it emanates from the only absolute certainty that we have in the world: our thought.

257

To take a simple example, how paltry is the realization of aircraft by comparison with the general presentiment that has obsessed humankind since earliest times: liberation from the force of gravitation; levitation, perhaps by virtue of will-power alone?

In a more abstract sense, are not the negation and inversion of all admitted natural laws as indispensable to the existence of those laws as flux is to reflux, shadow to light, aspiration to respiration and falsehood to truth?

Without death, life would have no more meaning to humans than to stones; without that which we call Evil, that which we call Good would no more exist in us than in natural phenomena; every thought and thing, like every sensation or position, can only exist relative to another and in opposition to itself.

Contradiction is rendering knowledge whole.

To deny or contradict is not to destroy knowledge but to render it whole, and the investigation of the absurd by the artist bears a strange resemblance, in the active mode, to the passive and penetrating *Credo quia absurdum* of Saint Augustine.[47]

What characterizes nature is the impossibility of the contrary within the same phenomenon or the same object, and one single exception to a law is sufficient to sweep away millions of experiences.

---

[47] The phrase *credo quia absurdum*, usually translated as "I believe it because it is absurd," was often used by Christian theologians as a defiant defense of religious faith against the otherwise-unanswerable assaults of rational argument. It probably originated as a misquotation from Tertullian, who argued that some stories are so inherently implausible that no one would bother to make them up, and that their implausibility might therefore count as evidence of their truth. Pawlowsky's citation of Saint Augustine is a common misattribution.

Conversely, what characterizes the domain of Mind is not only the possibility but the necessity of the contrary. Discovery always identifies that wholeness; that is the utility, if not the goal, of *Journey to the Land of the Fourth Dimension.*

What does "the Fourth Dimension" mean?

What, in fact, do we mean by the "fourth dimension?" It is the necessary symbol of an unknown without which the known could not exist.

The fourth dimension, in our world of three dimensions, is that variable whose existence is indispensable in every equation of the human mind, but whose quality vanishes on contact with numbers as soon as one attempts to give it a specific value. How, for instance, can geometry be made more flexible, permitting it to consider aesthetic curves other than by the official prohibition of research into the squaring of the circle? How can the artificial game of mathematics be humanized by introducing between the numbers, like cement, the continuity of life?

Again, how can movement be explained, other than by means of motionless points within the three rigid dimensions of space? Immediately we discern a providential unknown, a variable: time—and we attribute the role of fourth dimension to it, thus transforming it, on contact with space, into a known value satisfying the equation: a quantity which, alive though it is, becomes henceforth no more than a useful but mechanical mannequin, a symbol of that continuity without which all scientific conception is no more than a body without a soul.

How, in the domain of ideas, can the motionless movement of a work of art be related to the apparent movement of life? How can an immeasurable quality be related to measurable ones? How can the fusion of the past and the future in our subconscious, outside time, be related to the fluctuations of consciousness?

The certainty of the hypothetical fourth dimension will mark the place that can no longer remain empty—except that, the more our partial equations satisfy us, the more the symbol

259

flies away, always more ungraspable, deserting the cultivated fields for virgin terrain.

Behind each wall that is breached we find a new wall, behind which the fourth dimension already and necessarily lies: the eternal and indecipherable secret permitting the squaring of the ever-increasing circle of our knowledge.

I do not know how this quest for the absolute can appear illusory and deceptive to those who see nothing in the pursuit but its eventual success and who think, quite rightly, that a little circle will do as well as a big one to achieve the squaring of our knowledge. Is not the path we follow as interesting as the end? Just as Life does not consist of achieving its end in time—which is to say, Death—but of its duration, infinite and eternal in depth, so the value of the pursuit of the unknown is the internal treasures that it reveals to us along the way.

Revelation has been within us since the origin of the World.

Let us not, indeed, be mistaken: since the origin of the world, all possibilities and all future ideas have been in existence, as seeds of potential. It is, therefore, not to the future that it is necessary to look for revelation but the power of our memory. The poet of the enlightened land who conceived in very ancient times the symbol of the Earthly Paradise: God saying, after Adam had touched the Tree of Science, "He has become like one of us, knowing good and evil"—which is to say, the for and the against, the androgynous idea—"now we must make sure that he does not touch the Tree of Life and live forever", thus condemning man to material labor; was several thousand years ahead, not only of his own time, but of ours.

Humankind, as a whole, cannot follow the fulgurant course of an Idea; its progress is slower and "forward thinkers"—precursors—have to have the patience to wait until everyone else's ideas have caught up with theirs: a patience often difficult for the thinker who, after being madly elevated, must return to his point of departure and, estranged by what he has seen, feels like a foreigner visiting his own world.

The usefulness of precursors.

Is it necessary to conclude that these forward thinkers, these bold recognitions, are useless? Quite the contrary, for it is in bringing superhuman heroes to life, imagining the reality of facts whose prototypes remain latent in the world of ideas, that poets and researchers construct the frame of the world. Their exceptional follies of today will become the banality of tomorrow, and the crowd will eventually hasten to take the presently-accessible steps which they are carving out in the clouds—and that crowd, in its blind course, will have been upraised without knowing it.

Without changing position, the opposition of yesterday becomes the reaction of tomorrow, the exception becomes the law in its turn; only the Idea is immutable through its successive incarnations, its changes of material form: the relativities, in a word, that we call Life. It is for us to extract the substance from the shadow and seize the eternal element of things.

The Fourth Dimension is the Unknown without which the Known would not exist.

The eternal element of things, the immutable movement of thought, the permanent critique of transitory forms, the perpetual whiplash that prevents the realm of consciousness from crystallizing out and falling asleep, the unknown that must always be added to the known in order to complete it, the fourth measure without which the three others would not be able to take account of the whole universe, is what we call, for want of a better term, the fourth dimension.

Have we, quite simply, discovered God?

But, you might say, this fourth dimension, this unknown inaccessible to any human equation, this universal inconstant, this absolute to which we must all be relative, this judge of all our thoughts, this eternal subconscious that mysteriously nourishes our consciousness, this creator that realizes itself in every creature, has been known to us ever since humankind mumbled its first words! This eternal element of things is God!

Yes, but a God to be created.

Well, no, quite the contrary—and that is why we need a new symbol which differs from the idea of God as the integral calculus in mathematics, which progresses from infinitesimals to finite quantities, differs from the differential calculus which descends from finite grandeurs to their infinitesimal components.

Just as, in fact, it seems evident to us that in biology the synthesis of a living being would have consequences more important than the analysis of life, in philosophy, so the error of past centuries was, we believe, to exteriorize *a priori* the idea of God and, conceiving the world in reverse, to deduce by begging the question that the human mind is a result, instead of envisaging it as a cause.

In every epoch, thinkers act like shepherd's dogs, racing far ahead of the flock of ideas, perceiving, when they arrive at their destination, that one thing is missing: the flock that they were guiding; from there, they take these deceptive backward steps. As for the men of science, they count the flock where it is, install it and organize it, but do not bring it a single step forward. By going in quest of the fourth dimension, we intend to search man for the unknown that is nowhere but within him, to develop in man the divinity that is nowhere but within him, to create God by man and within him.

We shall come back to this point.

I remember a distant baccalaureate in philosophy that I rightly passed by hesitating to offer striking proofs of the existence of God. It is true that my dear teacher and friend Izoulet had disdainfully abstained from giving his course in Metaphysics, and that his young replacement, Professor Dumas, had substituted for Theodicy, with a smile, some enlightened views of experimental physiology.[48] On reflection, however, I cannot imagine that the best lessons would have ameliorated my condition. Proofs of the existence of God? Certainly, we shall have them one day: the day when the sons of the Tree of Science will themselves have achieved divinity—in many thousands and thousands of centuries, of superhuman labors and sublime thoughts, after many consoling errors, regressions and facile mirages!

Proofs of the existence of God? It is up to man to furnish them himself, and that might take a little time yet.

Leviathan imperils modern society.
Our fears have been confirmed by the War.

If the first chapters of *Journey to the Land of the Fourth Dimension* were designed to suggest ways of thought detached from hereditary prejudices, those which follow, dedicated to the *Leviathan*, carry the fight to present errors. They indicate the dangerous menace of collective conceptions that put the individual in second place, conceptions that the War has only served to materialize in a hideous and disturbing fashion. We are not speaking as a dreamer but as a witness, because we have gone through it, and if the war horrified us, it is not because it revealed, as is falsely claimed, a regression towards animality, but, entirely to the contrary, the terrifying progress of belief in an animal superior to man in the scale of being, in the Animal-State, which we have called the Leviathan—the named that Hobbes, its first inventor, gave to it.

---

[48] Jean Izoulet (1854-1929) was best known for his 1894 book on *La cité moderne et la metaphysique de sociologie*; he was a friend of Jules Bois, one of whose books he introduced. The "young" Professor Dumas who replaced Izoulet as Paw-lowsky's university teacher is difficult to identify; it cannot have been the famous chemist and pioneer of analytical physiology Jean-Baptiste-André Dumas (1800-1884) but might well have been a descendant of his.

It is evident, in fact, the modern warfare no longer responds to a need for natural selection between individuals and that it no longer bears any resemblance to those great autumnal winds which, in nature, break the dead branches and sweep away the yellowed leaves for the greater benefit of the tree. It is no longer a matter of letting the strongest—let alone the most intelligent—survive, but, on the contrary, of killing them and allowing the survival of the physically and morally defective elements that compose the cells of that inferior and monstrous animal which is called the State.

For, because the modern State no longer responds to any but the lowest needs and instincts of organic life, the privileged cells that compose it necessarily represent the most frightful selection for degeneration imaginable.

The Animal-State: a seductive thesis.

The thesis of the Animal-State is, in addition, not lacking in seductive logic. Without having sufficiently measured the extent of its irresponsibility, I was weak enough to defend it in 1897 in a little book entitled *A Definition of the State*.

I admit too that, 15 years later, having been informed by my dear friend Professor R. Prout on his return from America about the admirable work of Dr. Carrel,[49] I was forcibly struck

---

[49] I cannot prove any clearer identification of R. Prout but the more significant reference here is to Alexis Carrel, who became one of the first celebrity scientists by going to work in the USA and mastering the art of self-publicity; he won the Nobel Prize in 1912 for his work on growing animal tissues *in vitro*, which offered the (unfortunately false) promise of producing skin grafts for burn victims, growing organs for transplantation and producing meat without the requirement of livestock. His masterstroke as a self-publicist was to write his popular book on *The Culture of Organs* in collaboration with the famous aviator Charles Lindbergh. The various references in the *Voyage* to grafting, which now sound rather odd, are extrapolations of what Carrel was trying to achieve.

by the strange regressions that degrade—morally, one might say—tissues of a superior order when, separated from the human body and living independently in tissue-cultures, they no longer have to fulfill superior muscular or nervous functions.

Reduced to base alimentary functions, nourished, washed, purged each day by a nurse, having no other responsibility than general orders, no moral duty of command or information—no longer having, in a word, anything to do but live—such a tissue, previously superior, soon takes on the appearance of inferior tissues; it loses its personality, grows and begins to reproduce in a bestial and distressing fashion. What a facile and tempting social symbol, permitting the conclusion that man, the social cell, obtains all his superior qualities from the State!

This is nothing but an optical illusion.

Well, no, it is appropriate, especially in an era when forced Statism is even becoming revolutionary, to denounce more strongly than ever the absurd game of mirrors which, for the sake of analogy, makes us see in front of us what is in reality behind us. If only the great journey of humankind to the Land of the Fourth Dimension could be so quickly and so easily terminated, if Statism were the final terminus of our consciousness, if the Animal-State could fill the place that God has left vacant in the unknown immensity! Alas, though, the State of today is nothing other than the God of yesterday: a symbol of our desires rather than a reality, with the additional difference that yesterday's symbol was above us, while today's is beneath us.

Let no one be deceived, in fact: if the Animal-State offers so many striking analogies with the human animal, it is quite simply because it was constructed by man in his image—and we shall have more to say in due course about the tendency to anthropomorphism that quite justly denotes the inferiority of human creations with regard to man.

If the State were a being superior to man it would be more human than a thing. Now, not only is nothing superior to

265

human intelligence evident in the State, but, quite obviously, we find nothing in the State but the basest organic needs of human nature.

Love of one's country applies to individuals and their works, not to the State.

Let us finally take note, in this respect, that it is necessary to be wary of attributing to the State the beauties and individual virtues of the citizens that comprise it, these qualities being easily transmissible to another State—as one might suppose, for example, in the aftermath of some cataclysm causing the disappearance of all memories of the past and the emigration of the elite.

Yes, certainly, it is the economic organization of the State that permits the elite to develop in total security, to endow the country with those masterpieces of art and intelligence whose value is rightly inverse to their economic utility, but those humble or marvelous flowers that we attribute to our country could germinate in any favorable terrain, and the State, by itself, only ever plays the subordinate role of a mere field for the cultivation of individuals.

State organization has no other function than the diminution of forced labor.

In a doctoral thesis entitled *The Philosophy of Work*, which I defended in 1901, I decided to illustrate this distinction between the individual and the state by demonstrating that an identical human endeavor—whether intellectual or material—represents, in every civilization, either forced labor or free labor, depending whether it responds to the needs of the State or the individual.

The objective of all human life—the reason for the existence of any civilization—is to diminish or suppress by any means possible the sum of *forced labor* imposed by the needs of our physical nature, to acquire *leisure*—which is to say, the possibility of the free labor to which our moral being aspires.

In all religions, the idea of redemption from terrestrial slavery symbolizes this desire.

Thanks to such expedients as slaves working in mines, the hospitability of Piraeus, and so on, the social institution of slavery, Athens and Rome liberated their *citizens* from forced labor, leaving these recipients of State revenue entirely at leisure to occupy themselves freely. In our times, mechanization tends to the same result by means of the enslavement of matter, and, in all times, money represents forced labor negotiable in leisure.

It is by labor—material or mental, sportive or speculative—freely accomplished *external to any immediate necessity* that man rises above his physical condition and attains the splendid *useless* work of art; it is by this reduction of general expense, by the greater economy of co-operative organization, that the State legitimizes its existence and its rights.

One of the most evident social benefits of collective organization is the manner in which woman, the first object of the art of any civilization, lives in some way "outside the marketplace" in advanced societies. Let us only regret that the leisure afforded to the flowers of our civilization is equally afforded to its mushrooms—by which I mean idlers—but that is one of the faults of our legislation, which, unjustly socializing the benefits of the individual, has permitted inheritance.

The State, in a civilized nation, must pay the role of an economic manager charged with assuring our material life at the best possible price. It can ask much of us when the house is in danger, but it can never legitimately ask more of us than the house is worth, or require that, in order to live, we must sacrifice all our reasons for living. To protect these reasons for living, it can ask us to risk our lives, but solely in cases of legitimate defense against barbaric States. That is both the justification of republics, which are the servants of all their citizens, and the condemnation of empires, personal or popular, in which all men are slaves for the redemption of a single individual or a caste.

267

When the domestic State wishes to rise above matters of the hearth to govern salons and libraries—when, to ensure the forced labor of the community, it requisitions the free labor of the individual—we have a duty to renounce its services and leave it, to look after ourselves, as in the natural state.

The Individual is the ultimate end of any society. He has the right to rebel against the tyranny of the State.

The individual alone is king; nothing comes of anything but the individual; all social organization must ensure the liberty and the leisure of the individual, and when forced labor takes hold everywhere, we know that, either civilization can no longer bear fruit, or its fruits are in the hands of a group operating for its own profit. In that case, every individual has the right to break the contract, to rise up against the State, and to get rid of that evil servant. That is the history of all our public liberties, from the Panathenea of long ago, where Harmodios and Aristogiton were feted for killing the tyrant Hipparchus, to modern fascism.[50] The old Aristotelian and theological theory of tyrannicide has certainly evolved since the Middle Ages. We are no longer at the stage of John of Salisbury, Archbishop of Chartres, who, in the twelfth century, authorized every citizen to kill a tyrant by any means save by poison, unknown in the Bible, nor that of Saint Thomas Aquinas and the murder of the usurper—the *tyrannus absque titulo*—since the death penalty has been theoretically suppressed in political matters, and Victor Hugo himself hesitated in his

---

[50] Harmodios and Aristogiton were two youths who killed the Athenian tyrant Hipparchus during the festival of Panathenea in 514 B.C., after he had insulted their sister. The former was slain on the spot but the latter was captured and tortured; he then implicated various friends of Hipparchus' brother Hippias, who were promptly executed, but stopped naming supposed conspirators when—according to his own declaration—there was no one else he wanted to see dead except for Hippias himself.

Châtiments. It remains no less true, though, that the superior right of the individual against the State—a descendant of private vengeance, the first barbaric form of the penal right that became the judiciary duel—remains the basis of the history of liberty and has developed along with it.

From the theologian Jean Petit, justifying the murder of the Duc d'Orléans, to the theoreticians of liberty of the 16th century, we see the idea of national sovereignty forming, supported by the protestants for fear of the ruling power, by the Jesuits because of their hatred of any power outside the Holy See and by the *ligueurs* by virtue of their desire to seize power.[51] From the assassination of the Guises, followed by that of their assassin, Henri III—a murder commended by the Sorbonne—until the execution of Charles I and the revolution of 1688 proclaimed national sovereignty in England, there was always the same notion of control of the ruling power which, crossing the line after the last Estates-General of 1614, brings us to the 18th century, with the Encyclopedists preparing the way for the Estates-General of 1789 and the Revolution.

Scientific Tyranny must not replace Divine Right.

This kind of control was relatively easy while it was exercised upon a man—a sovereign; in our times it has become particularly delicate because the State, renouncing the puerile protection of an out-of-date politics, is clever enough to impose itself on individuals as if it were an indisputable scientif-

---

[51] Jean Petit (1360-1411) defended the assassination of the Duc d'Orléans by agents of the Duke of Burgundy, Jean Sans Peur [Fearless John], and was widely condemned for doing so. The Sainte-Ligue of the 16th century was a confederation of Catholics founded by the ambitious Duc de Guise, ostensibly to protect the Church from the protestant dynasty of Henri III (the *ligueurs* were eventually thwarted by Henri IV's conversion, although they had already lost popularity by making an alliance with Philip II of Spain).

ic necessity: a being superior to man, which surpasses and surrounds him.

The Leviathan? It is at our door, it already floats above our heads! Let us hasten to remove the human mask from this fabulous dragon and demonstrate the puerile works of this infernal machine that deceptive savants present to us as a living being.

Today, it is no longer a matter of killing a tyrant but a false idea, and the enterprise is perilous in a different way. Is it even possible at this moment in time? That is doubtful, and we should not retain any illusion about the outcome of the mortal combat that has been engaged for some time between the Individual and the State.

The world will soon be mechanized to the point that a simple grain of sand will be capable of stopping this formidable clock. Now, this grain of sand might be the most minimal individual attack occasioned by folly, hatred or despair. The simple rat of which we have spoken in one chapter of this book is symbolic of that.

A burdensome social discipline will therefore impose itself on the mechanized world of tomorrow. It will be difficult, for a long time, to prevent it being mistaken for a superior morality.

Next in the *Journey to the Land of the Fourth Dimension* come chapters whose humorous character has not always been sufficiently understood, and eventually, in order for us to escape the scientific nightmare, the final pages open windows to the Golden Eagle that look out upon possible futures, towards a definitive liberation in a world in which relativity no longer exists.

It is, I believe, the humorous aspect of certain chapters that most frequently gives rise to false interpretations, and that is a point I wish to stress. Few people today still understand the true role of humor, even though that mode of reasoning—for want of a better word—was employed a long time go, by the Eleatics and by Socrates, the first midwife of early thought.[52]

Humor is the sense of relativity.
This critical sense is applicable to the most elevated research.

Humor is the exact sense of the relativity of everything, the constant criticism of that which is believed to be definitive, the open door to new possibilities, without which no intellectual progress would be possible. Humor does not imply any conclusion, for every conclusion is an intellectual death, and it is this negative aspect that displeases many people, but it indicates the limits of our certainty, and that is the greatest service that can be rendered to us.

Imagine that no navigator had ever been able to set foot on the American continent, but that thousands of mariners, successively encountering different points of the coast, from which they took their bearings, had given us accounts of their findings. We would be able to construct, little by little, the exact contour of the unknown continent without ever having visited it. Humor fulfills an analogous role. Every time that man declares with satisfaction that he has established a certainty, whether in the scientific or moral domain, humor intervenes, in its mayoral manner, and, extrapolating the reasoning to its breaking-point, makes us see its relativity in a striking fashion.

Humor is not only applicable, as some seem to believe, solely to the vanities of current social life, but, even better, to the most elevated quests of the mind. It is what shows us the limits of the "exact" sciences, just as it shows us, on an everyday basis, the limits of moral "certainties." It does not guide us to a new world, but it proves to us that our world is limited

---

[52] The element of humor in the teachings of Socrates, as popularized by his pupil Plato, is often ignored, although, as Pawlowski observes in due course, the witty aspect of Zeno's paradoxes is still appreciated; the tale of Achilles and the tortoise is still told as a joke and is cited in many others.

and that something else must exist behind the wall that brings us to an abrupt halt.

It is therefore wrong to see humor as a simple sterile diversion of the mind; in all probability, no other criticism is capable of greater profundity or as fecund in its results.

The commonplace demands that we mistake it for apparent certainty.

Are you being serious? That question, too often asked of the humorist, might seem excusable on the part of a woman or a mathematician, whose instincts demand concrete representations, but it has always seemed to me to be lamentable coming from an artist or a thinker.

Speaking seriously, for the mass of men, is a matter of affirming gravely that one is getting to the bottom of things in every matter; it is to substitute for the sublime "What do I know?" of Montaigne the pitiful "I know everything" of today's scientific primers; to speak seriously is to lie to oneself and to others by taking for certain and universal verities whose reality is proven by mere common sense.

The Fine Arts Are Only Admitted as Diversions.

Why not put the question to novelists who please you with fabulous stories, dramatists who move you with their fictions in canvas scenery, poets whose imagistic comparisons seduce you, or sages who present you with apologues or parables?

The fact is that, from the silliest pun to the most beautiful poetic image, you vaguely sense the profound range of these analogies, comparisons, associations of ideas and rhymes, which operate as if lifting up a corner of the thick veil that conceals the mysterious relationships of things and the formidable continuity that is the world.

But then, when it is a matter of art or literature, *play* has been admitted since ancient times, for it is imagined that it is nothing but a game, a social diversion that has nothing to do with "reality."

272

Humor is like a disturbing moral anarchy when attacking "serious things."

Humor, on the other hand, seems dangerous, because it insinuates itself into "serious things"—into the accepted reasoning that is the very foundation of human knowledge—in order to extrapolate them to absurdity, using them to prove their own relativity.

Humor is not laughter. Laughter is a social tribunal that judges and condemns the ridiculous in comparing it to accepted verity that comprises law. Humor itself is not in the service of society but of the gods; it limits itself to marking the border between the known and the unknown.

Humor is thus incapable of pleasing those who wallow proudly and complaisantly in their certainties; it is, on the contrary, the little *frisson* of an intelligence that wants to take flight—but that frisson is always painful, because, as it opens its wings, the mind hurts itself on the bars of its cage.

The Idea of Genius is an Assault on Accepted Law.

Are you being serious? But is genius serious when, in some folly of the imagination, it amuses itself by overturning all accepted laws, all experiments made 100 times over, all centuries-old reasoning, in order abruptly to oppose to all human certainty the divine lightning-flash of an entirely contradictory idea?

Yes, undoubtedly, for the sake of human respect, the savant then follows every item with "the method that led him to his discovery," just as the artist then searches for the material support that will permit him to present his idea "seriously"—but all of that is merely social cosmetics; the idea of genius bursts forth in an initial lightning-flash of contradiction.

Achilles and the Tortoise.

Was Zeno of Elea serious when, having opposed two runners—Achilles and a tortoise setting off a few paces ahead of him—he affirmed that Achilles could never overtake the

273

tortoise, because, every time he covered the distance that separated them, the tortoise would have covered a further distance,
however small it might be, in the meantime? Even the gravest
textbooks of philosophy deign to re-raise this "joke" by a man
of whom the dialogues of Plato make much.

*Zeno of Elea was the first to denounce the relativity of mathe-
matics.*

Perhaps they are mistaken, as perhaps everyone is mistaken who sees nothing but a diversion of the mind in an attempted journey to the Land of the Fourth Dimension. Zeno, it
is said, attempted thus to prove that motion does not exist,
although movement proves itself by progressing...what pover-
ty!

Is it not evident, on the contrary, that Zeno, by means of
this objection, summarized the incapacity that still prevents
and always will prevent mathematics from attaining the entire
truth by means of one final somersault?

In the struggle that we must carry forward, in fact, under
threat of intellectual death, against the pretended certainties
that delight sleeping humanity, our first enemy is mathematical certainty, in the sense that it is commonly understood. It is
to this certainty that man appears most attached—where
would we be without it?—and it is with a shudder of terror
that one greets any attack on Pythagoras, Euclid, Leibnitz or
Newton, the protectors of human reason.

Mathematics is a close relative of Capital.

In the centuries-old labor of ideas, mathematics plays the
same role as capital in the history of societies: it is crystallized
intellectual labor, representing the wealth of which we are
proud: hard-earned security. It can even serve as the basis and
point of departure of new enterprises, but never takes part in
the enterprises themselves.

Philosophy, physics and the natural sciences, closely interrogating the continuity of life, attempt on a daily basis to
discover new fragmentary relationships between beings and

274

things, and whenever intuition reveals one of these relationships, they give mathematics the responsibility of fixing it in
memory by means of a symbol, as one might ask an emotion-
less stenographer to record a moving speech.

*The progress of mathematics is merely a reflection of other
kinds of progress.*

It is, therefore, illusory to speak of the progress of mathematics, but not to speak of the progress that it codifies,
which is due to investigations of nature.

In criticizing mathematics, we do not mean to demand its
suppression any more than we would attempt to suppress the
scaffolding necessary to the construction of a monument; we
simply wish to say that the scaffolding is not the monument,
as is commonly believed—that is all.

Calculation is a key that permits the same door to be
opened at will, but the key does not tell us what lies beyond
the door.

Public opinion, which blithely attributes an imprecise,
dream-like quality to the questing of the mind and gives an
ironic sense to the word "metaphysics," follows a false path,
just as it follows a false path in attributing a quality of reality
to mathematics.

The truth, entirely to the contrary, is on the side of the
imagination; as the immensity continues to escape us, though,
we fix a few partial symbols by means of calculation.

Mathematics, like the fine arts, is merely an algebraic representation of reality, but, while the fine arts summarize qualitative relations borrowed from life itself, mathematics only
conceives quantitative relations based in a game of numbers
that is fixed in advance.

Calculation is anthropomorphic.

Now, what finer anthropomorphic monument, elevated
beyond man in man's own image, could we find than the mathematical edifice? Based on the number 1, the only one that
we find in our consciousness, it is comprised of this number

reproduced infinitely around us, as if by mirrors: a comfortable, even fecund, hypothesis—a reassuring hypothesis, like so many others, since it permits us to obtain a certain victory, by playing a game whose rules we have established—but a limited hypothesis, incapable of integrating the continuity of the universe by means of its limited numbers.

Calculation only glimpses a fraction of reality.

I know full well that the ancients excluded arithmetical signs from their calculations, and that it was only after the Renaissance—or indeed, in more practical terms, after the invention of the metric system—that numerical measures were introduced into formulas. It is no less true, however, that mathematics, today as yesterday, even as it is elevated to the heights of philosophical speculation, never expresses anything but numerical grandeur.

Thanks to new physical observations, mathematics has been enriched by new formulas, just as a library is enriched by new books, but no library ever created a thought or gave birth to a book.

The imagination is a closer approximation of life.

The imagination is, therefore, the reality of which mathematics is only the memory.

Now, a memory is limited in certain respects, while a reality is not, in a world where everything is continuous and connected, and what we call illusion is often a better approximation of a superior reality than what we call certainty.

Let us attempt to make this notion more precise by means of some simple examples.

Perspective is a better approximation of our consciousness than a plan.

An architect imagines a monument: the colonnade of the Louvre, for instance. He conceives all its elements equally and in equilibrium; geometry and calculation immediately furnish him with the formulas corresponding to that intuition, and the monument is constructed.

A painter then comes with his easel to make a view of the monument, and the necessity of designing it in perspective immediately imposes itself upon his mind. Geometry and arithmetic, which are good daughters, and live at everyone's expense, immediately translate his desires into formulas and give him, with the same certainty, an elevation quite different from the one that they provide to the architect, with receding lines, unequal and deformed, but no less certain and exact. The monument is the same, but two opposed mathematical certainties render accounts of it according to the relative viewpoints of two observers.

But, you might say, reality is on the side of the architect, and optical illusion on the side of the painter. How do you know that, if not by the experience of your senses—as the phrase "optical illusion" indicates—and how do you know that perspective is not opening a domain to us even more real, more elevated and more universal in the material of art?

Laws of attraction of lines and masses, vaguely anticipated by ancient architects, led them to warp the two superior lines of a triangular fronton into a skyward bulge, to resist in their extremities the attraction of the base-line. These lines now appear to us to be rigorously straight, whereas, if they really were straight, they would appear to dip at their extremities, as in the modern fronton of the Madeleine. Analogous observations led them to incline their outermost columns in order that they should appear straight.

I ask you, where is the reality? In the conception that deforms, under the pretext of reality, or in the one that satisfies the secret laws of art, and renders a masterpiece perfect?

Other sensory deformations providing superior realities.

Another example: let us observe a moving automobile passing before us at top speed. The sound of the motor as it comes towards us is high-pitched, and immediately declines in pitch as it draws away. Nothing is simpler to explain, relative to us, but it requires a new notion of speed, independent of that of sound. Which is the more complete truth with respect to our consciousness? Evidently, the one that renders the more complete account of the sensations.

But that is nothing; this is what is important: the car's chassis, traveling at speed, appears to us to be shorter than it really is. As for the wheels, which we know to be round, they present to us the appearance of elongated ovals, inclined at the top in the direction of movement. A mere illusion, obviously, which is modified according to the position of the observer—but an illusion that is shared by the mechanical eye of a photographic apparatus, and an illusion that calculation can reduce to a formula. It is evident, in fact, that the top of the wheel is moving more rapidly than the bottom, since its movement is added to that of the car instead of being restricted by its backward movement—I mean, of course, relative to the observer, since it is obvious that the wheel's own movement is constant in all its parts, relative to its hub.

What can be deduced from such an apparently facile observation?

Simply this:

Firstly, that all observation in the physical domain is relative, and only has value in relation to the observer.

Secondly, that is it not appropriate to speak in terms of illusions or realities, reality being no more than an observation which one unthinkingly believes to hold all the necessary elements, and an illusion an observation from which one is aware that it is appropriate to detach new and unknown elements.

Thirdly, that the role of science is not to explain that unknown, but to attach a symbol to our observation that fixes the unknown in place, thus facilitating further research.

What might an optical deformation be in a two-dimensional world? A superior truth.

Let us now suppose, if you will, that we belonged to a two-dimensional world, and that our eyes, unaware of the accommodation, could only perceive plane surfaces.

Imagine a square-shaped sign turning towards us about a diagonal axis.[53] It appears to us progressively as an irregular diamond, and then vanishes completely, leaving only a straight line. Should we perhaps tell ourselves gravely that the plane has been reduced to infinity, or declare that it now only belongs to a world of one dimension? What would transpire then if a thinker, imagining the world in three dimensions, were to say that, not only did the original square still exist but that its revolution has encompassed a vaster and more comprehensive world? The defenders of reality would undoubtedly take him for a madman.

The Lorentz Transformation poses an analogous problem, solely accessible to mathematical vision.

An analogous adventure is in the process of turning contemporary science upside down.

We know that, in order to reconcile the phenomenon of Bradley's aberration (the image of a distant star being displaced in the telescope by reason of the movement of the Earth) with the no-less-certain Michelson and Morley experiment (establishing that the movement of the Earth has no influence on the velocity of light) Lorentz—anticipated by Fitzgerald—supposes that bodies contract in the direction of their movement. Every body in motion contracts, but that contraction is quite difficult to observe, since the Earth, for example, traveling at 30 kilometers a second, only suffers a contraction of 6 centimeters in a diameter of 12,740 kilometers—but that was sufficient to contract by one 50 millionth the bar bearing

---

[53] Only an observer in a three-dimensional word can see a square sign become diamond-shaped as it rotates and then present a straight line when seen side-on; when Pawlowski asks us to imagine that we "belong" to a two-dimensional world, he is asking us to imagine that sight only allows us to perceive two dimensions.

the mirrors in Michelson's interferometer, and thus to affect the experiment.[54]

Einstein draws us closer to physical reality.

Thanks to Einstein, these convenient hypotheses have recently acquired a singular amplitude. Based on the observations of Michelson, Einstein takes the speed-limit of our universe to be 300,000 kilometers a second, which is that of light. If we compare light to a swimmer, we observe, in effect, with Michelson, that its speed is the same whether it is swimming with or against the current.

Bodies in motion contract.

One cannot travel faster than light and no assistance can permit light to travel any faster than it does. Bodies in motion contract in the direction of their movement. They become progressively flatter as their movement increases; at 260,000 kilometers a second, they diminish by half; when they attain the limiting velocity of 300,000 kilometers a second they become infinitely flat.

Einstein informs us, moreover, that light has mass, since celebrated astronomical verifications prove that it is subject to

---

[54] James Bradley observed the aberration named after him in 1725. The famous experiment carried out by Albert Michelson and Edward Morley in 1887 was an attempt to calculate the velocity of the Earth relative to the "luminiferous ether" by comparing the speed of light arriving from a distant object when the Earth was moving away from the source at one extreme of its orbit and towards it at the other. The measured difference was less than the velocity of the Earth in its orbit, and was subsequently assumed to arise from instrumental error. In 1899-1904 Hendrik Lorentz and Joseph Larmor attempted to explain the result by means of the distortion that came to be known as the "Lorentz contraction," which became the basis of Albert Einstein's theory of special relativity, published in 1905.

gravitation. The density of the luminous particle must, therefore, be infinite by definition, as we already know that the mass of a particle whose speed attains that of light becomes infinite, according to the theory of Kauffman and Max Abraham.[55]

Our Earth, being in motion, is contracted. The measuring instruments that are located there are contracted in the same proportion—including, like all the rest, those which measure time. Our measurements are, therefore, correct relative to a system in motion; they would not be the same in a system animated by a different motion. Time is therefore modified by reason of motion, and there is no absolute time.

Time is a function of velocity.

A year passed on Earth corresponds to a shorter time on a body moving more rapidly, and a terrestrial eternity corresponds to an absence of time in a world moving at the velocity of light. As for the providential and mysterious ether, a sort of graph-paper that has served until now as the fixed basis on which all hypotheses are inscribed, it does not exist. Mass or energy is nothing other than movement; it increases or diminishes with it in the opposite sense to time.

---

[55] Walter Kauffmann and Max Abraham produced early theories of the electron; although Gustave Le Bon's *L'évolution de matière* was published in 1905, before Le Bon was able to acquaint himself with Einstein's special theory of relativity, it does include this observation regarding the variation of the mass of the electron with velocity, which tends to infinity as that velocity approaches the speed of light. Le Bon deduces from this that the electron and other "effluvia" are entities intermediate between mass and energy, demonstrating a transition between the "ponderable" and the "imponderable"—a rhetorical formulation echoed by Pawlowski, whose fourth dimension is a means of transition between the material and the ideal.

The time-motion relation varies between two infinities.

It therefore does not appear to us to be absurd to conclude that absolute immobility corresponds to eternity and an absence of mass occupying an infinitely large space, while absolute velocity corresponds to an absence of infinitely-dilated time and an immensely dense mass occupying an infinitely small space. Thus, our field of study extends beyond two infinities—which conforms quite well, it must be admitted, to a theory of relativity.

The interval ensures the equilibrium of the balance that weighs the universe.

Not the least praiseworthy aspect of Einstein's powerful theories is the coherency of their assembly. Thanks to them, our universe attains a marvelous order and equilibrium; it folds back upon itself in the form of an egg, the luminous rays completing a curve, since they are subject to inertia, returning to their point of departure. No unknown remains, since time and space are interrelated, as the two pans of a balance are by the beam, by means of the supreme theory of the *Interval*, the masterpiece and keystone of the system that advantageously replaces the obsolete notions of fixed space and absolute time.

Time becomes the fourth dimension.

From there to envisage time as being the fourth dimension of the universe is only a single step, and that step has been lightly taken. The dimensions of objects are modified by velocity, so time, the final co-ordinate, must be added to the other three and we conceive henceforth of a four-dimensional universe. Moreover, as Minkowski has remarked, such has always been a matter of current observation, for no point in space has ever been seen save from a certain moment, nor time perceived other than from a point in space.[56]

---

[56] Hermann Minkowski was the mathematician who pioneered the application of geometrical methods to number theory and developed a model of a four-dimensional universe—known as

The world is no longer Euclidean.

Let us finally add that our world is no longer Euclidean; the geodesic or alignment of the universe is no longer a straight line but a curve, which becomes the shortest distance between two points—and this leads us from the primitive principle of special relativity to the general theory of relativity that no longer recognizes any difference between a field of motion and a gravitational field.

Do Einstein's theories correspond to physical reality?

A difficulty of interpretation nevertheless crops up, which has not failed to divide our scientists. It has been repeatedly said that the Einsteinian doctrine is not translatable into everyday language and that its comprehension is only possible in the realm of pure mathematics.

Now, we have made the observation that mathematics, transcendent as it is, does not create any new verity and only furnishes useful symbols to glimpsed physical realities. If so, however brilliant Einstein's theories might be in their mathematical form, it is no less true that it is in physical reality that they must be verified.

The Lorentz contraction has a physical meaning.

This is so true that, for Einstein, the Lorentz deformation—or, better, transformation—is not merely a mathematical artifice, as its author thought, but that it has a physical meaning. He is less affirmative, however, where general relativity is concerned.

It is at this point that we arrive at the edge of the abyss whose existence I have not ceased to advertise since the beginning of this essay—that abyss or, more simply, that mysterious *turning* that we rediscover every time we take a tentative step towards the unknown.

"Minkowski spacetime"—which he integrated into Einstein's theory of special relativity in 1908.

Where, then, is the more important reality, as I asked above: in the plan of an architect or in the moving perspective of an architect? In the round form of an automobile wheel at rest or in its complex deformation at speed? In the cold representation of absolute time and space or in that of their variation and inter-connection? What shall I tell you now? What should we call the reality of preference: life in motion or its negation, immobility and death?

Perhaps, though, this physical meaning can only be translated in symbols.

But how can this moving and continuous life, which resides in the utmost depths of our subconscious, be transposed into broad daylight? How can its aspects be fixed, made graspable and intelligible? How can we make it communicable by one man to another, if not by means of sufficiently general symbols? These symbols, in the first place, are the words of the language, which have a different nuance for each of us, but which represent approximately the same things and the same ideas to everyone. Then there are the mathematical formulas which are to physical phenomena what the algebra of language is to ideas.

The reality is obviously not in the word or the formula, but it corresponds to that word or formula and remains inexpressible without it.

To immobilize ideas or things by means of verbal or mathematical formulas, as one fixes time in the divisions of a clock-face, is an act of primitive knowledge. To imagine, by contrast, in literature or in science, *moving symbols* representing in a more proximal fashion the moving mystery of nature, testifies, by contrast, to a superior culture—and the formula, in this case, becomes more powerful and more comprehensive than the word.

Words and formulas are only valuable in relation to reality, but they see further than our senses.

A mathematical formula is, therefore, a verb of superior power, but it is never any more than a *word*, whose power only comes from what it expresses and which, in defining the reality, entirely removes, by virtue of that very fact, its character of life and continuity.

If Einstein's Time-Space relationship were nothing but a pure mathematical artifice not corresponding to any physical reality, it would be of no more value than a pun.

It is therefore necessary that it rests upon a physical reality, but it is not necessary—quite the contrary—that the physical reality in question be directly graspable other than by reasoning, since it surpasses the range of our senses.

It responds, moreover, to a mental need that, by purely literary means and well before the popularization of Einstein's work, has suggested the necessity of such a relationship to us. One can take account of this by reading the chapters entitled "The Silent Soul," "The Innumerable Diligence," "Spatial Abstractions," "The Transmutation of the Atoms of Time," etc., absolute speed nevertheless being, for us, that of thought.

Time cannot be the fourth dimension completing the universe.

Is Time, therefore, the fourth dimension, as Einstein wishes? On this point, we cannot agree with him, and we think that literature, by the very reason of its imprecision, is more prudent and closer to the truth than mathematical formulation.

From the fourth dimension we expect, in fact, the explanation of all phenomena and their contraries, all qualities and their contraries—in a word, the total explanation of our world and its contrary. Now, Einstein's Time cannot bring us such integral notions. It varies so meekly as a function of space, incorporating itself by that token to the three dimensions, that one is finally led to ask whether it has not disappeared beneath the scarcely-glorious name of the Third Dimension when a body, hurtling at a velocity of 300,000 kilometers per second, no longer sustains anything more than a plane two-dimensional surface. That it is a fourth dimension—relative, symbolic—we are not ready to admit.

Einstein's Time has the marvelous virtue of being simultaneously time, energy, mass, density and velocity. In sum, what does it represent? All that is moving and mysterious in nature, all that elevates consciousness rather than the senses—with the exception, nevertheless, of consciousness itself. The union, by means of relative motion, of this moving domain with the three exhausted dimensions moving in space, thus reconstitutes the true model of a moving world of four dimensions.

Is this model complete? Will it permit us, for instance, to formularize qualities as well as quantities and to construct a work of art mathematically? It is permissible to doubt it. And even if we admitted it, would not that model of the world remain specifically relative to our system, since it does not conceive its contrary?

We rediscover here the eternal limit of mathematical hypotheses.

In truth, magnificent as the theories of Einstein are—permitting, for the first time, the conception in mathematical symbolism of all the physical forces—they appear to us, by the very reason of their mathematical character, to be subject to the traditional limits that the subtle Zeno assigned to the savants in pursuit of the tortoise.

Is not the insurmountable margin that prevents Achilles from reaching the tortoise always that *infinity* which never arises spontaneously in the continuous life of our consciousness, but which surges forth immediately as soon as a mathematician proposes the completion of a formula?

We have asked explicitly what the suppositions might be of an observer in a world of two dimensions, seeing a square sign elongate into a diamond and then reduce to infinity, without suspecting that it is turning in the third dimension. Our impressions are analogous, in our three-dimensional world; in the Lorentz transformation, a primitive round body (or very nearly round, since the movement of the Earth already affects the relationship of the circumference to the diameter) becomes oval as it gathers speed, then infinitely flat when its velocity attains that of light. Has this sign too "rotated" in a new dimension?

Yes, if we are permitted that rudimentary image; it has vanished into Einstein's fourth dimension—which is to say, into time—not forgetting that the infinite loss is comprised, thanks to the constant Interval, of an infinite gain in energy, mass and density.[57]

At 300,000 kilometers a second, the dilatation of time towards infinity will always be removed by a fraction.

Evidently, I hasten to say, such a compensation of infinities is scarcely in the mind of a pure mathematician. All that I want to retain is the single fact of limiting time, energy, mass, at a velocity of 300,000 kilometers a second, sufficiently to bring forth the purely negative notion of infinity, without, moreover, permitting its attainment, since a fraction of a second, however minimal it might be, will always separate us from the conclusive disappearance of time.

Does time no longer exist at the speed of light?

It still exists in infinitely small quantity, since the speed is conceived in terms of a space and time according to our measurement.

---

[57] Actually, no. The diminution of the object approaching the speed of light relative to the observer takes place along the observer's line of sight, so the visible profile of the object would not change. The notion that the Lorentz contraction is analogous to a "temporal rotation" whereby the "lost extent" has vanished into a fourth dimension is admirably bizarre, but false. Pawlowski seems to have been trapped in a false analogy by the careless remark he made earlier about the observer of a sign "belonging" to a two-dimensional world—by which he could only properly mean being unable to distinguish the third dimension by means of sight, not actually inhabiting a two-dimensional world.

At 300,000 kilometers a second, time no longer exists, save for infinitely small fractions of seconds and kilometers, but those fractions suffice for Achilles never to catch up with the tortoise—by which I mean the integral and continuous conception of the universe.

This simple observation cannot diminish in the least the extraordinary practical value of Einstein's theories and the rare penetration of mathematical symbols designed to enlighten a new era in the study of the physical world.

But if, as we believe, the fourth dimension must be—in the domain of pure quality and outside that of number—the living and mysterious unknown element that, by the union of opposites, explains and completes the universe, there is not now and never will be a mathematical symbol that can express it to us.

Einstein's space-time has no psychological quality.

Art, in this respect, opens up to us a domain that is vaster and more replete with promise.

In becoming a function of space and its fourth dimension, Einstein's mathematical time is transformed into space-time. It loses all its psychological and physiological qualities; it is no longer, for us, an idea complete in itself, a succession in the natural order. Following the rhythm of our reasoning, it is no longer permissible for consciousness to take itself as a system of reference.

For the philosopher who knows that all living reality is in consciousness and that mathematical symbols, like those of language, only represent it approximately, rather like a delegate representing his constituency, Einstein's theories, useful as they appear, are only a new mathematical prison in which the mind might fall dangerously asleep in a false certainty.

If the mind is to remain free, it will therefore find it necessary to resume the dolorous road of doubt—that doubt which, for want of a better word, we call humor, which is the pride of an independent mind.

The uncertain and dolorous highway of Art serves our journey better than the prison of mathematical certainty.

"Certainty" undoubtedly receives a better welcome from the crowd, which always dreams of immediate applications, but let us not forget this: the less useful something is immediately, the more serviceable it will be at length. That is the entire history of Art, whose range is in direct relation to its immediate uselessness.

Civilization is a work of art—a well-regulated comedy.

Let no one be mistaken, in fact: alongside the mathematical library where the symbolic measurements of life are crystallized out, art, since the origin of the world, has pursued its mysterious and patient synthesis of qualities—without our being aware of it, since our everyday life as civilized beings is already literature.

Our current ideas are inspired by the literary novel or by that other work of the imagination that we call history; our gestures are suggested by the examples of morality or the fine arts, magical formulas giving their prestige to rightness just as hypotheses serve as the basis for scientific equations in medicine. Civilization is, first and foremost, a work of art, a well-regulated comedy, and an intelligent man cannot avoid occasionally having the very clear sensation that he is, first and foremost, an actor forced to play a role on Earth that he has not scripted.

Let us not complain. It is by means of this progress in the artificial that the superior world of qualities gradually separates itself out, and that the imperceptible operation of the synthesis of life, linearity, space and movement becomes immobile and eternal thanks to Art—a synthesis that allows us, better than mathematical analysis, finally to attain what we call the fourth dimension.

Art is anterior to man. It is already found in the groupings of matter…

It is necessary not to forget, moreover, that art is anterior to the appearance of man. It already exists in the most humble groupings of matter, in the life of crystals as in the prodigious transmutations of matter effected by those alchemists of genius, plants.

Even before spontaneous generation—impossible only in pasteurized milieu—became manifest everywhere, abundant and miraculous, matter already grouped itself in the form of living beings, as the osmotic growths described by Stéphane Leduc prove, with their elegant plant-like silhouettes.[58] Since the appearance of matter, in fact—for want of any way to go further back—everything in nature has been *choice*, rational preference, research in form, line and harmony, pursuit of imponderable quality. Everything is alive, in a word, and the first manifestations of art appear to us in the primal groupings of matter.

Every living being comes from a living being; nothing is more natural if one is prepared to admit that matter is alive and that its sensibility and its mobility are what engender all living beings—without it being possible, as the evolutionists would like to do, to establish a hierarchy between its children and to declare, for example, that a *Protamoeba primitiva*, a

---

[58] Stéphane Leduc's *Théorie physico-chimique de la vie et générations spontanées* (1910; tr. as *The Mechanism of Life*) offered an account of the origin of life based on the observation that certain chemical intrusions into solutions form semipermeable membranes with extraordinary shapes. The Académie des Sciences had earlier refused to publish his work because the theory of spontaneous generation, which had been sternly opposed by Louis Pasteur half a century before, was considered inherently "unscientific," but Gustave Le Bon included an account of it in *L'évolution de la matière* and integrated it into his own account of that evolution, as Pawlowski does here. The phenomena Leduc observed and documented have been reincorporated into some modern hypotheses relating to the origin of life.

simple blob of protoplasm, a vague living nucleus in the Ocean, displays an ingenuity superior to that of a carnivorous plant or a crystal that nourishes itself, repairs itself, grows and reproduces.[59]

...and in the formidable intra-atomic activity.
The admirable discoveries of Gustave Le Bon concerning the dissociation of matter (too often attributed in the past to Becquerel and today to Einstein) have acquainted us with the potential grandeur of intra-atomic energy.[60]

A bronze sphere weighing a gram, with a radius of three millimeters, rotating with an equatorial velocity of 100,000 kilometers a second (the velocity of dissociated particles) would have an active force equal to the work furnished by 1510 locomotives of 50 horse-power. At the speed of light, which is closely approximated by the β particles of radium, that force surpasses 1,800 billion kilograms—and if that velocity is a speed limit, as Einstein proposes, that would similarly be the supreme value of the intra-atomic energy.[61]

---

[59] *Protamoeba primitiva* was a hypothetical "elementary protozoan" proposed by 19th-century evolutionists in the mid-19th century, when microscopes were not yet powerful enough to display bacteria and confirm the true complexity of primitive life-forms. The term was obsolete by the time Pawlowski was writing, but still recognizable.

[60] The Becquerel to whom Pawlowski refers here is Henri, the son of Alexandre and grandson of Antoine, all three of whom were noteworthy theorists in the field of electromagnetism.

[61] This exemplary calculation is taken from the same chapter of Le Bon's *L'évolution de la matière* as the example cited in the cautionary tale of "The Dissociated Dog," although it is slightly confused by Pawlowski's intrusion of a reference to Einstein; Le Bon was not aware when he gave the example that Einstein would soon propose that the velocity of light was an unsurpassable limit.

Let us take note, in passing, that, as in the gyroscope, a certain velocity is necessary to the stability of the atom and that it begins to dissociate when its velocity of rotation falls below a certain critical point. Perhaps it will be confirmed one day that life and thought are due to the deceleration and dissociation of an atom; let us hope, for the sake of our pride, that this dissociation is as slow and graceful as that of a milligram of *musk*, which, according to Berthelot, releases the innumerable particles of its perfume for 100,000 years before vanishing.[62]

Science ignores of progress in quality.

Science begins, as we have seen, by measuring in metrical symbols, thus to understand the energy of matter better, but it tells us nothing and never will be able to tell us anything about the prodigious intelligence that impels matter to group itself into ever-superior aesthetic forms, to transmute its "simple" bodies and to form beings therefrom that we call living in a more specific sense. This ardor for improvement, this choice of qualities, science ignores completely (for there is no better way of putting it) when it is a matter of extracting a human moral, for all that is imponderable remains foreign to it.

The fourth dimension represents the artistic side of life.

It is, therefore, to a fourth dimension that the concern reverts of completing our knowledge of the Universe, of symbolizing that domain of Art—immense, active, imponderable, immeasurable and mysterious—that we cannot remove from a general conception of the Universe without omitting that which constitutes the Universe's reason for existence, its evolution and its end.

The certainty that we mentioned above? But it is entirely contained in the subtle, mysterious, moving and continuous art of Life, in that Fourth Dimension, so close to us, which blinds us and prevents us from grasping it. The consoling illusion? It

---

[62] This reference is to the chemist Marcellin Berthelot.

is, on the contrary, in the mirror-play of mathematics, even while the mirror-play dazzles us by interweaving and deforming, before the enraptured spectator, the luminous rays of the rotating lighthouse illuminated by Einstein.

The fourth dimension is the sensation of the invisible in the presence of the visible.

The fourth dimension? Shall we understand, one day, that it is our only axis of reference, the touchstone that permits us immediately to *recognize* as sublime a masterpiece *that we do not know*, and which contradicts our sensory experience: the counselor that suggests to us the *against* in the presence of the *for* and permits us to judge equitably between the visible and the invisible. Shall we ever understand, in a word, what our consciousness is, sprung from the depths of the ages, completing and explaining the universe: an internal and impartial sense judging the other senses and their hypotheses; a sense that a poet does not hesitate to call *the sense of the divine*, and which a humorist calls, perhaps more simply, *common sense*.

The objective quest for certainty is nothing but facile cowardice. Let us not expect anything save from ourselves.

The term "common sense" will doubtless shock those who see elevated philosophical research or great scientific discoveries as the only means of attaining the Absolute and expend all their personal efforts upon it; that is what explains, moreover, why these reaches and discoveries always enthuse ordinary people.

How much more flattering the term "the sense of the divine" is to their mental sloth! One sole cry—*Deus, ecce Deus!*—and by the same token, our consciousness has covered, as by a single cry: *Vive Un Tel...* or the sound of a military march, sufficient to discharge us from the care and responsibility of thought.[63]

Simple common sense, on the contrary, falls back to reality, towards that humble everyday labor of thought which, by means of successive choices, slowly pursues the interminable road of progress! Having nothing to await—neither external prodigies nor divine intervention—knowing that all revelation is within us and can only come from us: what a crushing responsibility for the human mind, but what a sublime mission too!

Our external constructions, made in our image, are useful…

Since human beings came into existence, their principal occupation has been to discharge, at least in part, this heavy responsibility, by materializing around them the self-knowledge that they have been able to acquire and constructing the world in their own image. Without that anthropomorphic procedure, we hasten to say, no progress of the human mind would be possible and we could not conceive any model at all of the universe. Consciousness, devoted to itself, remains mute; it is necessary that it reflects itself in words, images, symbols, formulas or hypotheses in order to act, and the purely qualitative fourth dimension only expresses itself in contact with the three quantitative dimensions of our relative world.

Without the primitive hypotheses of our senses, without their personal interpretation, the external world would be neither resistant, nor sonorous, nor colored; there would be nothing but a collection of indiscernible movements and vibrations. Without the scientific hypothesis, no image of the world

---

[63] An appropriately unpretentious translation of the Latin exclamation would be "Look—there's God!" The French cry I have left *in situ*—whose pedantic translation would produce something like "Long Live Anyone"—is difficult to render into sufficiently punchy English, but "Bully for Him!" might suffice.

would be possible, just as a reasoning unordered by words would be impossible.

...provided that we do not take them for absolute objective certainties.

It remains no less true that these successive hypotheses, indispensable as they are, are only provisional and that the mistake of taking them for definitive certainties, immobilizes and considerably slows down the progress of ideas. While admiring them with all our heart, our duty is therefore to denounce their relativity, to demonstrate their limits and always to suggest new possibilities to the human mind.

This task is that of humorist when it is a matter of fixing the limits of a hypothesis by means of the absurd; it is that of the poet when it is a matter of proposing new aspects of imponderable quality.

It is this double task that we have attempted to realize in this book, solely with recourse to the symbols of Art.

Now, we live surrounded by reassuring idols.
We are the slaves of our creations.

We have shown above what a danger is posed to the movement of ideas by the mental paralysis that is false mathematical certainty, and we know how joyfully man complaisantly mires himself in the unity of the number that presents him with his own image—but this anthropomorphism is by no means specific to science, for we see the human Narcissus marveling at his creations at every step, and taking his portrait, caricature or shadow for objective, reassuring and certain models. We live, therefore, surrounded by idols in human form, like primitive savages.

Our houses, our furniture, our household objects, our machines and our scientific instruments are made in the image of man, with hair, arms, feet, arteries, bones, muscles, nerves and even senses. If we construct an automobile, for example, we conceive it, save for the wheels, in the image of a man, with an electrical nervous system, a respiration, a digestion, muscles, a bone-structure, arms that touch the ground, legs that propel, eyes and a voice. If we construct a moral entity such as the State, we similarly conceive it in the image of a man, with a brain, muscles, a digestive apparatus and a skeleton, which would be perfect if we did not then proceed, after the fashion of fetishists, to adore the idol that we have created and submit ourselves to its illusory superior powers.

We live, to put it bluntly, religiously, and are pusillanimously happy to serve the innumerable masters that we have given ourselves.

Without being aware of it, we become the slaves of our creatures, and, believing our lives to be transitory, we aspire to attach ourselves desperately to more durable creations of which we are the authors.

What a familial tenderness is maintained today by the movable property we possess, instead of the immovable property of old, and how many affections would be able to resist the admirable evangelical advice to "Sell all that you have, give the money to the poor and follow me?"

Which is the civilization that could similarly resist the destruction of its material and moral monuments, residues of the past?

The human mind is almost always satisfied with received precepts, established order and respected customs. Infinitely rare are its movements of independence and originality. In social matters, this dependence on idols is such that man, having come to that pass—as we have seen—willingly believes in the existence of a superior being: the Animal-State, and allows himself to become gradually less differentiated, like a mere specialized cell, like a cogwheel of the enormous organism that grips him.

Without refusing to recognize the material utility of these idols, the benefits of life in society and the useful hypotheses of scientists, it seems that the time has come to render to man his sovereignty and to turn his mind, not towards the world of his creations—which is to say, the world below—but towards the source from which all his ideas come—which is to say, all the intuitions that permit him, every day, to make progress, by proposing new and more elevated goals.

The most formidable and the most comfortable of our creations is that which we have made of God.

In this respect, however, one last obstacle arises, the most formidable of all: that of the internal idol, that of the divinity. As if by some mental cowardice, man, who is pleased to live among his creations, experiences an invincible sloth when it is a matter of elevating himself above his condition and understanding. It seems more convenient to him to create a Being superior to him, charged with all that he has not yet attained and which represents for him the unknown. And his humility, like his devotion, is similarly nothing but the evident mark of idleness or weakness, a sloth so extensive that man has preferred to bring God down to Earth rather than go towards Him.

On the day our Father dies, it will be necessary for us to take His place.

It has sometimes been observed that a man only becomes a man on the day his father dies. However old, active or independent he might be, it is on that day alone that he experiences a distressing sense of emptiness above him. He is now the responsible leader who marches ahead and who masks the unknown for those who follow him. No guide will any longer return in a bad situation to offer him a hand; he remains alone in life, facing the horizon over which death looms.

It is then that the man pauses for reflection, and looks back at those he must help. He becomes conscious of his worth and his responsibilities; he finally understands that nothing can come henceforth from anyone but him.

In the history of the world, the human mind will not be free of its infancy until the day when it will experience that crisis of distress, hesitation and mourning. On that day, a thinker or a poet will have the courage to pronounce these oppressive words: "Heaven is empty, my father is dead, or rather, never existed; it was my shadow, immeasurably magnified, that I followed along the road."

Above all, though, he will have the superhuman strength to add: "It is up to us, henceforth, to take the place of our dead father and to realize that necessary God to whom we have attributed all science, all wisdom and all providence."

I do not know whether many men would be capable today of making the prodigiously painful effort that would claim such an enfranchisement, and centuries might yet be necessary to discern the sense of it. On that day, we shall doubtless understand that no unknown exists outside ourselves and that it is within ourselves that all of the immense unknown must be sought.

But we are still nothing but little children.

Everything informs us, in fact, that the entire experience of centuries past is in the depths of our own consciousness, and that all the possibilities of the future are also there. If we were not still in prehistory, amid the first mumblings of humankind, if our minds were to become conscious of the formidable forces at their disposal, it is quite evident that we would only have to interrogate ourselves with enough force to know everything, although we still know almost nothing today.

Unfortunately, progress only happens very slowly, by virtue of the slothfulness, anguish and instinctive terror that our minds experience when we attempt to peer into that bottomless gulf. Everything in life still remains profoundly mysterious to us: the implacability of physical laws, the mobility of moral laws, a ray of light, a sound, an odor, a fugitive thought, and so many other subjects that suffice to plunge us, hardly aware of it as we are, into such an abyss of reflections that we sense clearly, from time to time, that there would be a sort of moral danger in peering too long into that abyss.

To take the place of the divinity—which is to say, to attain by oneself the explanation of every mystery—that is the formidable mission of man, a mission that even the best minds only fulfill, in the course of an entire life, for a few fugitive seconds of genius. Surrounding these few genuine useful lightning-flashes are missed steps, clarifications, eternal re-commencements, provisional certainties, relative absolutes, abortive actions or ideas, wasted passions, movements or endeavors! How many seeds whirl away in the wind for every one that germinates!

D. Berthelot[64] once offered, as an example to electricians, the luminous efficiency of the glow-worm, which is a 100%, while that of the Sun is only 14% and that of our lamps 21%; we wonder whether a similar example of efficiency might be proposed with regard to the human mind, while remembering that the worm only glows when it is in love.

A day will come when man will know himself.

When we finally understand that revelations can only come from ourselves and not from our anthropomorphic creations, when it becomes evident that everything in the world is relative, but relative to us, and that it is in ourselves alone that we can find the communal measure of the universe, perhaps then we shall finally understand ourselves and obtain consciousness of our worth.

One day, perhaps in millennia, the first man will come who, having the true power of thought, will possess the absolute science of the universe and the sources of life. It is necessary to content ourselves, in our primitive era, to play in that regard the very humble, and yet very enviable, role of John the Baptist.

This will be the Man-God.

That man and those of his race, according to the ancient prophecy, will be gods and will live forever.

---

[64] Unlike the previous reference to a person of this name, this one is to the physicist Daniel Berthelot, who was Marcellin's son.

That man will live, at the very least, for the time that he judges necessary to his full wisdom; he will be the God that we have designed, but who cannot exist outside of us, as we imagine, for he would otherwise have been able to create a new being superior to man long before.

Will he be the God of men, the God of the Earth, the God of the celestial immensities? It hardly matters, since he will know everything that concerns our universe. He will know the intimate constitution of matter, he will be able to create life, he will reproduce the mysteries of mimesis and all the other prodigies of natural history, he will know what electricity is, he will be able to transmute simple bodies solely by means of molecular displacement, he will utilize for his needs the prodigious forces of dematerialization, he will decipher thoughts at a distance, resuscitate the dead, heal the sick, journey into the past and future by interrogating his consciousness....

He will be, in sum, an exceedingly distinguished engineer.

He will be everything, relative to science... in reality, he will be nothing.

The God-scientist will know doubt, and will search for God.

For on that day, in the depths of his consciousness, the distressing mystery of the contrary with pose itself again.

Knowing the universe to the extent of its extreme limits, its intimate life and its construction, the new God will, however, understand that he only knows it from within, which is to say, from himself, and that he has none of the vision from without that a superior God, for example, might possess. And, beginning to doubt himself, the savant God will soon kneel down like his human ancestors before the great mystery.

Pensive, anxiously turning his gaze toward the Heavens, the new God would search for God. He will have done everything to understand the world, and he will have reconstructed it scientifically, piece by piece, in his own image, his will imposing itself on the universe—and, at the moment of attaining the absolute, of integrating all science, the magnificent edifice will fall into dust before the light breath of the *contrary*, which the poets of yesteryear would doubtless have named the Evil Genius, but which men of common sense simply call humor.

For the imagination always creates a contrary.

To construct a world whose relativities are all known, all measured: what a sublime, definitive, complete work....until the day when the necessity of the contrary awakes in the depths of consciousness: the possible existence, then conceived, of a world in which relativity would make no sense. For, as we said at the beginning of this critical analysis, everything imaginable exists, solely by virtue of the fact that it is imagined.

Already, certain conclusions can be derived from the preceding pages; let us attempt to offer a synthesis, in which we shall also try to find the symbol in the final pages of this book, devoted to the *Golden Eagle*.

The intelligence of the Universe is trying to know itself.

For reasons that are still unknown to us, that which we call, for want of a better term, universal intelligence, seems to be animated by a prodigious desire to know itself—which is to say, to realize itself.

In order to do that it needs a mirror, and that mirror is the World. A self-consciousness by itself remains, in effect, obscure, continuous, immobile, eternal and indiscernible. It can only act and realize itself by contradiction, opposition, reaction and limitation in a time and a space.

By creating symbols.

By what prodigious effort of creation has the consciousness of the world objectivized these partial movements and local energies that we call matter? How has it differentiated this matter, opposing it in groupings, and then in different beings?

That we still do not know, but we can find out by ourselves, since we are the superior and prodigious expression of that consciousness-in-progress, which permits us to glimpse its permanent qualities in transitory phenomena, and even outside them, since a fortunate relationship between two tones is not within the two tones.

For everything is connected in a world of the same origin and the same nature, and if, for example, the political views of a La Boétie writing the *Treatise on Voluntary Servitude* were correct, they would enable us to clarify, by analogy, the interest-groups in nature subordinating certain cells to the authority of one privileged cell.

Thus, on the one hand, there is a universal consciousness which seeks means of expression and which constitutes reality; and, on the other, there are means of expression that are only symbols of the reality, variations on the same theme, ingenious expedients permitting the arbitrary fractionation of the continuous.

Relative to the consciousness of the world, beings and things are only symbols, just as the words of languages and mathematical formulas are with respect to our consciousness.

Man is the most complete symbol of reality.

Man is the most elevated symbol of nature: its beloved son; its masterpiece, slowly built on heaps of cadavers in the course of countless centuries.

The unknown does not exist; there are only the possibilities of the known, which always increase, and it is in man that the highest possibilities exist.

It is not, strictly speaking, by his artistic knowledge of qualities that man is distinct from other beings; salt has its savor, a crystal the form that it maintains, an animal the beauty of which it is proud. Nor is it, precisely, by his awareness of contradiction; the strategy of a hunted animal requires psychological treasures in the world of sensations.

He is conscious of himself, like other beings but he is also conscious of the universe.

No, what renders man superior to everything else is the care that he takes, not only to persevere in his own qualities, which is the action of every created symbol, but also to acquire a subjective knowledge of what surrounds him, to incorporate himself in the very consciousness of the universe—an anxiety that is generally translated, in a touching fashion, into a desire for immortality.

We have previously examined the obstacles that man encounters on that superhuman road, which incite him slothfully to crystallize out false symbolic certainties of his own qualities, in taking his anthropomorphic creations for external reality.

We have also said that doubt and humor alone can permit him to resume his forward progress by showing him that the possibility of the contrary lurks behind each certainty.

This subjective consciousness of the Universe is impossible without the fourth dimension.

One last problem remains to be resolved: how can we, by means of our consciousness, attain this subjective consciousness of the world, and by means of an effort of thought—however prodigious it might be—enlightened in the course of future centuries by thousands of new symbols, arrive at a knowledge of the universe, as if we were the universe? Our consciousness, you might say, is individual, personal to each of us; it might permit us to know ourselves, but it is not the consciousness of the universe permitting us to know that universe subjectively.

This reasoning is perfect, if one considers consciousness as one does the heart or the liver in the world of our three-dimensional symbols.

Unicity, the conclusion of this book.

It is deprived of sense if one brings in, entirely to the contrary, the superior notion of the fourth dimension. Space and time, conveniently but arbitrarily fragmenting the real continuum, collapse like a provisional scaffolding when we retrieve consciousness of the real world, in which all is quality and in which quantity no longer exists—and it is thus that the fourth dimension leads us, for the first time, to a sound notion of the *Unicity of the atom*, the conclusion of this book and the point of departure of a new vision of the World.

"Our" consciousness? But a mere moment of reflection is sufficient to make us understand that is only ours to the extent to which allow ourselves to contradict, judge, approve or qualify the ideas or the judgments of our three-dimensional senses—for, from the viewpoint of the fourth dimension, there can no longer exist any but a single continuous Consciousness, of which each one of us is merely a new attempt at the realization of sublime hopes.

Only one consciousness exists in the Universe, which belongs specifically to every one of us.

Now, every one of us could be everything, if he wished, instead of being, as usual, a simple deception, great or small. All that is required for that is a lightning-flash of faith or genius.

Is that lightning-flash possible in a primitive era in which we are beginning to glimpse the scientific knowledge of the symbolic world of our three-dimensional sensations? We do not think so.

For centuries yet, humankind will worship its symbols as idols and mistake its anthropomorphic hypotheses for external reality. Only when the day comes that man knows the how of everything will he probably go in search of the why, and the aurora of God's goodness will succeed the dusk of the savant gods. While we wait, it is, we repeat, the prerogative of poets to prophesy future realities and the propriety of humorists to denounce the relativity of present pseudo-certainties.

But there are subjects that one can only examine in our day before a restricted public; for, as Zeno said to Socrates in the *Parmenides*, the crowd does not know that it is impossible to attain the truth without these quests and voyages through everything—and perhaps it is premature to inform school-children of the dubiousness of divinity.

The reign of goodness is only possible in the four-dimensional continuum; it will make us understand the universality of love.

Doubt is indeed a virtue of maturity for civilizations as for men; it engenders indulgence and disinclination to action; it should be a motive for discouragement for the ignorant, but the crown of all science for those who have learned everything.

Now, the reign of goodness will not be possible on Earth until the day when the language of the soul has replaced the provisional deception of formulas and words. And on that day alone will the profound and universal meaning be revealed of *love*: a symbol still infinitely relative and restricted today, but which will become the formidable continuous reality of the future world of four dimensions, as pain is that of the engendered world of three dimensions.

BLACK COAT PRESS

M. Allain & P. Souvestre. *The Daughter of Fantômas*
Anicet-Bourgeois. *Rocambole*
Guy d'Armen. *Doc Ardan: The City of Gold and Lepers*
Aloysius Bertrand. *Gaspard de la Nuit*
A. Bisson & G. Livet. *Nick Carter vs. Fantômas*
Félix Bodin. *The Novel of the Future*
Lucien Dabril. *Rocambole*
V. Darlay & H. de Gorsse. *Lupin vs. Holmes: The Stage Play*
C.I. Defontenay. *Star (Psi Cassiopeia)*
Charles Derennes: *The People of the Pole*
Alexandre Dumas. *The Return of Lord Ruthven*
J.-C. Dunyach. *The Night Orchid: Conan Doyle in Toulouse*
Paul Féval: *Anne of the Isles*
Paul Féval. *The Blackcoats: The Companions of the Treasure*
Paul Féval. *The Blackcoats: The Invisible Weapon*
Paul Féval. *The Blackcoats: The Parisian Jungle*
Paul Féval. *The Blackcoats: 'Salem Street*
Paul Féval. *Captain Phantom*
Paul Féval. *Gentlemen of the Night*
Paul Féval. *John Devil*
Paul Féval. *Knightshade*
Paul Féval. *Revenants*
Paul Féval. *Vampire City*
Paul Féval. *The Vampire Countess*
Paul Féval. *The Wandering Jew's Daughter*
Paul Féval, *fils. Felifax, the Tiger-Man*
Emile Gaboriau. *Monsieur Lecoq*
Arnould Galopin. *Doctor Omega*
V. Hugo, Foucher & Meurice. *The Hunchback of Notre-Dame*
O. Joncquel & Theo Varlet. *The Martian Epic*
Jean de La Hire. *The Nyctalope on Mars*
Jean de La Hire. *The Nyctalope vs. Lucifer*
Steve Leadley. *Sherlock Holmes - The Circle of Blood*
Maurice Leblanc. *Lupin vs. Holmes: The Hollow Needle*
Maurice Leblanc. *Lupin vs. Holmes: The Blonde Phantom*

Gustave Le Rouge. *The Vampires of Mars*
Jules Lermina. *Panic in Paris*
Gaston Leroux. *Chéri-Bibi*
Gaston Leroux. *The Phantom of the Opera*
Jean-Marc Lofficier. *The Katrina Protocol*
Jean-Marc & Randy Lofficier. *Edgar Allan Poe on Mars*
Jean-Marc & Randy Lofficier. *Robonocchio*
Lofficier. *Tales of the Shadowmen 1: The Modern Babylon*
Lofficier. *Tales of the Shadowmen 2: Gentlemen of the Night*
Lofficier. *Tales of the Shadowmen 3: Danse Macabre*
Lofficier. *Tales of the Shadowmen 4: Lords of Terror*
Lofficier. *Tales of the Shadowmen 5: The Vampires of Paris*
Xavier Mauméjean. *The League of Heroes*
William Patrick Maynard. *The Terror of Fu Manchu*
Frank J. Morlock. *Sherlock Holmes: The Grand Horizontals*
Marie Nizet. *Captain Vampire*
C. Nodier, Beraud & Toussaint-Merle. *Frankenstein*
Charles Nodier. *Lord Ruthven the Vampire*
Henri de Parville. *An Inhabitant of the Planet Mars*
John William Polidori. *Lord Ruthven the Vampire*
P.-A. Ponson du Terrail. *The Vampire and the Devil's Son*
Albert Robida. *The Clock of the Centuries*
Eugène Scribe. *Lord Ruthven the Vampire*
Brian Stableford. *The Germans on Venus*
Brian Stableford. *News from the Moon*
Brian Stableford. *The New Faust at the Tragicomique*
Brian Stableford. *The Shadow of Frankenstein*
Brian Stableford. *Sherlock Holmes - The Vampires of Eternity*
Brian Stableford. *The Stones of Camelot*
Brian Stableford. *The Wayward Muse*
Villiers de l'Isle-Adam. *The Scaffold*
Villiers de l'Isle-Adam. *The Vampire Soul*
Philippe Ward. *Artahe: The Legacy of Jules de Grandin*
P. de Wattyne & Y. Walter. *Sherlock Holmes vs. Fantômas*
David White: *Fantômas in America*